INHERITANCE

INHERITANCE IS THE first in a blood-drenched trilogy that tells the tale of the Vampire Counts, cruel undead rulers of the cursed land of Sylvania.

Within the horror-haunted human Empire, the rise to power of the dark and sinister Vlad von Carstein at first goes unnoticed. However, once he has established his rule in Sylvania, a plague of evil is set loose and the land is transformed into a domain of the undead. Can anyone save the land of the living from this bloodthirsty family of vampires and their terrifying undead armies?

More Warhammer from the Black Library

· **GOTREK & FELIX** by William King ·
TROLLSLAYER • SKAVENSLAYER
DAEMONSLAYER • DRAGONSLAYER
BEASTSLAYER • VAMPIRESLAYER
GIANTSLAYER

· **DARKBLADE** by Dan Abnett & Mike Lee ·
DARKBLADE: THE DAEMON'S CURSE
DARKBLADE: BLOODSTORM

· **THE BLACKHEARTS** by Nathan Long ·
VALNIR'S BANE
THE BROKEN LANCE

A WARHAMMER NOVEL

BOOK ONE IN THE
VON CARSTEIN TRILOGY

INHERITANCE

STEVEN SAVILE

For PJK who started it all.
Wish you could have seen this, sir.

A Black Library Publication

First published in Great Britain in 2006 by
BL Publishing,
Games Workshop Ltd.,
Willow Road, Nottingham,
NG7 2WS, UK

10 9 8 7 6 5 4 3 2 1

Cover illustration by Andrea Uderzo.
Map by Nuala Kinrade.

A CIP record for this book is available from the British Library.

ISBN 13: 978 1 84416 291 8
ISBN 10: 1 84416 291 5

Distributed in the US by Simon & Schuster
1230 Avenue of the Americas, New York, NY 10020.

Printed and bound in Great Britain by
Bookmarque, Surrey, UK.

See the Black Library on the Internet at
www.blacklibrary.com

Find out more about Games Workshop
and the world of Warhammer at
www.games-workshop.com

A cloaked figure sprang forward, unbalancing the king. His cloak played around his body like wings in the wind. Kallad knew the beast for what it was: a vampire. One of von Carstein's minions – perhaps even the undead count himself.

The vampire tossed its head back and howled at the moon, exhorting the dead to rise.

For a moment, Kallad thought his father turned to look at him through the black smoke and the raging flame. Every bone and every fibre of his being cried out to run to the old king's aid, but he had been charged with another duty. He had to see these women and children to safety, giving worth to the great king's sacrifice. He couldn't abandon them when he was their only hope. Down there in the deep they would die as surely as they would if he had left them in the great hall.

On the wall, the creature dragged Kellus close in the parody of an embrace and for a moment it appeared as though the two were kissing. The illusion was shattered as the vampire tossed the dead dwarf aside and leapt gracefully from the high wall.

Kallad turned his back, tears rolling down his impassive face.

The babe writhed in his arms. He lay the child on the floor, face down because he couldn't bear the accusation he imagined in its dead eyes. Tears streaming down his face, he took the axe and ended the child's unnatural life.

Smoke, flame and grief stung the dwarf's eyes as he knelt down over the corpse and pressed a coin into the child's mouth, an offering to Morr. 'This innocent has suffered enough hell for three lifetimes, Lord of the Dead. Have pity on those you claimed today.'

Kallad ran towards the safety of the mountainside and the caverns that led down into the warren of deep mines, across the open ground of the green and down a narrow alleyway that led to the entrance to the caves. The child didn't slow him. 'Come on!' he yelled, urging the women to move faster. There would be precious little time to get them all into the caves before the fire claimed the alleyway. 'Come on!' Some dragged their children others cradled them. None looked back.

'Where do we go?' the young boy asked. He'd drawn his toy sword and seemed ready to stab any shadow that moved in the firelight.

'Take the third fork in the central tunnel, lad. Follow it down. It goes deep beneath the mountain. I'll find you. From there, we're going home.'

'This is my home.'

'My home, lad. Karak Sadra. You'll be safe there.'

The boy nodded grimly and disappeared into the darkness. Kallad counted them all into the caverns. As the last of them disappeared into the tunnels, he turned to look up at the city walls.

Through the dancing flames he could see the battle still raging. The dead had claimed huge parts of the city but the manlings were fighting on to the bitter end. He scanned the battlements, looking for his father. Then he saw him. Kellus was locked in a mortal struggle. From this distance it was impossible to tell, but his axe was gone. He was on the back foot, the flames licking the stones around him, and being forced further back into the flames as the dead poured over the wall. The last vestiges of Grunberg's defences were breached. The white-haired King of Karak Sadra fought desperately, hurling the dead flesh of mindless zombies from the wall.

THIS IS A DARK age, a bloody age, an age of daemons and of sorcery. It is an age of battle and death, and of the world's ending. Amidst all of the fire, flame and fury it is a time, too, of mighty heroes, of bold deeds and great courage.

AT THE HEART of the Old World sprawls the Empire, the largest and most powerful of the human realms. Known for its engineers, sorcerers, traders and soldiers, it is a land of great mountains, mighty rivers, dark forests and vast cities. It is a land riven by uncertainty, as three pretenders all vye for control of the Imperial throne.

BUT THESE ARE far from civilised times. Across the length and breadth of the Old World, from the knightly palaces of Bretonnia to ice-bound Kislev in the far north, come rumblings of war. In the towering World's Edge Mountains, the orc tribes are gathering for another assault. In the east, the dead do not rest easy, and there are rumours of rats that walk like men emerging from the dark places of the world. From the northern wildernesses there is the ever-present threat of Chaos, of daemons and beastmen corrupted by the foul powers of the Dark Gods. As the time of battle draws ever nearer, the Empire needs heroes like never before.

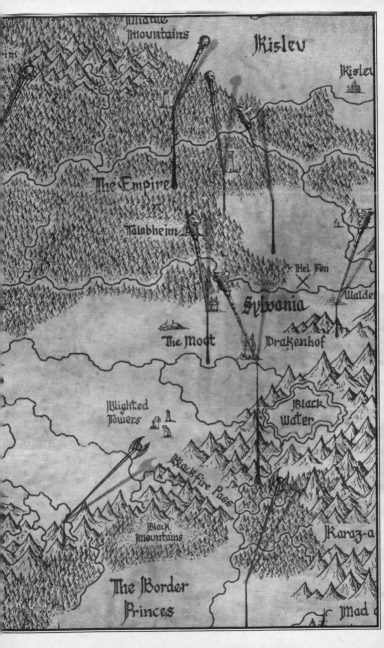

PROLOGUE
Death and the Maiden

DRAKENHOF CASTLE
Late winter, 1797

THE OLD MAN was dying an ugly death and for all their skill and faith there was nothing either the chirugeon or the priest could do to prevent it. Nevertheless they busied themselves by plumping the sweat-stained pillows that propped the old man up, and fussing like fishwives with candle stubs and curtains to keep the shadows and the draughts at bay, and still the bedchamber was bitterly cold. Where there ought to have been a roaring fire the stacked logs and kindling remained unlit. The two men lit smoke to ward off the ill humours and offered prayers to benevolent Sigmar. None of it made a blind bit of difference. Otto van Drak was dying. They knew it, and worse, he knew it. That was why they were with him; they had come to stand the death watch.

His bottom lip hung slackly and a ribbon of spittle drooled down his chin. Otto wiped at it with the back of a liver-spotted hand. Old age had ravaged the count with shocking speed. Otto had aged thirty years in as many days. All of the strength and vitality that had driven the man had fled in a few short weeks leaving behind a husk of humanity. His bones stood out against the sallow skin. There was no dignity in death for the Count of Sylvania.

Death, he finally understood, was the great leveller. It had no respect for ancestry or nobility of blood, and his death was determined to be as degrading as it could be. A week ago he had lost control of the muscles in his face and his tongue had bloated so much so he could barely lisp an intelligible sentence. Most of the words he managed sounded like nothing more than drunken gibberish.

For a man like Otto van Drak that was perhaps the most humiliating aspect of dying. Not for him the clean death of the battlefield, the bloodlust, the frenzy, the sheer glory of going out fighting. No, death, with its macabre sense of humour, had other humiliations lined up for him. His daughter had to bath him and help him go to the toilet while he sweated and shivered and barely managed to curse the gods who had reduced him to this.

He knew what was happening. His body was giving up the ghost one organ at a time. It was only the sheer force of his will that kept him breathing. He wasn't ready to die. Otto was contrary like that; he wanted to make them wait. It was one final act of stubbornness.

Using a cold compress his daughter Isabella leaned over the bed and towelled the sweat from his fevered brow.

'Hush, father,' she soothed, seeing that he was trying to say something. The frustration ate at his face, sheer loathing burned in his eyes. He was staring at his brother, Leopold, who slouched in a once plush crimson velvet chair. He looked thoroughly bored by the whole charade. They might have been brothers but there was no fraternal bond between them. Her mother had always claimed that the eyes were gateways to the soul. Isabella found them mesmerising. They contained such intensity of emotion and feeling. Nothing could be hidden by them. Eyes were so expressive. Looking into her father's now she could see the depth of his suffering. The old man was tormented by this degrading death but it would be over soon.

'Not long now,' the chirurgeon said to the priest, echoing her thoughts. He bent double over his case of saws and scalpels, rummaging around until he found a jar of fat-bodied leeches.

'Perhaps there is small mercy in that,' the priest said as the chirurgeon uncapped the jar and dipped his hand in. He stirred his hand through the leeches and lifted one out, placing it on the vein in Otto's neck so that it might feed.

'Leeches?' Isabella van Drak asked, her voice tinged with obvious distaste. 'Is that really necessary?'

'Bleeding is good for the heart,' the chirurgeon assured her. 'Reduces the strain if it has less to pump, which means it can keep on beating longer. Believe me, madam, my beauties will keep your father alive much, much longer if we let them do their work.' The young woman looked sceptical but she didn't stop the chirurgeon from placing six more of the blood-suckers on her father's body.

'All… talking about me… like I am… gone… Not… dead… yet…' Otto van Drak rasped. As though to prove the point he broke into a violent coughing fit before the last word was clear of his lips. He slapped ineffectually at the leeches feeding off him.

'Be still, father.' Isabella wiped away the mucus he coughed up.

'Damned… giving up… without… a fight.' Otto struggled to form the words. The frustration was too much for him.

Leopold pushed himself up from the chair and paced across the floor. He whispered something in the chirurgeon's ear and the other man nodded. Leopold stalked over to the window and braced his hands on the windowsill, feeling the wainscoting with his fingers. Listening to the old man's laboured breathing he dug his nails into the soft wood.

A jagged streak of lightning lit the room, throwing gnarled shadows across the inhabitants. Thunder rumbled a heartbeat later, the vibrations running through the thick walls of Castle Drakenhof. Leopold could barely keep the smug smile from his face. Rain lashed at the glass, breaking and running like tears through his reflection. He chuckled mirthlessly. Crying was the very last thing he felt like doing. 'You'll be damned anyway, you old goat. I'm sure the only reason you aren't dead already is that you are terrified they're all waiting for you on the other side. That's right isn't it, brother of mine? All of those wretched souls you put to death so cheerfully. You can hear them, can't you, Otto? You can hear them calling to you. You know they are waiting for you. Can you imagine what they are going to do to you when they finally get the chance at retribution? Oh my… what a delicious thought *that* is.'

Otto's eyes blazed with impotent rage.

'Come now, Otto. Show some dignity in your final hours. As Count of Sylvania I promise you I will do all I can to dishonour your memory.'

'Get… out!'

'What? And miss your final breath, brother mine? Oh no, not for all the spices in Araby. You, dear Otto, have always been an incorrigible liar and a cheat. Dishonesty is one of your few redeeming features, perhaps your only one. So, let me put it this way: I wouldn't be surprised if this was all one grand charade. Well, I won't be a laughing stock at your expense, brother. No, no, I'll wring the life out of you with my bare hands if I have to, but I won't leave this room until I've made sure you are well and truly dead. It's nothing personal, you understand, but I am walking out of here Count of Sylvania, and you, well the only way you are leaving here is in a box. If the roles were reversed I'm sure you'd do the same.'

'Damn you…'

'Oh yes, quite possibly. But I'll cross that bridge when I come to it, which looks like it will be a good while after you've already gone trip-trapping over it, eh? Now be a good chap and die.'

'Vile…'

'Again, quite possibly, but I can't help wondering what father would think if he could see you. I mean, no disrespect, but you are a mess, Otto. Dying obviously doesn't become you. It hasn't changed you much, either, for that matter. So much for learning the error of your ways. You are still too cheap to light a damned fire in your bedroom so we have to freeze while we wait for you to pop off.'

'Damn you… your children… damn all… rot… in pits… of hell. Never let you… be… count.' Otto clawed at the bed sheets, the skin around his knuckles bone-white. *'Never!'*

Lightning crashed once more, the bluish light illuminating the sickening fury in Otto van Drak's face. Twin forks struck somewhere along the mountain path between the castle and the town of Drakenhof itself. Fat rain broke and ran down the glass of the leaded window as another jag of lightning split the storm-black darkness. The wind howled. The wooden shutters rattled against the outer wall.

'I don't see that you have much say in the matter, all things considered,' Leopold said. 'That sham of a marriage you so conveniently engineered for Isabella with the Klinsmann runt, well it was laughable, wasn't it. I can't say I was surprised when the boy threw himself from the roof of the Almoners Hall. Still, all's well that ends well, eh, brother?'

Sitting down on the edge of the old man's bed, Isabella dabbed away the blood-flecked saliva that spattered his chin and turned her attention to her uncle. She had known him all of her life. At one time she had worshipped the ground he walked on but with age came the understanding that the man was a worm. 'And I suppose I have no say in the matter.'

Leopold studied his niece for an uncomfortable moment as she brushed the long dark hair back from her face. She was beautiful in her own way, pale-skinned and fine-boned. The combination crafted a glamour of delicacy around the girl though in truth she owned the foul van Drak temper and could be as devious as a weasel when the mood took her.

'None, I'm afraid, my dear. Would that it was otherwise, but I am not the law-maker. By accident of birth you came out... female. With no sons your father's line ends, and mine, as eldest surviving male begins. With your betrothed coming to such an... untimely end... well, that is just the way it is. You can't tamper with tradition, after all it becomes traditional for a reason. Though,' Leopold mused thoughtfully as though the idea had just occurred to him. He turned to look at the priest. 'Tell me, how does the benevolent Sigmar look upon the union of close family, say uncles and nieces, Brother Guttman? Being the kind of man I am, I might be convinced to make the sacrifice to set my dear brother's mind at rest. Wouldn't want to see the only good thing he ever managed to create forced into whoring on the street, would we?'

'It is frowned upon,' the aged priest said, not bothering to look at Leopold when he answered him. The priest made the sign of Sigmar's hammer in the air above Otto's head.

'Ah, well. Can't say I didn't try, my dear.' Leopold said with a lascivious wink.

'You would do well to mind your tongue, *uncle*.' Isabella said, coldly. 'This is still my home, and you are alone in it, whereas there are plenty of servants and men-at-arms here who remain loyal to my father, and in turn, to me.'

'A woman scorned and all that, eh? Well of course, dear. Threaten and bluster away. You know I love you like my own flesh and blood and would never see you suffer.'

'You would turn your back so you didn't have to watch,' Isabella finished for him.

'Damn, you've got spirit, girl, I'll give you that. A true van Drak. Heart and soul.'

'Hate… this. I don't… want… to die.' The leeches at his throat and temples pulsed as they fed on Otto van Drak. In the few minutes since the chirurgeon had placed them they had bloated up to almost a third again their size and still they sucked greedily at the dying count's blood.

'Pity you have no choice in the matter, old man. First you die, and then you will go to Morr and I am sure the Lord of the Underworld will delight in flensing your soul one layer at a time. After the kind of life you've led I can't imagine any amount of grovelling and snivelling by our friend the priest here will help you avoid what's coming to you.' Leopold said. 'Tell me, Brother Guttman, what says your god on this matter?' Leopold asked the stoop-shouldered priest of Sigmar. The man looked decidedly uncomfortable at being addressed directly.

'Only a repentant soul can be shrived of the taint of darkness,' the priest answered. Isabella helped the aged holy man kneel at Otto's bedside.

'And there you have it, brother, out of the mouthpiece of blessed Sigmar himself. You're damned.'

'Are you ready to unburden your soul of its sins before you meet Morr?' Victor Guttman asked Otto, ignoring Leopold's gloating.

'Get… away… from me… priest.' Otto spat a loose wad of phlegm into the priest's face. It clung to the cheekbone just below the old man's eye before slipping down into the grey shadow of his stubble. The frail priest wiped it away with a shaking hand. 'I have nothing … nothing… to repent. Save your breath… and mine.' Otto trailed off into a fit of raving, spitting out half-formed words and curses in a senseless torrent.

'Father, please,' Isabella said softly but it was no good, the old man wasn't about to be convinced to cleanse his soul.

'Oh, this is wonderful stuff, Otto. Quite wonderful,' Leopold gloated. 'Do you think I have time to summon the priests of Shallya and Ulric so you can alienate their gods, too? Any others you would particularly like to offend?' Another jag of lightning split the darkness. If anything the storm was worsening. The shutters clattered against the stonework outside, splinters of wood tearing free. The wind howled through the eaves, moaning in high pitched chorus from the snarling mouths of the weather-beaten gargoyles that guarded the four corners of the high tower. 'Every bitter word that froths from your mouth is rubbish, of course, Otto, but such marvellous rubbish. Give it up. All this breathing must be awfully tiresome. I know I am growing tired of it.'

The laughter died in his throat.

Three successive shafts of lightning turned the black night for a heartbeat into bright day. The storm lashed the countryside. The trees bent and bowed in the gale. Skeletal branches strained to the point of breaking. Thunder grumbled around the hilltops, the heavy sounds folding in on themselves until they boomed like orc war drums.

A shiver chased down the ladder of Leopold's spine one bone at a time. Behind him the priest pressed Otto to confess his sins.

'It's pointless,' Leopold said, turning to smile at the earnest priest. The old man's hands trembled and every trace of colour had drained from his face. 'If he starts at the beginning he won't make it out of his teens before Morr takes him. Our Otto has been a very bad boy.'

'Morr… take… you…' Otto cursed weakly as a fit of coughing gripped him. He hacked up blood. Brother Guttman took the towel from Isabella and made to wipe up the red-flecked saliva but Otto jerked his head away with surprising strength. 'Get… away from me… priest… won't have you… touch me.' Otto slumped back exhausted onto his pillows.

As though the sheer force of Otto's loathing had undone him, the priest staggered back a step, his hand fluttering up weakly toward Isabella to prevent himself from falling as his knees buckled, then swayed and collapsed. The side of his head and shoulder cracked off the rim of the bedside table with the sick sound of wet meat being tenderised.

Mellin, van Drak's chirurgeon, moved quickly to the fallen priest. 'Alive,' he said, feeling the faint pulse at Brother Guttman's throat. 'Though barely.'

Lightning rent the fabric of the bruise-purple sky, the incessant drumming of the fat rain stopped suddenly.

The frail priest contorted in a series of violent convulsions, almost as though his body were somehow earthing the raw electricity of the storm. And then he lay deathly still.

In the deafening silence that followed there was a single sharp knock and the door opened.

A terrified man-servant stood in the doorway, head down, humble. A hauntingly handsome man pushed past the servant, not waiting for his formal introduction. The stranger was easily a head taller than Leopold, if not more, and had to stoop slightly to enter the bedchamber. In his hand he held a silver-topped cane. The handle had been fashioned into the likeness of a dire wolf, teeth bared in a feral snarl. The shoulders of his cloak were a darker black where they were soaked through with rain and water dripped from the brim of his hat.

'The noble Vlad von Carstein, my l-lord,' the servant stuttered. With a wave of the hand, the newcomer dismissed the servant who scurried off gratefully.

The sound of rain rushed back to drown the silence in the very heart of the storm.

The newcomer approached the bed. His boots left wet prints on the cold wooden boards. Leopold stared at them, trying to fathom where the man had come from. 'Out of the storm,' he mumbled, shaking his head.

'I bid thee humble greeting, Count van Drak,' the man's accent was peculiarly thick; obviously foreign. Kislevite perhaps, or further east, Leopold thought, trying to place it. 'And you, fair lady,' he said, turning to Isabella, 'are quite enchanting. A pale rose set between these withered thorns.'

Her face lit up with that simple compliment. She broke into a lopsided smile and curtseyed, never taking her eyes from the man's. And such eyes he had. They were animalistic in their intensity, filled with nameless hungers. She felt herself being devoured by his gaze and surrendered willingly to the sensation. The man had *power* and he was not averse to exploiting it. A slow predatory smile spread across his face. Isabella felt herself being drawn to the newcomer. It was a subtle but irresistible sensation. She took a step toward him.

'Stop staring, woman, it is quite unbecoming.' Leopold snapped. 'And you, sir.' He turned his attention to the stranger. 'Thank you for coming, but as I am sure you can see, you are intruding on a somewhat personal moment. My brother is failing fast and, as you only die once, we would like to share his last few minutes, just the family, I am sure you understand. If you care to wait until… ah… afterwards, I would be pleased to see you in one of the reception rooms to discuss whatever business you have with the count?' He gestured toward the door, but instead of leaving the newcomer removed his white gloves, teasing them off one finger at a time, and took Isabella's hand. He raised it to his lips and let the kiss linger there, ignoring Leopold's blustering, the convulsing priest and the chirurgeon as they were clearly of no interest to him.

'I am Vlad eldest of the von Carstein family–' the newcomer said to the dying count, ignoring Leopold's posturing.

'I don't know the family,' Leopold interrupted somewhat peevishly.

'And neither would I expect you to,' the stranger countered smoothly. He regarded Leopold as though he were nothing more interesting than an insect trapped in a jar of honey, the sole fascination being in watching it drown in the sticky sweetness. 'But I can trace my lineage to a time before van Hal, to the founding of the Empire and beyond, which is more than can be said of many of today's nobility, yes? True nobility is a legacy of the blood, not something earned as the spoils of war, wouldn't you agree?' Vlad unclasped the hasp on his travel cloak and draped it over the back of the crimson chair. He set the wolf's head cane down to rest beside it, laying his white gloves over the snarling silver fangs, the wet hat on top of the gloves. His raven black hair was bound in a single braid that reached midway down the length of his back. There was an arrogance about the man that Leopold found disquieting. He moved with the grace of a natural predator stalking tender prey but equally there was no denying the fellow possessed a certain magnetism.

'Indeed,' Leopold agreed. 'And what, pray tell, brings you to us on such a foul night? Does my brother owe you thirty silvers, or perhaps he had your betrothed executed on one of his foolish whims? Let me assure you, as the new count, I will endeavour to make good on whatever debt you feel the family owes you. It is the very least I can do.'

'My business is with the count, not his lackey.'

'I don't see what–'

'There is no need for you to see anything, sir. I was merely in the vicinity, travelling to the wedding of a close friend, and I thought it right and proper to pledge fealty to the *current* Count van Drak, to offer my services in any way he might see fit.'

In the bed Otto chuckled mirthlessly. The chuckle gave way to another violent fit of coughing.

'Marry...' Otto's eyes blazed with vindictive glee. 'Yes,' the dying count hissed maliciously. 'Yes... yes.'

'Preposterous! I will not stand for this nonsense!' Leopold spluttered, a flush of colour rising in his cheeks so the broken blood vessels showed through angrily. 'In a few hours *I* will be count and I will have you drawn and quartered and your head on a spike before sunrise, do you hear me, fool?'

Otto managed something halfway between a cough and a laugh.

On the floor, the priest of Sigmar was gripped by a second, more violent, series of spasms. The chirurgeon struggled to hold him fast and prevent the old man from biting off or swallowing his tongue in the depths of the fit.

'Like... hell... will... see you *ruined* first!' Otto spat, an echo of his true self in his final defiance.

'Sir,' Vlad said, kneeling at the bedside. 'If that would be your will, I came to be of service, an answer to your prayer, and as such I would gladly accept the hand of your daughter Isabella as my wife, and would that you were alive to see us married.'

'No!' Leopold grabbed at Vlad's shoulder.

The priest's heels drummed on the floor punctuating Leopold's outburst.

'Excuse me,' Vlad said softly, and then rose and turned in one fluid motion, his hand snaking out with dizzying speed to close around Leopold van Drak's throat.

'You are annoying me, little man,' Vlad rasped, lifting Leopold up onto the tips of his toes, so that they were eye to eye. He held him there, Leopold kicking out weakly and flapping at Vlad's hand as the fingers tightened mercilessly around his throat, choking the very life out of him. Leopold struggled to draw even a single breath. He batted and clawed at Vlad's hand but the man's grip was relentless.

And then, almost casually, Vlad tossed him aside.

Leopold slumped to the floor, retching and gasping for breath.

'Now, we do appear to have a priest, could you rouse him?' Vlad von Carstein told the chirurgeon. 'Then we can get on with the ceremony. I would hazard that Count van Drak does not have long left, and it would be a shame to rob him of the joy of seeing his beloved daughter wed, would it not?'

Mellin nodded but didn't move. He was staring at Leopold as he struggled to rise.

'Now,' Vlad said. It was barely above a whisper but it was as though the word itself possessed power. The chirurgeon fumbled for his bag and knocked it over, sending its contents skittering across the floor. On hands and knees he picked through the mess until he found a small astringent salve. Shaking, he smeared the ointment on Brother Guttman's upper lip. The Sigmarite priest shuddered and came to, spluttering and slapping at his mouth. Seeing Vlad for the first time, the aged priest recoiled, reflexively making the sign of Sigmar's hammer in the air between them.

'We have need of your services, priest,' Vlad said, his voice like silk as his words wrapped around the priest, caressing the man into doing his bidding. 'The count would have his daughter wed before he passes.'

'You cannot do this to me! I won't allow this to happen! This is my birthright! Sylvania, this castle… it is all mine!' Leopold blustered. He needed the support of the wall to help him stand.

'On the contrary, good sir. The count can do anything – *anything* – that he so wishes. He is a law unto himself. If he bade me reach into your chest and rip out your heart with my bare hands and feed it to his dogs, well,' he held his hands out, palms up, then turned them over as though inspecting them. 'It might prove difficult, but if the count willed it, believe me, it would be done.'

He turned to Isabella. 'And what of you, my lady? It is customary for the bride to say "yes" at some point during the proceedings.'

'When my father dies *he*,' Isabella levelled a finger at the cringing Leopold, 'inherits his estate, the castle, the title, everything that by rights should be mine. All my life I've lived in the shadow of the van Drak men. I've had no life. I've played the dutiful daughter. I've been possessed – and now, my father is dying and I hunger for freedom. I hunger for it so desperately I can almost taste it, and in you, perhaps finally, I can realise it. So give me what I want, and I will give myself to you, body and soul.'

'And what would that be?'

She turned to look at her father in his death bed, and saw the malicious delight in his face. She smiled: 'Everything. But first, a token… A morning gift, I believe they call it. From the groom to the bride as proof of his love.'

'This is ridiculous!' Leopold shouted, his voice cracking with the strain of it.

'Anything,' Vlad said, ignoring him. 'If it is in my power to give, you shall have it.'

She smiled then, and it was as though she sloughed off the years of subjugation with that simple expression of pleasure. She drew him to her and whispered something in his ear as he kissed her delicately on the cheek.

'As you wish,' Vlad said.

He turned to face an apoplectic Leopold.

'I am a fair man, Leopold van Drak. I would not see you suffer unduly so I have a proposition for you. I will give you time to ponder it. Five minutes ought to suffice. Think about it, while the priest gets ready for the ceremony, and my wife to be makes sure her father is comfortable, and then, and only then, after five full minutes have passed, if you can look me in the eye and tell me that you truly wish me to stand aside, well then, I will have to accede to your will.'

'Are you serious?' Leopold asked somewhat incredulously. He hadn't expected the stranger to back down so easily.

'Always. What is a man if there is no honour to be found in his word? You have my word. Now, do you accept?'

Leopold met Vlad's coldly glowing eyes. The startling intensity of the hatred he saw blazing there had him involuntarily backing up a step. He felt the wall and the ridge of the windowsill dig into the base of his back.

'I do,' he said, knowing it was a trap even as he allowed himself to be shepherded into it.

'Good,' Vlad von Carstein said flatly. In four quick strides he was across the room. With one hand he picked Leopold up by the scruff of the neck, the other he rammed into the man's chest, splintering the bone as his fingers closed around the already dead man's heart. In a moment of shocking savagery he wrenched it free and hurled the corpse through the window. There were no screams.

The dead man's heart in his hand, Vlad leaned out through the window. Lightning crashed in the distance. The eye of the storm had passed over Drakenhof and was moving away. In the lightning's afterglow he saw the outline of Leopold's body spread out on a flat rooftop three storeys below, arms and legs akimbo in a whorish sprawl.

Isabella joined him at the broken window, linking her fingers with his, slick with her uncle's blood. But for the blood the gesture might have been mistaken for an intimate one. Instead it hinted at the darkness inside her: by taking his hand she was claiming him and the life he offered every bit as much as he was claiming her and the power her heritage represented.

The power.

'Your gift,' he said, offering the heart to her.

'Throw it away, now that it has stopped beating I have no use for it,' she said, drawing him away from the window.

Somewhere in the night a wolf howled. It was a haunting lament made more so by the wind and the rain.

'It sounds so... lonely.'

'It is missing its mate. Wolves are one of the few creatures that mate for life. It will know no other love. It is the creature's curse to be alone.'

Isabella shivered, drawing Vlad closer to her. 'Let's have no more talk of loneliness.' Rising onto tiptoes she kissed the man who promised to give her *everything* her heart desired.

CHAPTER ONE
A Fisher of Devils

A SYLVANIAN BORDER TOWN
Early spring, 2009

THE LAND WAS devoid of life. No insects chirped, no frogs croaked, there was no bird song, not even the whisper of the breeze stirring leaves in the trees. The silence was unnatural. The malignancy, Jon Skellan realised, infected everything. It was ingrained in the very earth of the land itself. Its sickness ate away at everything; decay only an inch beneath the surface. The trees, still bare despite the turning of the season into what ought to have been the first flush of spring, were rotten to the core. Scanning the skeletal branches overhead Skellan saw that the only nest was empty, and judging by the way the twigs had been unravelled by the weather, had been empty for a long time. It was a spiritual canker. The land – this land – was soaked in blood, cruelty and despair.

Skellan shuddered.

Beside him, Stefan Fischer made the sign of Sigmar's hammer.

The two of them were chasing ghosts but what better place to come looking for them than the barren lands of Sylvania?

'Verhungern Wood. Starvation Wood, or Hunger Wood. I'm not sure about the precise interpretation of the dialect into Reikspiel. Still, the name seems disturbingly appropriate, doesn't it?'

'Aye, it does,' Fischer agreed, looking at the rows of dead and dying trees. It was difficult to believe that less than two days walk behind them spring in all of her beauty was unfolding in the daffodils and crocuses along the banks of the River Stir. 'Forests are meant to be living things, full of living things.' And by saying it out loud, Fischer voiced what had been bothering Skellan for the last hour. There was a total lack of life around them. 'Not like this blasted, barren place. It's unnatural.'

Skellan uncorked the flask he carried at his hip and took a deep swig of water. He wiped his mouth with the back of his hand and sighed. They were a long way from home – and in more ways than simply distance. This place was unlike anywhere he had ever been before. He had heard tales of Sylvania, but like most he assumed they were exaggerated with fishwives' gossip and the usual tall tales of self-proclaimed adventurers. The reality was harsher than he had imagined. The land had suffered under centuries of abuse and misrule, which of course made their arrival here inevitable. It was their calling; to root out evil, to cleanse the world of the black arts and the villainous scum who dabbled in them.

The pair had been called many things; the simplest, though least accurate, being witch hunters. Jon Skellan found it interesting that the agony of grief could earn a man such an epithet. He hadn't made a conscious choice to become the man he was today. Life had shaped him, bent him, buckled him, but it had not broken him. Now, seven years to the month, if not the week, since the riders had come burning and looting to his home, here he was, chasing ghosts, or rather looking to finally lay them to rest.

'All roads lead to hell,' he said, bitterly.

'Well, this one brought us to Sylvania,' Fischer said.

'Same place, my friend, same godforsaken place.'

The ruining of one lifestyle and the birth of their new one had been shockingly quick. Skellan and Fischer had married sisters and become widowers within a quarter of an hour of each other. The highs and the lows of their lives were bound together. Fate can be cruel like that. Skellan looked at his brother-in-law. No one would ever mistake them for family. At thirty-six, Fischer was nine years older than Skellan, a good six inches taller and a stone heavier where the muscles had started to slide into fat, but the two men shared a single disturbing similarity: their eyes. Their eyes said they had seen a future filled with happiness, and it had been snatched away from them. The loss had aged them far beyond their years. Their souls were old, hardened. They had experienced the worst that life could throw at them, and they had survived. Now it was about vengeance.

A beetle the size of a mouse skittered across the ground less than a foot in front of his feet. It was the first living thing they had encountered in hours and it was hardly encouraging.

'Have you ever wondered what it might have been like if…' He didn't need to clarify the 'if'. They both knew what he was talking about.

'Every day,' Fischer said, not looking at him. 'It's like walking out of the storyteller's circle halfway through his tale… you don't know how it is supposed to end and you keep obsessing over it. What would life have been like if Leyna and Lizbet hadn't been murdered? Where would we be now? Not here, that's for sure.'

'No… not here.' Skellan agreed. 'No use getting maudlin.' He straightened as he said it, drawing himself upright as though shrugging off the heavy burden of sadness thinking about Lizbet always brought with it. It was, of course, an act. He could no more shrug off his grief than he could forget what caused it in the first place. It was simply a case of managing it. Skellan had long since come to terms with his wife's death. He accepted it. It had happened. He didn't forgive it, and he didn't forget.

There had been seven riders that day. It had taken time, almost seven years to be exact, but six of them were in the ground now, having paid the ultimate price for their sins. Skellan and Fischer had seen to that, and in doing so they showed the men no quarter. Like their victims, like Leyna and Lizbet and the other souls they sent to Morr in their frenzy, they burned. It wasn't pretty but then death never is. They caught up with the first of the murderers almost three months later, in a tavern drunk to the point where he could barely stand. Skellan had dragged him outside, dunked him in the horse's watering trough until the murderer came up coughing and spluttering and sober enough to know he was in trouble. The knee is a very delicate hinge protected by a bone cap. Skellan shattered one of the man's kneecaps with a brutal kick through the joint, and dragged him screaming into the room he lodged in. 'You've got a chance,' Skellan had said. 'Not a very good chance, but more of one than you gave my wife.' It wasn't true. Unable to stand, let alone walk, the man didn't have a chance against the flames and the smoke – and even if by some miracle he had dragged himself clear of the fire, Skellan and Fischer were waiting outside to see he joined the ranks of Morr's dead.

There was no satisfaction in it. No sense of a wrong having been righted or justice having been done.

It was all about vengeance and one by one the murderers burned.

At first it had been like a sickness inside him, and it had only grown worse until it became an all-consuming need to make the murderers pay for what they had done. But even their deaths didn't take the pain away, so for a while he made them die harder.

By the time they caught up with the fourth murderer, a snivelling wretch of a man, Skellan had devised his torture jacket. The coat had extra long sleeves and buckles so that they could be fastened in such a way that the wearer was trapped, helpless. The coat itself was doused in lamp oil. It was a brutal way to die, but Skellan justified it to himself by saying he was doing it for Lizbet and for all the others the murderer had tortured and burned alive. Lying to himself was a skill he had perfected over the seven-year hunt. He knew full well what he was doing. He was extracting vengeance for the dead.

It was guilt, he knew, that drove him. Guilt for the fact that he had failed them in life. Guilt for the fact that he hadn't been there to save them from the savagery of their murderers, and his guilt was an ugly thing because once it had wormed its way into his head it refused to give up its hold. It ate away at his mind. It convinced him that there was something he could have done. That it was his fault that Lizbet and Leyna and all of the others were dead.

So he carried with him his own personal daemons and didn't argue when he heard people cry: 'The witch hunter is coming!'

They walked on a while in silence, both men locked in thoughts of the past, neither one needing to say a word.

After a while the wind picked up, and carried with it a smell they were painfully familiar with.

Burning flesh.

AT FIRST SKELLAN thought it was his mind playing tricks on him, bringing back old ghosts to torment him, but beside him Fischer stopped and sniffed suspiciously at the air as though trying to locate the source of the smell and he realised the burning wasn't in his mind, it was here, now. There would be no burning without fire, and no fire without smoke. He scanned the trees looking for any hint of smoke, but it was impossible to see more than a few feet either way. The entire forest could have been on fire and without the press of heat from the conflagration he would never have known. The wind itself offered no clues. They had walked into a slight declivity that cut like a shallow U through the landscape. It meant that the wind was funnelled down through channel before folding back on itself. The tang of smoke and the sickly sweet stench of burned meat could have come from almost any direction. But it couldn't have come from far away. The smell would have dissipated over any great distance.

Skellan turned in a slow circle.

There was no hint of smoke or fire to the right, or where the valley spread out before them, and the withered line of trees masked any hint of smoke to the left but the fact that there were trees to hide the fire where everywhere else was barren told Skellan all he needed to know.

'This way,' he said, and started to run into the trees.

Fischer set off after him but found it difficult to keep up with the younger man.

Branches clawed at his clothes and scratched at his face as he pushed his way through them. Brittle twigs snapped underfoot. The smell of burning grew stronger the deeper into the wood they went.

And still there were no sounds or signs of life apart from Fischer's laboured breathing and bullish footsteps.

As he pushed on, Skellan realised that the press of the trees began to thin noticeably. He stumbled into the clearing without realising that was what he had found. It was a village, of sorts, in the wood. He pulled up short. There was a scattering of low houses made of wattle and daub, and a fire pit in what would be the small settlement's meeting place. Early spring mist clung to the air. The fire was ablaze, dead wood banked high. A body had been laid out on top of the wood, wrapped in some kind of cloth that had all but burned away. A handful of mourners gathered around the pyre, their faces limned with soot and tears as they turned to look at the intruders. An old man with close-cropped white hair appeared to be officiating over the ceremony.

Skellan held up his hands in a sign of peace and backed up a step, not wanting to intrude further on their grief.

'Peculiar ritual,' Fischer muttered as he finally caught up. 'Burning the dead instead of burying them.'

'But not unheard of,' Skellan agreed. 'More common during times of strife, certainly. Soldiers will honour their dead on such a funeral pyre. But this, I fear, is done for a very different reason.'

'Plague?'

'That would be my guess, though by rights an outbreak in a village this small would wipe the place out virtually overnight and burning the first victims won't matter a damn. How many live here? One hundred? Less? It isn't even a village, it's a handful of houses. If it is the plague, I pity them because they're doomed. I doubt very much whether this place will be here when we come back through these woods in a few months time. We *should* leave them in peace, but we're not going to. Let's give them some privacy to complete the ritual then I want to talk to some people. The burning of the dead has my curiosity piqued.'

'Aye, it is an odd thing, but then we are in an odd place. Who knows what these people think is normal?'

They waited just beyond the skirt of the tree line until the fire burned itself out. Despite their retreat out of sight the mourners were uncomfortably aware of their presence and cast occasional glances their way, trying to see them through the shadows. Skellan sat with his back against a tree. He whittled at a small piece of deadfall with his knife, shaping it into the petals of a crude flower. Beside him Fischer closed his eyes and fell into a light sleep. It always amazed the witch hunter how his friend seemed capable of sleeping at any time, in any place imaginable. It was a useful skill. He himself could never empty his mind enough to sleep. He worried about the smallest details. Obsessed about them.

Even this close to the small settlement the woods were disturbingly quiet. It was unnatural. He had no doubt about that. But what had caused the animals to abandon this place? That was the question that nagged away at the back of his mind. He knew full well that animals were sensitive to all kinds of danger; it was that survival instinct that kept them alive. Something had caused them to leave this part of Verhungern Wood.

Jon Skellan looked up at the sound of cautious footsteps approaching. Stefan Fischer's eyes snapped open and his hand moved reflexively toward the knife on his belt. It was the old man who had been leading the funeral; only up close Skellan saw that it wasn't a man at all. Her heavily lined features and close-cropped white hair had rendered the woman sexless over distance but close up there was no mistaking her femininity. There was a deep sadness in her eyes. She knew full well the fate awaiting her settlement. Death hung like a sword over her head. A heady mix of per-fumes and scents clung to her clothing. She was trying to hold the sickness back with pungent smelling poultices and essences of plant extracts. It was useless of course. The plague would not be fooled or deterred by pretty smells.

'It isn't safe for you here,' she said without pream-ble. Her voice was thickly accented, as though she were grating stones in her throat while she spoke.

Skellan nodded and pushed himself to his feet. He held out his hand in greeting. The old woman refused to take it. She looked at him as though he were insane to even contemplate touching her. Perhaps he was, but death held no fears for Jon Skellan. It hadn't for a long time. If plague took him then so be it. He would not hide himself away from it.

'I'll be the judge of that,' he said. 'Plague?'

The old woman's eyes narrowed as she looked at him. She transferred her gaze to Fischer, and rather like a mother berating an errant child scolded. 'And you can forget about your knife, young man. It isn't that kind of death that haunts these trees.'

'I guessed as much,' Skellan said. 'From the pyre. It brought back memories…'

'I can't imagine what kind of memories a funeral pyre would bring back… oh,' she said. 'I am sorry.'

Skellan nodded again. 'Thank you. We are looking for a man. He goes by the name of Aigner. Sebastian Aigner. We know he crossed over the border into Syl-vania two moons back, and that he is claiming to be hunting a cult, but the man is not what he seems.'

'I wish I could help you,' the old woman said rue-fully, 'but we tend to keep ourselves to ourselves here.'

'I understand.' Skellan bowed his head, as though beaten, the weight of the world dragging it down, and then he looked up as though something had just occurred to him. 'The plague? When did it first show up here? The first death?'

The old woman was surprised by the bluntness of the question.

'A month back, perhaps a little more.'

'I see. And yet no strangers passed through?'

She looked him squarely in the eye, knowing full well the implication of what he was suggesting. 'We keep ourselves to ourselves,' she repeated.

'You know, for some strange reason I am not inclined to believe you.' He looked to Fischer for confirmation.

'Something doesn't smell right,' the older man agreed. 'I'd be willing to wager our boy is tucked away in there somewhere.'

'No, he's moved on,' Skellan said, watching the old woman's face for any flicker of betrayal. It was difficult to lie well, and simple folk were more often than not appalling when it came to hiding the truth. It was in the eyes. It was always in the eyes. 'But he was here.'

She blinked once and licked at her lower lip. It was all he needed to know. She was lying.

'Did he bring the sickness with him?'

The old woman said nothing.

'Why would you protect the man who had, by accident or design, condemned your entire village to death? That is what I don't understand. Is it some sort of misguided loyalty?'

'Fear,' Fischer said.

'Fear,' Skellan said. 'That would mean you expect him to return…'

Her eyes darted left and right, as though she expected the man to actually be close enough to overhear them.

'That's it, isn't it? He threatened to come back.'

'We keep to ourselves,' the old woman repeated but her eyes said: *Yes he threatened to come back. He threatened to come back and kill us all if we told anyone about him. He damned us, either he kills us or the sickness he brought with him does… there is no justice in our world anymore.*

'He has a month on us. The distance is closing. I wonder if he looks over his shoulder nervously, expecting the worst? He can run for his life. It doesn't matter. It isn't his life anymore. It is mine. One day he will wake up and I will be standing over him, waiting to collect my due. He knows that. It eats away at him the way it ate away at his friends, only now he is the last. He knows that, too. I can almost smell his fear on the wind. Now, the question is where would he go from here? What are the obvious places?'

'Do you really think Aigner would be that stupid, Jon?' Fischer asked. He was talking for the sake of it. He was looking over the old woman's shoulder. The mourners were clearing away the ashes, gathering them into some kind of clay urn.

'Absolutely. Remember he is running for his life. That has a way of driving you forward without really thinking clearly. He sees limited choices. Always going forward, looking for shelter in the crush of people that civilisation offers. So,' he smiled at the old woman. 'Where can we go from here? Are there any settlements nearby big enough for us to lose ourselves in?'

'Like I said, we keep to ourselves,' the old woman sniffed, 'so we don't have much call for visiting other towns, but there are places of course, back on the main track. You have Roistone-Vasie four days' walk from here. It is a market town. With spring people will be gathering now. Beyond that you've got Leicheberg. It is the closest we have to a city.'

'Thank you,' Skellan said. He knew the lie of the land. The old woman had given them directions without having to betray her people. Sebastian Aigner had left here a month ago, heading for Leicheberg. It was a city, with all of the inherent distractions of a city: taverns, whores, gambling tables and the simplest things of life itself, food and a warm bed. Even running for his life it would slow him down. The press of people would give the illusion of safety.

Over her shoulder they were digging a small hole in the dirt for the urn.

'Might I?' Skellan asked, holding up the wooden flower he had carved while waiting for the funeral to end.

'It would be better if I did,' the old woman said.

'Perhaps, but it would be more personal if I laid it on her grave.'

She nodded.

Skellan took her nod as tacit agreement and walked across the small clearing. A few of the other villagers looked up as he approached. He felt their eyes on him but he didn't alter his stride. It took him a full minute to approach the freshly dug grave.

'How old was she?' he asked, kneeling beside the churned soil. He didn't look at anyone as he placed the delicate wooden flower on the dark soil.

'Fourteen,' someone said.

'My daughter's age,' Skellan said. 'I am truly sorry for your loss. May your god watch over her.'

He made the sign of the hammer as he rose to leave.

'I hope you kill the bastards that did this to my little girl.' The man's voice was full of bitterness. Skellan knew the emotion only too well. It was all that was left when the world collapsed around you.

He turned to face the speaker. When he spoke his voice was cold and hard. 'I certainly intend to.'

Without another word he walked back to where Fischer and the old woman waited.

'That was a kind thing you did, thank you.'

'The loss of anyone so young is a tragedy we can ill afford to bear. It was only a token, and it cost me nothing.'

'Truly, but few would have taken the time to pay their respects to a stranger. It is the way of the world, I fear. We forget the suffering of others all too easily, especially those left behind.'

Skellan turned to Fischer. 'Come, my friend. We should leave these good people to their grieving.'

Fischer nodded, and then cocked his head as though listening to some out of place sound in the silence of the forest. 'Tell me,' he said, after a moment. 'Has it always been this quiet here?'

'Quiet? Heavens, no,' the old woman said, shaking her head. 'And at night it is far from quiet. There's no denying that a lot of the creatures left with the coming of the wolves. They don't bother us and we don't bother them. They hunt at night, during the day they sleep.' She leaned in close, her voice dropping conspiratorially. 'Be careful though, when you are walking at night. Keep to the paths. Don't leave the paths. Never leave the paths. Verhungern isn't a safe place at night.'

With that final warning she left them on the edge of the trees. They watched her shuffle towards the mourners at the graveside. Fischer turned to Skellan. 'What on earth was that all about?'

'I'm not sure, but I am not in a hurry to find out, either.'

They kept well within the cover of the trees as they worked their way around the settlement until they came upon the narrow cotter's path that led through the trees back towards the main road and would eventually arrive at the market town of Roistone-Vasie. They had no more than a few hours of walking before nightfall and he had no intention of sleeping in the forest. It was a godforsaken place. The old woman's warning echoed in his mind. Keep to the paths. Skellan had his suspicions about what she meant. He was well aware of the horrors that walked abroad come nightfall.

They walked on awhile in silence, leaving the trees of Verhungern Wood behind. The road ran parallel to the forest for miles. The oppressive feeling that had been weighing the two men down since they entered the forest lifted almost as soon as they returned to the road. Neither man commented on it. Fischer dismissed it as nothing more than his nerves and imagination combining to play tricks on him. Skellan wasn't quite so quick to dismiss the feeling.

In the distance a dark smudge of mountains came into view but quickly lost its definition to the falling night.

THEY MADE CAMP by the roadside, not far enough away from the menace of the dark trees for comfort. Normally they would have eaten fresh meat, caught and killed less than an hour before they ate it, but there was no game to be hunted so they had to make do with the dry bread they had carried with them for three days since crossing the River Stir, and a hunk of pungent cheese. It barely touched their hunger.

Sitting at the makeshift fire, Skellan scanned the brooding darkness of the trees. It was disturbing how the shadows seemed to shift as he stared at them, as though something inside them moved.

'Not the most hospitable place we've ever visited, is it?' Fischer said. He chewed on a mouthful of hard bread and washed it down with a mouthful of water from his hip flask.

'No. What would make a man run into this blasted land? How could anyone choose to live here?'

'The key word is *live*, Jon. Aigner is hoping we'll lose him in this hellhole. And I can't say that I blame him. I mean, only a fool would willingly march into the wastes of Sylvania with nothing but mouldy cheese and stale bread to keep him alive.'

In the distance, a wolf howled. It was the first sound of life they had heard in hours. It wasn't a comforting one. It was answered moments later by another, then a third.

Skellan stared at the blackness beyond the trees, suddenly sure that he could see yellow eyes staring back at him. He shivered.

'They sound as hungry as I feel,' Fischer moaned, holding up what remained of his meal.

'Well, let's just hope they don't decide you're fat enough for the main course.'

'Hope is the last thing to die, you know that,' Fischer said, suddenly serious for a moment.

'Yes, always the innocents go first, like that girl back there.'

'Do you think he killed her? I mean, it doesn't seem like his style,' Fischer said, worrying at a string of cheese that had somehow gotten stuck in his teeth. The older man poked at it with his finger, digging it out.

'Who knows what depths the man is capable of stooping to. When you consort with the dead who knows what sicknesses you carry inside you? Aigner is the worst kind of monster; he wears a human face and yet he revels in depravity. He is sick to the core, yet he looks just like you or me. See him in a crowd and no one would be able to tell, but that sickness eats away at his humanity. An evil. He courts death. Is it any wonder he is drawn to the blackest arts? No, we will find our man, in Leicheberg or somewhere close, wherever the sickness of mankind is at its worst. That is where he will be And then he will burn.'

A chorus of wolves howls filled the night, the baying cries echoing all around them.

'It isn't going to be easy to sleep tonight,' Skellan muttered, looking once again at the shadows cloaking the fringe of Verhungern Wood.

'I'm sure I'll manage,' Fischer said with a grin, and he wasn't lying. Within five minutes of his head hitting the bedroll he was snoring as though he didn't have a care in the world.

Skellan gave up trying to sleep after an hour, and instead concentrated on listening to the sounds of nocturnal life stirring in the forest. He could hear the wolves, padding back and forth just beyond the tree line. He thought again of the old woman's warning to stay on the path. He had no intention of moving away from the dubious safety the path offered. It seemed, at least, that the trees acted as some kind of natural barrier that the wolves dared not cross.

It hadn't been his imagination. Sickly yellow eyes really were watching them from the forest. A wolf, a giant of a wolf, came close enough to be seen through the silver moonlight. The creature was easily twice the size of a big dog with a long snout and jowls that Skellan imagined curled back in a snarl, saliva flecking the animal's yellowed teeth. The wolf remained there, stock still and staring back directly at him, long enough for Skellan to feel his heartbeat triple as it thudded against his chest and his breathing become shallow with the onset of fear, but it didn't leave the shelter of the trees. Skellan didn't move. He didn't dare to. A single sudden movement could cause the animal to launch an attack and he was in no doubt as to who would come out on top in a fight between man and this particular beast. Beside him Fischer slept like a babe, oblivious to the wolf.

As quickly as it came, the wolf was gone. It ghosted away silently into the darkness. Skellan let out a breath he didn't know he had been holding. The tension drained from his body with surprising speed.

He heard more wolf howls as the night wore into morning but they were always distant and getting further away each time. He ached. His back ached, the base of his spine the focal point for the irregular jabs of pain that helped keep him awake all night. The inside of his arms burned from being always ready to reach quickly for his knife. The bones in his legs transmogrified to lead and weighed down through the tired muscle encasing them. With exhausted sleep there for the taking the sun rose redly on the horizon.

Daybreak.

Fischer stirred.

Skellan kicked him with the flat of his foot. 'Sleep well?'

The older man sat up. He knuckled the sleep from his eyes. Then, remembering, shuddered. He exhaled, hard. The breath sounded like a hiss of steam. 'No. No not at all.'

'Looked like you did all right to me,' Skellan said, unable to keep the bitterness of exhaustion out of his words.

'I dreamed... I dreamed that I was one of them, one of the wolves prowling the forest. I dreamed that I found you in the darkness, that all I wanted to do was feed on your flesh... I had to fight every instinct in my body just to stay still, to wait back behind the line of the trees because some part of me, the human part of the wolf, remembered you were my friend. I swear it felt like I stared at you for hours.' He stretched and cracked the joints in his shoulders, first the right shoulder, then the left. 'Morr's teeth, it was so real. I swear I could taste your fear on the air with my tongue… and part of me thought it was the most delicious thing I had ever tasted. I was inside the head of the thing but it was inside me too.'

'If it makes you feel any better you didn't move so much as a muscle all night, and yes, I was awake all night.'

'Doesn't matter. I'll be happy when we are away from here.' Fischer said with absolute conviction.

'I won't argue with you there.' Skellan rose stiffly. He hunched over, stretching out the muscles in his back. He grunted. He moved through a series of stretches, using the exercise to focus his mind. Fischer's dream disturbed him, not because he thought his friend had some latent psychic talent that stirred conveniently for him to enter the beast's mind, but because, perhaps the wolf, or whatever it really was, had found a way into his friend while he slept. That possibility made putting as much distance between themselves and Verhungern Wood their main priority.

They walked for the best part of the day, the wolves' howls receding into the distance, before exhaustion overcame them, forcing them to bed down beside a brackish river. Signs of life returned to the countryside. It was a gradual thing, a blackbird watching with beady eyes from a roadside hedge, a squirrel spiralling up a withered tree trunk, black-bodied eels in the river, but mile by mile and creature by creature the world around them was reborn, making the earlier absence of wildlife all the more disturbing.

The following evening the bony hand of Roistone-Vasie's infamous tower poked above the horizon. Even from a distance the tower was impressive in its nightmarish construction. Five bone-white fingers accusing the sky, their moonlit shadow reaching far out across the swampland beneath the imposing tower. Skellan hadn't seen anything like it before and he considered himself a man of the world. It was unique. It could have been a dead man's hand reaching through the mountainside.

A rancid stench emanated from the swampland. Marsh gas. The land itself bubbled and popped with the earth's gases. For all that, they ate well that night, in the shadow of Roistone-Vasie. Fischer trapped a brace of marsh hares, which he expertly skinned and filleted and boiled up in a tasty stew with thick roots and vegetables, and for the first time in two nights Skellan slept dreamlessly.

The market town itself, swallowed in the shadow of the great tower, was not what Skellan had been expecting. When the pair finally arrived at dusk on the fourth day, the streets were deserted. With grim resolve the two men walked down the empty streets. Skellan's fist clenched and unclenched unconsciously as he moved deeper into the eerie quiet. The houses were single storey wooden dwellings, simple in their construction but sturdy enough to withstand a battering from the elements. Windows were shuttered or boarded up.

'I don't like this place one little bit, my friend,' Fischer said, pulling at one of the nailed-down boards barring a ground floor window. 'It's not natural. I mean, where is everyone? What could have happened to them?'

'Plague,' Skellan said, looking at the sign painted over one of the doorways across the street. 'My guess is they ran to the next town, taking the sickness with them. Still, he's been here,' Skellan said. 'We're getting closer. I can feel it in my gut. We're close enough to spit on him.' He walked across the street and pushed open the first door he came to. The mouldering stench of rotten food met him on the threshold. He poked his head inside the small house. Light spilled through cracks in the shutters. The table was still set with an untouched meal of sour pork. Flies crawled across the rotten meat. Piles of white maggots writhed with a sick pulsing life where there should have been potatoes. The place had been abandoned in a hurry, that much was obvious. He backed out of the room.

Fischer faced him from an open doorway across the street.

'Ghost house!' he called over. 'It's as though they disappeared off the face of the earth.'

'Same here!' Skellan called back.

It was the same story in every house they explored.

On the street corner they heard the distant strains of melancholy music: the sound of a violinist's lament. They followed the elegiac melody, faint though it was, through the winding ribbon of streets and boarded up houses, tracing it to its source, the old Sigmarite temple on the corner of Hoffenstrasse. The façade was charred black from fire and stripped of its finery but it was still an imposing place, even if it was only a shell. The wooden steps groaned under their weight. The door had been broken back on its hinges where it had been battered down.

'Something happened here,' Fischer said, giving voice to the obvious truth. Temples didn't burn down of their own accord, and streets didn't lie deserted by chance. The Sylvanian motto might well be to leave the questions to the dead but Skellan wasn't some superstitious bumpkin afraid of the dark and forever jumping at his own shadow. Strange things were afoot and their very peculiarity only served to pique his curiosity. Inevitably the riddles would play out one way or another when they confronted the musician, and in doing so, no doubt, would lead back somehow to Sebastian Aigner.

They moved slowly, carefully, aware that they were walking into the heart of the unknown.

The music swelled, bursting with the musician's sorrow.

The damage to the outside of the temple was nothing compared to the systematic destruction of the inside. All signs of the religion had been scoured from the building. It had been gutted, pews stripped and broken up for firewood, in turn used to purge the life from the place. The stained glass windows were ruined, shattered into countless shards of coloured glass that lay melted and fused into ingots across the dirt floor. The lead had been stripped from the roof and sunlight dappled through like a scattering of gold coins. The altar had been cracked in two and the life-size statue of Sigmar lay on its side where the Man-God's legs had been shattered. The effigy's right hand had been broken off. Gahl-maraz, the Skull Splitter, Sigmar's great warhammer, lay in the dirt, the Man-God's cold stone fingers still curled around its shaft.

Sitting at the feet of the fallen idol an old man in a simple muslin robe played the violin. He hadn't heard them approach, so lost was he in the sadness of his own music.

Skellan's feet crunched on debris as he picked his way forward to the musician. The music spiralled in intensity then tailed away in a simple farewell. The old man laid the instrument on his lap and closed his eyes. Skellan coughed and the old man nearly jumped out of his skin. He looked terrified by the sudden intrusion into the solitude of his world.

'Sorry,' Skellan said. 'We didn't mean to startle you. We just arrived in town... we were expecting more... people.'

'Dead or gone,' the old man said. His voice was brittle with disuse, his accent thick and difficult to understand. Pure Reikspiel, it seemed, did not survive this far from the capital. The thick dialect would take some getting used to. 'Those that didn't succumb to the sickness fled to Leicheberg in hopes of outrunning it.'

Fischer picked up a piece of the fallen statue. 'What happened here?'

'They blamed Sigmar for not protecting their daughters from the wasting sickness. At first they came and prayed, but when their children continued to sicken and die, they turned on us. They were out of control. They came in the night with torches and firebrands and battered down the doors. They were chanting "Wiederauferstanden" over and over as they set fire to the temple.'

'The risen dead...' Skellan muttered, recognising the word and its cult connotations. 'Strange things are afoot, my friend. Strange things indeed.'

'Describe the symptoms of this sickness, brother,' Fischer prompted, sitting himself beside the old man. He had his suspicions already but he wanted them confirmed.

The old priest sniffed and wiped at his face. He was crying, Fischer realised. It must have been hard for the old man to force himself to remember. He was their shepherd after all, and his flock had scattered because he couldn't protect them.

'The Klein girl was the first to fall, a pretty little thing she was. Her father came to the temple to beg us for help because she was getting weaker and weaker, just wasting away. There was nothing we could do. We tried everything but she just continued to sicken. It all happened so shockingly fast. It was all over in a matter of a few nights. And then there was Herr Medick's eldest daughter, Helga. It was the same, no matter what we tried, night by night she literally faded away before our eyes.'

Fischer thought of the girl whose funeral they had stumbled across. A wasting sickness, the old woman had said. He didn't believe in coincidences.

'I'm sorry,' Skellan said. 'It must have been difficult. Nothing you did helped?'

'Nothing,' the old priest said. 'The girls died. There was nothing I could do. I prayed to benevolent Sigmar for guidance but at the last he turned his back on me and my children withered away and died.' There was an understandable bitterness in the old man's voice. He had given his life to helping others, and when they needed him the most he had proved helpless.

'How many?' Fischer asked, knowing that two or three deaths could still fall into the realm of chance.

The old man looked at him, eyes brimming over with guilt and tears. 'Sixteen,' he said. 'Sixteen before they finally fled from the wasting sickness. They were all girls. No more than children. I let them down. Sigmar let them down. The children of Roistone-Vasie are gone now; there is no hope for my town. I failed it.'

Fischer looked at Skellan.

Sixteen was well outside the realm of chance.

'You did all you could, there was nothing else you could do, you said so yourself.'

'It wasn't enough!' the old man lamented. He hurled the violin away from him. It hit the head of the Man-God and snapped its neck. Sobbing, the priest crawled across the debris to the ruined instrument,

'Come on,' Skellan said.

'Where are we going?'

'You heard the man, the survivors fled to Leicheberg. That means the cultists and Aigner. If we find one, no doubt we will find the other.'

They left the old man on his knees, cradling the broken instrument to his chest like a dying child.

CHAPTER TWO
Afraid of Sunlight

LEICHEBERG, SYLVANIA
Early spring, 2009

THE OLD LADY had been right; Leicheberg was to all intents and purposes a city, even by Empire standards, though its inhabitants hardly seemed like city-dwellers. Their faces were pinched and weathered by hunger, their eyes sunken with the familiarity of disappointment, their frames bowed with the burden of living from day to day. They lacked that spark, that vital flame that danced mischievously in the eyes of folks back home.

Back home.

They had no home.

They had forfeited it when they began the hunt for their wives' killers.

There was no beauty in their world now, so perhaps that was the reason the people they encountered looked so listless, so drawn, worn, beaten and broken? Perhaps it was a reflection of their own spirit they saw in these strangers' eyes?

The two strangers could walk the streets without attracting stares. Food queues lined up at the market stalls, thin-faced shoppers bickering over the last few morsels of not-quite-rotten vegetables. Puddles muddied the streets where the spring rain had nowhere to drain away. The place smelled of close-packed unwashed bodies, cabbage and urine. No one gave Skellan or Fischer a second glance.

The pair had been in Leicheberg for a week. They had rented a small room in a seedy tavern off the central square called The Traitor's Head. The name more than suited the establishment. It was a den filled with iniquities galore making it the perfect place to gather rumours. People's lips loosened when they drank. They talked out of turn. Spilled secrets. Skellan was not above listening to the drunken ramblings of braggarts and the pillow talk of prostitutes.

They had spent the first two days in the city in search of refugees from Roistone-Vasie, specifically those who had lost daughters to the mysterious wasting sickness that the old priest of Sigmar had described. Those few they found told the same sad story, how the sickness had come from nowhere, their daughters rising in the morning light-headed and woozy after a restless night, only to weaken over successive nights as the sweats and fevers gripped them, until they finally fell into a deep sleep from which they couldn't be woken. The parents spoke of candlelight vigils, useless prayers, fussing physicians and the same bitter swansong of death. There was precious little to be gleaned from delving into their sorrow. That much was obvious. While no one had anything to say directly about Sebastian Aigner, they had plenty to say about the Wiederauferstanden.

The Risen Dead was indeed a cult. Few would talk about them in any great detail for fear of retribution from unseen hands. It seemed the cult had infiltrated various levels of Sylvanian society, from the beggars and thieves at the bottom to the ranks of the nobility at the top. It was indeed tied to the worship of the undead. From what Skellan and Fischer could glean, the followers worshipped those abominations for being more than human. They *aspired* to be like these monsters.

The very thought of it left Jon Skellan cold; how could anyone in their right minds dream of being such an unholy parasite?

'You said it yourself, Jon, it's a sickness,' Fischer said.

They were walking through the market square looking for a trader the locals called Geisterjäger, the Ghost Hunter. His real name was Konstantin Gosta and he specialised in selling locks and chains he made himself from his small stall in the market place. He had a reputation for complicated mechanisms, the kind of thing you would use if you wanted to keep something precious safe from thieving hands. The Ghost Hunter was the best. He could design anything you wanted from tiny mechanisms to massively complicated combination locks that worked on convoluted mechanical techniques of cogs and tumblers having to fall into an exact predefined sequence.

'I just can't believe that people would willingly do that to themselves,' Skellan said, shaking his head.

'You mean you don't want to believe. We've both seen enough of it to know it's true.'

'Blood sacrifices to try and raise the dead.' He ran his hand through his hair and looked around the crowded square. 'The stupidity of it.' He spied the Ghost Hunter deep in conversation with a woman. She left without buying any of his wares. Rather than approach the locksmith immediately they stayed back inside the anonymity of the crowd and watched him. He was polite, said hello to passers by, but very few stopped to examine his wares and those that did, didn't part with any of their hard-earned coins. Judging by the few minutes they saw it was difficult to imagine the locksmith earning enough to make ends meet. The obvious answer of course was that he didn't, not legitimately. His knowledge of locks could be used not only to man-ufacture them, but also to open them. By day a locksmith, under cover of darkness the Ghost Hunter was a thief. There were few better in this day and age.

'A word, Gosta?' Skellan said, moving up beside the smaller man.

Without turning to see who was talking to him, the Ghost Hunter muttered, 'Take scruples, I've got no use for them. Better off getting rid of the word from my vocabulary.' He scratched at the palm of his right hand compulsively. The man was wound tightly, permanently fidgeting, shifting from foot to foot, scratching different parts of his body in a cycle from scalp, to cheek, to scalp and down to the fil-lets of his left arm, his side, the side of his face, just beneath the left ear, and back to the top of his head.

'Funny, Gosta, but not the word I had in mind.'

'No?'

'No.' Skellan leaned in close, making sure the Ghost Hunter appreciated the seriousness of his enquiry. 'I want to talk about Wiederauferstanden.'

'That's a mouthful,' he said, not meeting Skellan's eyes as he spoke.

'It is, so let's say the Risen Dead, if you prefer?'

'I do,' the smaller man said, shifting from foot to foot uncomfortably. 'Look, I don't know much. It isn't my thing, messing with the dead. I'm an honest criminal. What do you want to know? Maybe I can help, maybe I can't.'

'I want a way in,' Skellan said, not bothering to sugar-coat his most basic need.

'Not happening,' the Ghost Hunter said, shaking his head as though to emphasise the point. 'Not a prayer.'

'Are you trying to tell me that you can't name the right names? Put me in touch with the right person? I don't believe that for a second, Gosta.'

'Oh, I can name them all right, I can even tell you where they like to play their little games, that still won't get you inside the organisation though. They're the kind of group that comes looking for you; you don't go looking for them, if you know what I mean, stranger. They play their cards mighty close to their chests. And asking too many questions is likely to get you a cosy spot in a hessian sack at the bottom of the River Stir. You will, of course, have been chopped up into little pieces to make sure you fit in that cosy sack. That the kind of help you are looking for? I'm not going to help you kill yourself, least not without a good reason.'

'We can take care of ourselves. Give us an address then, I'm specifically looking for a piece of scum named Aigner, Sebastian Aigner. I don't know if he is part of this Risen Dead cult but from what I know of him, and the little I know about them, I wouldn't be surprised.'

'It's your death warrant, mister. Just as long as you understand that. I don't want no widow holding me responsible for your stupidity.'

'Just give me the address.'

The Ghost Hunter shifted uncomfortably. His eyes darted around furtively making sure no one who mattered was close enough to overhear what he was about to say.

'I ain't heard of your Aigner fella, but if he's mixed up with the Risen Dead, you'll probably find him down near the end of Schreckenstrasse, there's an old tower that used to be part of the Sigmarite temple. The temple's long gone, but the tower's still there. The Risen Dead use it because it still has access to the old catacombs. If you value your life you won't go anywhere near the place, mind.'

'Thank you,' Skellan said.

'Your funeral, big guy.' The locksmith turned away, eager to distance himself from Skellan and Fischer.

'I guess that means we're going for a walk,' Fischer said with a wry grin.

'Now's as good a time as any,' Skellan agreed.

They picked a path through the market-goers. The place smelled of urine and cabbage where it should have been filled with the heady smells of roasting pork, boiling bratwurst and sauerkraut. Famine took its toll in less obvious ways too. A woman sat on the stoop of a dilapidated building plucking feathers from a stringy-looking game bird. Her daughter sat beside her holding two more birds by the ankles. The two birds flapped and twisted in the girl's grip as though aware of what fate had in store for them. These three birds garnered the woman envious looks from those without the coin to buy even a few tough legs or sinewy wings. Two doors up a barber with a cutthroat razor trimmed and shaped an elderly man's beard. A wood carver was making some sort of pull-along toy on wheels while beside him his partner fashioned more practical things, the shafts for arrows, spoons, bowls and a miscellany of odds and ends that could be sold for cash including love tokens and trinkets.

'Do you trust him?' Fischer asked, stepping around a shoeless urchin playing in the mud. The child tugged at his trouser-leg, begging for coins.

'As much as I would trust anyone in this rat-infested hole. So not much, no. That doesn't mean his information isn't good though, just that his primary interest is survival at whatever cost. If selling us out pays well, you can bet that is exactly what Gosta will do.'

'So we could be walking into a trap?'

Skellan nodded. 'Absolutely.'

'Now there's a comforting thought.' Instinctively, Fischer reached down to feel for the familiar reassurance of the sword belted to his hip. Cold steel had a way of calming even the jitteriest of nerves. Right in front of him a woman with a young child cradled in her arms backed up a step and looked frightened enough to bolt. She was staring at his hand poised just above the sword's hilt. 'It's all right, it's all right,' he said, holding up his hands to show they were empty and that he had no intention of cutting her down where she stood. It didn't matter; the woman was already disappearing into the crowd.

He had sensed the same kind of nervousness in many of the citizens during their short stay in Leicheberg, as though they were used to the summary dispensation of brutal justice. Indeed the reputation of Sylvanian justice was one of the terrible swift sword, quick to anger, and unforgiving in its delivery. Fairness was not a word associated with Sylvanian society. For centuries the people had lived under the grip of the tyrannical van Draks, and they were familiar with the madness of their masters. Things had changed with the coming of the new line of counts, the von Carsteins, but next to the depravities of the last van Drak just about anyone would have looked like blessed Sigmar himself.

SCHRECKENSTRASSE WAS A long claustrophobic alleyway of close-packed houses that crowded into the street itself as the upper storeys leaned in close enough for the neighbours to touch fingertips if they reached through their open windows. Just as the Ghost Hunter had promised, the remains of the old Sigmarite temple were at the very far end of the street, on the furthest outskirts of the city. There was a tower, four storeys high, and some rubble. The tower stood alone, distanced from the rest of the buildings by the gap where the main chapel of the temple itself had once stood.

Skellan drew his sword.

Beside him Fischer did the same.

He looked at his friend and nodded. They matched each other step for step as they moved across the rubble. Skellan could sense eyes on him and knew they were being watched. It stood to reason that if the cult were using the tower for some nefarious purpose they would set lookouts – probably in the tower itself, and in one of the abandoned houses along Schreckenstrasse, an upper window with a good view of the door of the tower. He didn't look around or hesitate, even for a heartbeat. Three quick steps took Skellan up the short flight of stairs to the door. Rocking on his heels, he span and delivered a well-placed kick parallel to the rusty old lock mechanism that sent the door bursting open on buckled hinges. A hiss of noises and smells came rushing out from the darkness within.

Skellan stepped through the doorway. Fischer followed him.

Fischer was not overly fond of the dark or cramped spaces. What waited beyond the door tested the older man to the full.

The air was stale, thick with sweat and fear and the metallic tang of blood.

Precious little daylight spilled into the room, barely enough for Fischer to see much beyond his outstretched fingers with any clarity as he fumbled forward into the darkness, his eyes adjusting to the gloom, but he could hear slobbering sounds, and gasping, other noises too, whimpering, heavy things scrabbling about. None of the sounds were comforting. His hand gripped tighter around the hilt of his sword. He had no idea what secrets the treacherous heart of the darkness held, but knew he was about to find out. The sound of his own pulse was loud in his ears. He clenched his teeth and shuffled another step forward. A few chinks of light wriggled in through cracks in the boarded-up windows. They offered few clues as to the nature of the Risen Dead's business with the old tower. Someone groaned in the darkness. The noise raised the hackles along Fischer's neck. The sound was one of desperation; whoever had made it was suffering.

'I don't like this,' he whispered. His foot stubbed against something then. He toed it tentatively. It yielded. He kicked at it a little more forcefully. The voice groaned again. Fischer knew then what he was kicking: a body. 'Give me some light, damn it,' he cursed. He couldn't tell if the person was dying, drunk or drugged. He stepped over the body.

Skellan felt his way around the wall until he found what he was looking for, a torch. There was oil beneath the sconce. He dipped the dry reeds in the foul smelling liquid and then lit it with a spark of tinder. The air was moist but it didn't stop the reeds from catching and burning with a blue flame. He held the torch aloft. The flame cast a sickly light across the room. Fischer straddled a woman's body that had been bound and gagged. Dark patches showed through her clothing. Blood. There were rakes and hoes and buckets, hammers, saws and other tools from the tower's previous life scattered about the place. A staircase spiralled up into darkness, and down into deeper darkness. Skellan followed it down into a storeroom. Fischer followed a few steps behind him. Wooden shelves and barrels lined the small storage room but Skellan found what he was looking for:

In the centre of the floor was a three-foot by three-foot moss-covered trapdoor with a large iron ring in the middle.

He passed the torch to Fischer and gripped the iron ring with both hands. The trapdoor creaked on its rusty hinges as he pulled. The musty air of the grave escaped from the hole. Somewhere in the darkness beyond the torch, the moans and sighs swelled with excitement.

'I really don't like this,' Fischer repeated.

'It's the entrance to the old catacombs,' Skellan said.

'I know what it is, I still don't like it.'

'Aigner's down there.'

'You don't know that.'

'I can feel it. He's down there.' Skellan took the first step, crouching to descend into the darkness.

Fischer stood frozen.

Skellan took the torch from him.

With plaintive sigh Fischer followed him into the hole.

The stairs led them down deep beneath the ground. Fischer counted more than fifty steps. The tunnel was carved out of the earth itself and braced by aging timbers. They had to stoop; the ceiling was so low it was impossible to stand up straight. The sword offered little comfort against the press of the featureless darkness. At the bottom of the staircase the tunnel forked in three directions, each one leading off into a deeper darkness.

Skellan pressed a finger to his lips to emphasise the need for silence. He could hear something, in the distance. It took Fischer a moment to work out what it was: the low resonant rumble of voices chanting.

They moved cautiously down the centre tunnel, heading straight for the heart of the catacombs.

A horrendous cry cut through the tunnels. It was human. Female. Whoever was responsible for that scream, Fischer knew, was suffering. 'Come on,' he rasped at Skellan's back, driving the fear from his mind. The woman was alive and she needed them, that thought was enough to force the older man into action. They staggered forward. Suddenly the tunnel opened out into a chamber. There were corpses and bones everywhere, stacked one on top of another. Bodies wrapped in dirty bandages were piled into holes in the earth. Bare bones jumbled haphazardly; femurs, fibulas, tibias, scapulas and skulls made a sea of bones from the dead of Leicheberg. Some were broken, their ends ragged, others were sheathed in mould. Had these people ever been given a proper burial, Fischer wondered?

On the far side of the space an arch led into a second, bigger, chamber. Torches had been lit in the second room. In their light Fischer saw deformed shadows dancing on the earthen wall. They came together in one writhing mass.

In front of him, Skellan grunted, and stepped through the arch.

Gritting his teeth, Stefan Fischer followed him.

The sight that greeted them when they stepped through the arch was like something lifted straight out of their worst nightmares.

The woman who had screamed lay in the centre of the floor. There was a row of cages behind her but

Fischer only had eyes for the woman. She had been slit from throat to belly, and though still barely alive, six cadaverous wild-eyed creatures clawed over her, sucking greedily at her still-warm blood as it leaked out of her. Her blood streamed down their chins and smeared across their cheeks. Ghouls, Fischer realised sickly, watching the creatures as they sucked at their fingers and lapped at the gaping rent in her torso. It was impossible to believe that these monstrosities had ever been human; they had more in common with daemons drawn from the pit than with decent everyday people.

The woman was dead but shock and denial kept her heart pumping weakly for a few more minutes, prolonging her suffering.

Something inside Fischer broke. He felt it happen. A small part of his sanity splintered away and left him forever.

Fury swelled to fill the emptiness inside.

He charged forward, swinging his sword in a frenzy of slashing. It was a blur of steel in the flickering torchlight. The first ghoul looked up as Fischer's blade sliced through its neck; the thing's head lolled back exposing a second, ear-to-ear grin that had been opened by the sword. Blood bubbled in the gaping maw. The second saw the tip of Fischer's sword plunge deep into its own eye, burying itself in the ghoul's brain, before it slumped forward over the woman's eviscerated corpse. The ghoul's body was wracked by a series of shockingly violent spasms as the life leaked out of it. Fischer kicked the corpse aside, yanking his sword free of the ghoul's head and delivering a huge sweeping arc of a blow that cleaved clean through the neck of a third ghoul. Blood gouted out of the severed wound. The ghoul's still-grinning head bounced on the floor and rolled away. The sheer ferocity of Fischer's attack was monumental. The weight of the blow unbalanced the older man and sent him staggering forward, barely able to control his own momentum. He lurched two more steps, plunging his bloody blade into the gut of the fourth ghoul even as the monstrosity launched itself at the witch hunter. He twisted his wrist, opening the wound wide. The ghoul's guts spilled out of the ragged wound in its stomach. The fiend's clawed hands closed around the blade, pulling Fischer closer by drawing his blade deeper into its gut. It breathed in his face, grin wide as it leaned in to bite off part of Fischer's face. Its teeth had been sharpened into fangs. Its breath reeked of the sour fetid stench of the grave. Fischer recoiled instinctively, his movement jerking the ghoul off balance. It fell at his feet, dead, its guts spilling out across the floor.

Fischer was breathing hard.

Skellan said something behind him but he wasn't listening.

Two of the fiends remained.

He stared at them.

Judged them.

The last vestiges of humanity had gone from their eyes. One gazed listlessly into the air, intoxicated from the dead woman's blood. It had no idea that what remained of its life could be measured in a few heartbeats. The other matched his gaze with one of its own, filled with cold animalistic cunning. It was calculating the threat Fischer posed, whether it needed to fight, flee or feed. It was hard to believe the creatures had ever been human. They had descended so far from basic humanity that they wallowed in the realm of the monstrous.

They *were* monsters.

Fischer launched a second brutal attack. He held nothing back. He threw himself at the remaining ghouls. He slashed and cut and stabbed in a wild frenzy, hacking into the helpless creatures. He cut at their arms as they tried to protect themselves. There was no control, no finesse to his fighting. His sole purpose was to kill. Screaming, he span on his heel, bringing the sword round in a wide arc with the full spinning weight of his body behind the downward slice of the blade as it cleaved into the ghoul's neck and buried itself deep in the beast's chest. He couldn't pull his sword free.

Skellan dispatched the final ghoul with clinical precision. He stepped up behind the creature, yanked its head back and cut its throat. In the space between two heartbeats the deed was done. He rolled its corpse over with his foot. There were no marks or symbols carved into its flesh. Nothing to identify it as one of the Risen Dead, but the thing's ghoulish nature was in no doubt.

'How could anyone fall so far?' he asked, shaking his head.

Beside the dead girl Fischer fell to his knees. The sword slipped through his fingers and clattered to the floor. He gasped for breath almost choking between huge heaving sobs. Tears streamed down his cheeks. She hadn't just been opened up; the ghouls had feasted on most of her internal organs.

'You couldn't have saved her,' Skellan said gently, resting a comforting hand on his friend's shoulder. 'She was dead before we even entered the room.'

'Always... too late...' Fischer spat bitterly. He was trembling as the adrenaline fled from his body.

'Not always,' Skellan said, finally seeing the row of cages and the emaciated shadows huddled in their darkest corners. The cultists obviously intended to serve these poor souls to the ghouls for food. 'Not always.'

He stepped carefully around the corpses and opened the first of the cages. There were two women in there, barely older than children really, their faces smeared with dirt and caked with dried blood. They looked absolutely terrified. Skellan tried to calm them but they shook their heads wildly from side to side and pressed themselves further into the corner, out of Skellan's reach. They stank of urine and stale sweat.

There were six more women in the other cages.

Still weeping silently, Fischer helped Skellan release them.

Sigmar alone knew how long the poor wretches had been trapped in the catacombs waiting to be fed to the ghouls. The confinement had done nothing for their minds. They mumbled and talked to themselves and stared straight through their rescuers as they tried to shepherd them back upstairs.

They refused to go outside into the street. They started screaming hysterically and beating at their faces with their hands and scuttled back into the darkest part of the tower, pressing themselves desperately against the wall as though trying to disappear into it.

It took Skellan a moment to understand. 'They've been down there so long... they are afraid of the sunlight.'

CHAPTER THREE
A Knife in the Dark

LEICHEBERG, SYLVANIA
Spring, 2009

SEBASTIAN AIGNER WAS a phantom.

A ghost.

He wasn't real – or at least that was how it was beginning to feel to Jon Skellan after three weeks in Leicheberg. They were close, he knew, close enough for Aigner to feel them breathing down the back of his neck, but the closer they got to Aigner the more elusive the man became. They were always a step or two behind him.

Gathering any kind of reliable information had proven to be a nightmare. Every avenue turned out to be a blind one.

If the usual slew of information traffickers knew anything, they weren't talking. Greasing the bureaucratic palms wasn't helping either. The magistrates had nothing to say.

Aigner might just as well not exist.

The few hints and whispers Skellan and Fischer did manage to scare up quickly faded into nothing. The man had friends and those friends were influential enough to help him disappear. That in itself worried Skellan. Gossip spread. It was in people's nature to talk. Rumours developed a life of their own. The blanket of ignorance surrounding Sebastian Aigner was unnatural.

A lesser man might have given up the ghost and let Aigner simply vanish into thin air, but not Jon Skellan. Aigner was his obsession. The all-consuming need for revenge drove him. Aigner had led the band of looters who had murdered his wife, and for that there could be no forgiveness. Without forgiveness it was impossible to forget. Thoughts of Sebastian Aigner ate away at Jon Skellan night and day.

For three weeks they had been spreading the word, making it known that they would pay good currency for information about Aigner or the Risen Dead. They made no effort to hide their whereabouts. They wanted people to know where to find them when their tongues loosened by need or greed.

Fischer took a healthy swig of ale and slammed the empty tankard down on the beer-soaked table. He let out a rumbling belch and backhanded the froth from his mouth.

'I needed that!' Fischer made a big show of enjoying his drink.

'I'm sure you did,' Skellan said.

The Traitor's Head was full with its usual mis-matched clientele. Skellan didn't drink. At the beginning of the night he ordered a goblet of mulled wine then nursed the same drink until it was kicking-out time. He sipped at it occasionally, but Fischer was far from certain the alcohol ever touched his lips.

An open fire crackled in the hearth, the sap still trapped in the wood snapping and popping under the heat. A vagabond fresh from the road warmed his grubby hands by the fire.

The serving girl bustled between tables, platters of roasted fowl and stringy vegetables balanced precari-ously in her hands. Her blonde hair was plaited in a neat tail that coiled down to her ample breasts. The smile on her face was strained. She put two plates in front of Skellan and Fischer.

'Amos wants to see you,' she said, leaning in as she took Skellan's money from him. Amos was the owner of the Traitor's Head. It could of course mean any-thing, but Skellan chose to read it as a sign their luck was changing.

'Thank you, my dear.'

'Don't thank me, I'll be glad when you are gone. You boys are bad for business,' the girl said bluntly. 'Skulking in shadows and making people uncomfort-able with all of your questions. Sooner we're rid of you the better.'

Business in the tavern was slow. Between them they could have counted the number of drinkers on their hands and had a few fingers to spare. They were the only diners. The lack of trade was painfully obvious, as was the reason for it. The occasional furtive glance of the drinkers at the bar toward the witch hunters made sure of that. It wasn't uncommon for folk to fear them. In smaller hamlets where superstition ruled over common sense their arrival often led to unnecessary deaths, girls stoned or burnt for witch-craft as the accusations flew. Cities like Leicheberg were different, but not so much different. Very few places welcomed witch hunters.

The tavern door banged open, and a giant of a man came in out of the night. He kicked the dirt off his boots and dusted the road out of his hair. He had a lute strung across his back. He looked round the tap-room, nodded to a fellow at the far end of the bar, and walked briskly over to shake hands with Amos who was already drawing him an ale from the cask. The stranger's familiarity with the patrons and the tavern keeper put Skellan at ease.

'Deitmar!' Amos bellowed, the folds of fat around his three chins wobbling with excitement. 'As I live and breathe!'

The troubadour bowed theatrically, making a grand sweeping gesture out of removing his travelling cloak. He draped it over a barstool. 'Amos Keller, you are a sight for sore eyes! A beer, make it cold, and where is that delightful daughter of yours? Aimee? Aimee, come out here and give your uncle Deitmar a hug, lass!' He swept the serving girl up in a huge bear hug and span her round so that her toes barely touched the floor. Putting her down again he planted a kiss on her forehead. 'Damn, it is good to see you again, girl.'

Skellan watched the reunion with a hint of jeal-ousy.

'It's been too long,' she said, and it was obvious that she meant it.

Again Skellan felt a pang of envy at the easy acceptance the troubadour got; he was welcomed with open arms. It was a long time since anyone had welcomed either Skellan or Fischer so warmly.

'Seven years,' he said aloud, not realising he had spoken.

'What?' Fischer pressed, leaning in.

'I was just thinking out loud,' he said. 'It is seven years since anyone welcomed us home like that.'

'Makes you think about what you're missing, doesn't it? Seeing people happy.'

'Aye, it does. Makes you realise what was stolen from you.'

'That's another way of putting it.'

'It's the truth, no matter how you dress it up,' Skellan said. He hadn't taken his eyes off the newcomer. 'It was us that died that day, you know. Not just the girls. Aigner killed us. He took our lives away as surely as if he had stuck a sword in our guts. We aren't the men we would have been.'

'No, we aren't,' Fischer agreed. 'But that might not be such a bad thing, Jon. In the last seven years we have changed a lot of people's lives, and I honestly believe most of those changes have been for the better. That wouldn't have happened without... without...'

'I know,' Skellan said. 'That wouldn't have happened without Lizbet and Leyna dying. I know that but that doesn't make it feel any better.'

The troubadour sank into a threadbare velvet seat by the fire. He put his feet up on the small three-legged wooden footstool and began tuning his instrument, running his fingers through a series of off-key scales. He tightened the strings until he was happy with the music he made. Some of the drinkers turned to face the fire. A travelling singer was a rare treat in these parts.

'Now who in their right mind would travel to this godforsaken piece of the underworld?' Skellan wondered. The troubadour was well dressed for a traveller but not lavishly so; his clothes weren't heavily patched and the colours were still vibrant. He obviously didn't lack for coin which made even less sense. For a musician of any kind of skill there was money aplenty to be made in Talabheim, Middenheim, Altdorf, Nuln, Averheim and the Moot, and the other towns and cities of the Empire. The man could obviously play – the way his fingers moved through the warming up exercises proved he could more than ably carry a tune. 'Someone with no choice in the matter,' he answered his own question with the only solution that made any sense: the man was gathering information for someone. It was the perfect disguise for a spy.

Skellan thought through the possibilities: the troubadour was an agent, either of the Empire, perhaps the Ottilia or the Grand Theogonist, the two were always trying to gain the advantage over each other; or on the other side of the conflict there was the enigmatic Vlad von Carstein, the Count of Sylvania. The man was a mystery but few spoke against him because the atrocities of Otto van Drak's reign of blood and fear were still fresh in their minds. The man could, of course, be playing both sides. It was not impossible.

Skellan smiled to himself. Deitmar the wandering troubadour was someone worth talking to in this city of madmen and crooks.

The musician began to play, a rousing shanty to get the blood flowing. The drinkers banged their wooden tankards on the bar and stamped their feet apprecia-tively.

Skellan slipped away from his table, caught Amos Keller's eye, and gestured for him to follow somewhere quieter. The big man moved down the bar. He left the tankard he was towelling out on the counter and ducked through the door that led to the snug, a quiet part of the bar where men with money could pay for solitude.

'Your girl said you wanted me?' Skellan said, stepping into the room behind Amos. He had no idea what to expect from the encounter but for some reason he wasn't expecting good news. The troubadour's music picked up pace. The riot of sound swelled as the drinkers got into the spirit of things, banging their fists and stamping their feet ever more enthusiastically. No doubt Fischer was hammering his clenched fist on the tabletop and singing along at the top of his lungs.

'I ain't gonna beat around the bush. You and your friend are bad news. Real bad news. I put up with you because I feel sorry for you, but this morning things went past feeling sorry.'

'What do you mean?'

'Fella came in here, told me I had two choices, num-ber one was turf you out on your ear, the other was empty the place tonight, and leave the door open so some of his boys could come in and take care of you. You've made yourself some enemies, lad, and they want you out of their hair.'

'Did you recognise the man?'

'Aye, I did, but I ain't about to tell you who it was, I don't want to end up in the river in the morning, if you get my meaning.'

'So, you're asking us to leave I take it?'

'Got no choice, but I can tell you this much for nothing. The fella you are hunting, Aigner, he ain't been in Leicheberg for weeks.'

Skellan grabbed the barkeeper by the throat and pulled him close enough to taste the sour smell of his breath on his tongue. 'Are you sure?'

'Certain. He disappeared a few days before you boys arrived. He paid good money to keep folks quiet. He didn't want you following him.'

'And you knew all along?' Skellan's voice dropped to barely above a whisper. His eyes blazed with righteous fury. 'He bought your silence? How much was it worth, Amos? What value do *you* place on my wife's life? Tell me! How much was she worth to you?' He was shaking. The troubadour's music was loud enough to drown out his shouting in the taproom.

'Ten silver,' he said. 'And the promise of ten more where they came from for each week I kept you here. That's what the fella was here for, he came to pay Aigner's debt.'

After seven years of hunting the man, to be so close only to be lied to, cheated out of his revenge. It was too much. Skellan erupted: 'Give me one good reason not to kill you, right here, right now. One reason, Amos. Give me one reason.'

Beads of perspiration dribbled down the corpulent barkeeper's face. His fat lips trembled. His huge arms, like ham-hocks, had turned to jelly.

'One reason,' Skellan repeated. 'Why I shouldn't snap you in half right now?'

'Aimee.' Amos barely managed to say his daughter's name.

Skellan let him go. That was the difference between the hunter and his prey. Skellan was still a human being. He still cared about family and love and people, even if he was alone in the world.

He closed his eyes. 'Are they coming tonight?'

'Yes… an hour after lights out. I'm sorry. I didn't want this. I was frightened. They… They're going to kill you.'

'Well, they are going to try.' Skellan opened his eyes again. The red mist of fury had fallen away. He was thinking now, planning how best to stay alive to see dawn.

'Aren't you going to run?'

Skellan shook his head. 'No point, they attack here when I am expecting it, or they ambush me on the road when I am not. This way the odds are stacked slightly back in my favour. This is what I want you to do, act normally. You haven't spoken to me tonight. All right? Come lights out get Aimee and go sleep in the stables. I can't promise it will be safe but it has to be safer than your rooms.'

'What are you going to do?'

'The less you know, the better,' Skellan said, rather more harshly than he had intended. He softened. 'It is safer for you and Aimee that way.'

'I don't want any killing, not under my roof. That's why I warned you, to give you a chance to run before they arrived.'

'And I appreciate it, Amos. I do. But it is too late for that. Now we are playing last man standing and I intend to win.'

The barkeeper wiped the sweat from his brow with the same towel that he had been using to dry the pitcher with before. 'You're every bit as crazy as Aigner said you were…' For the first time there was a genuine cold-to-the-marrow fear in Amos Keller's voice as the stories of Jon Skellan's relentless hunt came back to him: the slaughter of Aigner's friends, the ritualised burning, the cold-blooded nature of the assassin. 'I shouldn't have said anything. I should have let you rot here trying to pry your answers from closed mouths until the Wiederauferstanden were ready to send your soul to Morr and gotten fat off the proceeds… But oh no, not stupid old Amos Keller… had to go and feel sympathy for the murdering lunatic in his lounge and try to warn him. Stupid, stupid fool, Amos, you should have just kept your nose out of it and let folks get on with killing each other.'

'Are you quite done?' Skellan asked, obviously amused by the barkeeper's rambling admonition of himself. 'People are going to be getting thirsty. Go do what you do. If you see one of my so-called assassins I want you to warn me. It will go badly for you if you don't. Do you understand? I want you to send me a drink over. I won't be ordering another one tonight, so any drink arriving at my table is a sign that a would-be murderer has entered the bar.'

Amos nodded reluctantly.

'Now, I am going back through to sit with my friend and listen to the music. I suggest you put a smile on your face. It shouldn't be so hard to do. Think about it this way, in the morning we'll be gone one way or another.'

Skellan pressed a silver coin into the barkeeper's fleshy hand. 'In advance, for that drink.' It was enough to pay for twenty drinks, with change. Amos took the money without a word. He pocketed it and left.

Skellan followed him through to the taproom a few minutes later.

The final few strains of a bawdy tale of a frisky tavern wench and a lusty sailor petered out to a round of enthusiastic applause. He slid into his seat. Fischer looked at him quizzically but he didn't answer. The next song was a ballad. The troubadour introduced it as 'The Lay of Fair Isabella'. It was quite unlike anything he had sung so far. His fingers played lovingly over the lute's strings, conjuring something of beauty from them.

Skellan closed his eyes and simply appreciated the music.

It was a love song of sorts.

A tragedy.

The troubadour's voice ached as he sang of the fair lady Isabella's sickness, her porcelain skin waxen as she faded in the arms of her love, beseeching him to save her even as she withered away to where death was the only answer.

The words washed over him and began to lose meaning, simply folding into each other. Deitmar's voice was mesmeric. He held the bar-room of drinkers rapt with his velvet tones. They hung on his every word as he played them like an expert puppeteer.

The nature of the music shifted, lowering an octave conspiratorially. Skellan opened his eyes. It was another trick of course, the troubadour manipulating them into thinking he was imparting some dark secret, but it worked, Skellan sat forward and listened intently as Deitmar whispered, barely above a breath, no rhyme or reason to his words:

'When in the long dark night of the risen dead
Callous Morr crept unto fair Isabella's bed
The lament lingered bitter on his lips
Even as he stooped low to kiss
Her broken soul
That one so fair should fall so foul
To waste away before her time
Fragile flesh and brittle bone
The treacherous remains
While love lay dying.'

And then, with a flourish, the music and the dying lady returned to vibrant life, resurrected by Deitmar's beautiful song. Two images caught Skellan's attention. Surely it was no coincidence that the troubadour mentioned the Risen Dead and the wasting sickness in the same breath.

'We need to talk to him before the night's out,' he said, leaning over to talk in hushed tones to Fischer. The other man nodded; obviously he had caught the oblique reference as well. 'And before the trouble starts.'

That caused Stefan Fischer to raise an eyebrow.

'Seems we've been played for fools, I'll explain it later.'

Fischer nodded.

The troubadour played nine more songs before taking a break to soothe his voice with a goblet of Amos's mulled wine. Skellan and Fischer moved to sit beside him at the fireside.

'If you've no objections?' Skellan said, sitting himself.

'Not at all, sometimes it is just as nice to share a drink with a stranger as it is to share one with a friend.'

'Indeed,' Skellan agreed. It was a refreshing to hear a man with a decent command of Riekspiel. Surrounded by the thick Sylvanian accents he had begun to forget what it sounded like. 'I must say I was quite taken with one of your songs. I assume you wrote it. I haven't heard it before… "The Lay of Fair Isabella" I believe you called it?'

'Ah, yes, though I fear my voice pales next to the beauty of fair Isabella herself.'

'Truly?'

'Truly, my new friend. Isabella von Carstein, the lady of Drakenhof. Fairer beauty and fouler heart you have never seen. To see fair Isabella is to lose one's soul. But what a way to die.'

'She sounds… interesting,' Skellan said with a wry grin. 'Not that I would ever trust a minstrel's romantic soul for a reliable account. You wandering spirits have a habit of falling in love daily, a new great beauty in every new town.'

Deitmar laughed easily.

'You know us so well. But believe me, in this case, what I say, that isn't even the half of it. She owns beauty enough to stop your heart dead should she so desire, and more often than not, she does. The woman is the most powerful in all of Sylvania and she is ruthless with it. Morr's teeth, even death itself can't take the woman. She has power over it, it would seem.'

'Indeed,' Skellan leaned in, listening intently. 'How so?'

'It's no secret, she was dying. She fell victim to the wasting sickness that is scouring the country. She fought it tooth and nail. Nothing the chirurgeons and the faith healers could do made the damnedest bit of difference. It was killing her. Just like all of the other girls across the land. The sickness was no respecter of her beauty or her power. To Morr, she was just another soul. Word was the priests even came to shrive her of her sins at the last. And you know what? The next afternoon, she rose from her deathbed, and she was radiant. More so than ever before. She was alive. The fever and the sickness had broken. It was a miracle.'

'Truly. I've seen the effects of this sickness. It isn't pleasant. Like you say, I have yet to encounter a survivor.'

'Isabella von Carstein,' Deitmar said with passion. 'Death holds no dominion over her.'

'Tell me,' Skellan said, as though the thought had just occurred to him. 'The night of the risen dead? You mentioned it in your song.' Mimicking Deitmar's trick with the song, Skellan leaned in and dropped his voice to a conspiratorial whisper. 'Would it have anything to do with the Wiederauferstanden?'

'The Cult of the Risen Dead?' If the troubadour was surprised by the question he masked it well. 'Only the obvious, that the cult believe there will be a night when the dead shall rise, when the barrier between this world and the next will fall. They call it the Night of the Risen Dead. Isabella von Carstein lives and breathes where all others afflicted with the wasting sickness rot in the dead earth. She is a beacon to their kind. They see an unholy miracle. She died at the hands of the priests and the chirurgeons, all their skills and faith couldn't save her, and yet she rose again. Death itself could not hold her. She is everything they dream of, everything they adore. The Cult of the Risen Dead worships the woman. To them Isabella von Carstein is reborn. She is death risen. She is immortal.'

'She is their leader?'

'Define leader, my friend. The misguided fools worship her heart, body and whatever is left of their blackened souls.' Deitmar said earnestly. 'Does that make her their leader? Perhaps, but then is Sigmar your leader?'

'I don't follow any so-called divinity. Give me ale, give me women with enough soft pink flesh to wrestle with, give me a sword, things I can see and touch with my own two hands, those are worth believing in. Thank you, my friend. Now, at least, I have a place to begin my search. Drakenhof.'

'It is three weeks' inhospitable travel. The roads are poor; the old counts were never ones to invest in things that didn't immediately reap rewards, and well, let's just say the countryside is at best unforgiving. I don't envy you the journey… but for one more look at fair Isabella it might just be worth it.' Deitmar winked at Skellan, a lascivious smile spreading up to his eyes. There was mischief written all over his face. 'If you know what I mean.'

'We are ever driven thus, are we not? Puppets to the whims of our hearts.'

'Exactly. And what shadow plays the heart does perform! Well, I should set about earning my keep before Amos decides better of it and turfs me out on my arse. It has been my pleasure, neighbour. May you find what you are looking for in Drakenhof.'

The troubadour played on deep into the night.

More customers came as the night wore on, but business was far from brisk.

After an hour or so Skellan leaned over to Fischer and said: 'I'm turning in for the night. I'll see you upstairs when you've finished up. We need to talk.'

Fischer nodded, took a deep swallow of his drink and pushed back his chair. He followed Skellan up to the plain room they rented above the taproom. It was a simple chamber with two beds, a chair, and a full-length mirror. There was a threadbare rug over the rough timbers of the hardwood floor. Sinking back onto his bed, Skellan explained the situation: that Aigner was gone, drawn to Drakenhof if this Countess Isabella really was the evil Deitmar claimed, and assassins of the Risen Dead intended to make sure they never caught up with him. Fischer listened. He moved the chair so that it faced the door.

'So they are coming tonight?'

'In a couple of hours, yes.'

'I assume we are going to surprise them.'

'Naturally.'

'All right, if you were them what would you do?' Fischer was already thinking through what he would do in the assassins' place. Sleep was their natural enemy. The longer the night wore on the less chance the witch hunters had of making it through to dawn. It stood to reason then that the assassins would come during the dead of night.

'I'd send three men, there are two of us but two on two there is always the chance that even with the element of surprise against us, we could somehow survive. Aigner knows us. He will have transferred his paranoia on to the rest of the cult. The third assassin adds a level of security.'

SKELLAN WAS RIGHT.

When they came, there were three of them. They moved quietly down the corridor, pausing at the door to listen. The door handle turned slowly. It was a simple ruse, but in the dark it would be effective. The pillows had been bolstered to look like the rough outline of sleeping men beneath the bedcovers. The trickery wouldn't hold up to close inspection but that didn't matter. There would be no time for it. The door opened, groaning slightly on dry hinges. The silhouette of a man filled the doorway.

He stepped into the room.

Another shape moved in behind him.

He was less than an arm's length from where Skellan stood, cloaked in the shadows behind the open door.

In the chair, Fischer waited, willing the third assassin into the small room. The man stayed back. Fischer's finger itched on the trigger guard of the small handheld crossbow he held levelled at the dark outline of the first man as he approached the bed. Moonlight glinted silver on the assassin's blade.

Skellan coughed, clearing his throat.

Fischer pulled the trigger. The bolt flew true, slamming into the gut of the assassin as he plunged his dagger into the bundle of bed linen. The man grunted in pain and staggered back, sagging against the wall. He slumped to the floor clutching the bolt in his gut.

Skellan moved quickly, stepping out of the shadows to press the point of his dagger up against the second assassin's throat.

'Do it,' the man rasped.

'With pleasure,' Skellan whispered in his ear as he rammed the knife home. The assassin folded in his arms, the life draining out of him. Skellan cast him aside. 'Come on my beauty,' he goaded, seeing the third assassin frozen in the doorway.

Before the man could flee, Fischer put a second crossbow bolt high in the man's thigh. He went down screaming in agony. Skellan dragged him into the room and slammed the door shut.

It was all over in less than a minute.

'Who sent you?' he hissed, grabbing hold of the shaft of the crossbow bolt and jerking it violently. The man shrieked in pain. 'Talk!'

'Go to hell!'

'Not nice,' Skellan whispered, pushing the bolt deeper into the man's thigh. 'You can die here, like your friends, or you can limp away. It is up to you. Now, who sent you?'

The colour had drained from the assassin's face. Sweat pooled in the creases of his neck. His eyes were wide with pain.

'I can make it worse, believe me. Now I am asking you again, who sent you?'

'Aigner,' the assassin said through clenched teeth.

'Better. Now where is the son of a bitch?'

The assassin shook his head violently.

'And we were doing so well,' Skellan said quite matter-of-factly as he yanked the crossbow bolt clean out of the assassin's leg. The man's screams were pitiful. 'I'll ask you again, last time. Where is Aigner?'

'The temple… Drakenhof.'

'Good.' Ion Skellan smiled mirthlessly. 'You should thank me.'

'Why?' the man cursed, clutching at the wound in his leg.

'Because I am going to give you the chance to see if you really can rise again. You shouldn't have come here tonight. You shouldn't have tried to kill me. That made things personal.'

'I am not afraid of death,' the assassin whispered, wrenching his shirt apart to expose his bare chest. 'Kill me. Do it!'

Mystical sigils had been scrawled across the man's flesh. The ink had seeped deep beneath the skin and into the muscle beneath.

'Do you truly believe they can bring you back? A few lines of ink?' Skellan pressed the tip of the knife into the man's chest, enough pressure behind it to draw a bead of blood.

'You know nothing, fool. Nothing!'

The assassin threw himself forward onto the knife. The blade buried hilt deep in his chest. The man shuddered once, a gasp escaping his lips, and collapsed into Skellan's arms.

He kept his promise to Amos. They were long gone come sunrise.

CHAPTER FOUR
Gathering Darkness

DRAKENHOF CASTLE, SYLVANIA
Late summer, 2009

VLAD VON CARSTEIN fascinated Alten Ganz.

The two of them watched ravens bickering over scraps in the courtyard below. Their dance was filled with savage beauty. The count watched the ravens, mesmerised by their wings and beaks as they fought over the crumbs put out by the cook.

'Fascinating, aren't they?' the count observed. 'So like us, and yet so different. This is basic nature, Ganz. This dance of wings and feathers is nothing more than the survival of the most desperate. It is a fight, every day. Feeding comes down to snatching the bread from the mouth of another bird. It is that or starvation. There is no sharing in their world. The bird willing to blind its brother for the sake of a piece of bread will feed like a king. The one that isn't, the one that won't fight for its life, will starve.'

At times there was an intense darkness to the way the Sylvanian count saw the world. He obsessed over the play of life and death. The dance of mortality, he called it. 'It is all about movement, Ganz. They dance toward the end of the song.'

'And life is the song,' the cadaverous young man finished, sensing where his master's thoughts were going.

'Ah, no, life is merely a prelude to the greatest of all songs.' Down below, the hungriest raven took flight, sleek black wings beating, its prize gripped firmly in its beak. The others were left to fight amongst themselves over the last few morsels. 'Death is the full rapturous movement. Never forget that, Ganz. Life is but fleeting, death is eternal.'

There were times when the count's predilection for darkness verged on the nihilistic. Like today, Ganz had found the man standing lonely vigil on the battlements of Drakenhof Castle. His quest for solitude was not uncommon. At sundown he would often come to the highest point of the castle and survey his domain as it unfurled beneath him. The wind pulled at his cloak, whipping it around his legs as he turned away from the squabbling birds.

'Have the cook put out double the amount of scraps tomorrow. I like the birds. They should have a home at Drakenhof.'

'As you wish, my lord.'

On some days the darkness seemed to radiate from Vlad von Carstein's heart and pulse outwards, consuming not only the man but many of those closest to him. The man was a complex composite of contradictions. Where on the one hand he was ruthless in dealing with those that stood against him, he had it in him to make sure the birds did not go hungry. It was a tenderness he didn't convey to his fellow man.

In that the Count of Sylvania was an enigma, even to his chancellor.

It wasn't arrogance. It wasn't even a symptom of power. It was a genuine indifference to his fellow man.

He walked slowly along the narrow battlements, pausing every few steps to look at some peculiarity he saw in the landscape below. Ganz mirrored his pace step for step as the count moved away from the courtyard to brace himself against a parapet towering over a razor of jagged rocks far, far below. He stayed a hesitant step behind von Carstein. The count was talking, in part to himself, in part to the wind, and of course, to Ganz. He listened to the count's musing. He never knew what he might hear next: a fragment of long forgotten poetry; an element of philosophy; history so wrapped up in story that it sounded like a cherished memory; or on a day like today, a death sentence.

'Rothermeyer is a thorn in my side, Ganz. He has a greatly inflated opinion of his importance in this life and the next. I want him taken care of. Make him the same offer you made Sturm and Drang. Be persuasive. He has two choices, I do not particularly care which of the two he takes. After Heinz Rothermeyer, pay a visit to Pieter Kaplin. Kaplin is doing his best to make a mockery of my generosity, Ganz. He is playing me for a simpleton, and that cannot be allowed to happen. There will be no choices for Pieter. You will make an example of him. Others will quickly tow the line. If not, they can always be replaced. Just make certain they are in no doubt as to what will happen to them if they continue to defy me.'

'My lord,' Ganz nodded, shuffling back a step. The drop from the battlements was a long one to the rocks below and while von Carstein obviously enjoyed flirting with death, Ganz much preferred the safety of solid ground. His balance was not as unerringly good as the count's. The man ghosted around the battlements with the preternatural grace and precision of one of those black-winged birds he was so fond of. 'It will be as you wish. Pieter Kaplin will rue the day he incurred your wrath.'

'You make me sound like an animal, Ganz. Remember, there is beauty in all things. Is the wolf driven by wrath when it stalks its tender prey? Were those birds down in the courtyard driven by blood fury?' He shook his head to reinforce the point he was making. 'No, they kill through necessity, through nature, they are killers through need. The gods made them and placed that basic need within their spirit. They need to kill. So they make a beautiful dance of the savagery, they don't seek to tame the wild beast within them. In that they are so unlike humans. Humans seek to subvert nature, to tame the savage beast that lurks within their soul. They build monuments and temples to gods who knew the darkness of their own souls and used it to their advantage. They revere Sigmar and his mighty warhammer, conveniently forgetting that that very warhammer was a tool of death. They wall themselves in. Build houses of sticks and stones and call themselves civilised. Humans are weak, they fear what might happen if their bestial nature is unleashed. They forget that there is beauty in *all* things – even the darkness – when they should be embracing it.' Von Carstein lapsed into silence, lost in thoughts of death and beauty.

This was another aspect of the count's personality: his mood could swing abruptly from merely thoughtful to this deeply melancholic brooding as he lost himself inside his own labyrinthine thoughts. It afforded him an air of introspection. The man was quite obviously brilliant, blessed with an intellect verging on sheer genius, he was well read and versed in every subject he cared to talk about and quick enough of wit to read people as well as he read those books.

Alten Ganz had never encountered anyone even remotely like Vlad von Carstein.

'Have Herman Posner accompany you, along with a few of his most trusted men. I have a feeling Posner is the perfect mixture of violence and cunning to tip Rothermeyer over the edge. Tell me, Ganz, do you believe Heinz will bend his knee and accept my rule? I tire of all this petty squabbling.'

'He would be a fool not to,' Ganz said, without really answering the question.

'That is not what I asked though, is it?' von Carstein said. He toyed with his signet ring as he spoke, turning it so that it was back-to-front on his ring finger, then completing the turn again. It was the closest thing the count had to a nervous tic. He toyed with the signet ring when he was deep in thought or puzzling through a problem. It was a habit Ganz had seen demonstrated on many an occasion.

'No, my lord.'

'So tell me, Ganz, honestly. Do you believe Heinz Rothermeyer will finally bend his knee to me?'

'No, my lord. Rothermeyer is a proud man. He will fight you to the last.'

Vlad von Carstein nodded thoughtfully, his gaze off somewhere in the middle distance where the night consumed the town of Drakenhof far below their vantage point.

'I agree,' he said at last. 'So, you know what you will have to do.'

'Yes, my lord.'

'Then go, time is fleeting, I would have these thorns picked from my flesh before they bleed me further.'

GANZ LEFT VON Carstein alone on the battlements. There was no telling how long the count would remain out there, the man craved solitude. Few in Drakenhof Castle dared approach their lord and he seldom sought out the company of others, save his wife Isabella and Ganz.

Isabella von Carstein was her husband's equal in every way. She was beautiful and cruel, a dangerous combination. Unlike Vlad she was predictable in her cruelty, though. Ganz had long since found her measure. She craved power in all shapes and forms. It was a simplistic desire compared to the confusing nature of her husband, but in that she proved the perfect balance, the perfect foil, the perfect mate. When the count had thought he had lost her to the wasting sickness he had been desolate. At first he had railed at the chirurgeons and the physicians, urging them to find the miracle that would cure his wife, and then when medicine failed he sought a higher salvation. He stood lonely vigil on the highest stones of the castle wall, night after night, as though proximity to the gods in the sky might somehow convince them to save his beloved Isabella. It was only on the final evening, when her carers feared her spirit had passed too far into Morr's kingdom to ever find its way out, that Vlad banished everyone from her chamber and sat the loneliest of vigils, the death watch for his own wife.

But she didn't die.

The count emerged the next day exhausted, physically drained to the point of collapse, and sent the gawkers on their way. My wife will live, was all he said. A simple four-word announcement. His wife did live. He was right. That night, looking better than she had in months, Isabella von Carstein emerged from her bedchamber to show the world that truly, she would live. By the grace of the gods she had conquered the wasting sickness that had so ravaged Sylvania.

The narrow stone stairwell led to a gallery still high above the main house of the castle. The walls of the gallery were lined with portraits of von Carstein by some of the nation's most beloved artists, each one seeking to capture on canvas some of the count's most hypnotic qualities. It was the eyes they focussed on. Some might have considered the obsession with his own image vanity, but the more he grew to know the count, the less Ganz believed he was a vain man. No, it was just another dichotomy within the man. There were no mirrors in the castle, none of the usual trappings of narcissism that went with self-obsession.

The paintings were obvious things of beauty and the count was an admirer of all such creations. He spoke often about great beauty being a gift from the gods themselves, a blessing, so he chose to surround himself with the pictures just as he surrounded himself with fine porcelain and marble statuettes, adorned himself with delicately crafted jewellery and furnished his home with plush velvets and brocades.

It was about collecting things of beauty.

Hoarding them.

Oddly, there were no portraits of his wife in the gallery.

Ganz walked briskly through the long room, pushing aside the thick red velvet drape at the far end and descending a second tightly spiralled stair into the servants' quarters. Unlike the refinements elsewhere, there was an edge of decay about these rooms. The tapestries on the walls were worn a little threadbare in places. The colour was spotted and uneven after years of sunlight had leached them of their vibrancy. They showed scenes of the Great Hunt, some nameless, faceless van Drak count leading yapping dogs and men on a chase after wild boar. Given the mad van Draks' well deserved reputations as barbarous fiends, Ganz suspected the invisible prey ran on two legs rather than four. The stained glass window at the far end of the hallway scattered a hypnotic array of yellows, greens and reds across the carpet.

Ganz stalked down the hallway. Halfway along, two servants' staircases led to different levels of the castle, the longest one descending directly into the kitchens, the shorter one leading to another gallery, this one overlooking the main hall.

Ganz took the short staircase two and three steps at a time.

He was out of breath by the time he reached the bottom.

The gallery was designed to show off the grandeur of the main hall and the count's obsidian throne. This was Ganz's favourite place in the whole castle. From here he could observe the comings and goings of the count's court unseen. Life played itself out in the room below, the scheming of the petty barons, the pleas for clemency, the terrible swift sword of the count's justice, the everyday life of Sylvania, it all happened down there.

From here Ganz watched, studied, and learned. He was not so different from Isabella von Carstein, he too craved the power his close association with the count conferred, but he wasn't so ignorant as to believe himself irreplaceable. Far from it, he harboured no illusions as regards his own beauty: he was not something the count would willingly choose to have about his person. He had to *make* himself irreplaceable. That meant gathering knowledge, knowing each and every man in the count's court, knowing their weaknesses and how to exploit them.

The count was right; life in his court really was very much like the ravens they had watched squabbling over scraps of food. Survival came down to being willing to sacrifice others in order to ensure your continued existence.

Alten Ganz was a survivor.

It was in his nature.

The main hall was abuzz with activity. Some lesser noble from the outer reaches of the county had taken it upon himself to make a pilgrimage to Drakenhof to petition Vlad von Carstein for aid in feeding his own people. The count had laughed in his face dismissively and told him to get on his knees and beg. When the noble did as he was told von Carstein laughed even harder and suggested that he might as well kiss the dirt at his feet for all the respect he had for a man who would beg at the feet of another. Instead of aid, von Carstein disenfranchised the noble, allowing him to leave Drakenhof with the shirt on his back and nothing more, no shoes, no trousers, no cloak to guard against the elements, and promised to send one of his most trusted family members to the man's home to rule in his stead. 'A man should be able to care for his own, not prostrate himself at the feet of strangers and beg for mercy. It is a lesson you would all do well to learn.' That was the count's judgement and the ramifications of it were still playing out in the main hall hours later.

GANZ FOUND HERMAN Posner in the drill hall, running a number of the count's soldiers through a series of punishing exercises. Posner was taller than Ganz by a good six inches, and had a much heavier build, all of it due to his well-defined musculature. While the others looked on, Posner duelled a younger soldier. Posner used two short slightly curved swords while his opponent opted for a longer blade and a small shield. Posner's swords wove a dance of death between the two men, keeping his opponent at bay with dizzying ease. The blades shimmered in the torchlight. Such was Posner's skill that the two blades appeared to blur into one, so quick was the movement.

As Ganz stepped onto the duelling floor Posner's left-hand blade snaked out to nick the young soldier's cheek, drawing a line of blood with the shallowest of cuts. He bowed to his opponent and turned to Ganz who was applauding slowly as he walked across the floor.

'Very impressive,' Ganz said.

'If it isn't von Carstein's esteemed chancellor. To what do we owe the pleasure, Herr Ganz?' Posner said, his sepulchral tones echoing loudly in the vast emptiness of the drill hall.

'Work. We are going to visit Baron Heinz Rothermeyer. The count would have him brought to heel.'

'Hear that, men?' Posner said to the men who had been watching his duel with the young soldier. A feral grin spread slowly across his face. 'The count wants us to instil just the right amount of terror in the baron's heart to convince him mend his ways, eh?'

'Something like that,' Ganz agreed.

Posner sheathed his twin blades in the scabbards slung low on his back.

'When do we leave?'

'Sunrise,' Ganz said.

'Too soon. We have to make preparations for the journey. Sundown. We can travel under cover of darkness.'

'So be it, sundown tomorrow. Be ready.' Ganz turned on his heel and left. The echo of steel on steel rang in his ears before he was halfway across the duelling floor.

'Better!' he heard Posner encourage one of his men. The count had selected Posner for a reason, and for all that Ganz disliked the man, he was the first to admit that Posner was among the best at what he did.

And what he did was kill people.

CHAPTER FIVE
Something Wicked This Way Comes

ACROSS SYLVANIA
Early autumn, 2009

FIVE BLACK BROUGHAM coaches rolled through the night.

Horses' hooves drummed like thunder on the hard-packed dirt of the makeshift road.

Clutching the reins tightly in their fists the five coachmen driving the broughams hunched low over the footboard irons, their occasional whip cracks spurring their teams of horses on to greater speeds. The coachmen wore heavy road-stained travel cloaks and had hoods pulled high over their heads and scarves wrapped around their faces.

The brougham coaches bore the crest of von Carstein on their doors.

The further north they travelled the worse the condition of the roads became. Three of the five coaches had had to be re-wheeled after rocks in the road had broken the existing wheel's felloe. One coach had needed its elliptical spring replaced and the other had developed cracks in its axle and had broken a lynch-pin. None of the carriages had escaped unscathed.

The coaches afforded the travellers some small luxury, with Herman Posner and his men sharing four of the broughams, leaving Ganz alone in the fifth. Even so, tempers among the passengers had long since worn thin, and several frayed to breaking point. It was inevitable, Ganz realised. His travelling companions were killers. They craved space and solitude, perhaps to contemplate or come to terms with the murders they were prepared to commit in the name of their master, or perhaps simply to clear their minds of the tedium of the endless road.

After a month cooped up in the carriages it was inevitable that a few fights would break out, but whenever they did Posner was quick to stamp them out. The man ruled his soldiers with an iron fist and backed his threats up with the steel of his twin blades. Few pushed the arguments once Posner interjected himself into them. It was part fear, part respect, Ganz realised, appreciating the man's leadership skills. He was very much like the count in that regard, commanding the love and the fear of his servants.

They travelled by night and slept in the velvet darkness of the brougham coaches by day. It was a peculiar arrangement and Ganz found himself missing the touch of the sun on his face but he was growing used to it.

At sundown every day Posner put his men through a rigorous series of exercises aimed at minimising the effects of the journey on their bodies and keeping their minds sharp. Much of the exercises looked, to Ganz, like an elaborate form of dance, with Posner focussing on the footwork of his seven warriors as he drove them through a punishing series of blocks, strikes, parries and cuts.

Posner practised what he preached. He matched his men exercise for exercise and then pushed himself further still, focussing on his body dynamics and balance. The man was the consummate athlete. He manipulated his own body with preternatural grace. Without doubt, the man was a deadly adversary.

The eight of them together would be more than a match for local militia.

Rothermeyer's barony, Eschen, was one of the smaller outlying territories along the north-west border of the province, between the Forest of Shadows and the fork in the River Stir, a mere four days' travel from Waldenhof, Pieter Kaplin's home. The coaches might easily have been travelling through the Lands of the Dead for all the life the land offered. Given the season, the trees ought to have been a thousand shades of copper and tin. Instead, they were thick with lichen and mould, while others were lightning split, stumps of rotten trunks and dead wood. On the roadside dilapidated buildings crumbled to rock dust and rubble, and barren fields lay where there should have been a bountiful harvest waiting to be reaped. The sickness had spread to the very soil itself, poisoning the province.

Ganz rode alone in the last carriage. With plush red velvet banquettes and padded backrests the interior was luxurious, the drapes were thick enough to block out the sun, even at the height of the day, and the banquettes were more than comfortable enough for sleeping on.

He had thought through what he was going to say to Rothermeyer a thousand times, couching it in terms as disparate as a friendly warning and a pat on the back to outright threat and physical violence, playing through all of the wayward baron's possible responses in his mind. It was like an elaborate game of chess, trying to see through to the endgame with the best possible strategy. Soon enough it would move out of the realm of the imagination and become all too real. And it would come to blows, as he had told the count. Rothermeyer was no fool, and being on the very fringe of the count's territory it was little surprise the man felt invulnerable.

Vlad von Carstein's reach may have been long, but Rothermeyer must have been gambling on the fact that it was almost impossible to exert any real control on his barony over such great distance. The miles were his greatest protection from the count. They could also, just as easily, prove to be his death warrant as they had proved to be for Pieter Kaplin.

No doubt Rothermeyer knew they were coming. The five black broughams bearing von Carstein's crest had raised more than a few eyebrows as they cut through the night, and their practice this evening had been witnessed by a handful of farmers and their curious families from Eschen's outlying farmsteads. The strangers would most certainly be the topic of conversation for miles around and it was only to be expected that the lesser baronies they had swept through along the way would send word of their passing. It was part of the culture of fear that enveloped Sylvania. The black coaches could only mean ill news for someone further up the road. The word would spread by messenger birds: von Carstein's men were coming.

Those barons yet to fall in line with the count's rule would hear of the black coaches coming their way and would know fear.

Ganz admired the simplicity of the count's manoeuvre. Instead of travelling like any anonymous wanderer trudging the roads of the province by foot or horseback, the sumptuous brougham coaches not only afforded comfort, they made it plain exactly who was travelling in them. The knowledge that the count's men were abroad would be more than enough to stir the ever-present fear and self-loathing of the Sylvanian people.

The coachman rapped on the ceiling of Ganz's carriage, three sharp knocks.

The chancellor rolled up the velvet curtain, drew down the glass window and leaned out through the opening.

'What is it, man?' Ganz shouted over the noise of the wheels and the horses' hooves.

'Just crossed the River Stir, sir, and that's Eschen in the distance. We'll be there by dawn.'

Ganz strained to see through the gradually lifting darkness but it was impossible to make out more than a smudge of deeper darkness along the line where the land met the night sky. Sunrise was little more than an hour away. Eschen would be a hive of activity already, bakers preparing the day's bread, grooms readying the horses, stable boys mucking out the stalls, servants slaving away to make their work of the day appear effortless. How the coachman could possibly know that that inky smudge on the horizon was Eschen baffled him but Ganz was gradually coming to suspect that there was more to this peculiar entourage than met the eye.

In the month they had spent on the road the coachmen had barely said a word to each other, though they occasionally spoke to him in low inflectionless voices, and they did not fraternise with Posner's men. The five drivers were vaguely disquieting. It was something about them, a peculiar quality they all shared. Five deeply introspective men, almost identical in build, focussed so utterly on the road as though their very lives depended upon mastering it, permanently wrapped up against the elements despite the fact that it was late summer, drifting into autumn, and the nights were pleasantly balmy. Little more than the arch of their brow and the shadowed recesses of their eyes were exposed, and still they were capable of seeing for miles in the dark with greater clarity than Ganz could during the day.

Slowly, as the first blush of the sun began to rise and the distance to the town narrowed, the outline of Eschen came into focus.

It was a daunting silhouette, far grander in scale than Ganz had expected this close to the edge of the province. Not as vast as Drakenhof, Eschen still verged somewhere on the border between being called a town and a city. Spires rose into the reddening sky, and the rooftops of two and three-storey buildings crowded in on each other. Ganz's knuckles whitened as his grip on the sill of the carriage door tightened.

Eschen Keep rose on a mile long crag and tall mount behind the houses, a brooding sentinel watching over the streets and houses below. Most surprising of all though, the thing that Ganz had most definitely not expected, were the high walls. Eschen was a fortified town.

It made sense, given the proximity of the Kislev border. Fortifications would act as a deterrent to prospective raiders.

As they drew closer Alten Ganz's suspicions began to crystallise.

The walls were new and had nothing to do with keeping raiding parties at bay.

Rothermeyer's rebellion was more serious than von Carstein suspected. The man was making preparations for civil war. Walling his city was a declaration of intent. Ganz could only wonder how many more of the border barons were with him in this. It would be a foolish man who stood alone against the might of Vlad von Carstein, and from the little Ganz knew about Heinz Rothermeyer the man was a lot of things, stubborn, honourable, curmudgeonly, but he was not a fool.

The coaches thundered on towards the gates of the walled town.

Ganz forced himself to reassess the situation. When they embarked it was to warn an errant baron from stepping out of line, not put down a burgeoning rebellion. Suddenly he felt like a fly crawling into the spider's sticky web.

Two soldiers standing square in the middle of the road blocked their entry through the Eschen Gate. More soldiers in the livery of Rothermeyer lined the battlements above them. Ganz studied the men. They ranged in age, two were very young, and another was well into his fifth decade. They were nervous. It was in their body language. They were tense. Expecting trouble. With good reason, considering the fact that their baron had obviously been plotting his coup for some considerable time. The next few minutes were going to be interesting.

'Hold!' one of the guards blocking the road demanded.

The front coach slowed to a complete stop, the horses' flaring nostrils mere inches from the guard's impassive face. The man didn't so much as flinch. His companion stepped around the front of the horses and walked up to the door of the front carriage.

Ganz reached through the open window for the door handle and opened the door. He climbed out of the coach cautiously, stiff from the long hours of travel.

'We seek an audience with the baron,' Ganz said, walking up to the soldier. 'I trust you will see to it that word gets up to the keep so we are properly welcomed, as befits our status as emissaries of the count himself.' Ganz craned his neck to look up at the soldiers on the battlements, meeting their gaze one by one and letting them know that he was taking care to remember their faces.

'Baron Rothermeyer does not recognise the claim of your master, sir. If I allow you to enter Eschen it is as a common traveller. Have you coin to pay for your food and board? We won't allow vagrancy, baron's rules.'

Ganz looked at the soldier, and shook his head very slowly from side to side. A slow smile reached his lips.

'Listen carefully,' Ganz said. 'I am going to pretend you haven't opened your mouth just yet. First impressions are so very important. Now, let me tell you who I am. My name is Ganz, Alten Ganz, and I am chancellor of the Count of Sylvania's court. That would make me one of the most powerful men in the land, wouldn't you agree? Now, I am going to let you into a secret, and then we can begin again. The last person who used a similar tone when addressing me currently resides within the cold dirt of one of the many cemeteries in Drakenhof city. So, should we try again? We seek an audience with the baron.'

'Like I said, *chancellor*, the baron does not recognise the legitimacy of your master's rule. You are welcome to visit our city as a traveller. There is not, I am afraid, very much to see, but you must understand that any audience will be on the baron's terms, if indeed he should choose to grant one. I am also to inform you that there is, unfortunately, no room for your entourage in the keep itself, though there is a single chamber that has been made up for you and your man. Might I recommend the Pretender's Arms for your companions, it is a fair-sized tavern about halfway up Lavender Hill.' He pointed over his shoulder in the direction of the crag-and-tail rock formation leading up to the keep.

'This is preposterous,' Ganz said, shaking his head in disgust. 'Does the baron not realise the implications of such an affront to the count? Never mind, don't answer that. Of course he does. For every action there is a reaction, it is predictable. Rothermeyer knows full well that von Carstein will look to extract punishment for this stubborn display of resistance, and yet he goes ahead with it. Very well, soldier, open the gates.'

The second soldier stood aside. Together the two men raised the huge wooden brace barring the gate, and pushed the doors open to allow the black brougham coaches to pass.

The leading coachman cracked his whip above the horses' heads and the carriage lumbered forward. Likewise, the others followed in tight procession through the gate and into the cramped streets of Eschen. The steel-wrapped wheels clattered on the cobblestones and the horses' hooves clip-clopped loudly in the relative quiet of the early morning. The streets were tight and wound narrowly in a series of twists and turns like the meander of a great river. The spectre of Eschen Keep was ever-present, looming over the procession as it moved slowly up the incline of Lavender Hill toward the keep itself.

The Pretender's Arms was indeed almost half way up the long tail of the hill. Two stable boys and a dour faced groom waited for them by the coach house gates. The boys looked as though they had just been dragged rather violently out of bed and hauled down to the courtyard. The soldier from the gate must have sent a runner on to warn them that they were coming. No doubt he had some sort of reciprocal arrangement with the tavern. Ganz's coach pulled level with Posner's as it peeled away toward the tavern's courtyard. He saw Posner's impassive face staring out through a chink in the curtained window.

The man looked anything but happy at the baron's affront. Ganz gestured for him to pull down his window so that they could talk.

'I will have word sent down to you when I am settled. Get some sleep, tonight we will sort out this idiocy of Rothermeyer's.'

'Indeed we will,' Posner said coldly.

The manner with which he said it sent a shiver the length of Ganz's spine. Herman Posner was not inclined to offer forgiveness; it was not a part of the warrior's personality. He would answer the slight in his own way, Ganz had no doubt about that. Posner pulled up his window again and let the curtain fall so that he could no longer be seen.

'To the keep!' Ganz shouted up to his own coachman, and sank back into the velvet banquette to wait out the final few minutes of the ride. He closed his eyes.

When he opened them again the coach was slowing down at the gates of Eschen Keep. Again, two soldiers blocked the coach's path. A third soldier came around the side of the coach and knocked on the door. Ganz drew the black curtain aside.

'Yes?' he said, any hint of civility gone from his tone.

'The baron bids you welcome to Eschen, Herr Ganz. The chamberlain will take you to your room, and a girl has been assigned to see to your… ah… needs during your stay at the keep. Your coachman is to return to the tavern where the rest of your companions are staying. The baron trusts that this will meet with your approval.'

Ganz sighed. 'No, of course it doesn't meet with my approval, soldier. But I will show good grace and accept the decision. For now.'

The soldier banged on the side of the carriage and the brougham rumbled forward beneath the barbican. Eschen Keep was a formidable bastion, immune to assault from three of its four sides thanks to the jagged rocks of the crag it was built on. Though the mile-long tail of rock formed a gradual incline, the keep itself was several hundred feet above the town below. The wind was strong in the narrow bailey, the curtain wall doing little to prevent a battering from the elements. The coach rolled to a stop and Ganz opened the door and clambered out. The air tasted fresh. It stung his cheeks as he turned to survey his surroundings.

Eschen Keep was undoubtedly built for war. Unlike many of the baronies of Sylvania whose keeps and castles were ostentatious displays of wealth to separate themselves from the commoners, Eschen with its wall walks, murder holes and narrow arrow slits was made to hold off a full frontal attack. It wasn't a home, it was designed for protection during the strife of war. No doubt within the keep itself measures had been taken to survive a prolonged siege as well. Despite himself, Ganz could not help but admire Rothermeyer's audacity. The man had almost certainly bled his coffers dry in this last stubborn defiance of von Carstein's rule.

It was a pity that the gesture was futile.

A raven flew overhead, cawing raucously. Ganz couldn't help but think back to that evening on the battlements with the count and wonder if it was a sign. An acceptance of superstition came naturally to most Sylvanians.

The chamberlain and the girl waited on the steps of the keep. The man could have been Ganz's doppelganger; it was like looking at himself only thirty years older, the same cadaverous features, sunken cheekbones and hollowed-out eyes, and a willow-thin frame that was all awkward angles. The man's white hair was brushed back over his scalp and instead of a fringe he wore a harsh widow's peak. The girl on the other hand was, as the count would have said, a thing of beauty. She had an olive tint to her complexion and almond-shaped eyes. Her oval face was heartbreakingly pretty, high cheekbones and lush full kissable lips. But Ganz's eyes were drawn back to hers. At first they appeared to be green in the dawn's early light but the closer he looked the more certain he was that they were in fact a kaleidoscope of colours and it was the colour of her shawl and the sun that made them look green.

The man bowed stiffly as Ganz approached, the girl curtseyed. She moved as pleasingly as she looked.

'Greetings,' the chamberlain said, holding out his hand to take Ganz's travel cloak. Ganz unclipped the hasp and with a flourish draped it over the man's outstretched arm. 'Follow me, please.'

'Lead the way,' Ganz said, moving into step beside the girl.

His first impression of Eschen Keep was that he had had the right of it when he assumed Rothermeyer had emptied his treasury making the place as defensible as possible. The place was spartan. There were no wall hangings or tapestries or other decorations aimed solely at being easy on the eye. Everything about the keep was functional, the corridors narrow and the ceilings low to make swinging a sword difficult, tight spiral stairways, the corkscrew of stairs favouring the right-handed defenders fighting a retreat. Ganz followed the chamberlain to a small room on the second floor.

'Klara will draw you a bath so that you might wash the road from your skin, and I will have your luggage brought up to the room. Rest. You will be summoned when the baron is ready to greet you. If there is anything you need, Klara will see to it. I trust your stay will be a pleasant one, Herr Ganz. If there is nothing else I will leave you to Klara?'

'Thank you. That will be all,' Ganz said.

'As you wish.' The white haired man bowed again, as stiffly as before, and left the two of them alone.

'I will see to your bath.' The serving girl's voice was husky and thickly accented. Where some might have seen it as a flaw, for Ganz it only added to her curious appeal.

'Please,' he said, moving to the window. The view from the window was surprisingly similar to the view from his window in Drakenhof Castle, but then, he reasoned, how different could an endless cluster of rooftops, towers and spires look? The room itself was smaller though, and like the corridors leading to it, it was bare of ornament or decoration. There was a large metal tub in the corner of the room, and a cauldron of water bubbling in the hearth. Four large porcelain jugs filled with cold water were lined up beside the tub, a fifth jug stood empty. Klara took this jug to the cauldron and filled it with steaming hot water, which she poured into the metal bath. The water hissed against the cold steel.

'If you would like to undress, I can prepare the bath and bathe you?'

'Ah… no. It's all right, I can manage by myself. Just fill the tub up, leave some lye so that I can scrub the dirt out of my skin, and I will be more than happy.'

'I am to care to your every need, herr. I would not wish to disappoint my baron.'

'Disappoint is a word for lovers, not servants, girl. You displease your master or you give him pleasure. It would please me greatly if you drew a nice hot bath and then left me in peace to savour it, understood?'

'Yes, herr,' Klara said, lowering her eyes. She drew a second jug of steaming hot water from the cauldron and emptied it into the bath.

It took her a few minutes to fill the tub and cool the water sufficiently for Ganz to submerse his whole body. She left him alone to undress.

The bath was good. Being on the road, forced to live like an animal for the last month, made soaking in the hot water all the more luxurious. Ganz closed his eyes and tried to enjoy the feel of the water on his skin. He remained that way, head back, eyes closed, simply savouring the sensation of being clean, until the water was barely tepid. He soaped himself, rinsed the lather of acerbic lye off with icy cold water from the final jug, and clambered out of the bath and towelled himself dry. He wrapped the wet towel around his waist and stood by the window once again, this time paying special attention to the layout of this side of the keep and the streets below. He locked certain landmarks in his mind, using them to orientate himself. Knowledge of what could become hostile surroundings was invaluable.

He turned away from the window at the sound of a knock on the bedroom door.

'Come in,' Ganz said, expecting Klara to have returned from whatever errand she had fetched herself off on. It wasn't the almond-eyed servant girl who opened the door.

An elderly man, frail-boned, with snow-white hair fastened in a topknot, corsair style, leaned on a silver-tipped cane in the doorway. His hands were liver-spotted, the skin hanging loosely on the brittle bones beneath. The old man was frail but he wasn't weak. There was a difference. Ganz knew who his visitor was immediately.

'Baron,' he said by way of greeting. 'You have me at a disadvantage.'

'As was my intention, Herr Ganz. A naked opponent has, ah, less chance of hiding things, so to speak.'

The old man's eyes were bright and hinted at a sharp mind at work in his old body, which was so rarely the case with the aged. The old baron came into the room and closed the door behind him. He lowered himself gingerly down onto a hard wooden chair. 'Now, let's get something straight, shall we? I don't care for your master and I have no intention of kowtowing to his every whim. I am the lord of my dominion. These are my people here. I care for them. Your master in his cold empty castle hundreds of miles away is nothing to me.'

'Ah, now, you see, Baron Rothermeyer – may I call you Heinz?' without waiting for the baron's consent, Ganz went on: 'You see, Heinz, you have put me in a difficult position here because I *do* care for my master and he sent me to you to give you a chance. Every mile of this godforsaken journey I have fervently hoped there would be a wise man waiting at the end of the road, not a fool. Stubbornness will only get you killed, Heinz. Surely you can see that.'

The old man stiffened slightly in his chair. 'Do not presume to threaten me in my own home, young man. You are alone here. Your erstwhile assassins are in a tavern half a mile away. I am surrounded by people who love me and would willingly die doing my bidding. You on the other hand, well, no one would so much as hear you scream.' Rothermeyer coughed, hard, dredging up a lungful of phlegm. It rattled in his throat before he swallowed it back. 'Am I making myself clear?'

'Abundantly,' Ganz said, adjusting the towel. His semi-nakedness made him feel far more vulnerable than he would have leaning over a tabletop in some diplomatic chamber in the heart of the keep. 'But perhaps I am not making *myself* quite so clear, Heinz. I live for my count and likewise I would willingly die for him. I am sure that if you so chose you could have your men make me scream. The prospect does not frighten me even half so much as disappointing my count. That, I believe is a mark of my devotion to him. He is a righteous man, a powerful man. He is good for this nation of ours. But Heinz, I have to tell you that your stubbornness has ceased to be amusing to von Carstein. I was told to offer you a choice. It is the same choice the count has offered other errant barons, and it is a simple enough one: bend the knee to him during the festivities of Geheimnisnacht or face his wrath. If you swear subservience, your petty rebellions will be forgotten, that is his promise. He is a man of his word, Heinz.'

'It won't happen,' the old man said flatly.

'That is a shame. Might I urge you to think it over? What is it they say? Decisions made in haste are most often repented at leisure.' The cold had begun to draw goose pimples out of Ganz's bare skin but he made no move to cover himself.

'The decision was made a long time ago, son.'

'And you set about preparing to defend yourself from its ramifications? Is that what the wall is all about?'

'Something like that, yes.'

'And now judgement has come to your door. I pity you, Heinz. Honestly, I do. If you kill me, another will come, and another after him, and they will keep coming until Eschen has been purged from the face of the world. He won't spare you because of your age. He won't humour a senile old fool. Have you no sense of what you are doing to those people you claim to love? You are signing their death warrants. Is it worth it? The death of everyone who loves and respects you? I can't believe it is. I can't. But trust me, this petty show of defiance guarantees that it is only a matter of time. So, because of you, I pity them, too. The count is not by nature a merciful man.'

Rothermeyer stood awkwardly, his weight on the cane. 'You speak very prettily for a thug, son. What are you, von Carstein's pet scholar?'

'I don't want anyone to suffer unduly.'

'But what constitutes unduly in your eyes?'

'People dying needlessly, which is exactly what will happen,' Ganz said with a surprising amount of passion in his voice.

'Better to die free than enslaved to a monster like Vlad von Carstein. Haven't you realised that yet?' Rothermeyer walked slowly over to the door, and then paused with his hand on the handle, as though something had just occurred to him. 'I don't see that we have anything else to talk about. Erich, my chamberlain will see you are fed, and returned to your men by sundown. I expect you out of Eschen by nightfall. And, in time, expect you to return with your armies to crush what you see as my petty rebellion. If death by a thousand cuts awaits me, so be it. I will meet Ulric in the Underworld with my head held high that I lived as a man and died as one.' The old man invoked the name of the warrior god. 'As you so rightly said, I am an old man. Death does not frighten me the way it used to.' Heinz Rothermeyer closed the door behind him as he left.

'Why waste a thousand cuts, you old fool, when one will do?' Ganz muttered at the wooden door.

The meeting hadn't proceeded the way he had hoped it would but it had gone very much the way he had expected it to.

Ganz unwrapped the damp towel and dressed in clean clothes from his travelling chest.

Klara didn't return.

He lay on the bed and closed his eyes, content to doze for a few hours before rejoining Posner at the Pretender's Arms.

Food was brought to the room an hour before noon: a plate of fresh fruit, pumpernickel bread, aromatic cheeses and thick slices of various cold meats. It was a platter fit for nobility. Ganz ate ravenously. He hadn't realised it had been so long since his last real meal. The melange of flavours on his tongue was mouth-wateringly delicious. He ate until he was sated then he checked the sun through the window. It was a few hours past the meridian.

'Time to end the dance,' he said to himself. He looked around the room for some kind of bell-pull to summon the chamberlain but there was nothing of the sort that he could find. He opened the door. The passageway was empty. He walked back the way the chamberlain had led him a few hours earlier. Ganz found a servant boy walking hurriedly up the main staircase.

'Boy!' he called. The youngster stopped in his tracks and turned to look back quizzically. 'See my bags are brought from my room and have my coachman ready my carriage.' The boy nodded and skipped back down the stairs. Saying nothing, he hustled down the passageway Ganz had just left. Ganz made his way out to the courtyard. A few servants were busy with whatever chores their daily life forced on them. He crossed the courtyard to the stables. His black brougham was parked outside. The moribund coachman sat on the flatbed, reins wrapped tightly in his fist as though he had been expecting Ganz's imminent return. With a shiver, Ganz realised the man had in all probability never left his seat since dropping him off earlier.

'We are going to meet up with the others at the tavern down the hill, a boy is tending to my luggage.' He opened the door and clambered into the velvet cool darkness of the carriage.

He was seething by the time he found Posner, asleep in his own carriage in the courtyard of the Pretender's

Arms twenty minutes later. Posner and his men hadn't bothered with renting out a dormitory. Instead they chose to sleep in their broughams just as they had done every day for the last month. No doubt Posner had decided that whatever the outcome of Ganz's treating with the old baron, Rothermeyer would be dead come morning and they would be back on the road, so there was no point in making themselves comfortable. Giving the circumstances of his return from the keep he couldn't fault Posner's logic.

The soldier was laid out in a state of what looked like peaceful repose when Ganz opened the door to his coach and clambered in. Posner lay on his back, arms folded across his chest, heels together, on the velvet banquette. He was amazed the man could sleep like that. The carriage smelled stale – damp earth and mildew. It was a graveyard reek.

'He wasn't prepared to give so much as an inch,' Ganz said, sitting himself down on the bench opposite Posner's makeshift bed.

'You didn't seriously expect him to, did you?' Posner said, without opening his eyes.

'No,' Ganz conceded grudgingly.

'Then why the long face? You gave him his chance; he chose his own fate. It is more than many people get to do, remember that, chancellor. The consequence of his choice might be a visit from my men but it was still his choice. In his place I like to think I would have the courage to make the same choice. It is uncommon for an old man to have the courage to die gloriously. They prefer to slip into their dotage and dwell on things that once were and might have been but for one twist of fate, one bad decision, one love lost, one mistake made. Now, however, it is out of his hands. Come nightfall death will walk in his house. I fully expect that he has left the door open for us.'

'Just make it quick and clean,' Ganz said, a bad taste lingering in his mouth from the whole business. 'He is an old man.'

'It won't be either,' Posner said. 'Now leave me in peace, I must clear my mind for the killing to come.'

Ganz waited out the hours to nightfall in his own carriage. The minutes and hours dragged by, giving his guilt time to fester. The plain-speaking old man had gotten under his skin. He was fully aware of the consequences of his stupid rebellion and yet he refused to simply bow to the rule of von Carstein, which would have been enough to save his life. Instead he chose to stand up against the storm of the count's wrath even though it meant his own death. He didn't know if it was bravery or stupidity but whatever it was, it made Ganz respect the old man as much as he pitied him.

Somewhere during the long wait he fell asleep. He awoke to the frenzied sound of wolves baying in the distance. He opened the carriage door and staggered out into the night. A sickle moon hung in the clear sky. He had no idea how long he had been asleep or what time it was. The four other carriages were empty. For once, the coachmen were nowhere in sight. Their absence disturbed Ganz more than it ought to have, but the more he thought about it the more he realised that he had never seen the strange men leave the coaches.

The wolves howled again, a lupine chorus that echoed around the hilltop. He had no idea how many of the beasts there were out there but it was certainly a hunting pack and judging by the rabid baying they had scented their prey.

The sound caused the fine hairs at the nape of Ganz's neck to rise like hackles, prickling with the black premonition of fear. He knew, unreasonably, what they were hunting, long before the first wolf came loping back into the courtyard of the Pretender's Arms, the baron's blood still fresh on its muzzle. More of the great beasts came padding back into the forecourt, jowls slick with the blood of Heinz Rothermeyer and those unfortunates who loved the old man enough to die with him.

A huge wolf, almost twice the size of the others, came bounding into the courtyard. Ganz backed up against the side of one of the brougham coaches, feeling the door handle dig into his spine. The great wolf veered towards him, head thrown back as though driven crazy by the smell of his fear. Less than a foot from Ganz it raised up onto its hind legs and slammed its fore paws into the carriage door either side of Ganz's face. Its foul breath stung his eyes. He squirmed but there was no way he could wriggle out beneath the creature's claws before its jaws closed on his neck and ripped his throat out if it so desired. The wolf's feral eyes regarded him as though he was nothing more than a slab of meat.

Posner's words came back to him, ghosts in his mind: *It is uncommon for an old man to have the courage to die gloriously.*

There was nothing glorious about it, he realised. Death was dirty. He felt the warm trickle of urine dribbling down the inside of his leg.

The wolf's huge gaping maw appeared to stretch as the beast arched its back and let out an almost human howl. It was as though the wolf had raked its claws over his soul. Ganz felt his knees begin to buckle and the world around him began to shift and lose its shape and definition as it swam out of focus.

He fell amongst a curious mix of howls and laughter from all around the courtyard. He blacked out. He had no idea how long for. Seconds. Minutes. It was impossible to say.

When he looked up he saw Herman Posner standing over him, smears of fresh blood around his mouth and across his cheek. Of the wolf there was no sign.

'The baron is dead,' Posner said, scratching behind his ear. 'As are most of his household. It is time we left town, chancellor.'

There was something about Posner's eyes as he stared down at him that stirred up Ganz's most primal fears.

He realised what it was.

They were feral.

CHAPTER SIX
The Night of the Dancing Dead

DRAKENHOF
Early winter, 2010

IT HAD BEEN a hard year for Jon Skellan.

Failure weighed heavily on him.

The agony of dead ends and false hopes were etched now in every crease and wrinkle of the witch hunter's face. His eyes betrayed the depth of his suffering.

Jon Skellan was a haunted man.

His ghosts were not kindly spirits come to shape his future, they were bitter revenants that came tearing up from his past with hate enough to turn any heart black. Wearing the guises of loved ones they taunted him with his failure. They threw it in his face, branding him useless, their accusations dripped with the venom of self-loathing because that, after all, was exactly what these ghosts he carried with him were: projections of his own self-loathing, his own bitterness, his own hate. It was Skellan who couldn't bear to look at himself in the mirror anymore.

He knew that and yet still he let them get to him.

He obsessed on one unassailable fact: Sebastian Aigner was still out there. Still alive.

The murderer's continued existence taunted Skellan day and night.

It was as though the pair were locked in some perverse game of cat-and-mouse that was being played on the streets of Drakenhof. Several times since their arrival in the city Skellan and Fischer had come within a whisker of confronting Aigner, Aigner having moved on mere minutes before their arrival. They were close enough they could smell the man's rank body odour in the musty air of the taverns and gambling dens, only for them be left scratching their heads with the murderer having seemingly vanished into thin air by the time they made it back out onto the street.

A long time ago Skellan had reached the only reasonable conclusion he could: that some very powerful people were shielding his wife's murderer.

It wasn't a pleasant thought. It made him doubt who he could trust, made him spurn help where it was offered and made him turn on those who offered friendship.

So he stayed, and he waited, forcing himself to find patience where there was only the desperate need for resolution and restitution. He listened to the stories surfacing almost daily. First it was tales of the wasting sickness ravaging the Sylvanian aristocracy, and the tragic accidents that befell those who sought to oppose the rule of Vlad von Carstein, and then it was the anti-Sigmarite outbreaks that saw more and more of the old temples defiled.

More and more of the whisperers offered their own copper coin's worth of wisdom along with the rumours. Every third or fourth gossip fastened on the Cult of the Risen Dead and how they were not so slowly removing all traces of Sigmar from the Sylvanian countryside. Some could not hide their glee at the return to the older faiths; others remained more sceptical, sensing that there was more to this religious purge than simply some resurgence of the old ways and pointed to the name chosen by the cult, the Risen Dead. It played on centuries of fear, something the peasantry were all too familiar with.

Perhaps the most telling gossip revolved around the miraculous recovery of the count's wife Isabella and the fact that, unsurprisingly, she was a changed woman after the sickness, forever wan and pale. The gossips spoke about how she never left the chambers she shared with her husband, save by night.

Even now, almost a year on, Skellan remembered well the clandestine meeting he and Fischer had had with Viktor Schliemann, one of the two physicians who had attended the countess during her prolonged illness. The man had been terrified, always casting glances back over his shoulder as though afraid of who might overhear their conversation. The most memorable thing about the meeting though was the fact that Schliemann was adamant that Isabella von Carstein's heart had stopped. That she was in fact dead when he left the room. This was immediately before the count had called the physicians fakes and dismissed them from his service.

Schliemann had been brutally murdered the morning after that meeting with Skellan.

Skellan had no fondness for coincidences. It was obvious that Schliemann had paid the highest price for his loose tongue.

Someone had wanted him silenced, which only went to convince Skellan that he had been telling the truth, that Isabella von Carstein had died and been resuscitated. It was no wonder that she had become so important to the followers of the Risen Dead. She was one of them. She had crossed over to the other side, she had breathed the foetid air of Morr's underworld, and yet she was back, walking amongst them once more, pale-faced and afraid of sunlight. She was a creature of the night, a human owl.

The old temples destroyed, the dead risen, the nobles falling victim to the same peculiar wasting sickness that meant that the castles across the land had become home to sallow-skinned nocturnal folk, these rumours all pointed to the same fundamental truth: that there was something rotten in the province of Sylvania.

Skellan made the sign of the hammer reflexively, and gazed up at the spectre of the count's gothic castle perched like some bird of prey on the mountainside, all sharp edges and jagged black towers with their blind windows staring back down at him. The castle was like nothing he had ever seen teetering there on the sheer face of the rock. The bird of prey analogy was a good one, Skellan thought wryly, though it could easily have been some misshapen gargoyle perched up there instead.

With money running low they had had a small stroke of good fortune and taken to lodging with Klaus Hollenfuer, a wine merchant in one of the less run-down parts of the city. Hollenfuer was a good man, sympathetic to their quest for justice. He could have charged them an arm and a leg for the spacious room above his wine cellar but instead of taking money he had them work off the rent, running the occasional delivery, but more often than not simply guarding his stock.

Hollenfuer didn't need them, he had a small legion of guards on his payroll and there were plenty of boys in the city who could have run his errands. They both knew that Hollenfuer kept them around because he felt sorry for them. The merchant had lost his own wife and daughter to bandits on the road to Vanhaldenschlosse a few years earlier. Part of him, he confessed one drunken evening over half-empty glasses, envied Skellan and Fischer for their relentless pursuit of Aigner and his murderous band of brothers and wished he had the guts to do the same to Boris Earbiter and his filthy horde of bandit scum.

The three of them were in the attic rooms above the wine cellar on Kaufmannstrasse. Skellan, his back to the other men, stared intently out of the small round window.

A low-lying fog had begun to settle in, it masked the city streets with a real peasouper thickness that made it difficult for him to see more than a few feet when he looked down at the streets below. Looking upwards though, toward the castle, the air was still bright and clear. The fog, however, was rising. In a few hours it would shroud the castle as completely as it already did the city streets.

He couldn't have wished for better weather for what he had in mind.

It was the perfect cloak for the subterfuge he was hoping to employ.

A steady procession of coaches and carts carrying the rich and the beautiful had been making their way up the curving road toward the black castle's lowered drawbridge all day. From a distance the gateway looked like a huge gaping maw waiting to swallow them. Totentanz, quite literally the Dance of Death, or at least a masquerade in honour of the departed, marked the eve of Geheimnisnacht. Vlad von Carstein had seen to it that absolutely anyone who was anyone would be under his roof to see in Geheimnisnacht.

Many of the coaches' passengers had travelled from the furthest reaches of the province to pay tribute to the count and his beloved Isabella, and in the process witness the unveiling of the artist Gemaetin Gist's portrait of the countess. That Gist, an old man deep into his final years, had undoubtedly created one final masterpiece was cause for jubilation. Gist hadn't accepted a commission in over a decade and many thought the old man would never hold a brush again until he was creating art for Morr in the halls of the dead. It was no small marvel that the count had somehow coaxed the man into doing one final portrait.

But then, the count was persuasive.

Drakenhof had been alive with talk of Totentanz for weeks. Seamstresses and tailors worked their fingers to the bone hurrying to create gowns to rival the beauty of their wearers. The vintners and dairy farmers crated and casked up the finest of their wares, delivering them up to the castle, the bakers and butchers prepared fresh meat and delicacies to make the mouth water. It seemed as though everyone had a part to play in the masked ball apart from Skellan and Fischer.

'Are you absolutely sure you can't be talked out of this?' Fischer asked, knowing that his friend had well and truly made his mind up and there was nothing he could do about it. He didn't like it, and he had being making his unhappiness plain ever since Skellan had shared his plan but the only thing to do now was to go along with it – ride the wave and see where it took them.

'Certain,' Skellan said, scratching his nose. It was something he did when he was nervous and didn't know what to do with his hands. 'He's up there, my friend. I know it. You know it. Can't you feel it? I can. It's in the air itself, so thick you can almost touch it. It's alive… It feels as though there is some kind of charge… A frisson. If I close my eyes I can feel it seep into my skin and cause my heart to hammer. It makes my blood sing in my veins. And I know what it means: he's close. So close. Here's my promise: it ends tonight, after eight long years. One of us will meet with Morr face to face.'

'Can you promise me it won't be you?'

'No,' Skellan said honestly. 'But believe me, if I go, I will do my damnedest to take the murdering whoreson with me.'

'Good luck to you, lad,' Hollenfuer said coming up behind him to rest a hand on his shoulder. 'It's a brave thing you are doing tonight, walking into the beast's lair. May your god guide your sword.'

'Thank you, Klaus. All right, let's go over this again, shall we?' Skellan turned away from the window. 'The final delivery is in little more than an hour, thirteen casks of various wines, two will be marked as Bretonnian. Those are the ones Fischer and I will be hiding in. Your man is waiting at the other end to uncork us, so to speak. A third cask, marked with the seal of Hochland, will contain our swords, and twin hand-held double shot crossbows along with eight bolts in two small belted sheaths. The weapons will be wrapped in oiled skins and floating in the actual wine.'

'We've been over this a thousand times, my friend,' the merchant said placatingly. 'Henrik is already up at the castle unloading an earlier shipment, your weapons are wrapped and ready to hide in the barrel. The last cart is loaded. All that remains is for you to go downstairs and for me to seal you in an empty cask of Bretonnian white. The journey to the castle will take an hour, perhaps a little more. Worry about what you will do once you are inside the castle. Let me worry about getting you in there.'

'I'm still not entirely happy about this,' Fischer said. 'I've got a bad feeling. It just keeps niggling away at the back of my mind and it won't go away.'

'That's your "old woman" instinct,' Skellan said, with an exaggerated wink at Hollenfuer. 'You know it *is* rather overdeveloped. When this is all over you'll make a wonderful harridan or shrew, my friend.'

The merchant didn't laugh. In part because he shared Fischer's misgivings but he wasn't about to voice his concerns. 'So, what say we get to work, lads?'

'Aye, the day isn't getting any younger,' Skellan said.

The three men went down four flights of stairs to the cellar where the dray was already loaded, the two carthorses harnessed and ready to roll. The barrels on the flatbed were various sizes and showed different signs of age and wear, a few of them were a dark wet brown and branded with the maker's mark while the others were made of pale dry wood. The two Bretonnian casks were barely big enough for them to squeeze into. Hollenfuer had reasoned that the smaller casks would be less suspicious than the larger beer barrels, though if an over-enthusiastic guard decided to help unload the cart he would be in for a hefty surprise.

Skellan climbed into one of the barrels, drawing his knees up tight to his chin and lowering his head. Hollenfuer pressed the lid down then hammered the seal into place. He had drilled two small air holes just beneath the second metal band cinching the barrel's girth somewhere near where the stowaways' face ought to be, but they were so small they would let precious little air into the suffocating confines of the barrel. They were big enough to keep him alive though.

It was dark and claustrophobically uncomfortable.

An hour in there was going to be nothing short of hellish.

After a few minutes he heard the banging of Fischer's cask being secured, and then the third lid being nailed shut on their weapons. One weapon didn't make it into the third cask. Skellan wore it on a leather thong around his neck, the glass phial cold against his skin as he cradled it close to his chest. It had cost him almost all of the money he had left but if it helped Aigner burn it would be worth every last coin of it.

And then they were moving. The slow gentle sway of the cart quickly became nauseating. Skellan tried to clear his mind of all thoughts but they kept coming back to the same thing – the face of the man he intended to kill.

Sebastian Aigner.

The cask muffled the sounds of the world. It was impossible to tell where they were along the road. He caught occasional snatches of Hollenfuer whistling. The man couldn't carry a tune to save his life.

Every few minutes, the sweat pooling in the hollows of his collar and the base of his spine and behind his knees, Skellan twisted around to suck in a few precious mouthfuls of fresh air. The inside of the cask was choked with the bouquet of rancid wine. Several times he had to fight back the urge to gag. Before long he found himself getting dizzy on the intoxicating fumes.

The cart jounced and juddered on the roughshod road, bouncing Skellan around in the dark. Numbness, like a thousand stabbing pins and needles, seeped into his arms and legs as his blood stopped circulating properly.

And then, after what felt like an eternity, he felt the cart begin to slow and eventually come to a standstill.

He could barely make out the strains of muffled conversation. He used his imagination to piece it together: the guard questioning the wine merchant, demanding his bill of lading, then satisfied, telling him where to leave the delivery using an unseen passage so as to avoid being seen by the steady stream of guests.

Someone banged three times in rapid succession on the lid of Skellan's barrel.

His heart stopped.

He didn't dare breathe or move.

Everything hung in the balance. It could all be over in the matter of a few seconds. Years in pursuit of justice come to nothing. He closed his eyes, waiting for the inevitable shaft of sunlight as the guard cracked open the lid of his hiding place – but it didn't come.

The cart rumbled forward again.

A shaky sigh leaked between his lips. They were inside the castle walls. They were rapidly approaching the critical moment, transferring the barrels from the cart into the count's cellars. If anything were going to go wrong it would be in the next few minutes. Skellan sent a silent prayer to Sigmar.

The barrel bumped sharply as the cartwheel rattled over a jagged stone and for a moment all sensation of movement ceased – then suddenly the barrels were being manhandled off the cart and rolled down planks into the cellar. Skellan caught himself on the brink of crying out. The shock of the violent disruption to his surroundings was both nauseating and agonizing as his body slammed into the barrel's inner wall and squashed his face up against the lid. As suddenly as it began, the turbulent spinning stopped and the seal was being broken on the lid of his wooden prison.

As the lid came off Skellan arched his back and pushed upwards, desperate to get out of the claustrophobic barrel. Like a diver surfacing after too long beneath the surface, he gasped, gulping down the musty cellar air greedily. He retched, almost choking on the air.

Hollenfuer's cellar boy Henrik hunched over the second Bretonnian white cask. He wore a look of steady concentration on his face as he worked the tip of the metal crowbar between the seal and the wood and levered it loose. From inside Fischer pushed up with both hands, forcing his way out of the barrel.

Skellan's legs buckled as he tried to stand. He caught himself on the supporting strut of a peculiar wooden contraption that was halfway between a harness and a winch. He stood there for a long moment, shaking. Henrik helped Fischer stand. In the small rectangle of failing light at the top of the gangplanks leading up out of the cellar Hollenfuer nodded once, and banged the storm covers closed. Moments later they heard the distinct crack of a whip and the creaks and groans of the cart making a slow circle before returning back to the wine cellar on Kaufmannstrasse.

Skellan looked around the cellar. The cold stones were impregnated with years of damp and limned with creeping black mould. Henrik handed them their weapons. Skellan sheathed his sword and clipped the hand-held crossbow onto his belt. The extra bolts he slipped into a boot sheath. Beside him Fischer did likewise. With his sword at his side his sense of vulnerability subsided. He clapped his friend on the back.

The ceiling was low enough to force Fischer to stoop. The bigger man moved awkwardly toward the door leading up to the kitchens.

'No retreat, no surrender,' Skellan said, taking a deep breath and following him.

They paused at the door. Sounds of frantic activity filtered down to them. The hordes of kitchen staff were no doubt working madly to get everything perfect for the count's feast.

'If we don't make it out of this,' Fischer whispered, fear glistening in his dark eyes, 'what kind of existence would you choose in your next life?'

'The same life I had once before in this one: an unknown farmer living in an out of the way corner of the Empire, a good wife, happy. I would give anything to go back to that time. To be the man I was, not the man I became.'

Fischer nodded his understanding.

'I would like to go back to that day,' he admitted. 'Though I think I would choose to die with them second time around, rather than live like this.'

This time it was Skellan who nodded.

'Enough talking, my friend. Death awaits.'

So saying, he hefted a small cask of port wine onto his shoulder and pushed open the door and walked confidently up the narrow servant's stairway. Fischer followed, two steps behind him. Skellan ignored the looks of the kitchen staff and walked straight up to the man who looked as though he was in charge.

'Where'd you want it, squire?' he said, tapping the cask with his fingers.

The cook turned up his nose and waved him away. 'Over there, with the others by the door. Then go get yourself cleaned up. You're filthy, man. The count will have your hide if he sees you like that.'

Skellan grunted and turned away. There were several small barrels and one larger one stacked against the furthest wall. He put the cask down beside the others, and walked straight out of the kitchen door. The passageway divided into three, one fork going left, another right, while the third continued straight on. Without knowing which way to go, he opted to go straight on for sake of expediency. It would be easier to find his way back if it proved to be the wrong choice.

They moved quickly through the belly of the castle in search of a stairway leading up. It wasn't difficult to find one.

Noise drew them toward the great hall. The passageways increased in richness, going from cold stone to tapestry-lined walls with various depictions of hunting and reclined beauties, each passage opening into a wider one until it finally opened into the great hall itself, the buzz turned into a roar of noise.

The great hall was alive with a swarm of people flitting from place to place, the buzz of conversation constant. All of the guests wore peculiar skull masks, making it appear as though they themselves had risen fresh from the grave. As Skellan and Fischer entered the hall two young serving girls swooped down seemingly out of nowhere and pressed masks into their hands. Skellan took his gratefully and quickly covered his face.

'How in Sigmar's name are we going to find him if he's wearing a bloody mask?' Fischer cursed behind him.

The hall was already stiflingly hot, the air thick with humidity. Given the amount of people already present it was hardly surprising. Skellan noticed more than a few ladies fanning themselves almost constantly as they turned and turned about to survey the gathering. The place was a riot of clashing colours. Beside the count's obsidian throne a row of violinists and cellists conjured a symphony of music, the third concerto of Adolphus, the blind Sigmarite monk, each note resonating with a pure unblemished simplicity that bordered on the divine. Skellan stopped in the middle of the press of people and let the music wash over him like a crashing wave. It was beautiful; there really was no other word to describe it.

On the opposite side of the obsidian throne a large dais hand been constructed and on it stood Gemaetin Gist's portrait of Isabella von Carstein, hidden beneath a plain scarlet curtain.

There was a fluid grace to the way the guests moved across the floor as though they were all part of some huge orchestrated dance, but where it aimed at sophistication there was something decidedly more tribal and ritualistic about the whole performance.

Skellan scanned the dizzying array of facemasks hoping to catch a glimpse of the people lurking behind the bone. Cold certainty settled in his gut: Aigner was among them. He knew it. One of those masks hid the man who murdered his wife.

Skellan pushed deeper into the crowd.

Fischer struggled to match his momentum.

The music surged. Bodies swarmed and pressed on all sides.

Skellan stared at mask after mask, a hideous dance of death being played out before his eyes. It was hopeless. To be so close, within touching distance at least once, almost certainly, and not being able to recognise his quarry. He clenched his fists. More than anything at that moment he wanted to lash out with frustration.

The tempo of the music shifted into something more melancholy. Skellan stood in the centre of the great hall, looking left and right. And then, he looked up, at the gallery overlooking the floor. A cadaverous young man braced himself on the mahogany balustrade, studying the dancers as though he were watching a swarm of flies crawling over the carcass of some long dead animal. His distaste was obvious. Behind him were five men, two of whom bore a striking resemblance to the count himself. Some sort of family, Skellan reasoned. The other three were muscle, ready to interject if things on the dance floor got out of hand thanks to a rowdy drinker or an angry borderland baron making a scene.

Skellan scanned the second gallery behind him. Again it was lined with attentive spectators, well dressed but obviously guards. One wore twin blades in a curious double sheath on his back. While the blades were interesting it was the shaven head of the man beside the sword-bearer that stopped Skellan dead in his tracks.

The years had not been kind to Sebastian Aigner.

Far from it. In the eight years since he had ridden into Skellan's village with his murderous brethren the man had aged twenty. He looked different, not just older. It was something about the way he held himself. He looked like a man resigned to his fate. That was it. Skellan had seen the look before in those he had condemned to a fiery death. The mark of damnation hung over Aigner's head.

It was all Jon Skellan could do not to unclip the hand-held crossbow at his side and bury a metal-tipped bolt in the man's throat there and then. He imagined himself doing it, raising the small crossbow slowly, squeezing down on the trigger mechanism and watching the deadly bolt punch into Aigner's throat, the momentary look of shock, bewilderment, before the blood pulsed out of the wound, through his desperate fingers as he clutched at his throat trying to keep it back. An icy satisfaction settled like a smooth sided stone in Skellan's gut. It ended here, tonight.

'I see him,' he said just loudly enough for his words to carry to Fischer.

Fischer turned and quickly scanned the gallery. He almost didn't recognise the man. His shaved head and the heavy criss-crossing of scars on his scalp made Aigner look very different.

'It's him,' Fischer agreed.

He looked around the great hall for a stairway that led up to the gallery but there were nothing obvious. Several of the stone columns around the room were covered by thick velvet drapes, and magnificent tapestries hung from two of the four walls. Any one of them could have hidden a door or a staircase.

Skellan pushed toward the edge of the great hall, his head swimming with thoughts of vengeance. Bodies closed around him, cutting him off from Fischer. He kept pushing forward, squeezing through gaps that weren't really there. The time signature of the music shifted again, into a heady cantante, the violins replacing the voice of the singer as the music spiralled into its triumphant crescendo.

In the second of awed silence that followed, a collective gasp escaped the lips of the milling dancers. The count, Vlad von Carstein and his beautiful wife

Isabella stepped through the oaken doors behind the obsidian throne. The man moved with predatory grace, the woman like his shadow. The pair were so perfectly in time with each other. The count raised his wife's hand high, and bowed low to a ripple of applause.

There was something about the man that set Skellan's skin crawling. It wasn't anything obvious. There was no mark of Chaos hanging over him. It was subtle but it was there. A faint nagging something. In part it could have been down to the arrogance with which the man carried himself, but that was not it, at least not all of it. He might not have been able to divine the cause, but the effect was plain to see, the partygoers viewed the count with awe. Death masks slipped down to reveal wide-eyed adoration. Vlad von Carstein owned these people body and soul. He had a mesmerist's draw on them.

Skellan knew that von Carstein was no different from a great puppet master: every one of the people in the great hall would dance to his whim. The woman on the other hand, was easy to read. There was a raw sexuality about her and she knew it. A measured look here, a slight smile there, a teasing touch, the tip of her tongue lingering just slightly too long on her fulsome lips, a toss of the head to accentuate the swanlike grace of her neck and the cascade of her dark hair as it spilled down her back. She played with them almost as well as her husband did, but where he carried a faint air of melancholy with him she radiated the self-assurance of power. Real power.

The crowd parted to let them pass.

Skellan used the distraction of von Carstein's arrival to slip away unnoticed. He glanced back over his shoulder. Toadying guests all hungry to get close to the count and his lady fenced Fischer in. Skellan had no choice. He couldn't go back for him and he couldn't risk waiting. The choices of a warrior were simple: in a difficult situation, press on, when surrounded, look for weaknesses in your enemy's strategy that can be exploited, when confronted with death, fight. He had no choice. Skellan left Fischer staring helplessly as his back as he disappeared through the crowd.

Behind him, Fischer tried to barge his way through the bodies but the sheer weight of people pushed him back.

'Friends,' von Carstein said, his voice cutting through the falling hubbub. 'Be welcome in my home, for today we celebrate the most fragile of things and the most finite, life, and revel in the infinite, death. We come together as faceless constructs, bare bones that make us indistinguishable from one and other, in that we are equal.' There were a few murmurs of ascent. 'Equal in life and in death. Tonight we throw our inhibitions to the wind and give ourselves over to the music of these fine players. We are blessed with wonderful food and wine brought in from the very finest corners of the province. So, I urge you to surrender to the spirit of Totentanz. It is, after all, the dance of the dead, and who are we mere mortals to withstand such august company? Raise a glass to the restless dead, my friends! To the ghosts, the shades, the ghouls, the wraiths, the wights, the banshees, the liches, the mummies, the nightmares, the weres, the shadows, the zombies, the spectres, the phantasms, and of course,' he slowed down, letting his voice sink to the merest whisper. The count didn't need to shout. His voice carried to each and every guest, raising goose pimples of anticipation along their flesh, 'the vampires.'

A burst of applause greeted von Carstein's toast. Cries of: 'To the dead!' echoed around the room.

Skellan reached the first of four red velvet curtains bearing the crest of Sylvania. One of them, he hoped, would reveal a short flight of stairs leading up to the gallery. He paused to look up at Aigner. The man appeared almost bored by the proceedings. Aigner leaned on the mahogany balustrade clenching and unclenching his fists. Beside him more of von Carstein's cronies were chuckling.

Skellan pushed aside the curtain. As he had suspected, the red cloth hid a passageway. This one led off deeper into the castle but there was no sign of a staircase leading up to the gallery so he let the curtain fall closed again. The second curtain hid a barred door. The third opened on to another passage that disappeared into the darkness of Drakenhof's lower levels. He slipped behind the final curtain and into a tight embrasure that turned into an even tighter staircase.

The music started up again behind him.

SKELLAN CLIMBED THE stairs. Countless thoughts chased through his head like blind runners stumbling across each other. He couldn't think straight. It didn't matter. He didn't need to. His hands trembled with anticipation as he pulled the leather thong over his head. The glass phial was all that he needed.

He was glad Fischer had become trapped within the surging crowd. He hadn't been entirely truthful. He knew the risks coming here. He was going to kill Aigner in front of hundreds of people. He didn't expect to walk out of Drakenhof. It didn't matter. All that mattered was that Lizbet was finally avenged, that the circle of violence closed here, tonight.

Death had long since ceased to frighten him – after all, what was there to be afraid of? Lizbet would be waiting for him in the Kingdom of Morr. They would be together again. In that, von Carstein had been right when he said death was cause for celebration.

He paused before he stepped out onto the gallery. The violins rose in shrieking chorus, masking the sound of his footsteps.

There were four men on the gallery with Aigner.

Skellan didn't care, he only had eyes for Aigner. The others were insignificant. His fist closed around the glass phial. One of the others, the shortest of the four, turned and saw him. A look of distaste spread across the man's face.

'Downstairs, you ain't allowed up here.'

'I go where I please,' Skellan said.

Aigner turned at the sound of his voice.

For a moment Skellan fancied he saw a glimmer of recognition in the murderer's eyes, but more likely, he saw it because he wanted it to be there. A cunning smile spread across the shaven-headed man's skeletal face.

'You do, do you?' Aigner said. His voice was every bit as hateful as Skellan remembered. 'Well, not today. Back downstairs before I decide to teach you a lesson you won't quickly forget.'

'I don't forget anything.' Skellan moved forward two more steps until Aigner was just beyond arms reach. 'Not my wife, not my daughter, not my friends.' He touched his temple. 'They're all in here. Like the murdering scum you brought to my village. They're in here. Burning.'

'Ahhh,' Sebastian Aigner said, realisation dawning. 'So *you're* the witch hunter, are you? I was expecting someone… taller.'

'Is this going to be a problem, Sebastian?' The swordsman with the twin curved blades asked. He instinctively moved to put himself between Aigner and Skellan.

'No,' Aigner said, shaking his head. 'No problem at all, Posner. Our friend here was just dying.'

Aigner's slow smile flashed in to a dangerous grin. His lips curled back on sharp teeth.

'You first,' Skellan said, taking one step forward and slamming his fist up into Aigner's face. The glass phial shattered spilling its contents into Aigner's eyes and down his cheeks.

Aigner's hands flew up to his face, slapping and clawing at the acid as it seared into his skin. Pink froth sizzled between his fingers. Blood ran down the backs of his hands. Skellan didn't move. Aigner staggered forward a lumbering step. His mouth moved but the incessant violins drowned out his screams; violent music to match Aigner's violent contortions as the acid ran into his mouth and down his throat, eating away at his flesh as it did so. He lifted his hands away from his face. Half of his right cheek was gone, dissolved in a mess of blood and bone. A rash of pustulent blisters seethed across his cheeks, chin and neck, popping, sizzling and spitting as the acid continued to melt into what was left of his face. Rage burned in his one good eye. The other was gone, black and blind where the acid had burned through it.

Skellan moved quickly. He reached for the hand-held crossbow at his waist, unclipped it and levelled it squarely at Aigner's chest.

'You killed my wife... Death isn't good enough for you.'

He squeezed the trigger mechanism twice in quick succession. Two feathered shafts slammed into Aigner's chest, punching him back off his feet. He sprawled across the gallery's floor, blood and gore leaking from the wounds. Writhing on the deck, Aigner gripped one of the bolts in his bloody fist and yanked it free. His face contorted with pain.

Standing beside him, Herman Posner drew one of his twin blades and tossed it to Skellan. 'Finish him off. This isn't pretty.'

'It shouldn't be pretty,' Skellan said flatly. He stepped over Aigner's body and raised the bor-rowed sword. None of the others moved. It was as though a spell held them transfixed. 'And it shouldn't be fast.' He plunged the blade into Aigner's gut, wrenching it left and then right to open the wound wider, then pulled it out.

'That won't do it,' Posner said. 'Take his head off.'

Skellan hesitated.

'Do it.'

Suddenly, Aigner reared up, his face contorted in a mask of rage. The skin had dissolved around his cheeks and lower jaw, baring razor-sharp fangs. His claws raked blindly toward Skellan's face.

Skellan stepped sideways and back a step, bringing the sword around in a savage arc. The wickedly curved blade cut clean through the murderer's neck and spine, sending his decapitated head bouncing and spinning across the floor. There was precious little blood, considering the wound. A trickle rather than a fountain. One of the count's men stopped it with his foot. Aigner's dead eyes stared accusingly at Skellan. For a heartbeat Aigner's body continued to rise before it slumped to the floor, dead.

The waspish violin music swarmed around them as the musicians played on, oblivious to the killing that had taken place mere feet from them.

Skellan stood over the corpse of the man who had ruined his life. This final vengeance did not taste sweet. There was no satisfaction in the slaying. He looked down at the ruined face, still hissing and sizzling as the acid burned away more and more of the fatty tissue. Given time the acid would strip the head of all its soft tissue and dissolve the brain so all that remained would be the clean white bone plates of the dead man's skull.

'That was personal, was it?' Posner asked.

'Yes.'

'And it is over now? Finished?'

'Yes.'

'Good. That is good. My man did wrong by you and you claimed your justice, I can respect that… but it leaves me with a problem.'

'How so?'

'You killed my man, I can't let you walk away from here without recompense.'

'I understand.'

'And yet you aren't grovelling pitifully for your life. I can respect that as well.'

'I am not afraid to die. I came here tonight expecting to. It doesn't matter to me if I walk away from here. I have done what I set out to do. From now there is no purpose to my life. The sooner I die, the sooner I am reunited with my wife.'

'Ahhh, so that is your story? I understand. But if I were you I wouldn't look forward to any tear-filled reunions in the halls of the dead just yet. What is your name?'

'Jon Skellan.'

'Well, Jon Skellan, you killed my man. As I said, this causes me a problem.'

'And I said kill me,' Skellan said.

'In time. But you see, killing you doesn't *hurt* you. You've said it yourself, you want to die. You are finished here. You have avenged your loved ones. So killing you doesn't give *me* my justice.'

Skellan saw Fischer lurking in the door behind Posner's shoulder. He had come up a different way to the gallery. His hand rested on the handle grip of his own short crossbow. Skellan shook his head. This wasn't what he wanted. This was about his life, not his friend's. He turned, as though to look over the balcony at the guests of the count's masquerade.

Posner followed the direction of his gaze.

'Oh, their time will come. But you, Jon Skellan, what to do with you? My instinct, I must admit is to kill you, but as we've established, I can't do that, and besides killing you doesn't solve the fact that I am a man short.'

'Just do what you want to do and have done with it.' Skellan said. Posner's curved sabre slipped through his fingers and clattered to the floor. 'I'm finished here.'

The music down below lapsed into momentary silence.

'No, you're not,' Herman Posner said thoughtfully. 'It's just beginning.' His grin revealed predatory fangs. In the lull between arrangements, with the others laughing, Posner's face shifted, his smile disappearing as his features stretched. His cheekbones lifted and the bones beneath his face formed and reformed as though liquid. His jaw elongated and the line of his ears sharpened as the animal beneath his skin rose to the surface.

The transformation complete, Posner's roar was purely animalistic.

He flew at Skellan, slapping aside his ineffectual defence, grabbed a fistful of hair and yanked his head back, exposing his neck. For a full five heartbeats Posner held him like that, locked in a parody of a lover's embrace, before he sank his teeth into the soft, ripe flesh and drank greedily.

Skellan's limbs flapped, for the first few seconds, fiercely as he fought for his life, and then more and more weakly as his will to live faded into oblivion. He felt himself slipping away, his sense of self fragmenting into innumerable shards, parts of his life, forgotten memories of childhood, of Lizbet, of happiness, sadness, anger, and all he could think was: *so this is death…*

Then he felt the warm sticky wetness in his mouth as it filled with blood. His own blood and Posner's blood mingling.

Sated, Posner threw his head back and howled before hurling Skellan's limp body over the balustrade and into the middle of the revels below.

It took a second and then the shrieks and the screams began.

From the doorway Fischer loosed two crossbow bolts; one fired high and wide into the ceiling of the great hall, the other embedded itself in the neck of one of Posner's men. He didn't fall. Reaching up the man wrenched the bolt free of the wound in his neck even as a tiny dribble of blood oozed from the gaping wound. The man snarled and dropped into a crouch, his face undergoing the same hideous transformation Posner's had moments before.

Fischer turned and ran for his life.

Down below, Vlad von Carstein's voice cut through the pandemonium. 'Ah, first blood has been drawn. Yes. Yes. Reveal yourselves. Let out the beast within! The festivities can truly begin! Drink! Drink the wine of humanity!'

From both galleries above the great hall von Carstein's vampires leapt over the balcony and fell upon the revellers.

What followed was nothing short of slaughter.

CHAPTER SEVEN
Kingdom of the Risen Dead

CASTLE DRAKENHOF
Early winter, 2010

GANZ HAD ALWAYS known the truth.

But knowing and believing were two very different beasts.

They were animals.

No. They were worse than animals.

When the music stopped there was only the sound of the screams.

The fiends leapt from the galleries and fell upon the terrified revellers in a frenzy of feeding. Their teeth and claws ripped and rent at the pretty dresses and the pale flesh tearing their prey apart piece by bloody piece.

Alten Ganz looked away.

On the gallery opposite him Herman Posner watched the slaughter with disinterest, as though he had seen it all before, which, Ganz realised with a shudder, he probably had. The man's face had metamorphosed into that of a beast: the beast within. Posner wasn't a man any more than the count was, or Isabella or any of the others. The night travelling, the thick velvet curtains to keep out the day, his preternatural grace, it all made sense. Ganz thought of all the evenings he had stood on the battlements listening to von Carstein lament the transient nature of life, his obsession with beauty, even the portrait gallery, the countless paintings of the count. It all made sense.

Posner saw him staring and, teeth bared, flashed him a dangerous grin.

Ganz looked away again.

People were dying all around him. There was nowhere he could look without seeing some act of brutality. Death, this death offered by von Carstein's vampires, was not pretty. It was bloody and wretched. There would be nothing left to bury but bones.

The count was in the centre of it, detached from the bloodlust of his kin. Unlike the others, his face had not undergone a grotesque transformation. The countess, though, had given herself to the feeding frenzy. Her gown was soaked in the gore of countless partygoers' lives and still she threw herself into the slaughter. The carnage was incredible.

In a matter of minutes they were all dead.

Only then did Posner join his monstrous kin on the killing floor. He walked through the bodies without thought for who or what they had been.

'Was it everything you dreamt it would be?' Posner said, his voice echoing weirdly in the suddenly silent hall.

'And more,' Isabella answered. She was on her knees, her face smeared with the blood of the newly dead aristocracy. She jumped up and rushed over to the dais where her portrait had been knocked to the floor in the fighting. She knelt over it, staring at the face she hadn't seen for so long. 'Do you think I'm pretty?'

'It does not do you justice, countess,' Posner said.

'You think?' A flush of happiness brought a smile to her bloody lips.

'Gist is a master, but even a master cannot hope to render such flawless beauty with a clumsy brush.'

'Gist is dead,' Isabella said, lost suddenly in the memory of it. 'I ate him.'

'Is, was, it matters not, countess. The choice of words is nothing more than semantics. The proof of his labours is there in your hands, a timeless reminder of your beauty. If you forget yourself you need only gaze upon it as it hangs on the wall to be reminded. And for us beauty never fades.'

'Yes.' Isabella mused. 'Yes. I should like that. I am beautiful, aren't I?'

'Yes, countess.'

'And it will always be this way?'

'Yes, countess. For eternity.'

'Thank you, Herman.'

Posner turned to see the count reaching out to his wife. There wasn't a single fleck of blood on him. 'Come,' he said. She rose and picked a path through the corpses like a butterfly flitting from flower to flower. Posner followed her and von Carstein to the battlements. Alten Ganz knew where the count was going – there was only one place he would go – so he

raced up to the rooftops via the servants stairs, panting and gasping as he pushed himself to keep on
running up the different staircases. He was already
there when von Carstein arrived. The battlements
were thronged with ravens nesting along the crenella-
tions and in the eaves and crevices of the gothic
architecture. Feathers ruffled and wings beat as the
count burst out onto the roof with Posner and
Isabella trailing in his wake.

'Geheimnisnacht,' von Carstein said, no hint of
breathlessness in his voice. 'A night like no other. Do
you have it, Ganz?' He held out a hand expectantly.

Ganz reached inside the folds of his cloak and drew
out a single sheet of parchment. His hand trembled
as he handed it over to his master. He had looked at
the parchment and though he couldn't read most of
the arcane scrawl he recognised it for what it was: an
incantation.

'My thanks. This single piece of paper will change
the world as we know it.' His words snatched away by
the rising wind, von Carstein savoured the thought.
'No more will we walk in fear, no more will we hide
in shadows. This is our time. Now. With this single
piece of paper we change the world.'

Isabella wrapped herself around her husband's side,
her hair streaming in the wind, naked hunger in her
eyes.

Posner stared out over the battlements at the city
below, shrouded in fog and darkness.

Ganz didn't move. He stared at the brittle
parchment in his master's hand. Only it wasn't
parchment or paper or even vellum, he knew, it was
flesh and blood, or rather skin and blood. The

incantation written in blood on a sheet of cured human skin. The letters were the faded rust of blood and the texture of the parchment was unmistakable.

'Read it, my love,' Isabella whispered.

'Do you know what this is?' Vlad asked. Without waiting for an answer, he continued. 'One page from the nine Books of Nagash. Hand-written by Nagash himself, the blood on this page was shaped with his own hand. This is but a fraction of his wisdom, a hint at the wonders that held the key to his immortality. These words unlock the Kingdom of the Dead. This one page is precious beyond money. This one page… the power in it… The words give life, revification of the flesh… They offer a way back for all those who have gone – imagine – with this there can be no death. Not as we know it. Not as a meaningful thing, the end of a life lived to the full. With this the dead will rise to stand at my side. If I will it they will fight at my side as I march across the Empire of mortal men. Death shall have no dominion. With these words I shall command the flesh. I shall return life where I see fit. Fight me, face my wrath, I shall kill my enemies and then raise them to fight *for* me as I conquer the world. With these few words I shall raise the dead from their earthly prisons. I shall speak and in speaking become a dark and hungry god. I, Vlad von Carstein, first of the Vampire Counts of Sylvania, shall have dominion over the realms of life and death. As I say, so it shall be.'

'Read it,' Isabella pressed. She nuzzled in close to Vlad, her tongue trailing luxuriantly across his cheek, kissing and nibbling up to his ear. She breathed heavily into his ear before the trail of hot wet kisses led to the Vampire Count's neck, her teeth closing to bite in a sensuous re-enactment of her own siring.

'No,' Ganz said. He held out his hand as though asking for the parchment back.

'You would that it stays the way it is? The way it has always been? With my kind forced to hide from daylight, vilified by the stupid masses? Hunted by fools with stakes and garlic cloves like wild animals fit for nothing but slaying?'

'No,' Ganz repeated. He was visibly trembling. Still he held his hand out as though he truly expected the Vampire Count to surrender the incantation without unleashing its curse on the world.

'Are you afraid, Ganz? Are you afraid of a world full of the risen dead? Are you afraid that they will see you as I see you? As meat?'

Ganz looked at them all one at a time, studying them and seeing them for what they were for the first time in his life. They were nature's predators. They hunted to survive. The slaughter downstairs was evidence of that. What was he to them? He knew the answer. The truth. He always had.

Prey.

They weren't equals. They weren't even comparable. They had eternity where he was a mote caught in the eye of time. One blink and he was gone.

'Kill me,' he said, looking the Vampire Count in the eye. 'Make me like you.'

'No,' von Carstein said, breaking eye contact.

'Why? Aren't I good enough? Haven't I proved my loyalty?'

'You are nothing more than meat,' Posner said, not bothering to hide his distaste of Ganz's humanity.

'Quiet, Herman. Of course you are loyal, and valued. It is precisely because of that that I cannot – no I will not – turn you. I need a man to walk in the world of day, to be my voice. I trust you Ganz. Do you understand? You are more valuable to me as you are.'

'As meat.'

'As meat,' the count agreed.

'When this is over?'

'It will never be over. Not truly.'

'And if I throw myself off the battlements?'

'You will serve me in death, a mindless automaton. Would you wish that upon yourself?' von Carstein asked in all seriousness. 'Would you choose an undeath as a shambling zombie?'

'No,' Ganz admitted.

'Then be happy with what you are, and serve me with all of your heart. Or I might let Herman eat it.'

'I'll be the last of my kind... the last living man in the Kingdom of the Dead.' The thought of it was more than he could bear. Ganz sank to his knees, and lowered his head until his forehead touched the cold stone of the castle's rooftop. 'Kill me,' he pleaded, but von Carstein ignored him.

The Vampire Count stood upon the highest point of the castle, the mountain's teeth rising into the moonlight behind him like ghostly fangs.

'Hear me!' he called out into the darkness. 'Obey me!'

And he began to recite the incantation. Even as the first words left his mouth the heavens above split with a mighty crack and the first fat drops of rain began to fall. The ravens exploded from their nests, cawing frantically as they circled, a seething mass of black wings. From nothing rose a storm so violent it ripped and tore at the roof slates of Drakenhof and sent the loose ones spinning into the night to shatter on impact as they fell from the sky. Posner stood implacably in the midst of the driving rain. Beside him Isabella's expression was one of delicious expectancy. Vlad's obsessive chant was caught and ripped away into the night by the rising wind, the impact of his words carried to the farthest corners of Sylvania. Driven, he plunged on, calling out to the vilest forces in the universe, demanding they bend to his will.

Ganz raised his head to stare at the man he revered. The winds howling around the battlements rose to gale force. Sheets of rain pounded the mountainside. Amid the eye of the storm the Vampire Count threw back his head and bellowed another command from Nagash's damned book. The words meant nothing to Ganz. The wind tore at von Carstein's clothes and hair, buffeting and battering him. He read on, caught up in the sheer power of the incantation, his words tripping over themselves in their eagerness to be free of his mouth. Thunder crashed. A spear of brilliant white lightning split the night.

The transformation of Vlad von Carstein was highlighted in another jag of lightning; in the space of a few gut-wrenching syllables his face elongated and hardened into the bestial mask of the vampire, the contours of his brow sharpened, a feral snarl curling his lips, baring long canine incisors. The Vampire Count threw his head back against the wind, demanding the dead rise and do his bidding.

'Come to me! Rise! Walk again my children! Rise! Rise! Rise!'

And across the land the dead heard his call and stirred.

Bodies so long underground the flesh had been stripped by maggots and worms clawed and scratched at the confines of their coffins, chipping and splintering their skeletal fingers as they tore through first the cloth shroud and then the coffin lid. In their mass graves, newly dead plague victims sighed and shuddered as the agony of life returned to their revived corpses, the sickness that had stolen their lives, eaten away at their flesh and stilled their heart not enough to deny the call of the Vampire Count. In secluded corners of the province, forgotten by all but the murderers who left them there, the dirt of the unconsecrated graves hidden in forests and fields and roadside ditches rippled and churned as their restless residents gave themselves to a slow painful rebirth.

And below them, in the great hall of Drakenhof Castle, the revellers stirred and sighed and found life once more in their bodies, their souls denied eternal rest, the demands of von Carstein's magic bringing them back as nothing more than mindless zombies; all that was, save for one.

Jon Skellan.

He tasted the blood of the vampire on his tongue where it mingled with his own, and felt the aching need to feed, the burning hunger that accompanied his damnation and the madness of knowing, of understanding, suddenly what Posner had done to him. Skellan knew what he had become and finally understood the tragedy of it: how his last greatest peace had been stolen from him. There would be no reunion with Lizbet in this life or the next.

Skellan's tortured screams rent the night in two.

CHAPTER EIGHT
Into the Barren Lands

SYLVANIA
Winter, 2010

STEFAN FISCHER RAN for his life.

He staggered and stumbled and forced himself to run on. Hunger ate away at him. Some days he was lucky and feasted on the meat of a giant rat or long nosed tapir, other days he subsisted on roots from plants, there were no fruits or berries. On the worst days he went hungry.

After three weeks of running the snows came. At first gentle, they didn't settle but as the climate continued to drop the snow stopped melting as it fell. Winter arrived.

It would be the death of him if he didn't find warmth and shelter soon. A few roots and bugs weren't going to be enough to keep him alive. And that was what it all came down to: staying alive.

He stumbled on, into the boggy marshland west of Dark Moor, the spectre of Vanhaldenschlosse black in the distance like the ghostly claws of a revenant shade. Insects and mosquitoes swarmed all over him day and night, biting and sucking at his blood. For every one he slapped away or killed, ten more swarmed in to take its place feeding on his fresh meat. The only respite he got from the blood-sucking insects was at night, if he managed to gather the fixings to make a fire. The smoke drove them away.

By cover of night he stole a coracle from a small settlement on the outskirts of the marsh and for the last three days had been poling the small boat slowly through the reeds and rushes. He had eaten nothing for two days. Hunger left him dizzy and delirious. In the delirium he remembered snatches of Geheimnisnacht, the masquerade, the beautiful people in their bone masks, and the slaughter that followed. There was a nightmarish quality to it but that was no surprise, every minute of every day since Geheimnisnacht had been part of one long unending nightmare.

His only thought now was that he had to escape Sylvania. He had to make it back to the Empire so that he might warn people of von Carstein's true nature.

Not that he expected anyone to believe him.

The dead rising from their graves, the count and his cohorts gathering an army of the damned to their side. Who in their right mind would believe him? It was hard enough for him to believe and he had lived through it. It was still fresh in his mind –

and it always would be. The images of death and destruction had seared themselves into his mind's eye.

FISCHER STUMBLED DOWN *the narrow stairs, his heart hammering in his chest. Skellan was dead. That… that… thing had thrown his corpse over the gallery rail. The Totentanz was a trap and Skellan's death acted as the spring that sent the jaws slamming down. He staggered out of the stairwell. A woman still clutching her bone mask stumbled into his arms. Her throat had been torn out. The blood and the gore spilled from the open wound, down the front of her dress. She died in his arms, her lifeblood oozing out all over him. The great hall was in chaos. People screaming, running, dying. The vampires descended in a feeding frenzy. Flight was impossible. Everyone who ran for one of the exits from the great hall was chased down and slaughtered by one of von Carstein's vampires. He was going to die here, in this foreign place, unmourned, food for one of the damned. He staggered forward. The woman's dead weight dragged her from his hands. People were dying all around him. There was nowhere to run. Nowhere to hide.*

Something slammed into his back, propelling him off his feet. Fischer sprawled forward, arms outstretched to break his fall, and landed in a bloody pool of spilled viscera. The blood was still warm on his hands and face. The screams were unbearable. He slipped and slithered through the gore, pulling a dead man across his body and lay there under the gutted corpse, staring blankly up toward the ceiling and praying fervently that the vampires would miss him. It was almost impossible not to gag on the wretched stench of death. He wanted desperately to breathe but

couldn't, not more than a sip of corrupt air at a time. It
was all he could do not to cry out in revulsion. Tatters of
flesh were stripped and thrown around the death room.
Blood sprayed over everything. The feeding frenzy went on
unabated, the vampires playing with the last few revellers,
spinning them from vampire to vampire, cutting them and
pushing them away until they tired of the game and bit
their victim's throats out and drained every last ounce of
blood before they discarded their corpses like rag dolls.

The vampires moved through the room, pulling trinkets
and jewellery from the corpses and arguing over the spoils
after von Carstein disappeared upstairs. He was lucky -
they weren't looking for survivors, they were sated from the
feeding and interested in gold and jewels. He had neither
on him so he was left alone. The silence was unerring but
it did not last long. Long minutes later it was replaced by
cracks of thunder and the sound of rain lashing at the windows as a storm raged outside.

Still Fischer didn't move, even as around him the nightmarish scene of slaughter became a macabre resurrection,
one after another the gutted, slashed, and gored partygoers rose awkwardly, answering some unheard call. In the
midst of it all he saw Skellan rise, his hands going to the
wound on his neck where Herman Posner had bitten him.
Mimicking the dead, Fischer pushed himself jerkily to his
feet. He wanted desperately to go to his friend – for a
moment he though that it really was Jon Skellan there,
that somehow he had survived the slaughter, where the
others shambled about the great hall like mindless zombies
Skellan appeared to be thinking, remembering what had
happened. Then he screamed and his scream was far from
human. It was the last trace of humanity fleeing from his
vampiric form. Silent tears slid down Fischer's cheeks as he

said a final goodbye to his friend. With the milling corpses bumping into each other as they struggled to retain control of their awkward limbs Fischer slipped behind one of the velvet curtains, moving slowly, like one of the lost souls he had just abandoned. No one followed him as he snuck into the kitchens and then down again into the cellars. And then he was out into the fresh air, the rain soaking him and washing the blood from his face as he staggered about in the darkness looking for a way out.

He stole a black stallion from the count's stables and rode it into the ground. The horse died beneath him. He cut the dead animal open, filleting a few cuts of meat from it, which he stuffed into his pockets, and then he ran.

THE RESURRECTIONS WERE not contained to the revellers either. In the six weeks he had been running Fischer had come across pockets of shambling undead, recently raised from gardens of Morr and mausoleums across the countryside, the dirt of the graves still clinging to their rotten flesh, all moving unerringly in the direction of Drakenhof Castle.

They were answering von Carstein's call.

The Vampire Count was drawing the dead to him, summoning them from the grave to his side. More and more bodies, almost as though he were raising an army... a monstrous undead regiment. But why? And it came to him then. Von Carstein could only have a single purpose for raising an undead army: to wage war on the Empire.

Fischer pushed the pole deep into the saturated ground, propelling the coracle deeper into the marsh.

He had to survive.

He had to warn people what monsters were coming their way.

Without his warning town after town would succumb to the same bloody slaughter that he had lived through on Geheimnisnacht.

He wouldn't – couldn't – allow that to happen.

He had to survive.

CHAPTER NINE
Succubus Dreams

SYLVANIA
Winter, 2010

THE INSECTS WERE gone and the air was fresh for the first time in more than a week.

Fischer was weak with hunger. The last thing he had eaten was a water rat that he had caught by dragging the net he had found beneath the wooden seat of the coracle through the marsh water. He had been hoping to find some kind of fish but for a starving man meat was meat. He ate it with relish only to throw most of it up less than an hour later.

He lay on his back in the small boat, looking up at the sky. Ravens circled above his head, drifting silently on high thermals. The winter sun was bright in the clear blue sky. Not for the first time he regretted not having returned to his room above

Hollenfuer's wine cellars. As the winter deepened the risk of hypothermia heightened. The cold was his greatest enemy now. He had pushed himself to the point of exhaustion knowing instinctively that sleep could be as deadly as a knife in the gut. Not that sleep was something he welcomed now; every dream, no matter how fleeting, took him back to Geheimnisnacht and the slaughter in the great hall, the faces of the dead as they came back from whatever hell their souls had been consigned to, the bone masks scattered across the floor, slick with the blood of their wearers, and the vampires.

It was a constant struggle though, not giving in to the lure of exhaustion.

A smudge of black smoke on the horizon gave him a surge of fresh hope. Fire.

He pushed himself to his knees and grasped the wooden pole, sinking it deep into the muddy bottom of the marsh waters, his gaze focussed on the smoke in the distance, a litany of mumbled prayers tripping off his lips. Smoke promised habitation, a settlement of some sort, a place to get real food, warm clothing, and a real bed for a night.

Turgid brown water lapped against the side of the coracle as he propelled it toward the column of smoke.

As he neared he began to make out more shapes and details. It was a settlement, the thatched roofs glittered yellow in the sun. The realisation that he would be sleeping under a dry roof, out of the elements, for the first time in almost two months was almost too much for him to bear. He drew the pole out of the water, and hand over hand, plunged it back

Into the murky water, pointing the small boat closer to the settlement. He began fantasising about roast meat and vegetables, a cooking fire with a grill spit and a haunch of wild boar turning over the flames, dripping fat that sizzled on the coals beneath it. Such was the intensity of the imagined sight Fischer began to salivate at the very thought of it.

He moored the coracle up against a small wooden jetty and clambered out. There were fifteen houses in total and they were all built on stilts so that they rested above the water level. Gangplanks and rope bridges joined the buildings, and each had its own small jetty where coracles and canoes were moored. Fischer had no idea why anyone would choose to live in the marsh, but at that moment he was not about to start complaining. The smoke was coming from one of the central houses, which was slightly larger than the others. The rope bridge swayed beneath Fischer as he traversed from one building to another. He lost his footing twice but didn't fall. His vision swam as dizziness threatened to overwhelm him.

He opened the door and stumbled into the welcoming warmth of a small communal hut. There were tables and chairs and a fire crackling in the hearth. There were three men in the room, who looked up, surprised by his sudden arrival. He knew what he must have looked like, collapsing through the door, his face and neck swollen with bites and stings and smeared with blood from his constant scratching at them, his hair tangled and foul with stagnant rain and sweat and his clothes utterly filthy with ground-in muck and gore, hanging off him as though he were a bag of bones, so much weight had he lost since fleeing Drakenhof.

Fischer staggered forward then stumbled and fell to his knees. He reached out a hand to grab on to something for support then fell forward. He blacked out. He had no idea how long for but when he came to he was lying on a makeshift pallet by the fire and there was a ring of concerned faces looking over him.

'Give the poor fellow some air, woman.'

'Hush your chatter, Tomas Franz, he's waking up.'

'Where?' Fischer's voice cracked. He hadn't spoken for so long it was difficult to form the words. 'Where am I?'

'Right 'ere. Middle of nowhere.'

'Take no notice of Georg. Welcome to our little village, stranger. You are, in Sumpfdorf. Vanhaldenschlosse is two days walk north-east of here, once you are out of the marsh. From there, it's maybe five days on to Eschen, ten due north to Waldenhof. A better question might be what brought you to us?'

He didn't have an answer – at least not one he cared to share. 'Trying to get... home.'

'Magda, fetch the poor man some broth. Jens, run to my house and get Olof to give you our extra blankets.' The woman commanded. She turned to Fischer, her voice immediately softening. 'What's your name, love?'

'Stefan Fischer.'

'Well Stefan, welcome to our home. You look like you need a place to rest your head. We ain't rich and we ain't proud but we don't mind helpin' folk in need. So rest up. We'll talk when you've had some of Magda's broth.' She smiled at him, and for a moment at least, the nightmares of the last few months faded away into the background. He was safe.

The boy, Jens, returned with a thick warm blanket that smelled of the woman's home: of smoke from the fireplace, of her skin, of food cooked and spiced and long since eaten. He accepted it gratefully. A shy young slip of a girl approached his bedside with a wooden bowl filled almost to the brim with steaming soup. He tried to take it from her but his hands were shaking so badly she ended up spoon-feeding Fischer while he slurped and swallowed greedily. The broth smelled delicious and tasted better. He burnt his mouth in his haste to swallow mouthful after greedy mouthful. There were vegetables in it, and some kind of stringy meat.

When he was done, the woman came and sat by his bedside and shooed the others away.

'So, Stefan Fischer, tell me your story. Nobody ends up in Sumpfdorf intentionally. Are you running away from someone or to someone? It is always one or the other.'

Fischer closed his eyes. She obviously thought he was some kind of criminal on the run from an angry magistrate. He didn't know where to start. Part of him desperately wanted to tell her the truth, all of it, just to unburden his soul, but a larger part insisted that this little haven would be safe from the insanities of the Vampire Count, that they didn't need to know about the slaughter and the gathering undead army. The horrors of the world would surely pass them by. He closed his eyes as he began to smudge the truth.

'I came to Sylvania with my friend. We were looking for a man. Now I am going home and… and my friend is dead. All I want to do is go home but I think… I think I can't… because I don't think it is there anymore… He was my home as much as any place was. We'd been together forever and now we

aren't. So now I just want to get out of this godforsaken province.'

'A sad story, but then I expected nothing less. You
are welcome here, Stefan Fischer. We don't have
much, but what we do have is yours to share. Stay as
long as you need. The world will be waiting for you
when you leave. It doesn't go away, however much we
might like it to.'

'Thank you. I don't even know your name.'

'Janelle.'

'Thank you, Janelle.'

'You are most welcome, Stefan.'

'Fischer. Call me Fischer. My friends do.'

'Fischer. Sleep, rest. If you need anything call Magda
or my son, Jens. When you are recovered, if you still
want to get out of Sylvania, I will have Jens escort you
out of the marsh and put you on the road. Carry on
to Warten Downs and eventually you'll come to Essen
Ford, where you can cross the Stir back into Talabecland.'

THEY WERE KIND to him.

He stayed with Janelle and the good people of
Sumpfdorf for five days, gathering his strength, eating
well for the first time since leaving Hollenfuer's
home, and sleeping. Sleep was a blessing. Only on
one night did he dream of Skellan. It was a strange
dream, tinged with nightmarish qualities but it
wasn't frightening, only sad. In his dream Skellan's
lost soul found him in the marsh and begged him for
directions to Morr's Kingdom. The most haunting
aspect of the dream was Skellan's sadness as he
begged his friend. After years of searching for that

final closure his soul was out there, cast aside, to wander in limbo for eternity while his soulless shell lived on, infected by von Carstein's evil. When the shade moved on its way Fischer was left with an uncomfortable sense of having failed his friend. Come morning he wished he had the courage to hunt down the vampire his friend had become, to release his friend from his torment, but daylight didn't bring with it false courage. The sun rising redly over the marsh only succeeded in convincing him that the whole world was going to hell and he was just one man, and alone there was nothing he could do to stop it.

True to Janelle's word Jens escorted him out of the marsh and onto the Warten Downs road. The parting was bittersweet. In Sumpfdorf he had found something he hadn't had for a long time, contentment. His spirit was at rest.

'You are welcome to come back to us, Fischer, when you have finished running. I want you to understand that. There will always be a place for you here.'

'Thank you, Janelle. I will come back one day, I promise.'

'You should not make promises you cannot keep. Say instead I will come back, if I can. Let there be no lies between us.'

Fischer smiled. 'I will come back if I can, Janelle. I think I found somewhere I could one day call home and that is something I never thought to have again.'

'You are a good man, Fischer. You will do what you have to and then you will come back to us. We will be waiting.'

Make no promises you can't keep, Fischer thought, remembering the farewell.

He was alone again, shadows on the road behind him, shadows on the road ahead of him. They had given him a fur-lined skin coat, and cleaned the filth out of his clothes. He had a pack with enough food for two weeks on the road and fresh air on his face. He felt almost human again.

Still, the road ahead promised to be a long soul-sapping journey.

'One foot in front of the other,' he said and started to walk.

THE DREAM OF Skellan haunted him, even under the full glare of the winter sun. He couldn't help but feel that he was running out on his friend when, perhaps more so than ever before, he needed him. That feeling of desertion stayed with him for the long days ahead. At the end of his third day on the road a garish gypsy caravan slowed as it was in the process of overtaking him. The travellers were in good spirits, singing songs in a language Fischer didn't understand. There were three of them up front on the flatboard seat of the painted wagon, a man, well-groomed with his fair hair wetted down and slicked back off his forehead. He was perhaps a little older than Fischer. On either side of him sat two women, one, fair like the man, who was obviously his daughter, while the other was dark and bore almost no familial resemblance. She was dangerously beautiful with pale skin and emerald green eyes. It was difficult not to stare.

'Evening, neighbour,' the man called down as the wagon drew level with Fischer.

'Evening.'

'You're on the road late, where you headed?'

'Home.'

'Indeed, and where would that would be?'

'Talabecland.'

'You are a long way from home, neighbour. Want a ride? There's room up here for one more. We don't bite.'

The dark-haired young woman leaned forward, her hair falling in front of her face. She brushed it aside slowly, her smile the first thing to appear from behind the cascade of raven black hair. 'Unless you ask us to,' she said mischievously.

'Saskia!' The man shook his head as though to say, 'What can you do?'

'If it's no trouble,' Fischer said, reaching a hand up. The man grasped it and hauled him up to the flatboard seat. The women slid along to make room for him.

They travelled well into the night.

The conversation was full of places the unlikely trio had travelled, from Kislev to Bretonnia and Tilea, far to the south of the Border Princes. They were entertainers, jongleurs. Their act was filled with music, juggling and acrobatics. During the night the man, Kennet, recited *Das Leid Ungebeten* in its eerie entirety. The Ballad of the Uninvited was the perfect ghost story for a dark night and Kennet's performance was spellbinding. His voice ached as he spoke, carried away by the keen lament of the restless dead. Ina, Kennet's other daughter, was quiet most of the time, content to listen to her father and play second fiddle to her sister. They drank cider and bitter wine, joking and telling stories. Fischer found it hard to imagine good people like these surviving in Vlad von Carstein's Kingdom of the Dead. During the ride he found his eyes wandering back to Saskia. There was something utterly compelling about her pale skin and emerald green eyes. Even though she was less than half his age Fischer found his thoughts wandering to places they hadn't visited for a long time. Desire was an emotion he had thought long since lost to him. Unlike Janelle who had made him feel safe, warm, content to be alive, Saskia set his blood on fire. Had he been a younger man it would have been easy to surrender, as it was, Fischer was not about to make a fool of himself so he contented himself with stolen glances and carnal imaginings.

That night Fischer slept fitfully, his dreams fragmented and troubled. The most disturbing snatches of them threatened to wake him. They revolved around Saskia, her dark hair falling across his face, her fingernails dragging down his chest as she nuzzled into his neck, her teeth nibbling, teasing, her breathy promise, 'Unless you ask us to' hot in his ear as her teeth sank into his neck.

He awoke in a feverish sweat, his clothes in disarray. Instead of feeling refreshed from a good long sleep he was exhausted. He felt as though he could sleep for another eight hours comfortably. He was alone inside the caravan. The caravan itself moved to the gentle sway of the road. He touched the curve of his neck, half expecting to feel a stab of pain from bite wounds. It was unblemished.

'Stupid old man, Fischer. Dreams are just dreams.'

He stretched and rearranged his clothing, making himself decent before he opened the back door. He climbed out and used the ladder on the side of the door to climb up onto the roof and join Kennet and the ladies in the driving seat. The sun, he noticed, was already setting.

'Why didn't you wake me?' he scratched his head as he sank down beside Saskia.

'We thought you needed your sleep.'

'Seems you were right. I haven't slept well lately. A lot on my mind.'

'I know. You talk in your sleep.'

'No.'

'Oh yes. You must have been having some pretty colourful nightmares. At one point you were screaming and clawing at the blankets. Were you being buried alive?'

He had vague memories of the nightmare, but all of the fragments of his dreams were disjointed. After Saskia fed off him he found himself back in Drakenhof's great hall, facing his friend over the corpses of the fallen, Skellan urging him to join him in von Carstein's vampiric horde, and then the bodies on the floor had begun to seethe and writhe as the undead slowly began to rise.

Fischer shook off the memory.

He broke his fast on a chunk of hard bread and cheese and watched the evening world go by.

As with the day before, Kennet told stories to help the time pass, and the girls sang songs. One in particular stood out. The troubadour, Deitmar Köln, had sung it in the Traitor's Head back in Leicheberg: 'The Lay of Fair Isabella'. Saskia's voice held Fischer mesmerised as it wove though the tragic story of the Vampire Count's bride, though in their telling

Isabella was more than a victim, she was the instigator of her own sickness, hungry for the power of eternity. The retelling was revolting given what he knew – what he had seen with his own eyes: the countess covered in blood asking for reassurance that she was pretty, even as the monsters fed on the dead and dying. He wondered what death had done to her mind. Was she the same scheming power-hungry woman she had been in life? Or had death unhinged her mind and turned her into something far more dangerous?

'Stop,' he said. He was physically shaking. 'Stop. I don't want to hear this.'

But Kennet just laughed and the girls sang on.

Several hours down the road they came to a fork, one turning point leading away toward Hel Fenn, the other into Grim Wood. Kennet steered the caravan into the forest. Fischer lay back on the flat roof of the caravan, listening to another of Kennet's sagas. The leaves of the trees twined and intertwined overhead forming a perfect canopy. He couldn't see so much as a sliver of moonlight through them. Sleep soon claimed him.

Again, his dreams were troubled with hallucinogenic splinters of memory fused with the conjurations of his imagination, and again, woven in and out of those splinters of memory were fragments of dream that verged on the erotic: Saskia's lips touching his cheek, his neck, finding the hollow where his pulse was so close to the surface, and feeding off him. He struggled to pull himself out of the dreams but the more he struggled the more Saskia drank and the weaker he grew.

* * *

HE HAD NO sense of time when he awoke. The leaves of Grim Wood kept out the sunlight as well as they fended off the moonlight.

The jongleurs sat together upfront, singing a haunting refrain from the 'Trauerspiel von Vanhal', the tragedy of the great witch hunter himself. It was a melancholy song, and though Fischer knew it well he had not heard it sung since he was a young man. It was one of those pieces that had fallen out of fashion as he had grown older. It was surprising that these travelling entertainers knew it, and so many of the older ballads. There couldn't have been a huge call for this kind of material in the taverns and taprooms of the Empire.

Fischer felt utterly drained. He reached into his pack and ended up eating three days' worth of his food without entirely satisfying his hunger. He felt light-headed. The movement of the wagon made him feel vaguely sick.

His dreams on the third night were the worst of all.

In one jagged splinter of memory-cum-imagination he dreamed he was a man who dreamed he was a wolf who dreamed he was damned for all eternity to be locked in the flesh of a man. He dreamed of Saskia too. Her gentle touch and the sheer sensuality of her lips as she kissed his skin caused his pulse to trip and skip erratically. The smell of her as she leaned in, the sensation of her teeth sinking into his neck and sucking the very lifeblood out of him was intoxicating. And through it all, the laughter of Jon Skellan rang in his ears, taunting him as he surrendered to the blackness of oblivion.

He came awake with a start.

Sweat streamed down his forehead and chest. Again his clothes were in disarray, the buttons open. Red bite marks and abrasions covered his chest. Instinctively he touched his neck where Saskia had fed on him in the dream. He felt the sharp rise of a swelling just above the hollow between his neck and collarbone and within it the serrated edge of bite marks.

Panic flared in his mind. He scrabbled around looking for his sword, his knife, anything to defend himself with. They were gone. His pack was there, with its dwindling supply of food. He looked around the inside of the gypsy caravan but couldn't see anything that could be used as a makeshift weapon. He was groggy and struggling to think straight. The rational part of his mind insisted it had all been a dream, that in fact he was still dreaming, but the cold hard truth pressed against his fingers when he touched his neck.

He was trapped in a wagon travelling with at least one vampire through dense woodland thick enough to turn day into night, and he was defenceless.

He tried to listen to see if he could hear anything but through the wooden walls and over the trundling wheels it was impossible. His every instinct screamed: flee!

Fischer grabbed his pack and slung it on his back. He crept over the mattress and the tangle of sheets to the door, cringing at every creak and shift the wooden floorboards made beneath his weight. He braced himself inside the small doorway with his hand on the doorknob.

He closed his eyes and counted silently to ten, gathering his courage and mastering his breathing. The next few minutes were going to be vital, he knew. Whether he lived or died at the hands of these blood-sucking fiends depended on what happened next. He twisted the doorknob and eased the door open inch by cautious inch until it was wide open. The caravan was juddering as its wheels bounced over ruts and stones in the so-called road. The branches dragged down low in places, almost scraping the roof of the wagon. Fischer crouched down and watched the road, trying to judge a rhythm so that he could best time his jump.

'One... two... three!'

He sprang from the open doorway, hitting the dirt road hard, and rolled.

'Hey!' Kennet cried.

Fischer struggled to get his feet under him and hared off into the undergrowth, hoping the trees would give him cover enough to run for his life. He scrambled forward, slipped and had to use his hands to keep him on his feet as he barrelled forward deeper into the trees. Branches and leaves slapped in his face. Brambles tore at his arms as he pushed through them. Behind him Fischer heard the cries of pursuit as they crashed through the forest after him.

'I can *smell* you, Fischer! You can't hide. There is nowhere to go and your fear *stinks*! So go on, run!' Kennet's voice taunted loudly, goading him into running faster. 'Run 'til your heart bursts! Your blood will be good and hot. Soon enough we will all feed!'

Please no, Fischer prayed, pumping his arms and legs harder. It was almost impossible to run properly in the forest. His lungs burned. Fire flared through his thighs and calves. He slipped on a mulch of dead leaves and tripped over a piece of deadfall lying across his path. He barely succeeded in keeping his feet as he ducked beneath a huge overhanging branch. Pushing a swath of leaves out of his face he careened into a rotten tree trunk, pushed himself off it. Gasping for breath, Fischer continued his frantic flight. All the while the taunts of Kennet grew closer, harrying him. He stumbled and staggered on even when his legs wanted to buckle and collapse.

He heard them all round him, playing with him as they shepherded him toward wherever it was they had decided to kill him: Kennet behind him, Saskia to his left, Ina to his right. They called out to him, pushed him in different directions until his legs collapsed under him.

Sobbing, Fischer looked up as Kennet approached, his face twisted into the mask of the monster he actually was. Saskia no longer looked like some heavenly creature; her face was hard, daemonic and Ina's grin was feral as she moved to stand beside her bestial kin.

'Mine,' Saskia said, crouching down beside Fischer. She reached out and tenderly stroked his cheek. 'He always was.'

Fischer spat in her face.

'I'd rather die!'

'Oh you will, believe me, you will.' Her fingers sought out his pulse as it fluttered through his neck. She drew in a slow breath through her nose, savouring the feel of his life beneath her fingertips. 'Blood... such sweet music it makes.'

'Do it,' Ina urged.

'Come on then,' Fischer said stubbornly. 'Finish me, you freak! Do it!'

Saskia pricked his cheek with a fingernail, drawing a ribbon of rich red blood. She leaned in and laved the blood up with her tongue, playing with the blood across her lips.

Fischer went cold. He didn't move. He didn't panic. He didn't close his eyes.

He met her gaze and rasped: 'Do it, damn you!'

He felt her teeth close on the soft flesh of his throat and in that last second as he waited for death heard a sound, like a sharp intake of breath. Fischer winced as the first prickling of teeth sank into his throat but it wasn't matched with the agony of the vampire's feeding. Instead Saskia's head jerked back, her eyes flaring open. The blooded silver tip of an arrow protruded through the front of her throat, the fletching of the shaft tangled in her beautiful hair. He touched his throat. It was wet with a trickle of blood from where the arrow had scratched him. A second arrow thudded into her back, its tip piercing through her breast. Saskia's mouth worked in a silent scream. She slumped into Fischer's terrified arms. He held her, not knowing what else to do.

More arrows rained into the clearing, taking Kennet high in the chest, spinning him around and dumping him, dead, on his back. Ina took three arrows in the chest, and one in the face.

Six men stepped into the clearing. Quickly and efficiently they decapitated the vampire jongleurs and began to dig two separate shallow graves, one for the three heads, the other for the bodies.

'It's your lucky day,' one of the men, a flaxen-haired youth, said, slinging his bow over his shoulder and helping Fischer to rise.

He felt an unwelcome hollowness inside at Saskia's death. It was as though he had lost something. A part of himself. It felt wrong in so many ways. She had been inhuman. A monster. She had been feeding off him for days, bleeding the life out of him. And yet, there was an ache where she had once been. He shook his head, trying to dislodge the unpleasant feeling. She was dead. He was alive. That was it. End of the story.

'Let me have a look at that,' the archer said. Fischer titled his head to expose the shallow wound. The archer prodded and probed the gash. 'Sit.' Fischer did as he was told. The man drew out a small sewing kit, and a hip flask. 'Drink a good swallow, it'll take the sting out. We need to stitch this up otherwise it'll never heal properly.'

Fischer uncorked the bottle and took a hearty swig. The liquor burned as it slid down his throat.

The archer talked while he doctored the wound.

'You're a lucky man, my friend. Another minute and we'd have been chopping your head off and burying you with the other fiends. Makes you believe in Sigmar, doesn't it?'

'I don't tend to believe in much of anything anymore.'

'Don't talk, it pulls at the stitching. I'll try and answer your questions without you having to ask them. My name is Ralf Baumann. I serve in the Ottilia of House Untermensch's grand army, beneath Hans Schliffen. For the last month we have been experiencing an uprising of sorts, undead, all along the Talabheim borderlands and the Ottilia herself ordered us into the field to police the situation.'

'It is worse than you fear, by far. Undeath is an epidemic in Sylvania.' Fischer said, ignoring the archer's instructions. 'The dead are rising to the call of Vlad von Carstein. The man is a monster. Man. Gah! He is no man. His humanity is long gone. The Vampire Count is a monster. He has slaughtered thousands only to bring them back as mindless zombies. I saw it with my own eyes on Geheimnisnacht. It was butchery. Anyone who has stood against him, he has seen them cut down and replaced by one of his own kind, a bloodsucking fiend. And once dead they get no rest. Oh no, he is raising an army of the dead to do his bloody work!'

Baumann remained impassive as he finished stitching the gash but the second he tied off the final stitch he exploded into action, running across the clearing to where his fellow soldiers were burying the dead and animatedly explaining what he had just heard. An army of the dead being raised by a Vampire Count was more, by far, than this small battalion of soldiers were equipped to handle.

Being caught in this no-man's land between the two factions, living and dead, would mean their death, no one harboured any illusions about that. And as they were all coming to understand, death at the hands of von Carstein was not the clean death a soldier deserved. It was the vile unending 'undeath' of a zombie resurrected to swell the ranks of the Vampire Count's immortal army.

They had to return to the main body of the Ottilia's army.

Schliffen had to know what they were facing.

And for that to happen they had to survive.

CHAPTER TEN
The Storm Before

ESSEN FORD, SYLVANIA
Winter, 2010

THE MORE HE got to know him, the more Ralf Baumann reminded Fischer of Jon Skellan.

It was the little things at first, gestures, throwaway comments, the way he talked of life and his philosophy of living, of his daughters back home in Talabheim, and of the wife he had lost to sickness two summers gone. They suggested the two men were not so dissimilar, yet the true mark of their brotherhood came in the form of their damnation. Neither Baumann nor Skellan were fully at peace with the world around them. They had lost their place in it. It was the most basic thing a human being had, the knowledge of his own place in the world, that sense of purpose that came with knowing who you were, but because these men lived on while those they loved rotted in the dirt, the serenity that came with innocence was lost to them.

Haunted by old ghosts who loved them too much to leave them alone, both men were victims of the survivor's curse.

It weighed as heavily on Baumann as it had on Skellan.

Given the choice of grief or action, Baumann, like Skellan had before him, chose to fight back and gave himself to it body and soul. It was in how they dealt with all the things they had in common that made the two men different. The fact that Baumann was not given to the same brooding introspection and fits of violent temper that plagued Skellan, but rather was quick of wit and passionate in his camaraderie made him a good companion for the long journey. The more he thought about it, the more Fischer came to think that the two were twin aspects of the same soul, darkness and light.

He found himself liking Baumann, a lot, and felt as though he had known the man far longer than he actually had.

It HAD SNOWED for seven consecutive days without letting up.

Every day the seven of them pushed on, matching the weather with their own stubborn determination, through valleys and along ridgelines of precarious rock, across frozen streams and snow-laden glades. It was tough going but on the evening of the eighth day they met up with outriders from Schliffen's force. They were camped outside of Essen, close to the fording point of the River Stir, waiting for the main body of the Ottilia's army to cross over from the Talabecland side of the water.

A pile of bones replaced the campfire.

'We're taking no risks,' Frank Bernholz, one of the outriders, explained. 'Twice now we've had to fend off these creatures. The fire attracts them. They aren't smart enough to stay away from Mouse's mace so he ends up grinding them down one at a time while we do our damnedest to keep the rest of the buggers at bay.'

Mouse, the smallest of the crew, grinned and patted the hefty studded mace by his side. 'Big pile of walking bones ain't no match for Bessie here.'

'I can well imagine,' Fischer said.

'When are you expecting the general, Frank?' Baumann asked, settling down on a stone beside the outrider. He cracked a piece of hard travel bread and started to chew on it.

'Yesterday. I sent Marius out to see what was holding him up. I don't like being marooned out here like some kind of sitting duck. Not my idea of a fun way to pass the time. I like it clean and honest. I like to know what I am fighting and to be able to look my enemy in the eye, knowing that he has as much to lose as I do when it comes to the crunch. Can't do it with these... these... *things*. We've lost three scouts in the last week, Ralf. Three good men.'

'It's a dirty business, for sure.'

'And it's only getting dirtier.'

'You do know what's coming, don't you?'

'I've got my suspicions, yeah. Not looking forward to facing whatever it is they decide to throw at us. It's not like fighting men. Men you know, you know the fear pulsing through their veins, you know the exhilaration, the weakness, you know when doubt sets in and more importantly you know when they are broken. A pile of walking bones doesn't think for itself and those walking corpses… They just keep coming and coming and coming. What have they got to lose? They're already dead. They don't know fear or doubt. They just keep on coming, wave after wave of them, and eventually even a good man will break. Maybe not on the first day or the second or even the third but the time will come when exhaustion wears him down, when doubt gnaws away at the back of his mind, when he makes a mistake and then what happens? He dies. Only it doesn't end there… Oh no, his corpse swells the ranks of the enemy and minutes after his death he is fighting against his friends. It's ugly.'

'Ain't that the truth.'

'They're out there now. You'll hear them when the sun finally goes down. Wolves howling at the moon and this eerie keening moan that seems to float all around the camp. We're in the jaws of a trap here and Schliffen knows it. We're his bait. That's why he's late.'

'That's a pretty cynical way of looking at the situation, my friend.'

'Is it? Take a look around, this is the ideal battleground, or as close as you're likely to get around here. You're not exactly wide open to surprises. This way Schliffen is picking the battleground. He knows the fight is coming. Like any good soldier he wants to make the best of what he's got. The water at our back means we're only vulnerable from three sides, and we're between two major branches of the hill so von Carstein can only bring his army over piecemeal, buying us time to dig in. We've been fortifying for a week. There's some nasty surprises out there beneath the snow, for what good they will do us.'

'Every little bit helps. So, honest opinion: when's this all going to go down?'

'Reckon you boys got here in the nick of time. The natives are restless. They're gathering all around us, have been for the last few nights. They fall into some sort of daze during the day, but like I said, come sunset you can hear them and there are lots of them. The noise has been getting louder every night, as more of them gather. It's creepy as hell, let me tell you. I heard them feeding last night. It isn't a sound I particularly want to hear again. It's like pigs at the trough, but, well, they aren't pigs are they. They're just like you or me. Or they were. Once. Anyway, sundown tomorrow would be my guess, unless they are waiting for something special.'

'I assume Schliffen will be thinking the same way.'

'I've long since stopped trying to second-guess the general but I certainly hope so. Morr's balls, I've got no desire to end up shuffling around with strips of rotten flesh hanging off me. That isn't a way I want to go.'

Baumann patted the outrider on the back and rejoined his own men, filling them in on the situation. He painted a bleak picture.

'So we've become the bait in the trap?'

'That's about the sum of it.'

'Nice,' Fischer said ironically.

The men ate in silence, watching the sun dwindle and finally disappear beneath the horizon.

A cold wind blew through the camp. Baumann busied himself by sharpening his sword on a whetstone. The regular *scheeeel scheeeel scheeeel* of his stropping motion rang out into the darkness. It was met by the ululating cries of the undead as they crowded in around the camp. Fischer caught glimpses of them in the darkness, bone-white flashes picked out by the moon, darker shapes shambling inside the shadows. In the most basic of ways they reminded him of wild animals playing with their food. They weren't trying to hide. They wanted to be seen. Being seen inspired fear in the minds and hearts of the soldiers.

By nature men who dealt in death were a superstitious lot. They believed they would hear an owl call their name the night before their own deaths and insisted on having their sword in their hand as they died as though the blade itself would prove to Morr's attendants that they were warriors, and always when they went into battle they would carry two silver coins to pay their passage into Morr's halls should they fall. Burdened with these superstitions it was hardly surprising that the men saw the shuffling corpses as a promise of the fate that awaited them on the battlefield. Today those putrefied zombies were their enemy, but tomorrow they would be their sword brothers.

More and more as the night lengthened they heard the low keening echo around them. The enemy were moving and they were blind to it. Bernholz had them prepare firebrands to fight off any of the creatures who stumbled too close to the camp but he wouldn't allow his men to light them for fear that the fire would attract the zombies, wraiths and wights like moths.

Fischer thought the man was an idiot. Those things out there weren't human and they weren't moths attracted by curiosity to the bright light. They were either oblivious to it or they were afraid of it. Dead or alive, they still burned. So as he saw it fire was their one and only friend. He didn't speak out against the Bernholz though.

The listless apathy of resignation had settled about the small camp. The conversations were muted, the men slipping into their own thoughts as they prepared for the inevitable battle. They knew that Hans Schliffen was sacrificing them in order to draw von Carstein's undead out onto the battlefield of his own choosing. They accepted it. It was what they did. They were soldiers. They sacrificed themselves for the greater good. It was a simple maxim: soldiers died for what they believed in. Every one of the men in the camp that night knew it and accepted it.

They were even coming to accept the fact that their general had condemned them almost certainly to an afterlife of living death in order to give the rest of his men the best chance of survival. There were always casualties during any engagement. Tough decisions had to be made. People would die: friends, brothers, fathers, no one was immune to the bite of a sword or the punch of an arrow. While they honed the edge of their weapons they did their damnedest to empty their minds. None of them wanted to dwell on the day ahead. They might accept what Schliffen was doing to them but they didn't have to like it. They were soldiers. They followed orders; even ones they knew would get them killed. There was no point in arguing with the strategy. Schliffen had made his mind up, and in his mind baiting the trap was their best hope of defeating von Carstein's horde.

All they could do was wait.

Fischer pressed his back against one of the cold stones the outriders had ringed around the empty fire pit and closed his eyes. He was asleep in moments, this time dreamlessly. The younger men lay awake most of the night, unable to sleep. The calls of the dead plagued them and their own black thoughts tormented them. They envied veterans like Fischer their ability to sleep with the sword of Morr hanging over their heads.

Before dawn the snow gave way to rain: a few spots at first and then more persistent. An hour after sunrise the sky was still dark with steel grey clouds, bulbous thunderheads, and the rain sheeted down turning the snow into slush and the soaking the ground beneath. By noon, Schliffen's precious battlefield was mired. Fischer picked his way toward the centre but walking was almost impossible as every step sank into the sludge almost as far as his knees.

He scared a single raven up from the muddy field and sent it cawing off into the torrential rain.

Fighting in this was going to be a nightmare.

Their one hope had disappeared with the mud – their mobility. Now they were going to be slopping about in the mire, flailing around for balance and moving like zombies themselves. A bitter part of him wondered if von Carstein wasn't somehow behind the foul turn of the weather. The man was a daemon after all, why shouldn't he have mastery over the elements?

The mud soaked up his calf and over his knee as he struggled another step forward. He turned to look behind him. There was no sign of the body of the Ottilia's army. There were, however, plenty of signs to suggest the encroaching presence of the Vampire Count's. Thousands of them. Tens of thousands. Sprawled out all across the killing ground between him and the line of the second tributary that formed Essen Ford.

Bodies.

Fischer stood, rooted to the spot, as his feet sank deeper into the sludge.

From what he could see the dead had simply collapsed where they stood and lay in a sprawl of limbs. He wanted to believe that whatever hold von Carstein had over them had failed, that they were safe. But he didn't believe it, not for a second. They were puppets, their strings had been laid aside but von Carstein could easily pick them up again and make them dance to whatever whim he saw fit to satisfy. Even with Schliffen's rearguard they were doomed. No quarter would be asked or given. The Vampire Count would bring the full wrath of his army down on their heads come sunset and all of the strategies and all of the gamesmanship in the Old World wouldn't save them.

He slumped forward onto his knees.

The thought of running crossed his mind but he dismissed it before the idea was even half formed. After all this running there was nowhere left to run to. He had done what he had set out to do. He had spread the word. Vlad von Carstein's secret was out in the world now. The people who needed to know it knew.

And yet tears streamed down his cheeks.

The tears surprised him. He wasn't afraid. He had always known this day would come.

Tonight he would stand beside Baumann and Bernholz and the others and he would be proud to do just that. War made heroes out of normal people. Here, on the fields of Essen Ford, heroes would be born.

And heroes would die.

CHAPTER ELEVEN
The Swords of Scorn

ESSEN FORD, SYLVANIA
Winter, 2010

THE SOUNDS OF the battlefield were all wrong.

There were screams as soldiers fell and fierce battle-cries answered by the stampede as swords clattered off shields, the cacophony intended to instil fear in an enemy that knew no fear. Despite the screaming, the drumming and the stamping feet there was no ringing clash of steel on steel.

The fight was no ordinary fight.

Swords slashed through the torrential rain, cutting at the dead arms as they clawed and scratched and pulled at the soldiers. The dead stumbled forward and the living lurched backwards desperate to evade their outstretched arms and suffocating embrace. The ground beneath their feet was treacherous. It was virtually impossible to fight. They were reduced to trying to stay alive. They staggered and lurched as they struggled to fend off the dead, their movements mimicking von Carstein's monstrous regiment as they struggled to keep their balance.

No matter how desperately the Ottilia's soldiers fought, the dead kept on coming, surging relentlessly forward without fear or concern for their own safety.

Fischer fought for his life beside Baumann, the flaxen-haired archer proving himself as deadly with a sword as he had shown he was with a bow. There was no smile on his face now though, only grim determination to stay alive as the dead threw themselves at them. Twice already during the fighting Baumann's blade had deflected a blow aimed at sweeping Fischer's head clean off his shoulders.

Fischer ducked under a wild blow, jamming his sword up into the gut of a woman. Half of her face had been eaten away by maggots. He wrenched the sword left and right violently slicing deep into her spinal cord. Her torso buckled, folding over itself. Fischer dragged his sword free. Unable to support itself her body collapsed at their feet but still she clawed at them, tugging at their feet. Her clawed hands hooked around Baumann's ankle and almost succeeded in toppling him before Fischer's sword cleaved through her wrist. He kicked her severed hand away as another zombie trampled over her writhing corpse. There was no time for thanks.

The pair fought on, lungs and arms burning with exhaustion. The sheer weight of numbers was overwhelming. The dead climbed over each other to get at them.

All across Essen Ford it was the same.

The dead were a tidal wave, an undeniable force beyond the limits of nature sweeping everything away in their path. Von Carstein's army was relentless and lethal. They had no need of weapons. They threw themselves bodily at the terrified soldiers, dragging them down into the sinking mud and once they had them down the dead swarmed over them, clawing, biting and rending at their flesh until they had stripped the fallen soldier of his humanity.

It was barbaric.

It wasn't a battle, it was butchery.

Ghouls, once men like Fischer and Baumann before they sank so far as to become cannibalistic eaters of the dead, picked over the corpses as the combatants trampled them into the mud. The vile creatures stripped away fillets of fresh meat and gorged themselves on it. Friends, foes, the ghouls were indiscriminate in their feeding.

Fischer parried a raking claw aimed at putting his eyes out and rammed the point of his sword into a woman's throat. Her blood-matted hair fell across her face. Where she should have had eyes were empty sockets stitched up with mortician's thread. She threw herself forward onto the sword, trying to snare him in her deadly embrace. Fischer couldn't drag his sword free. Her bloody locks fell in his face as she threw all of her weight at him. Fischer felt himself buckling under her.

Screaming, Fischer heaved himself upright and sent her spinning away across the muddy field, his sword still stuck in her throat. She bucked and thrashed trying to wrench Fischer's sword out. He cursed and hurled himself forward, landing on top of the blind woman. He punched at her face, slamming his fist into it again and again until it felt like he was pounding a slab of raw meat. Still she clawed at the sword. Fischer pushed himself to his feet as another two undead grabbed at him. He slammed an elbow into the face of the first hard enough to rupture its nose and spray blood into its eyes. He grabbed the hilt of his sword before the second dead man could stop him.

Baumann cut the dead man down before Fischer could turn to meet the challenge.

More came to fill the gap left by the fallen dead.

There was no end to it.

Around them good men died only to rise again and turn on them.

IT HAD BEEN like that for six hours. Even before the first blow had been struck whispers spread through the ranks, the Vampire Count had offered the outriders clemency should they abandon the Ottilia and serve him. None did. Schliffen had arrived on the field of battle an hour before von Carstein unleashed the full might of his horde. It didn't matter. More than half of the outriders had fallen and been absorbed into the ranks of the undead before Schliffen and the body of the Ottilia's army arrived. Their horses were useless in the muck and mire. They couldn't run and the mud only served to bog them down and topple them giving the ghouls more meat to gorge themselves on. There was no questioning their bravery though, even when von Carstein himself entered the fray, his nightmare steed snorting licks of fire from its flaring nostrils as the Vampire Count's wailing blade cleaved through terrified ranks of human defenders. The shrieking of the sword as it cut through the air was mortifying. The soldiers who weren't cut down fled and dragged more down in their panicked wake as they tried to escape the hungry blade. Von Carstein himself mocked them, laughing manically as he cut and hewed through the living and almost negligently raised them in his wake, bringing them into his legion of the damned.

Fischer stared in awe at the nightmare.

It was an awesome beast, blacker even than true black and easily five hands higher than the biggest horse Fischer had ever seen. Everything about the mount and its rider radiated pure unmitigated evil. The creature reeked of it. Von Carstein's mane of black hair was matted with the rain. He twisted in the saddle, standing on black iron stirrups and learning forward. His sword wailed its hideous threnody as it sheared through the neck of a terrified Imperial soldier. The man's head fell beneath the nightmare's hooves and was sucked into the mud.

More vampires came behind the count, led by a giant of a man who had no need of a nightmarish steed to inspire terror, his twin curved blades were more than enough. The vampire's face was splashed with blood, none of it his own. He licked his lips and savoured the taste of his defeated foes. The treacherous battlefield didn't appear to hinder him as he ghosted through the living and the dead, his twin blades blurring into a single steel blue arc. His vampires and wolves trailed in his deadly wake.

Some of the risen dead recovered weapons from the fallen, skeletons with swords and pikes and spears came at them.

In a flicker of movement in the corner of his eye Fischer saw Bernholz was in trouble. A revenant shade had risen up behind him, ethereal claws coming down to rake through body and soul. The shock of the cold would be enough to throw Bernholz's focus, giving the three putrefied corpses crowding around him the chance they needed to bring him down. He couldn't shout. The warning would go unheard over the sounds of carnage and feeding. He had to do something.

Without thinking about what he was doing Fischer grabbed a handful of mud-clogged hair on a decapitated head and heaved it up into the air so it arced through the air and came down hard on the shoulder of one of the zombies crowding in on Bernholz and landed at its feet in a splash of snow and sludge. Bernholz backed up a step. It saved his life. The revenant shade's claws sheared through his back and out of his chest causing the soldier to scream in shock and pain but his backwards step had given him space enough to regain his composure as the zombies lurched forward. The outrider gutted one and decapitated another. Even then there was no letup for him as dire wolves snapped at his legs and dregs clawed their way through the mud seeking to bring him down.

Something slammed into Fischer's back and sent him sprawling forward and his sword spinning out of his hand. He tasted the mud and the blood of the fight as his face ploughed into the sodden ground.

His sword had fallen tantalizingly out of reach of his fingers. He scrabbled toward it but before his hand could snatch it a heavy foot came down on his back, pinning him in the mud.

'Well, well, well, look who we have here.'

Despite its mocking tone he knew the voice.

Fischer squirmed beneath the crushing weight of the foot. He craned his neck to see the twisted features of his best friend sneering down at him: Jon Skellan. Only it wasn't Skellan. It was the soulless, heartless, dead thing wearing Skellan's bloodless corpse. It might have his memories and share his skin but it wasn't his friend. It was an animal.

Skellan kicked Fischer. 'Up, my friend. Time to die like a man.' Blood clung to Skellan's teeth where he had fed. His eyes were searing pits of anger.

'You're not my friend, not anymore.'

'Have it your own way. Up. I've got no patience for cowards and you stink of fear, Fischer. You absolutely reek of it. Now get up.'

Skellan kicked him forward as he struggled to rise so he kissed the blood-soaked dirt. Fischer put his hands under him again and started to stand only for Skellan to kick him off-balance again. He lay there in the mud, utterly drained. He lacked the will to move. Around him the sounds of the battle muted and lost their clarity as his senses narrowed their focus to the space between him and Skellan, shutting out all of the screaming and the dying, the driving rain, the keening of the undead and von Carstein's hideous wailing sword.

'So this is how it ends then?' Fischer said looking up at Skellan.

The vampire sheathed his sword and offered his hand.

'It doesn't have to. Take my hand. Join us. We can always use a good man. The Blood Kiss will set you free, believe me. I am a different man. Before it was all petty vengeance. My life was consumed with it. Posner freed me of the shackles of mortality. Now the strength of death flows through my veins in place of blood. The weakness is gone. There is no pity, no compassion, and no stinking mercy. I am vampire. I am immortal, what need have I to fear anything? It is a gift. The greatest gift.'

'No. You don't believe that. It is a curse and you know it. It is an abomination, even nature refuses you a reflection now so repugnant are you to the world. And you forget in your new arrogance, Skellan, you can die. You can die very well. Like Aigner. Remember him? Remember the man who murdered Lizbet? Remember the monster he was? That is what you are. How does it feel? You didn't slay the beast, you *became* the beast.'

'He was weak.'

'He was strong enough to destroy everything you loved.'

'And what is love if not weakness?' Skellan sneered, baring razor-sharp fangs. His features contorted, burning with bestial anger. 'I am not the man I was. I am more than that. I am immortal. I will be here when you are dust. I will see the rise and fall of empires. I am immortal.'

Suddenly, oddly, Fischer realised that the rain running down his face could well be the last thing he ever felt. He tilted his face up to meet it, savouring it for a moment before answering Skellan.

'So you keep saying, but you forget there are countless ways you can die a final death, and when you do
you will be condemned to eternal torture in the realm
of the dead, so cling to your unlife, Jon Skellan, live
in fear of that final terrible judgement.' He reached
into his shirt and pulled out the silver pendant Leyna
had given him on their wedding night: the hammer
of Sigmar.

Skellan recoiled, a look of utter revulsion on his
bestial features. 'You and your miserable Man-God!'
he spat. 'Stay as meat, you ignorant fool! You are
nothing more or less than cattle to us.' He swept his
arm out in a grand gesture, encompassing the whole
field. 'You are part of our herd, Fischer. You are bred
for one specific purpose: so that we might feed on
you.'

Fischer's fist closed around the silver trinket.

'Then feed, *friend*. You wouldn't be the first to. Hell,
you wouldn't even be the prettiest. Drink! Here's my
throat, I am offering it to you. Drink damn you!
Drink!'

'What are you waiting for?' Herman Posner asked
curiously. He had come up behind the pair without
either of them noticing. The man moved like a ghost
across the battlefield. The fighting had all but died
out in several parts of the field. A gibbous moon hung
in the air behind Posner's head. Without turning,
Posner rammed one of his twin blades into Bernholz's chest as the outrider came up behind him,
sword raised ready to deliver a huge killing blow. It
was coldly done. Posner didn't even acknowledge the
dying man as Bernholz's eyes flared wide and blood
bubbled out of his mouth as it sagged open in shock.

The sword slipped from his fingers and fell into a puddle of mud and blood. The man was dead before he hit the dirt.

'Well? He's meat. Feed, lad. Don't let good food go to waste. Didn't your mother teach you anything?'

Before Skellan could respond the cries went up across Essen Ford: the Ottilia's forces were routed, the battle was won and there were still hours to go before the sun rose redly on the killing ground and the dead sank back into whatever hell held them once more. It was over.

Posner's crew moved amongst the living and the dead, spreading the word: the Vampire Count wanted the survivors.

All of them.

Skellan hauled Fischer to his feet and pushed him forward, driving him hard toward the pavilions the dead were erecting for their master away from the worst of the carnage. He staggered and stumbled through the mud. He wasn't alone. The survivors – of whom there were precious few – were being herded like cattle toward von Carstein's pavilion. He saw Schliffen, beaten and battered, his head down as he shuffled toward the tents, and Baumann, cut and bleeding but head raised defiantly as two of Posner's vampires jabbed him forward with the bloody tips of their swords. The vampires were beaten bloody; one's face was badly disfigured where Baumann had put his eye out and shattered its nose, and the other had lost half of its jaw where Baumann had almost cleaved its head in two.

Fischer saw countless bodies hunched over the fallen. He knew what they were: ghouls picking over the corpses, feeding. Normally he would have expected the survivors to gather the dead for burial, but not this time. The dead of Essen Ford would swell the ranks of the Vampire Count's monstrous army.

They had lost more than just their lives.

They had lost their deaths.

CHAPTER TWELVE
Spilling Tainted Blood

ESSEN FORD, SYLVANIA
Winter, 2010

VON CARSTEIN WALKED down the line of prisoners.

He moved slowly, taking the time to examine each of the men facing him. Ganz walked two paces behind him. Buoyed up with the bloodlust of victory he felt like one of *them*. He felt immortal. Eternal. He felt the thrill of victory course through his veins. He felt the vitality of life pulsing through his body. He was alive. For the first time in years he felt it. He experienced it all as one huge sensory overload: the rain on his face, the tang of blood and dirt as he breathed, the sudden richness and clarity of the colours that made up the world around him, the infinite shades of greens and browns, even the coppery taste of his own blood in his mouth, all of it came together in one exaltation of life. And that was when he realised that he had more in common with the cattle von Carstein had lined up for inspection than he did with the Vampire Count and his hellish minions. He was human. Humanity was weakness.

Ganz looked at the row of faces, the resistance beaten out of them, the resignation to their fate written harshly in their dulled eyes.

They were meat.

Meat for the beast.

'You,' von Carstein said. 'These are your men, yes?'

The man nodded.

'I will give you a choice, a simple one. Think carefully before you decide. I am not in the habit of letting people change their minds. You spurned my offer of clemency so your life is forfeit. That is not in doubt. Your choice is this, serve me in life, or serve me in death. It matters not to me. Either way, I own you.'

Hans Schliffen stiffened physically. 'You cannot be serious.'

One of Posner's vampires moved up behind the general, hissing in his ear as he gripped his arms and pinned them behind his back. 'The count is always serious.'

'Indeed. Ganz, pick a soldier, any soldier, and cut his throat. Show the good general here just how serious I am.'

Ganz walked the line, relishing the looks of pure terror in the soldiers' eyes as he paused in front of them, each one silently begging him not to choose them, to move on and take one of their friends instead. He stopped in front of Baumann because unlike the others there was no fear in his gaze, only defiance as he stared Ganz down. A slow smiled spread across Ganz's face. He stepped forward and, with one swift twist of the wrist, grabbed a handful of the man's hair and yanked his head back. He brought his other hand up and rammed the dagger he had concealed in it deep into the archer's throat. Baumann gagged, blood burbling through his fingers as he clutched at the wound. It was a surprisingly slow death. No one dared move, least of all Ganz. He stared with sick fascination as the man he had just stabbed died.

Von Carstein held out his hand, palm up and made a slow lifting gesture. Baumann's body twitched and jerked in response as the newly-dead muscles answered to his will. Less than a minute later Baumann was standing back in his place in the line, his head lolling back slackly on his slashed throat, the life burned out from his eyes.

'In life or in death, general? I am quite serious.'

'You... I can't...'

'Allow me to help you some more, general. You see I own you all. How I dispose of you is my prerogative. You should have thought about that before you crossed me. You, you, and you,' von Carstein said, selecting three of Posner's vampires, including Skellan. 'Choose one of the cattle and feed.'

The three vampires came forward, looking over the line of prisoners. Few had the strength left in them to even look at them as they walked the length of the line, slowly, adding an edge of menace to the execution by drawing out the selection of their victims.

Skellan stopped behind Fischer and leaned in to whisper in his ear: 'You should have joined me, my *friend*, but it is too late now.'

'Couldn't even face me, could you?' Fischer said. They were the last words he ever spoke. Skellan sank his fangs into Fischer's neck and fed greedily, sucking the very lifeblood out of him. Fischer's body stiffened, spasmed violently and then slumped as the life left it. Skellan continued to drain every precious ounce of blood from him, swallowing the thick warm liquid hungrily.

Along the line the two other vampires fed, then threw the empty corpses to the floor.

Von Carstein raised the three dead men with an almost negligent flick of the wrist. Their bodies jerked and spasmed as the Vampire Count manipulated them back into their places in the line. Their movements were a grim parody of life.

'Now, general. Pick one of your men.'

Schliffen shook his head. 'No. I won't. This is... You are a monster. This is barbaric.'

'Do not try my patience, general. Pick a man. If you don't, I will.'

Schliffen shook his head crazily, not willing to sacrifice any of his surviving soldiers.

'Why do you insist in making everything so difficult, general?' von Carstein sighed. 'Very well, I will choose for you. You, come here.' The Vampire Count singled out a young man, no more than nineteen or twenty years of age. The young man shuffled forward. He sniffed. Snot and tears streamed down his cheeks.

'It is your lucky day, soldier. I am not going to kill you but I am going to kill each and every one of your friends here. I want you to run back to the Empire and tell everyone that Vlad von Carstein is coming. Make them understand that I am hungry for blood and that I am tired with living in the darkness and shadows. I want you to tell them what kind of monster I am. How I executed the survivors of your army. I want you to tell them how I fed my pet vampires with your friends and how when everyone was dead and the ghouls had sated themselves I raised each and every one to serve me in death. Do you understand me?'

The petrified young soldier nodded.

'Then go before I change my mind.'

The young man stumbled away, staggered and started to run. Von Carstein laughed at him as he slipped and fell, pushed himself up and managed four more steps before he fell again. He turned to Posner.

'Kill them all.'

'With pleasure, my lord,' Posner said. 'You heard him men, feeding time!'

The vampires descended on the line of prisoners in a feeding frenzy.

In the chaos Hans Schliffen broke free his guard's grip and dragged the wailing sword from the sheath at von Carstein's side. The blade screamed a warning even as Schliffen brought it around in a brutal arc. It was all over in a single heartbeat. Posner saw the blow coming and tried to push the count out of the way but von Carstein stiffened and snarled at his warrior. That snarl froze on his dead face as Schliffen's blow clove von Carstein's head clean from his shoulders.

The Vampire Count's tainted blood sprayed out of the gaping stump.

As one the risen dead fell where they stood.

Posner reacted first, dragging his twin curved blades free of their sheaths and hurling himself at Schliffen. The general aimed another wild swing at Posner but the vampire danced beneath it and rose, snarling, both blades coming together to shear through Schliffen's arms only inches above the wrists. Screaming in agony Schliffen stared as the stumps of his arms pumped out his lifeblood.

'Bind him and burn him,' Posner rasped. 'I want the man to suffer.'

Two of Posner's vampires dragged the screaming general through the mud to where a third was lighting a brazier. When the flames leapt to angry life they forced Schliffen's bloody arms into them. The stink of burned flesh and the general's shrieks filled the air. The vampires ignored Schliffen's screams and held his arms in the fire until the stumps were dry and caked with charcoal, the wounds cauterised.

Posner came over to where Schliffen lay curled up on the floor cradling the blackened stumps protectively to his chest.

'You'll wish you were already dead, soldier. The count might have offered you a mercifully quick death. I won't.' There was no sign that Schliffen heard him. Posner turned to the three vampires standing around the brazier listening to the general's juices spit and crackle in the roaring fire. 'Four horses, bind the man to them arm and foot... and then lash the damned animals until he's been ripped limb from limb. Do it slowly. I want him to know. I want him to feel it as he is pulled apart. It is the least I can do for the count.'

He turned his back on the whimpering general. He walked back toward the white pavilions where the rest of his vampires were done feeding on the prisoners. Their thirst for blood slaked the vampires threw the corpses to the ghouls to finish.

He smiled to himself. He would take von Carstein's signet ring and use it as a sign of power, to validate the transition between one ruler and the next. And then there was the crazy bitch von Carstein had saddled himself with, Isabella. He would take her too. He would make her scream his name: Herman Posner, Count of the Vampires!

The land would hear her screams and quake at his coming.

Posner had expected to see that sycophant Ganz weeping over von Carstein's body, tearing at his hair and wailing, but Ganz was gone.

More worryingly, there was no sign of von Carstein's corpse.

CHAPTER THIRTEEN
King of Dust

ESSEN FORD, SYLVANIA
Winter, 2010

GANZ FLED FROM the battlefield, carrying the dead count's body and severed head in his arms as he stumbled toward the safety of the trees.

His grief was absolute.

He staggered forward, talking over and over mindlessly, saying the same things.

'It will be all right. It will be all right. It will be all right.'

No matter how many times he repeated the promise a distant part of him knew that things could never be all right again. Von Carstein was dead. His count was dead.

He cradled the lifeless body in his arms.

It seemed inconceivable that a wreck of a man like Schliffen could slay the Vampire Count in his moment of triumph. It wasn't right. Von Carstein was man of vision. He saw beauty in all things. In all...

That wasn't true. That was his grief speaking – it was all he could hear. The world around him was dead. A wasteland. The Vampire Count had proved his ruthlessness and in doing so turned Alten Ganz into a cold-blooded killer. He couldn't think for the incessant yammering of his guilt inside his head. On and on and on. Snatches of conversation came back to him, and in every one at least one voice was always the count's. Tears streamed down his face. Tears of grief and guilt. He had seen Schliffen wrestle free of his guard's grip and lunge for the count's sword but he hadn't done anything. He had simply stood there and stared like a rabbit caught in the hunter's sight, waiting for the killing blow to thud home. If he had done something... if he had at least tried... the count might still have been alive.

He had no idea what he was doing.

Ganz plunged blindly into the forest, stumbling into tree trunks and tripping over trailing roots. Thirty paces in, where the undergrowth thickened into an impenetrable tangle, he fell to his knees and laid the dead Vampire Count on the blanket of mildewed leaves and rotten twigs. He knelt there sobbing until the grief dried itself out and there were no more tears left to fall.

He arranged the count's clothes, making him look presentable. The count was always so careful with his appearance. He held the dead man's head in his hands. Brushed the long black hair back so that it didn't fall across the eyes, and laid it reverentially in place. Ganz couldn't bear the look of shocked betrayal in the count's dead eyes. He reached out and closed them. Von Carstein's skin was cold. Far too cold for someone who had died such a short while ago, he knew.

'But he didn't just die... He's been dead as long as I have known him.'

Ganz folded the count's arms across his chest.

The von Carstein signet ring was caked in blood.

It could have belonged to anyone; enough blood had been shed that night, von Carstein in the thick of the fighting. But it didn't belong to just anyone, Ganz knew. It was the count's blood.

The thought of taking the ring, keeping it for himself, entered his mind.

'Robbing the dead's not right,' he muttered.

Ganz gathered leaves and branches to cover the count's body. The ground was too hard for him to dig even the shallowest of graves with his bare hands so instead he made a cairn, piling dead leaves, branches and stones over von Carstein's body to protect it from hungry animals.

He stood over the cairn. He didn't know what he was supposed to do. So he did nothing.

'Goodbye.'

He walked slowly back toward the white pavilions.

Posner was struggling to subdue Isabella. She was in a rage the like of which Ganz had never seen before. She frenziedly tore at her own hair, at her clothes, and at anyone unfortunate enough to be within arm's reach. Three of Posner's vampires lay in the pool of tainted blood at her feet. Her claws had shred their faces and her fangs had ripped their throats out.

Ganz couldn't begin to imagine how she felt, her love, her eternal love, cut down in a single blow. Surely the loss would unhinge her already fragile mind.

CHAPTER FOURTEEN
Of Swords and Ashes

ESSEN FORD, SYLVANIA
Winter, 2010

POSNER'S RISE WAS bloody and brutal.

He cut down any and all that stood against him.

Loyalty amongst the lords of the undead was not a natural thing; the shadows had grown dark in their hearts. They were kindred but that didn't mean they would even so much as shed a tear for a fallen brother. Few would miss von Carstein and all, without exception, would relish the opportunity to rise in his place. That lack of basic loyalty to the old count and his widow meant that few around the camp grieved. While Isabella sobbed her heart out and railed against the heavens at the unjustness of it all, each in their own way were wondering and planting hooks that might lead to alliances and in turn power.

They hungered for it.

There is no vampiric society, no aristocracy or blue-blooded royalty amongst the undead. Vampires crave power, and through strength and cunning they take it. Frailty is punished by death: final, true death. There is no natural succession amongst those left behind. No birthright. No passing of the torch from generation to generation. Power is taken with strength.

Herman Posner understood that.

He walked through the subdued camp, seeing the alliances taking shape around him. Seeing potential pockets of rebellion rising up. Before they could bear fruit he crushed them. Those who refused his right to rule the dead were given one chance, a choice, much as Vlad himself had done only hours before with the cattle.

Where von Carstein had said 'Serve me in life or serve me in death,' Posner offered a slight variation to his brothers: serve me in life or serve me with your death.

His men culled the ranks of the vampires that night, shedding the weak and those most loyal to the old guard. The killing left behind a core he could, in some small way, trust.

It was not a luxury he would rely on.

Treachery, Posner knew, lay close to every vampire's stilled heart.

Still, he savoured his moment of victory.

He would find Isabella and make her an offer she would be a fool to refuse, cementing his place as the new count.

With the worst of the storm gone, and the rain drizzled out, the night was brightening. Storm clouds had blotted out the stars but they returned as a restless wind chased the clouds away. The wind rustled and mumbled through the encampment. A ruddy glow came from the embers of the campfire the vampires had built to burn the various parts of Schliffen's corpse. The dying light cast a reddish glow over the faces of the vampires who still stood around the fire ring, watching the murderer burn to ash and smoke. They had not spoken or moved as long as the fire had been burning.

Posner left them to their vigil.

He drew back the flap on the main pavilion and ducked inside.

The pavilion was opulent with gothic splendour. The count, as ever, had surrounded himself with things of great beauty, rugs from Amhabal and Sudrat in distant Araby, scents in the oil burners from Shuang Hsi in far-off Cathay, decorative clamshells from Sartosa, bone candelabra hand-carved in Ind, and much more. Von Carstein had been a collector. He had gathered souvenirs as others gathered memories. Posner picked up a jewelled egg von Carstein had stolen from the palace in Praag.

It was surprising the things von Carstein had chosen to keep near him during the march on the Empire. The egg was priceless, like so much of von Carstein's art. It had a name... Azovu? Posner marvelled at it. The egg was carved from a solid piece of heliotrope jasper, and decorated with yellow and white gold scrolls set with brilliant diamonds and chased red gold flowers. There was a tiny drop ruby clasp that opened to reveal a miniature replica, in gold and diamond, of Arianka's glass tomb. There

was a perverse irony in the design. He assumed it was
Walpurgis's work. The man was twisted enough
inside that he would have made a truly great vampire.

He put the egg back on the wooden dresser where
he had found it.

In this tent alone there were treasures enough for
him to live like an Emperor for years.

He had no use for von Carstein's trinkets.

Only his power.

The count had possessed a page from one of the
nine great books of Nagash. If he had one page there
would be more, surely. Posner could only imagine
the possibilities those books would open up if a single page could raise the dead into an unstoppable
army.

That was the kind of power that Posner craved.

Real power.

Not petty little treaties and pacts that relied on
backstabbers to remain trustworthy.

Von Carstein's wailing sword lay on the table in the
centre of the pavilion. The man's blood was still on it,
dried into a caked layer like rust on the dark blade.
Posner picked it up and examined it in his hands. The
sword let out a gentle keening moan.

Posner smiled, hefted the sword and tested it with
a few quick swings. The balance was exquisite, quite
unlike anything he had ever wielded. It was as though
the blade itself possessed a will of its own; its preternatural balance and timing no more than its own
selfish lust for blood and slaughter. After four dizzy-
ingly fast passes, high and low parries and thrusts, the
wailing blade was crying out for blood and Posner
found it almost impossible to lay the blade aside. It

was inside his skull crying out to be fed. He dropped the sword and backed away from it in disgust.

The thing was alive.

A vampiric sword for a Vampire Count; it was a bloody partnership forged in the pits of Morr's underworld for sure.

'What do you want?'

He hadn't even seen Isabella huddled in the corner, clutching one of her dead husband's shirts to her heaving breast.

'You,' Posner said without a trace of irony or passion.

'I can smell him on it,' Isabella said, lost for a moment in the sensory deception of the shirt. 'He's still here. He hasn't gone. He hasn't left me.'

She was a wretched mess huddled on the floor, pressed up against the edge of von Carstein's elaborately carved coffin. Her eyes were rimmed red and the veins showed bluely through her pale skin. She looked like death.

Posner knelt down beside her and reached out tenderly to brush her hair back where it had fallen into her eyes. 'He's gone. I can't believe it either but he's gone. Now it is time for you to stand up and be strong, Isabella. Beautiful Isabella. There isn't a creature out there tonight who wouldn't see you dead, do you understand that? You are the last link to the past, to Vlad. They would bury you beneath a Sigmarite temple if they could.'

She shook her head violently, reacting to his tone if not his actual words. He looked deep into her eyes but she showed no sign of understanding what he was saying. She had receded somewhere deep inside herself. He didn't know how to reach her. All he could do was talk.

'I can help you,' he said, trying to put as much conviction into his voice as he could. 'Walk out of here with me. Stand by my side. Join with me and none can stand against us. I can protect you from them, sweet beautiful Isabella. I can keep you safe. I can be your count.'

'No,' she said, wriggling around beneath his hand. 'No. No. He wouldn't leave me. No. He's coming back. He *loves* me!'

Posner did his best to stifle his exasperation. He stood and hauled her up to her feet.

'Come out with me. Let them see us together. You don't have to say anything. Just stand there and be beautiful, Isabella. Can you do that? Can you do that for me?'

'No,' she said again.

Posner slipped his arm through hers. 'Lean on me.'

'No.' It was as though it was the only thing she could say. An endless stream of denials. No. No. No. No. No.

Gently, he guided her out of the tent.

They were all looking at him, he knew, the darkness couldn't hide their curiosity. They were looking at him to make a mistake. He didn't make mistakes. He was Herman Posner.

'It ends here, now. I claim this woman as my bride by right of strength. Any who would dare to challenge that right, speak now or forever hold your silence.'

'I challenge you,' said a voice Posner had thought never to hear again.

CHAPTER FIFTEEN
From Dust Returned

ESSEN FORD, SYLVANIA
Winter, 2010

HE WAS LOOKING at a ghost.

It wasn't possible.

Death for a vampire was final, there was no return from the torments of eternity. It was the end.

Your soul was shredded. There was no rest. No resurrection. No return. You were an empty vessel. There was nothing that *could* come back.

And yet…

Vlad von Carstein stepped through the crowd. His mane of black hair was blown back in the wind, exposing the line of dried and flaking blood that marred his neck.

But it couldn't be von Carstein. Posner's mind ran wild, impossible thoughts tumbling over each other in their clamour to be heard. One thought though was louder than all of the others: von Carstein was dead.

Posner had seen it with his own two eyes. Schliffen had taken the Vampire Count's head clean off his shoulders with that damnable wailing blade. It was impossible. He couldn't be alive. It had to be Ganz. The weasel had to be behind this charade somehow. Posner couldn't see the man.

This had to be some kind of trick. It had to be.

'I would be grateful if you would unhand my wife,' von Carstein said casually. Posner felt the coldness of his stare.

'You aren't him. He's dead.'

'Aren't we all?'

Some of the vampires chuckled at the count's gallows humour. Posner didn't raise so much as a smile. It felt as though his hastily-constructed world was coming down around his shoulders.

And then he did smile, and it was full of cunning; a predator's smile.

'You've got nothing here. Your sycophants are gone. Even the weasel Ganz has abandoned you. My vampires are all around you. Mine. They are loyal to me.'

'Loyal?' the Vampire Count said mockingly. 'What do any of us know of loyalty, Herman? You especially. I would have thought you knew better.'

Posner pushed the woman away from him. 'You want her? She's yours. You have,' he glanced up at the sky, 'until the cloud has passed completely across the face of the moon to run for your life. Otherwise I will strike you down where you stand. You already died once. Killing you again shouldn't be so difficult if one of the cattle can manage it. Go on, run.'

'No.' It was Isabella, stumbling through the mud toward von Carstein. 'No. No.' She repeated. She ran into him, hammering her clenched fists on his chest and shrieking hysterically: 'Nononononono!'

Von Carstein didn't flinch.

'I *liked* you, Herman,' he said, his voice laced with disappointment. 'But we all make mistakes.'

The Vampire Count snarled, releasing the beast within. The bones in his face cracked and elongated, his jaw distending to reveal lethal fangs. He pushed Isabella aside and dropped into a fighting crouch.

'Fight me.'

Posner reached back and with a hiss drew his twin blades. The moonlight glittered off the silver. He circled warily, eying the count. 'You intend to fight me with your bare hands, Vlad?' His grin was maniacal. The twin blades danced in his hands, weaving a hypnotic pattern of death between the two combatants.

And then he heard it: the keening wail of von Carstein's damned sword.

He couldn't turn. He daren't take his eyes off the Vampire Count as he slowly circled, looking for a weakness in Posner's defence.

He saw the cadaverous figure of Ganz out of the corner of his eye. He had the wailing sword in his hands.

Posner launched a lightning-fast assault. He threw himself forward, his swords whickering through the air either side of von Carstein's head but the count, with ungodly timing, rolled away from both lethal cuts without seeming to actually move. Posner dropped and swept out a leg, looking to topple his opponent, while matching it with the left-handed blade, slicing it in perfect time with the leg sweep. The manoeuvre would have eviscerated a lesser man. Von Carstein leapt backwards in a tightly controlled somersault and landed easily. He held out his hand for Ganz to give him his sword while Posner regained his balance.

'Herman, Herman, Herman.' Von Carstein hefted the wailing blade, switching it from right hand to left and back again. He moved up onto his toes then rocked back onto his heels. 'You're a man of few words.'

Posner's answer was silence.

Deep within himself Posner heard a sound. It repeated itself over and over. A *howl*. It was animalistic. Its grip on his soul was absolute. His face shifted as the beast within, the vampiric side of his nature, was unleashed.

'Death is too noble for a piece of filth like you.'

Posner sprang forward and lunged in a single fluid motion. It was so incredibly fast it was virtually impossible to see his blade as it flicked out in search of von Carstein's heart. Steel rang on steel as the count turned his blade away with an almost negligent flick of the wrist. In response, von Carstein's sword slipped inside his guard and twisted up toward his throat. Posner's parry was a blur. His left-handed blade caught the count's wailing sword and locked it there for a split second, giving his right-hand blade the fraction of a heartbeat it needed to lance inside von Carstein's defences and drive the tip toward his stomach.

Von Carstein caught the blade in the palm of his right hand. Posner stared at the blood as it leaked between the Vampire Count's fingers and across his signet ring.

The distraction was all von Carstein needed.

He stepped in, his left hand deftly disengaging his blade from Posner's and unleashing a high swing that buried the edge of the wailing sword deep in Posner's neck. At the last moment he pulled the ferocity from the blow, deliberately preventing it from cleaving through the man's neck.

Posner staggered sideways, his eyes wide with the shock of agony as his tainted blood gouted from the gaping wound. His left hand spasmed and his fingers lost their grip on the curved blade. It slipped through his fingers and fell. It landed tip first in the mud and stuck, quivering. His hand went to his neck as though trying to staunch the flow of blood. He tried to speak but all that came out was a strangled gurgle.

He saw the weasel Ganz standing beside Isabella.

It was all so close.

He could almost touch it.

He raised his right hand and hurled the sword end over end, like a dagger. The remnants of a smile twitched across his lips as he saw the heavy blade slam into the centre of Alten Ganz's chest, shattering the bone and piercing his heart.

Ganz staggered back. Posner saw him try to right himself before he toppled. It was a reflex action. He was already dead.

'Never did... like... you,' Posner managed. He broke off into a bloody gurgle of coughing. He raised his eyes to meet von Carstein's condemning gaze. 'Finish it then.'

'No,' Isabella von Carstein said, lucid for the first time in hours. 'Let me.' She held out her hand for her husband's blade.

The Vampire Count gave her the sword willingly.

Posner lowered his head, waiting for the final killing blow to fall.

And then he was dead.

CHAPTER SIXTEEN
The White Wolf

SCHWARTHAFEN, SYLVANIA
Dead of winter, 2049

DEATH WAS A constant companion.

It had been a long and bitter war. At times the Empire emerged triumphant and other times the forces of darkness swept over the living mercilessly. Death was never far away. They lived hand to mouth. They dared not look to the future. Still, in the darkness, a flicker of hope refused to be extinguished. They had lived with this evil, many of them, their entire lives. A few, the oldest of the men, could remember a time before the threat of the Vampire Count, von Carstein, of Sylvania. It had become something of a myth amongst the soldiers.

They had all lost someone to the conflict: brothers, fathers, friends, sisters, wives, mothers, daughters and lovers. Death was no respecter of sex. It didn't limit itself to the battlefields and the trenches. It spilled over into the streets of their home towns. Food was scarce even with the women planting and reaping the harvest. The bakers, the butchers and the grocers made best use of what little they had, eking out the precious ingredients like misers in the hope of fending off famine.

The war was harshest on the children and the elderly; those who knew no better and those who still remembered the life before, when fresh fruit and meat and dairy produce had not been luxuries money couldn't buy.

Sickness was prevalent. Disease flourished in the wretched conditions with scurvy claiming victims daily when food stores ran dry. Cholera and dysentery did the work of von Carstein's army, killing thousands.

The people of the Empire lived with it. They had no choice. Death was all around them, wearing many guises.

Forty years of fighting.

Forty years of dying.

Forty years of losing loved ones.

Forty years trying to cling on to the hope that one day, one day, they would be free of the blight that was Vlad von Carstein, Vampire Count of Sylvania.

Forty years.

Jerek Kruger shuddered at the thought. The undying count had been an ever-present bogeyman throughout the White Wolf's life. The dark was coming. The grand master could not remember a time in his life when he hadn't considered darkness the hour of the enemy. He wasn't a superstitious man; he had yet to meet a foe his two-handed warhammer couldn't vanquish. Even the dead could die, a fact that came as no great surprise to the warrior. Those things were animated, like puppets, they weren't *living*, and they didn't *breathe*. Cut the strings and they fell down.

He scratched at his wild beard. The cold sting of the wind numbed his face. It wormed its way beneath the heavy pelts he wore over his red lacquered armour. The waiting was the worst. He had lost a lot of good men over the years and seen them come back to haunt him in a way that most leaders could never imagine – on the battlefield, shambling forward, clutching the weapons that had failed them in life, their spirits crushed, their souls gone, he prayed, to a better place. Ulric protected them; that is what the men believed as they threw themselves willingly into the slaughter.

Jerek Kruger planted the carved head of his huge two-handed warhammer into the snow between his feet. The rune of Ulric sank more than halfway into the pure white. He knew full well what awaited him and his men over the coming hours. It had passed beyond glory. They were fighting for survival. It was a desperate fight and only grew more so as every casualty added one more to the Vampire Count's horde. If they fell here, if the Knights of the White Wolf failed on the fields of Schwarthafen, the gateway would be open all the way into Altdorf itself, the very heart of the Empire.

'We will not fail,' the grand master said, his voice like flint. Beside him his second-in-command, Roth Mehlinger, grunted his agreement.

'We cannot.'

This was his test, Kruger knew. This was the moment that would give meaning to their lives. These coming days the Knights of the White Wolf would face their greatest foe since their inauguration in the wake of the Chaos Wars. This was the moment they had been born for.

And yet the seed of doubt was there in each man's mind. Their foe was immortal. He had been struck down time and again only to rise with vengeance and unholy fury. No sword, no axe, no hammer could banish the fiend. Kruger couldn't allow himself to think that way. Thinking about von Carstein as eternal sealed his own fate and the fates of all of the men who looked to him for leadership. Von Carstein was a vampire. The beast possessed unholy strength, cunning, gall, but was a beast nonetheless. Johann van Hal, the witch hunter, had first named the evil, and naming is the first stage in slaying it. For all its power the beast suffered from the Hunger, the thirst for fresh, warm blood. They *had* to feed to survive. That was their weakness. For all their cold and cunning they were still driven by the most primal of all instincts, survival.

And to survive they had to feed.

Which meant they could not hide.

The sunlight was deceptive. It offered the illusion of safety. The white pavilions of the Vampire Count were visible across the battlefield. The dead were there, lying where they had fallen, waiting for night to rise again. Most sickening of all, though, were the humans who had flocked to von Carstein's banner. The fools allowed themselves to be fed on, night after night, and guarded the undead by day. These were men and women, innocent, stupid. They saw some tragic romance in the vampire's plight. They flocked to the undead lord, no doubt desperate to be given the Blood Kiss and join the ranks of his true followers. Jerek Kruger couldn't bring himself to think about their stupidity. These were the people he was fighting to *save*.

Sadness smouldered in his soul.

They could not see; they were children lost in a wilderness of mirrors where the hunters cast no reflection.

It was his duty to protect them, to save them from the darkness within themselves and guide them out of the maze of lies and deceits they had lost themselves inside.

He had sworn an oath to the Elector of Middenheim. He was a knight protector. They all were. Each and every wild-haired red-armoured warrior on the field of Schwarthafen. They were not there for glory. They were not there because some ancient principle of honour had been slighted. They were there to protect those that could not protect themselves. They were the last chance.

The last hope.

And they were a long way from home.

Middenheim with its lofty viaducts and deep catacombs was an impregnable fortress on a sheer-sided pinnacle of rock rising out of dense forestland. That was a fortress built to withstand almost any assault. Drawing up the wooden bridges effectively cut the city off from the outside world. But they weren't in Middenheim; they were in the

Ulric-forsaken wastelands of Sylvania and they were lining up to face the greatest evil known to man. It was a fool's fight.

Kruger knew it. Mehlinger knew it.

And every other man out there that evening knew it.

Still they stood there implacably, ready for the fight of their lives.

The mood in the camp was sombre. Some men busied themselves tending to their mounts, rechecking the barding and the braces, the stirrups and the girth, while others oiled their platemail or knelt in prayer and supplication, offering devotion to the warrior god.

'Walk with me,' Kruger told Mehlinger.

Together they moved down the line, offering words of encouragement to the younger knights, sharing fond reminiscences with the older ones. Jerek Kruger was, among many things, a leader of men. They looked to him for guidance in this dark time. He made a promise to himself that he would not let them down. He knew them all by name and face, he knew their families, their stories. He was their father, for many of the men the bond was stronger than it was to their own flesh and blood. He took an interest in their lives, in them as people.

Mehlinger moved silently beside him. Kruger knew the men called him the Grand Master's Shadow. There were worse epithets for a knight. He was taciturn and dour, preferring his own company or the company of Aster, his horse. People were a burden, they thought and did strange things, acted in peculiar ways, and more often than not let you down. Mehlinger needed things he could trust around him, and in the Knights of the White Wolf he had a brotherhood he *could* trust but trusting still came hard to the man, Kruger knew. They all had their weaknesses but it was their strengths, when combined, which set them apart. Alone they were weak, together they were giants.

That was what made them what they were. They thought and acted as one. United.

That was what made the Knights of the White Wolf the most feared and revered fighting force in the Empire.

Nothing could stand against them. Nothing.

Until now.

He stood alone at the head of the army, gazing out into the lowering dark at the white pavilions of the Vampire Count. They were a thorn in his soul, drawing blood every time he moved within their shadows. The von Carstein banner snapped in the wind, the sigil impossible to make out from this distance. Kruger knew it well. It was a vile loathsome icon.

'When this is over, Mehlinger, I'll burn that damned banner and dedicate whatever years I have left to purging this blighted province of its taint.' He said it forcefully enough to be heard by a few of the men who were using oil and rags to tend to their warhammers.

'And we'll be right there with you!' one of the knights, a flame-haired bull of a man, Lukien Karr, roared.

Kruger nodded. 'Damn right you will be.'

He turned his back on the pavilions and looked up at the sun, already setting behind the hills and the treeline of Ghoul Wood. He slammed a gauntleted hand off his breastplate, saluting the men as he passed them on the way back to his command point.

'Ready the men. We ride when the sun dips beneath the horizon. I want every second rider equipped with burning brands, for the first pass their warhammers will be their secondary weapon. Understood? I want–' he very nearly said chaos but that wasn't right, he didn't want to invite chaos into the battle. He raised his voice so it carried down the line, a rallying call. 'Von Carstein's army is a shambles. These creatures burn, so we burn them. We purge their ungodly taint from the world. We hammer them into the ground and we sear them off the face of the earth. These things aren't human. They aren't our friends, our loved ones. They are diabolical shells, shades sent to taunt us, to draw out our grief and unman us. Well, no more. We will purge this wretched land of their daemonic taint with oil and fire if we must, but purge it we will. We ride tonight for more than valour, we ride for everything that is *right*. We ride for every innocent child of the Empire so that they might live in a world worthy of them! We ride for the survival of all mankind!'

Up and down the line the battle-hardened Knights of the White Wolf responded to Kruger's impassioned speech vigorously, hammering their breastplates with gauntleted fists over and over until the beating became deafening, and then, when the hammering was at its loudest, howling like the very beasts they took their name from.

Kruger slammed his gauntleted fist once against his breastplate and lifted it in salute to his men.

'We fight!' Mehlinger cried. 'Mount up! Night falls!'

'The White Wolves ride!' the chant went up. 'The White Wolves ride!'

Roused, they were an awesome sight.

Nothing could stand against them, Kruger promised himself. Nothing.

He turned away from his men. Mehlinger was right, where he had assumed they had a final hour, they had barely minutes as the sun dipped behind the treelined hills. Already shapes were emerging from the white pavilions: von Carstein's vampires.

On the ground the dead stirred.

CHAPTER SEVENTEEN
Riders on the Storm

SCHWARTHAFEN, SYLVANIA
Dead of winter, 2049

AT FULL GLORIOUS charge the Knights of the White Wolf were an awesome sight.

The thundering hooves of the warhorses sent shivers coursing through the earth itself. The cacophonous tattoo of their charge rent the night.

Rank upon rank of majestic chargers came at the rows of undead with flaming brands and warhammers swinging.

'For all of humankind!' Mehlinger bellowed, his words snatched away by the wind.

Kruger drove his spurs hard into his horse's flanks, urging her to open up into full gallop. The waiting was over: the helplessness of it, the doubt gnawing away at a man's courage, the uncertainty. Fighting was better. The old Wolf lived for the thrill of it. There was nothing in the world even remotely like the vitality of it: man and beast as one. The charred earth crunched under his horse's hooves. Grimly, Kruger wiped the sweat from his eyes with the fur cuff of his gauntlet.

Mehlinger blew his warhorn, trumpeting the command to full gallop.

The discipline of the line was precise; when the grand master gave his horse her head the rest of the line followed, matching their momentum beat for beat.

Kruger's smile was grim.

There was no evil in the world that could not be thwarted by men brave enough to stand up against it.

There was no fear here today. This was what they lived for.

His warhammer sang in the air as he whipped it round above his head.

The cry of carrion birds overhead matched it hungrily; the birds had some sixth sense, flocking to the killing ground long before the first blood was spilled.

The air reeked of sulphur, sharp and repugnant.

No waning of the light marked the arrival of night. Moments before the charge a bloom of blue light above the white pavilions chased up into the heavens, like lightning in reverse as it gathered into a luminous sphere. The ball of lightning shifted colour almost continuously as it climbed until it met the clouds with a clash of steel and a belly-deep rumble of thunder that rent the sky. Immediately the rain came down, hard. The fat drops bounced five and six inches off the battlefield, turning it quickly to sludge beneath the horses' hooves.

Kruger had heard stories of the Vampire Count resorting to sorcery to turn the tide of his battles. Von Carstein could conjure hordes of ravaging daemons for all he cared. They would die just the same. Kruger was nothing if not a practical man. He knew what the blossoming blue radiance was but, unnatural or not, rain was rain and his men were more than capable of riding through a storm. The redolent sulphur, the ball lightning, the sudden fury of the storm itself, all of it might be unnerving, Kruger thought maliciously, but they were incomparable to the sight of the White Wolves bearing down on you.

The white-hot fire of battle filled his senses, coruscating through his entire body.

This was what being alive was, at its very grandest. Here, now.

And then the battle was joined in a horrifying destruction of flesh, blood and bone as the Knights of the White Wolf hit the ranks of the dead head-on, warhammers crashing into thick skulls and mashing through dead arms as they clawed out. Firebrands flew high into the air, arcing, some burning out in the torrential rain, others descending on the mass of undead with lethal fire, igniting on the desiccated skin of the zombies.

The dead met the charge kicking and screaming as they were trampled beneath the horses' hooves.

Already the ghouls had a feast of corpses to gorge themselves on. Bodies sprawled in pools of congealing blood. Some had lost arms, legs were crushed, heads stoved in. The ghouls treated them all the same: as meat.

Kruger's warhammer smashed into skulls and shoulders, cutting a swathe through the dead. This was his day. This is what he had been born to do. *He* was the immortal on the field, not von Carstein. The blood fury sang through his veins. He bellowed a fearsome battle-cry and threw himself into the fray. He booted a shambling zombie in the face so hard that the creature's jaw caved in, and lifted another, a child with dead eyes, off its feet with the staggering force of his hammer blow. The boy slumped with his arm hanging loosely at his side, forced himself to his feet only for Kruger's hammer to stove in his skull. The air around Jerek Kruger ripped and crackled with violence. He savoured it, channelling it inside, feeling it course through his veins and turning it into his own strength. That was his magic. He was a fighter.

He sought out von Carstein across the field of slaughter and found him.

'FACE ME!' the grand master roared, challenging the Vampire Count. His taunt carried across the fighting and was met by a sneer from the pale lips of von Carstein. Kruger stood in the saddle and roared his challenge again: 'FACE ME!'

Mehlinger's warhorn sounded three times in short succession, drawing the second rank of knights in a sweeping arc across the battlefield and sending the third rank in their wake to pick off the pieces while the front rank broke the back of the undead's force. The dead scattered aimlessly, lost for direction as the Vampire Count rose to meet Jerek Kruger's challenge, his sword wailing and shrieking like a daemon possessed as he wheeled his mount around and spurred the nightmare beast into a rash charge.

Kruger's heart slowed, his pulse, the noise of the battle, everything around him slowed as though trapped in molasses. He saw von Carstein riding at him, saw the carrion birds circling overhead hungrily, saw the dead falling beneath his horse's hooves, but it all happened so slowly. His heartbeat thundered in his ears. His battle-cry stretched out into one long deafening howl.

And then the world snapped violently back into place.

Kruger's warhammer sang as it whistled through the air. The white pavilions were battered by the wind and rain but still that damnable banner snapped and flapped tauntingly against the black sky.

The Vampire Count's horde was in disarray. The Knights of the White Wolf hammered them down, crushing them ruthlessly.

Kruger only had eyes for one foe: the Vampire Count.

Von Carstein's tainted blade cried out for blood as the Vampire Count flung himself forward. Ripples of moonlight shimmered on the cursed blade as it scythed through the air, aimed high at Kruger's neck.

The grand master took the blow on the shaft of his huge warhammer, the jarring impact shuddering through him. He slammed a fist into von Carstein's face. There was nothing pretty about the move. It was pure brutality. It was a bone-crunching blow that had the vampire reeling in his saddle.

Kruger pressed his slim advantage, bringing the butt of the warhammer's shaft to bear. He jabbed the end of it into von Carstein's face as he struggled to shift his balance. The vampire was quicker. He rolled

under the blow, taking it on his shoulder, his sword
snaking out and slicing uselessly off Kruger's breastplate. The speed of the counter was dizzying. No
sooner had the wailing blade clattered off Kruger's
mail than von Carstein brought it to bear again and
again in two lightning fast nicks, either side of the
grand master's face, drawing blood on both cheeks.
The wounds dripped into Kruger's unkempt beard.
They were marks of humiliation, nothing more, nothing less.

Kruger roared, his entire musculature driven by
controlled fury. He brought his warhammer down
in a crushing arc. The blow was clumsy. It missed
von Carstein and cracked sickeningly into the head
of the Vampire Count's nightmarish steed. The animal shied, bucking and twisting, as its hind legs
buckled and spilled von Carstein from the saddle.
The undead count leapt clear, landing lightly, a
look of intense displeasure on his face. He brought
the wailing blade to the centre, taking it in a two-
handed grip, then waited, implacable, deadly.

Kruger wheeled his mount around and charged
for von Carstein, his mind filled with the image of
the count's head bursting like an overripe water-
melon beneath his hammer blow.

Again von Carstein was too quick. He dived and
rolled beneath Kruger's lethal hammer and
between his mount's deadly hooves, coming out on
the other side in a tight crouch, horse blood dripping from his sword where he had gutted the
animal on the way through. The horse managed
five more steps before it realised it was dead and
collapsed. Kruger barely managed to roll free

before the dead weight of the beast pinned him in the mud.

Von Carstein was on him in an instant, followed by a pack of howling ghouls who threw themselves on the dead horse, biting and tearing with their teeth and bare hands. Gouts of blood pumped from the animal's gaping stomach, soaking the vile creatures as they fed.

'You're a parasite. Your time here is done, vampire,' Kruger said, his grimace hard as he weighed the warhammer in his huge hands.

'And you're wasting your precious breath trying to goad me, savage. Time to die.' The vampire unleashed a lethal reverse cut, feinting first high to Kruger's left then pulling the blow a fraction before the White Wolf's block and dropping his right shoulder, rolling the cut so it actually came from underneath, shearing up for his throat. Kruger barely got out of the way in time to save his life as the wailing blade sliced away the lobe and more than half of his ear in a bloody mess. The pain was blinding.

He staggered back a step and countered with a punishing right cross, his meaty fist snapping the vampire's head back. One fang snapped under the impact, spraying blood. Kruger sprang forward raining blows on either side of von Carstein's head, slamming his club-like fist into the vampire's ear and his nose but the Vampire Count was strong, impossibly strong. After the initial shock of the blow von Carstein unleashed the beast within, sacrificing all pretence at humanity, and roared on the offensive, his bloody blade slashing and arcing between them.

They circled each other warily, each judging the other for signs of weakness, looking for the kill. Death was very close and Kruger did not care. He had never been more alive.

Von Carstein feinted left and lunged, the tip of the wailing blade slicing at Kruger's stomach. The knight slammed the cut away and launched himself two-footed at the vampire, his booted feet crashing into the Count's face. Von Carstein staggered back. Kruger rolled to his feet as the vampire reared up, sword slashing wildly in the air between them. The knight threw himself forward, blocking blow after blow with the shaft of his warhammer and answering each with a devastating counter aimed at the Count's head until the rune of Ulric slammed into the side of von Carstein's face, hurling him from his feet. He lay there in the pool of horse's blood, ghouls all around him feasting, as Jerek Kruger, chest heaving, stood over him.

'Today I conquer death, destroyer of worlds. Go back to the hell that spawned you, fiend.'

With that Kruger beat the life out of the Vampire Count, pounding his bones to a bloody pulp with his mighty warhammer. The carrion birds cackled and cawed, circling vindictively overhead.

Mehlinger's horn trumpeted. The Vampire Count had fallen and the remnants of his army were routed.

The tide of the battle had turned. Kruger sank to his knees, utterly spent. Dawn was still hours away. It didn't matter. They were victorious. The night was won.

CHAPTER EIGHTEEN
A Wolf to the Slaughter

MIDDENHEIM
Spring, 2050

But one night does not a war win when the enemy refuses to die. The sad truth is that victory on one field can easily turn to defeat on another.

Where the open fields of Schwarthafen suited the glorious chargers of the Knights of the White Wolf, the cramped serpentine streets of Middenheim imprisoned them. It was impossible to ride their horses and unseated they lost not only their mobility but their cohesion as well.

Without their powerful mounts the knights were nothing more than glorified infantry with unwieldy weapons unused to fighting at close quarters.

They were vulnerable to von Carstein's undead.

The city's isolation on the huge plateau, the Fauschlag, only served to hinder them all the more because their enemy was neither mortal nor flesh and bone. In his heart Kruger knew there was no way to fend off von Carstein this time. What use was iron and steel against the ghosts conjured by the Vampire Count?

Von Carstein held back his zombies and skeletons, crowding them on the viaducts into the city itself and in a vast ring around the base of the plateau.

Instead he unleashed the revenant shades, the wraiths and the wights and the ghasts and the ghouls, ethereal undead that ghosted through wood and stone as though it didn't exist. Middenheim was every inch the great fortress city that Ulric foresaw but in a matter of hours von Carstein turned it into a necropolis.

Middenheim, City of the Dead.

Lukien Karr was the first casualty. Brave, foolish Lukien. Bellowing the battle-cry of the White Wolves, the knight stepped into the path of a ghastly shade and met it steel for insubstantial talons. The wraith entered Karr, sank into his skin and chilled his heart and turned his blood to ice, then ripped itself free of the dead man, ectoplasmic ribbons of ichor fanning out behind the wraith as it screeched off up the narrow street toward the plague monument. It was over in a heartbeat. Karr fell to the cobbles, a look of abject terror frosted onto his face.

More died the same way, the spirits shrieking and laughing as they tore through the flesh of the knights, making a mockery of their life as the helpless warriors hurled their hammers and struggled vainly to fight off an enemy as insubstantial as thin air.

The cry went up for priests, the desperate hope that faith and holy water would stand firm where iron and steel had proved useless.

Jerek Kruger stood in the centre of it all, watching his men die and helpless to do anything about it. He burned with impotent rage.

The ghosts of von Carstein tore through the streets, they drifted, they flew, they emerged from solid stone walls, they came from everywhere and there was nothing Kruger could do but swing his warhammer and wonder why the revenant shades claimed the lives of those around him but left him alive. They swarmed through the Pit with its warren of decrepit shacks and tumbledown buildings. They swept through the makeshift hovels as easily as they did Middenpalaz, the graf's palatial home. They poured through the squares, moonlight shining through their transparent forms, and down the streets, an endless sea of incorporeal souls spilling out of the shadows and the spaces between. In the Graf's Repose succulents and hardy perennials choked and withered as the cold flush of death lapped over them in foetid waves. Von Carstein's dead army threatened all life.

The priests came shuffling into the streets, cowed by the terrifying might of the wraiths and the ghasts as they snuffed the life out of the knights trying vainly to protect them as they stumbled over lines of exorcism and banishment rituals. They joined together from all denominations: Ulric, Sigmar, Shallya, Myrmidia, Verena and Morr, bringing their bells and holy books into the streets, spraying blessed water at the shades and shadows, though fear had them cowering and tripping over the lines of the rituals, allowing the mellifluous wraiths to slide into their flesh and chill their blood to ice, culling the one defence the city of Middenheim actually had from the Vampire Count's wrath.

The high priest of Sigmar suffered the worst. As the old man raised his eyes to the Middenheim Spire he saw the implacable figure of Vlad von Carstein squatting amid the buttresses and the gargoyles. It was impossible for him to make out the sardonic mockery in the pale count's expression but still the old priest was overwhelmed by the sudden repulsive touch of the vampire's base evil. The priest knew that von Carstein only resembled a human, that his nature was in fact something far older, and far more malignant in origin. His tainted blood was ancient and far crueller than any living being's.

He revelled in savagery, in death, in sadistic slaughter and sacrifice. He excelled at it. He was the Lord of Death and he hungered for mortal flesh, mortal blood. The priest felt the taint of his hunger, felt himself succumbing to it, being overwhelmed by the bloodlust of the beast perched up amongst the gargoyles, mocking their heroics.

The cobblestones around the Sigmarite's feet frosted with rime, touched by the unholy cold of the hungry dead, ribbons of frost crystallising and crusting over the stone walls of his temple, solidifying into ice. The priest's breath fogged in the air in front of his face as he struggled to give voice to the words of banishment, merging with the spectral forms, his own breath giving shape and definition to the dead. And then they were inside him, not one wraith, but a whole ungodly host, devouring his eternal soul even as they congested his lungs and blocked his throat with ice so that he could not breath or talk, choking him slowly and painfully to death even as the Vampire Count's mocking laughter rang through the streets. As the cold wormed its way into the silver hammer around his neck, the holy relic cracked and split in two. The shards fell to the cobbles and shattered like glass. The priest clutched at his throat, clawing at his own tongue, trying to pull it out so that he might swallow one last desperate mouthful of air before he died.

Kruger watched helplessly, feeling wretched, responsible and helpless at the same time. The fact that the wraiths came shrieking into his face and then pulled away to claim another soul tormented the grand master. He bellowed his rage and chased the bodiless entities into the open square beneath the Middenheim Spire, slipping and stumbling on the frosted cobbles as the shadows writhed and good men died.

'IT'S ME YOU WANT!' Kruger yelled, his cry whipped away by the icy wind. He had killed von Carstein once, but death held no dominion over the count. He had heard the stories of Bluthof where five lances had skewered von Carstein to the ground before the Count of Ostland had buried his Runefang deep in the beast's heart. Three days later von Carstein returned to order the crucifixion of prisoners outside the town gates. At Bogenhafen Bridge a cannon ball had decapitated the Vampire Count. An

hour later the cannon crew were dead and Bogen-hafen was overrun, Vlad von Carstein at the head of the conquering army.

The beast refused to die.

Von Carstein's mocking laughter haunted Kruger until he finally saw the monster crouched between the leering gargoyles of the spire hundreds of feet above. Kruger didn't hesitate. He charged into the vault of the cathedral, the massive wooden doors banging closed behind him, the echoes folding in on themselves as they reverberated through the massive dome above his head. Stained glass images of Ulric and the White Wolves let in a wondrous array of hues, reds and golds and greens dappling the stone floor like a scattering of coins.

Kruger ran down the aisle. The leather grip of his warhammer was soaked with the cold sweat of fear; its reminder spurred him on. He crashed through the door at the rear of the temple and started up the spiral stairs two and three at a time. There were two hundred and seventy-six in total, curling up almost two hundred feet to the bell tower. The grand master's lungs were burning before he was halfway up, his legs on fire, but guilt drove him on viciously. Kruger gasped for breath as he slammed the door to the bell tower open.

Von Carstein was there, ringing a death knell with the hilt of his damnable sword on the huge brass bell, the sonorous clang resonating through the very fabric of the tower.

Kruger sucked in a deep breath, battling to regulate his breathing. He wasn't a young man anymore. He felt every one of the stairs he had just climbed.

'I wondered how many you were prepared to sacrifice before you remembered you were a man and came to face me,' von Carstein said, amicably. He sheathed his sword.

'All of this was to get me?' Kruger said, images of the slaughter flashing through his mind. He shook his head, trying to dislodge them. He focussed on the undead count's sardonic smile, his cold eyes that delved deep inside, stripping away secrets and fears as though they were layers of clothing draped over a soul. He gave his hatred for the monster facing him time to fester.

'So it seems, does it not?'

'I killed you once before, von Carstein. Who's to say I won't do it again?'

'Well,' the Vampire Count said, appearing to give the question serious thought, 'me. You interest me, something most humans fail to do. You have... qualities that it is easy to admire. I could use a man like you.'

'Over my dead body,' Kruger spat.

'That was the general idea, yes.'

The Vampire Count moved away from the prayer bell. He came toward Kruger, his smile widening with each step closer. He moved like a spider, cautious, with predatory cunning.

'If you kill me, this ends. You have your revenge. Let my men live.'

'Too late for that, I am afraid. My pets are hungry. I promised them some succulent morsels to eat and nothing tastes better than fattened wolf meat, believe me.'

'You disgust me. You aren't human.'

'Don't you ever feel it, Wolf? The thirst for blood? Oh, I can see it in your eyes. You do. You do. You feel it now. You feel it on the battlefield when you ride for your precious honour. You hide behind your fatuous code of chivalry but we aren't so different. You choose to justify your violence and thirst for blood behind mysticism, claiming devotion to your pathetic warrior god so you can make it holy. At least I am honest about it. I allow myself to delight in the hedonistic rush of killing. I revel in the naked savagery of death. It is in you already, Wolf. The beast is in your soul. You keep it caged but it comes out every time you hold that hammer of yours. Believe me, you would make a good vampire. You already have the taste for blood.'

'I am nothing like you.'

'No, of course, you are the honourable and decent savage whereas I am just the savage.'

'Shut up!' Kruger hissed, lashing out with his warhammer.

Von Carstein didn't move. He didn't even breathe.

Kruger lunged forward two steps, the old wooden timber beams of the floor groaning under his weight. He swung again, wildly.

Von Carstein exploded into brutal, astonishing, action. He sprang at the White Wolf, his black cloak billowing out behind him. His economy of movement was both lethal and hypnotic; there was a brutal precision to his kicks and punches as they came, hard and fast. It was all Kruger could do to ward off the first few. In the space between heartbeats he was driven to his knees by a rain of punishment so shockingly violent it was irresistible.

He threw up his warhammer desperately but it made no difference. An open-handed strike to the throat had Kruger choking as he swallowed his tongue. Vlad stepped back, watching curiously as the grand master choked slowly to death.

'No,' he said, shaking his head. 'You don't get away from me that easily, Wolf.'

He reached down and grabbed the pelt around Jerek Kruger's shoulders and hauled him effortlessly to his feet. The grand master's eyes flickered convulsively as he hovered on the edge of death. Von Carstein waited until his enemy was a second from death and sank his teeth into Kruger's throat. He drank hungrily, savouring the hot sweet coppery taste of the White Wolf's blood as it trickled down his throat. He pulled back before he completely drained the grizzled old warrior, grabbed a handful of hair and yanked his mouth open. Slowly, savouring the final delicious irony of the moment, the Vampire Count sank his teeth into his own wrist, drawing blood. He held the wound over Kruger's mouth, letting it drip down his throat.

Kruger's body shuddered, every ounce of the man's being revolting against the tainted blood as it pooled in his mouth… and then he swallowed and his eyes flared open as he gagged and gasped a first desperate breath in minutes.

He lurched away from the Vampire Count's Blood Kiss, reeling as his legs betrayed him. Clutching at a low beam, Kruger staggered toward the moonlight as it poured in through an open arch.

He turned to look back at von Carstein.

'It ends here.'

He turned back to the arch. He felt the kiss of the fresh air on his face, savoured it, one final proof that he was alive, and threw himself from the height of the great spire.

CHAPTER NINETEEN
Alone in the Dark

MIDDENHEIM
Spring, 2050

HE AWOKE IN claustrophobic darkness. He couldn't move. His arms were crossed over his chest. He could move his legs sideways about six inches. No more.

The darkness pressed down on him. He tried to move his arms, sliding them down his chest, working them around to his side. It felt worse. He was trapped. He couldn't think.

Then, in hallucinatory flashes it came back to him. The wights, the wraiths, the rime of frost across the city – his city – as the ghosts of the conquered ravaged it and up above, the mocking laughter of von Carstein as his friends – no, men, he didn't have friends, his men – died, and then he was falling. The space in between was blank. Each fresh revelation stripped away another little piece of his humanity. He felt no grief, only curious detachment as his life came back to him fragment by bloody fragment, his identity establishing itself there in the dark.

He had been Jerek Kruger. That was before. He didn't know who he was now. Or what.

Only that he was something else – something altogether alien to the man he had been, though he possessed all of Kruger's memories and longings and no doubt wore the dead man's skin and bones.

Jerek Kruger was dead. He knew that with cold certainty.

Von Carstein's taunts came back to him: *It is in you already, Wolf. The beast is in your soul. You keep it caged but it comes out every time you hold that hammer of yours. Believe me, you would make a good vampire. You already have the taste for blood.*

The fall…

He tasted something sour in his mouth. It took him a moment to realise what it was: dried blood. *You already have the taste for blood.* He knew then what had happened to him, what the taste of rust in his mouth signified. He writhed about in the tight confines of the coffin, kicking and gagging at the same time. His feet drummed dully on the wooden lid of the coffin, the weight of the earth dampening the sound to a dull thud. He was underground. They had buried him. Panic flared in his mind. He wasn't just trapped he was buried beneath tons of dirt. The sudden understanding was suffocating. The thing that had been Kruger shrieked its terror, bucking and writhing against the tight confines of the coffin.

He worked his hands around until they were either side of his face.

The darkness was all consuming.

Through the haze of fear one single need emerged: hunger. He needed to feed.

The thought simultaneously revolted and excited him. He could taste the blood in his mouth and it tasted good. He wanted more. He needed more. Fresh blood.

He had to find a way out of this prison. He had to feed.

Von Carstein had turned him into a monster... or had he always been a monster? Had the vampire been right? Had the beast always been shackled within his soul just waiting to be set free?

He knew who he was. It came to him with shocking clarity. He was a vampire, like von Carstein who had fathered him.

He was von Carstein, as much as any son was part of its father: by blood.

Jerek von Carstein. He tasted the name in his mind. Jerek von Carstein.

They would pay for doing this to him. All of them.

Anger blazed inside him. White-hot fury. He had fought monsters all his life and in doing so had become the worst sort. He roared in pain and frustration, and pushed at the wooden lid with his feet and his knees and the flats of his hands. The thin wood cracked and began to splinter beneath the strain. A trickle of dirt spilled into the coffin, hitting him on the chest. He roared again and pushed with all of his might but the lid didn't give another inch. The hard-packed earth kept it lodged in place.

He was trapped. Buried alive… Only he would be alive forever.

Forever trapped in the suffocating darkness, unable to move, unable to do anything but think. It would drive him to madness.

But it would save lives up there… The thought came to him unbidden. As long as he was a prisoner in his earthly tomb they were safe up there: his men, their families, the people he had fought to protect against the beast that was von Carstein.

But their safety would be his undoing. He wasn't strong enough. He knew that already.

The taste of blood was metallic on his tongue, taunting him.

He didn't just need to feed, he *wanted* to. Von Carstein had turned him into a monster.

He beat his knuckles raw and bloody against the splintered wood in frustration. Clawed at the splinters, tore his nails scrabbling at the wooden lid trying to tear through it. Jags of wood cut into his fingers, shredding the flesh and paring it down to the bone in places.

And then the dirt came. Like rain.

The lid gave way, a huge crack opening down the centre, and the mud and the worms and the stones spilled into the coffin, trapping Jerek von Carstein completely. He opened his mouth to scream and the dirt poured into it, filling him.

He lashed out wildly but could barely move. *Choking*, he thought desperately as he swallowed mouthfuls of dirt. *Can't breathe… Can't…*

But there was no pain in his lungs. No light-headed dizziness. No desperate retching for breath. He didn't need it. He was dead already. The thought ripped away one of the final shreds of his sanity.

He raged against the suffocating press of the soil and the jagged splinters of the coffin lid, tearing at the dirt, clawing upwards, dragging himself through the hard-packed earth until, finally, his face broke the surface.

He was born again.

Born into death in a brutal parody of the way he had been born into life, the earth yielding him up, his mother in this undead life.

He opened his eyes to see his father looking down at him.

Jerek coughed up a lungful of worms and black dirt.

'Why?' he managed to ask. 'Why did you do this?'

'Because you owed me a death. Because I lost a good man but in you I found a better one. Because I saw into your soul. Because you were already a wolf. All of these reasons and none of them. Because I *wanted* to. You will work it out, in time. Now come, let's feed. There is a world of flesh and blood out here. Satisfy your hunger, Wolf.'

Vlad gripped Jerek's wrist and hauled him free of the grave.

CHAPTER TWENTY
Dusk Chorus

ALTDORF
Winter, 2051

JON SKELLAN HAD all but forgotten what it was like to be human.

It had been so long since he last felt anything.

That was what he missed most, the simple sensation of feeling the air in his lungs as he drew a deep breath, of smelling the fresh cut grass and the bread rising in the baker's oven, the kiss of sunlight on his face.

Sunlight.

He had taken it for granted all his life. The sun rose, the sun set. It was as simple as that. He was sixty-nine years old, though he hadn't aged a day in decades. Skellan hadn't felt the sun on his face in forty-one years.

Forty-one years.

He couldn't remember what it felt like.

The only thing he did feel now was hunger. It was a dark desperate sensation that gnawed away inside him constantly, demanding to be fed and with an appetite that could never truly be sated. He wasn't the man he had once been; the base lust for revenge that had driven him for so long had faded with the death of Aigner and his siring. The traces of humanity had faded gradually over the years, being subsumed by the fundamental vampiric urge: the need to feed. He had come to enjoy the hunt and the kill. A predatory smile spread across his face. He could taste it, thick in the air:

Blood.

The coming days promised slaughter; a rare feast of blood, old, young, innocent and soured by bitter experience. The city of Altdorf offered a smorgasbord of death fit for the entire vampiric aristocracy of Sylvania. Von Carstein's malignant kin swelled the undead army for the final glorious assault on the heart of the Empire itself.

Altdorf. The Imperial capital stood on a series of islands amongst the broad mud flats at the confluence of the Reik and Talabec rivers.

The city's defences were pitifully inadequate. In desperation the fools had dug ditches and planted stakes as though they expected the vampires to rush forward and throw themselves blindly on the sharpened wooden spikes. More old wives' tales had driven the citizens of the capital to redirect the flow of the Reik itself so it formed a moat of running water. Inside the city walls the riverbeds had run dry and the defenders had taken to using them as expedient footpaths. It was quite ingenious how they had managed it but then, the city was renowned for its learning.

The effort was unnecessary, of course. Superstition turned them all into fools. They prayed blindly to their impotent gods for salvation and turned to legends, needing them to be true. They bent the Reik because they needed to believe doing so gave them immunity from the vampires; that the count and his kin couldn't cross a river of fast-flowing water.

Holed up in their damp cellars, hidden behind planks and boards that blinded their windows, the Altdorfers deliberately forgot about the zombies, the ghouls, the ghasts, and other revenant shades at von Carstein's disposal. They had little hope. Mothers cradled their babies in their arms, shivering, backs pressed against the cold stone walls, listening for the sound of the vampires coming, trying to summon the courage to kill their own flesh and blood rather than give them over to the monsters to feed off. Desperate sobs haunted the darkest places of the city. This was their doom.

Skellan thrived on it.

War had accelerated the process of decay; what could fail and powder and flake and rust and collapse, did. Nature had already begun the long process of ridding the land of the pestilential hand of man. The first stage was rendering the once-grand buildings to dust returned. Vines and creepers crawled up the sides of the great surrounding walls, undermining the strength of their foundations as they rooted in between the cracks where the stones mated, working them wider and making them weaker.

What nature started they would finish.

Mankind would suffer in its final hours.

Skellan looked up at the sky. Dawn was less than an hour away. He could sense the complacency creeping into the defenders as they manned the battlements. The archers knew that they were safe, for a few hours at least; von Carstein would not launch an attack so close to sunrise.

Safety was an illusion.

He turned to look behind him. Along the mud flats tens of thousands of mindless automata were crowded, piles of bones and rotten flesh gathered in an endless wave of violence waiting to crash against the defenders, and at the lumbering siege engines rolling slowly forward to the front line. Von Carstein's army appeared endless, stretching as far as the eye could see. He could only imagine the effect it had on the morale of the men facing it, waiting, grimly relieved that at least they had another day of living allotted to them, thinking that they would get to return home to their wives and children one last time before the nightmare was turned loose.

How wrong they were.

The sky remained black as the heart of night, no sign of dawn's first blush of light.

Skellan turned to the grizzled old wolf of a man beside him, as Jerek von Carstein in turn shifted to look at the first of the massive siege engines of fused body and bone lumbering into position. Skellan didn't entirely trust the count's pet even if Vlad himself seemed to think the White Wolf had been entirely tamed. There was something about him that rankled, though it was impossible for Skellan to put his finger on what it was. Of course duplicity and deceit were hardly strange bedfellows for any member of the vampiric aristocracy; they were all a bunch of murderous liars, cheats and thieves, Skellan included. Trust was not something to be blindly given.

The first of the huge siege engines lumbered into place, hundreds of von Carstein's zombies hauling on ropes to drag it forward. The vampires patrolled the lines, whipping the creatures to greater and greater efforts. The infernal machine was like some freshly rendered vision of hell, a confusion of arms and legs and screaming contorted faces fused together in an impossible jumble that towered over the battlefield. Carrion crows circled overhead, drawn by the stench of death that clung to the monstrous trebuchets and catapults.

Mouths moved, still screaming. The constructs were alive, or at least alive in death, animated by dark magic. Their screams echoed the caws of the carrion birds.

Eight machines were locked in place, in range of the high city walls, another eight waiting in reserve.

The sun showed no sign of rising. There would be no dawn to save them.

He wondered when the defenders would realise that in their final hours night had become eternal.

Skellan walked a slow path through the dead to von Carstein's white pavilion, where the count sat, the wailing blade in his lap, toying with the signet ring on his left hand, rolling it slowly around his long thin finger. Von Carstein looked up, his already pale features emaciated now with the strain of war. It was obvious he needed to feed. Skellan drew one of the count's aides aside and instructed him to bring fresh blood that he might share with von Carstein before they delivered the ultimatum. The swarthy manservant scurried off.

'Can you taste it?' von Carstein said without looking up from his sword. The blade moaned slightly beneath his fingertips.

'The fear? Oh yes, delicious isn't it. They are waiting for their precious sun but it isn't coming.'

'Everyone is afraid of the dark, Skellan. It is a primal fear. It goes back to when we lived in caves and used fire to keep the monsters of the night at bay. We could sit here for a month, in perpetual dark and then walk into Altdorf unmolested because fear will have done the fighting for us. I can feel it already, undermining them. They huddle in the dark places praying death will pass them by.'

'They know nothing,' Skellan said.

The manservant returned with a young girl. Her feet and face were covered in grime and she was trembling uncontrollably.

'Ask her,' von Carstein said. 'Ask her what is more frightening, being here with us now, or being locked in the dark waiting to be dragged before us. Well girl, which is it?'

'Yes,' Skellan said, moving in close to stand just behind her, his hand touching the softness of her cheek as silent tears fell. His accent shifted into a much purer Reikspiel, and he began talking to the girl in her own tongue. 'Which is it? The wait or the kill? Which frightens you more?'

The girl shook her head.

Skellan tangled his fist in her hair and yanked her head back. 'I asked you a question, I expect an answer.'

'W…w… waiting,' she stammered.

'That wasn't so difficult was it,' Skellan said, almost tenderly. 'Now, let's get you cleaned up shall we? Can't have you covered in mud like this. Manners cost us nothing.' He gestured for the lurking servant to bring a wet cloth and gently cleaned the grime from the girl's face, lingering over her tears. Done, he turned her around. 'Better, and now you only stink of fear, not mud,' he said approvingly, and sank his teeth into her neck. Even as she screamed and fought against him, until the strength left her limbs and her arms hung slackly at her side. Her eyes rolled up into her head. Skellan broke away, gasping as he swallowed the last mouthful of warm blood and tossed her over to von Carstein to finish off.

'Feed,' Skellan said. 'You need your strength.'

The count drained the last of the girl's blood and threw the corpse to a ghoul who dragged it outside so that it could strip the flesh from the bones and feast out of sight of its master.

Von Carstein stood, sheathing the hungry sword and fastening his cloak about his shoulders. He looked at Skellan and nodded. 'It is time.'

With that, he walked out into the eternal night, Skellan two paces behind him.

The Vampire Count moved through the ranks of the dead, eyes fixed on the city walls.

Skellan studied his master as he led the way. For all that he had come to admire von Carstein's ruthlessness in the pursuit of his vision of a Kingdom of the Dead the man was deeply flawed. He was not the perfect monster. He could be insufferable with his brooding and his philosophising. It was melancholic and introspective and had no place in the armour of a great leader. It was too human; too close to weakness and those other damnable human traits. It was a game to Skellan, and whether the cattle played by the rules or broke them the results were the same, he fed off them. He didn't care about them. They were just meat. Von Carstein's attachment to them left him with a cold feeling in his gut. And the woman, Isabella, she was nothing short of insane. Her instability however made her interesting. She understood, in some basic way, the game.

Skellan had heard tales of her habits, bathing in vats of virgin blood to preserve her good looks, drinking thirty and forty maidens in a single night in a glut of ecstasy, painting the walls of the palace with the blood of her victims after an orgy of killing and an hour later complain that she was lonely in the draughty old castle. That she was alone.

Von Carstein stood on a stone butte amid the mud flats and called out: 'Who speaks for your city?'

His voice carried easily, his accent thickening even as it amplified. It sounded brutal in Skellan's ears, lacking any refinement or culture. But that was the way of the new world: the monsters ruled.

There was a bustle of activity on the battlements, the guards obviously unsure how to respond to the situation. Von Carstein waited patiently, as though he had all the time in the world. Skellan knew well enough what they were trying to do. Soon enough they would learn that stalling for time was going to get them nowhere. The sun wasn't going to save them this time.

After a few minutes, a man wearing a simple white shift with the hammer of Sigmar emblazoned on it appeared. He looked surprisingly tranquil given the massive army of undead spilled out across the mud flats as far as the eye could see. Beside him stood an effeminate dark-haired fop who, even from a distance, looked mortally afraid. Skellan smiled to himself. The old man was a priest but he carried himself like a warrior, the simpering fool by his side, more likely than not, Ludwig von Holzkrug, pretender to the Imperial throne. Skellan ignored him and stared at the priest. He knew who he was. The man had aged in the years since they had last met but he was still recognisable as Wilhelm von Ostwald. The last time Skellan had seen him the man was a fanatical witch hunter. It seemed that the fanatic had found religion. It was a shame it wouldn't save his immortal soul.

'I, Wilhelm III, Grand Theogonist of Sigmar, speak for the people of Altdorf,' the old priest called down coolly.

'I, Vlad von Carstein, come in faith to make you an offer I urge you to consider and answer for the best of your people.'

'Speak then.'

'The sun will not rise today, the long night has begun. This is my offer to you, serve me in life, or serve me in death. The choice is yours. There will be no mercy if you chose to stand against me.'

The fop looked visibly shaken, imagining no doubt the unlife of servitude, a mindless zombie at von Carstein's beck and call. The priest on the other hand was unmoved.

'That is no offer, vampire. That is a death sentence. I will not sell my people into slavery.'

'So be it,' von Carstein said flatly.

He signalled for the siege engines to fire the first volley of flaming skulls into the heart of the Empire.

CHAPTER TWENTY-ONE
Curiosity Killed the Thief

ALTDORF
Winter, 2051

ONE FINAL JOB, the thief promised himself, and then it's time to get out.

It was all about portable wealth. Felix Mann was a rich man by anyone's measure. He had assets: he had invested wisely in property in the Empire's capital, a society house close to the Imperial palace and the Sigmar monument in Heldenplatz, on the border of the affluent Obereik and the Palast districts. The property was worth an Emperor's ransom but it couldn't exactly be packed up on a cart and shipped out to Tilea or Estalia. He could see the great bronze statue of the Empire's patron deity from the window of his bedroom. He wondered what the Man-God would think about the fate that was befalling his city.

'All good things come to an end,' he said to himself. Talking to himself was a bad habit that he had developed recently.

There was a ship waiting in Reiksport that would spirit Felix out of the doomed city before it succumbed to the inevitable and fell. It was all down to timing, circumstance and taking that final opportunity. Felix wasn't a greedy man. He had no need of exceptional wealth; for all the majesty of his house and its finery, the trappings of the rich held no interest for him. Theft was a game where he pitted himself against the wits of his victims, the wealth he walked away with nothing more than a way of keeping score.

The thousands of undead feet shuffling across the mud flats sent vibrations running deep through the heart of the old city, tiny tremors of revulsion where nature shied away from the unnatural touch of the dead. Flaming skulls shrieked intermittently over the high walls, smashing and burning where they landed, spilling vitriolic fire throughout the timber-framed houses, and terror through the citizens. The skulls brought the horrors of the war home to them. Those skulls belonged to people who had stood against the Vampire Count. Tomorrow or the next day it might be *their* skulls shattering against the walls of the Imperial palace, their brains scooped out to feed von Carstein's ghouls. Felix found it all quite barbaric.

He walked slowly, thinking, planning. One last job. Portable wealth. He knew full well what he intended, a crime so audacious it would live on in the folklore of Altdorf as long as the city itself. The walls above were thick with archers but the streets themselves were virtually deserted. It wasn't like that everywhere

in the city, of course: in Amtsbezirk the Tower Prison
and Mundsen Keep were surrounded by people desperate to liberate their loved ones so that they might
flee, or free the vile murderous scum locked up
within their walls so that they might be fed to the
count's ghouls as an offering in the belief that it
might save the rest of the populace. It was desperate.
Hopeless. In Domplatz they stood at the doors of the
Tempel Haus begging the handful of Knights of the
Flery Heart to ride out and save them despite the
overwhelming odds and the impossibility of their
survival or success. In Oberhausen they petitioned at
the jet-black building of the Temple of Morr for the
god of death to protect their souls.

In Süderich the fish market was long abandoned,
the fishmongers with no wares to sell due to looting
in the first days of the siege, and in Reikhoch the Ruh-
statt Cemetery was the scene of desecration with
many of the tombs and crypts of the dead exhumed,
the bodies burned and destroyed so that they might
not rise up against the living and bring down the city
from within.

His wandering took him down narrow alleyways
and wider streets to Kaiserplatz on the opposite side
of the Imperial palace. The gallows was the only thing
left in the vast square. He skirted the edge of the Hof-
garde barracks, his feet leading him toward the
Imperial mint and counting house. The street was
empty so he took the opportunity to really look at the
Kaiserliches Kanzleiamt. In this part of Altdorf it was
near nigh impossible to tell how the city's population
had swollen with thousands of refugees from the surrounding countryside, the road wardens and the

militia had crammed them down in the poorer districts of the city, allowing at least the patina of civilisation to remain intact where there was money to appreciate it.

One last job, he promised himself, his smile wide.

In the distance men were barking like dogs, shouting out orders, screaming as the fires caught and burned fiercely, the echoes of flame haunting the empty streets. Felix wasn't surprised the majority of Altdorfers had scurried off into hiding like rats; look at the example their spiritual leader had set – the Grand Theogonist had disappeared into the bowels of the huge Sigmarite cathedral three days ago, though differentiating between day and night had become a thing of the past. Night was eternal. Felix had heard fools blathering about how von Carstein had the power to prevent the sun from rising which was patently absurd but the idiots believed what they saw, and what they saw was night's black heart.

The counting house was a three-tiered masterpiece of stone and wood, as secure as any building ever built. It reminded Felix of a mastiff: squat, determined, stubborn, unbreakable, like some immensely powerful beast that would take every ounce of his nous to tame, but that was what made the game fun. Anything else would have been boring.

With all eyes turned outwards to the Vampire Count's undead on the mud flats the watch patrols had become lax.

A flash of fire whistled overhead, the skull crashing into one of the high towers of the Imperial barracks and showering flame. The fire clung to the stone but it burned itself out quickly. In that moment though the flaming skull was every bit as brilliant as a sun, throwing its light over Kaiserplatz. Felix stood stock still, trapped in its red glare, waiting for a cry that never came. It was amazing how a few days could undo the discipline of years.

More blazing skulls arced high over his head, showering sparks and trailing tails of fire as they lit the night. Despite the horror of what was actually happening there was a curious beauty about the fire set against the black sky.

It was only a matter of time before the dead scaled the city walls and the desperate efforts of the archers and swordsmen along the battlements wouldn't be enough to repel them. Everyone in Altdorf knew it but few were willing to accept it, hence the near anarchy in some parts of the city with shops being looted and stalls stripped of any kind of food that might help some hidden family last another day or two of the siege. It was as though the Vampire Count was deliberately stripping them of their humanity, turning them into rats, scavengers.

The speed with which so called civilised people sacrificed the rule of law and order was dizzying. Thousands turned to Sigmar and the other gods for deliverance but an equal number turned to crime, helping themselves at the cost of others. For an ordinary decent thief like Felix, for whom there was honour and a certain panache to their criminality, this descent of mankind into the pits of degradation and despair was sickening. He wanted to shake people and force them to see that their selfishness was only accelerating von Carstein's victory.

Signs of the dead were everywhere he looked. Von Carstein was playing with them, like a cat playing with a rat before feeding time. Felix knew the stories of how Middenheim had fallen to the wraiths, and how the Ottilia's army had been swept away by the zombie tide. There was no magic that made Altdorf immune. Cities could fall. Empires could fall.

He needed to get out before the walls came crumbling down and the dead flooded the cramped streets. The instincts of civilisation wouldn't stand up to more than a few hours of that heinous horror before it succumbed to the dark side of its own nature. He wasn't a fighter. He lived by his wits, by the sharpness of his tongue, not his sword. He was a rogue.

Felix turned his attention back to the counting house. He wasn't interested in money – a vast sum of coins would be impossible to ship out in a hurry. What he wanted was gems, pure cut and uncut pieces of flawless quality: a fortune that could be carried in his pocket. The value of precious stones was universal.

The guardhouse outside the courtyard was empty where ordinarily there would have been five skilled swordsmen patrolling the courtyard alone.

Felix walked casually across the street, resisting the urge to look to the right and left first. The secret was in making it look as though he had every right to be there. He peered in through the glass of the guardhouse window. The fire in the hearth had burned out and there was no sign that the guards had been there for days. Probably manning the walls, Felix reasoned, liking the way his train of thought was leading him. It was logical of course that with such a visible threat on the other side of the wall few eyes would be turned inwards.

He walked a slow circuit around the counting house, looking for points of ingress and egress. 'There are more ways to skin a dead cat,' Felix said to himself, rounding the corner back into Kaiserplatz. A good thief always knew all the options available to him, and didn't merely rely on the front and back doors, or even first or second floor windows. He craned his neck to measure the distance between rooftops in various places, several of which were probably jumpable. People tended to forget about rooftops when planning the security of their houses. Of course, given the heavy manning of the battlements, entry via the roof was not the most secluded of the options available to him. He had no wish to be seen by some distracted guard who just happened to turn to look back longingly at his home, or needed spiritual strength so turned to the spires of Altdorf's cathedral.

There were too many opportunities for things to go wrong for his liking so he turned his eyes to lower, less overlooked ledges and the darker crannies where the building butted up against others.

And then there was always underground, but Sigmar alone knew how many of the denizens of the once fair city had taken to living like rats underground in the sewers believing themselves safe. Out of sight out of mind was not, as far as Felix knew, relevant when it came to fleeing the hordes of death.

It was, he decided, far from impregnable. But then, it wasn't supposed to be a fortress. It relied upon manpower to keep even the most ardent thief out, which was an act of hubris Felix was sure that the chancellor of the Imperial counting house would come to regret over the coming days.

There would be patrolling guards, and alarms; that was a given considering the nature of the building. The question was what the alarms would do. A literal alarm would summon help but given the paranoia of the extremely rich he half-expected some kind of lethal payback for having the temerity to rob the Imperial counting house.

He needed someone on the inside.

Unfortunately time was against the kind of subtlety that kind of infiltration required. His hands were proverbially tied. He needed to get in without taking the time for the niceties of the con. The job would be lacking the element of finesse a good caper had but it would be efficient and no one would get hurt. That was important. Thugs used brute force; a decent thief used his brain and left the brawn at home. The alarms, Felix rationalised, would be located around the sewers, and the ground and first floors. If he had been designing the security that is what he would have done. There were very few good second storey thieves working the city nowadays. It was an art long forgotten. Coarse crimes like muggings and pick-pocketing were the vogue. The skill had gone out of the grift. People weren't prepared to work for their money. They wanted it easy and quick.

Not Felix Mann though, he belonged to the old school. He was a gentleman thief. A connoisseur of crime. He was a throwback, one of the last of the true grifters. His skill lay in making his society believe he didn't exist. In Middenheim he was known as Reinard

Kohl. In Talabheim he was Florian Schmelder. In Bogenhafen his name was Ahren Leher. In Kemperbad he was Stefan Meyer, and in Marienburg, Ralf Bekker.

In any given city in the Old World he had countless names and countless dowagers and wealthy widows eating out of the palm of his hand, showering him with trinkets for favours, desperate for even a few minutes of his attention. He made them feel special, reminded them what it felt like to be young, to be loved. He broke their hearts but in doing so he gave them something back, pride, a sense of self-worth, his gift was making them fall in love with themselves once more, and he made a pretty penny in the process. Wealthy merchants wined and dined him believing him to be of their ilk. His successes were the talk of every town, and his lies so big everyone just had to believe them.

Carrion birds had settled along the crenellated roof of the barracks. Their beady eyes unnerved him.

He needed to think.

Any weaknesses for him to exploit would more likely than not be on the second and third storeys. There had to be a way in. Had to be.

He walked slowly back towards the Domplatz district trying to clear his mind.

It was like one of those elaborate Cathayan finger traps, the more he worried and pulled at the problem the more the small details sprang out to snare him, which of course had him wrestling all the details which stubbornly refused to be solved. The secret was to draw his fingers out slowly and smoothly. Or in other words to empty his mind; think about something else.

The problem was if he wasn't thinking about the job, the reality of the undead army crowding the Meadows Gate swamped his mind and the instinct to run became overwhelming. As with so many others, the fact that the Grand Theogonist had disappeared into the vaults of the great cathedral did nothing to comfort him. The priest had told the congregation he was retreating to pray for wisdom and enlightenment in this dark time.

The crowds were still gathered before the great doors of the cathedral, waiting patiently for their spiritual father to emerge.

Felix was sure the man had retreated into the bowels of Altdorf and used the complex warren of catacombs and the sewers to escape the city. Without his robes of office few would recognise the man. It certainly wasn't impossible that he might have made his way as far as Reiksport unmolested and taken a ship from there to anywhere in the known world.

It was, after all, what he would have done.

He had expected to find a few stragglers still camped outside of the octagonal cathedral. Hundreds had converged on the place of worship: penitents, worshippers, the fearful and the desperate. To his left a group of women who looked as though they had just crawled out of the sewers knelt in huddled prayer.

There was an almost hysterical reaction from the crowd as the doors of the cathedral began to open, and then a huge sigh of disappointment as they saw it was the lector, not the Grand Theogonist himself who emerged. The man was older by a few years and had the bearing of a scholar and the body to match. His face, however, was plain and open; a face you could instinctively trust. He moved stiffly, as though each step cost him heavily. The hubbub grew.

He gestured for silence.

A gentle murmur whispered through the crowd. He was going to address them. Felix could read the excitement in the rows of faces. As one they all thought the same thing: surely this meant Sigmar had spoken! An air of anticipation rippled through the onlookers. Felix caught it and moved closer, curious to hear what the lector had to say.

The lector coughed, clearing his throat.

'Three days gone our benevolent brother descended into the vaults to pray for guidance. He abstained food and water believing his faith in the lord our god would sustain him. He emerged this morning with the words we have longed to hear: beloved Sigmar has granted our holy father wisdom. With this knowledge our soldiers can slay the beast! He has given us the key to our survival!' The lector raised his hands in benediction.

A huge cheer rang out as people hugged each other, believing themselves saved.

Felix grinned. It was difficult not to be carried away by the lector's enthusiasm. Now he understood why it was the lector addressing the crowd and not Wilhelm himself. Wilhelm's sharp nose and narrow eyes were harder than the lector's, less forgiving, but then he had seen things the lector could not even imagine in the darkest corners of his heart. The lector breaking the news of Sigmar's intervention was a stroke of genius. Felix's grin spread. He knew a good grift when he saw one. This was no case of divine intervention; on the contrary, it was a divine con. But that was the magic of the best grifts, convincing the rubes to believe the impossible. The bigger the lies, the more outrageous the lies, the more desperate the masses were to be gulled by them, especially if there was a little divinity thrown into the mix. This was a new angle for him to think about.

A ripple of movement in the shadows behind the lector caught his eye.

He was about to dismiss it when he saw it again, ten feet away from where he had first seen it: a crease in the shadows, a slight blurring of the wall as something passed in front of it. He wouldn't have been able to see it if he hadn't been looking for it, but now he knew what to look for it was not particularly difficult to follow. He knew what it was: the first layer of the divine grift peeling away before his very eyes. There was someone in the shadows, creeping away from the cathedral. He wasn't sure how the deceit worked, a glamour perhaps?

Curiosity piqued, he followed, keeping close to the shadows cast by the scant moonlight. The peculiar light anomaly moved slowly. He matched its pace, dampening the sound of his footsteps on the cobbles. He knew what he was doing was stupid. It was none of his business. The Sigmarites could pull the scam to end all scams for all he cared. He'd be gone in forty-eight hours. But he was curious. It was what made him a good thief. He didn't take things at face value. He didn't swallow the easy lie. There was a grift going down here and curiosity be damned, he wanted to know what it was all about.

'Killed the cat, though didn't it?' Felix muttered, disgusted with himself as, in the darkness of an alleyway two streets over from the Sigmar cathedral, the figure of a tall, thin man took shape within the shimmering dark. The stranger peeled back the hood of his cloak and stopped mid-step. He had obviously heard Felix. He turned and stared directly at him. Felix winced. They were barely fifteen feet apart. Felix had been careless, gotten too close. He had been so caught up in trying to unravel the sting that he had walked right into one of the central players. He tried to look casually lost, like an innocent passer-by but it was a pointless ruse. They both knew why he was there.

The look the stranger gave Felix sent a shiver soul deep. It was the man's eyes. They were ancient, knowing, and so, so cold. They stripped away the layers of lies and identity and delved deep into the core of who he was. They *knew* him.

'You would do well to forget you ever saw me,' the stranger said, and strode away into the everlasting night.

CHAPTER TWENTY-TWO
Answered Prayers

ALTDORF
Winter, 2051

CURSING HIMSELF FOR a fool Felix Mann retreated to his house in the Obereik district.

His heart was hammering. His hands were trembling. The encounter had shaken him badly.

He couldn't get over the way the man's eyes had dissected his soul. That was exactly what it had felt like: as though the man had taken a chirurgeon's blade to his very sense of self and stripped it with brutal efficacy, slice after bloody slice.

'Forty-eight hours,' he promised himself. Forty-eight hours. One last job and it would all be over. He looked up at the sky, as though hoping to see validation of his vow in the stars but all he saw was the damned darkness. It was far from reassuring even though he knew, rationally, that it wasn't a natural night, this seemingly endless dark. The sun was blocked, it hadn't disappeared. Von Carstein hadn't spirited it away. He wasn't that powerful. It was up there somewhere blazing with radiant intensity. A few miles away, he was sure, it was bright beautiful daylight. It surprised him how much he missed it. He felt its absence in his blood. It wasn't as though he was a stranger to the night. He lived in the dark. As much as anywhere in this godforsaken city it was his home but it was different now. He couldn't trust it anymore. It held secrets.

The man had used it to cloak himself, moving virtually invisibly through the city. That, more than anything else, scared the thief. He didn't like things he couldn't explain and grift or not he knew he was standing on the fringe of a very dangerous game. He couldn't even begin to imagine the stakes but he knew the smart money was on running for the hills. He who turns and runs away lives to fight another day, and all of that.

'Forty-eight hours,' he promised himself again, knowing full well he wasn't going anywhere until the counting house job was done.

A new, horrific dimension was added to von Carstein's bombing of the city during his walk home. Limbs, arms, hands, whole legs, feet, rotten and gangrenous, rancid with plague and other sickness, were catapulted into the city along with the flaming skulls. Felix picked a path through the detritus of human flesh, wondering how long they would be left there to fester, and how long it would take for the disease to spread.

He shot the bolts on the door, locking himself in, but even knowing he was secure, he couldn't sleep. He lay for an hour in the darkness, staring at the ceiling, thinking.

The man hadn't been human, he realised with something akin to dread settling in the pit of his stomach. It was the eyes. They gave him away. There had been no trace of humanity in them, only the ruthless cunning of a killer. Felix held his face in his hands. The Sigmarite priests were treating with the enemy; that was how desperate things had become, that was how much trouble he was in.

'Forty-eight hours,' he said again, knowing that he didn't have forty-eight hours. Time was a luxury he could ill afford.

He pushed himself out of bed and paced around the room restlessly. He didn't like it. He didn't like it one little bit. Circumstance was manipulating him into going faster than he felt comfortable. Rushing a job meant taking risks, taking risks meant making mistakes. The question wasn't if he was going to make mistakes, it was if he was going to get away with them.

A great thief wasn't defined by skill alone, a great thief was lucky. The greatest thieves of all time rode their luck like a dockside doxy.

'To hell with it,' Felix Mann said. He dressed quickly, in dark colours, but not blacks. He avoided black because the darkness wasn't pure, black stood out against it more than deep homespun browns and forest greens. He knelt, sliding two long thin dirks into their sheaths in his boots. He felt beneath the mattress for the canvas wrap and pulled it out. The case was a little smaller than his hand and it contained the tools of his trade. Felix unwrapped the canvas, checking through each pick and sawtoothed metal file methodically before wrapping the small canvas case back up and securing it to his belt. A second canvas wrap contained three coils of copper wire, wax and tallow as well as the fixings for tinder.

He smeared an oil-based salve across his face, the components of the salve rendering his skin dark, in patches deep brown, in others almost olive green with hints of a purer black around the eyes, and tied his hair back with a thin strip of black leather. He greased the toes of his supple leather boots in sticky tar. Next he blacked up any exposed skin he could see in the full length body mirror, including the backs of his hands, smoothing the salve up past his wrists and well under the cuffs of his shirt so that even when he stretched and the fabric rode up there would be no telltale white skin to betray him. His palms he left white. He pulled on a supple pair of leather gloves, stretching his fingers deep into them. He drew a series of deep breaths, regulating his breathing.

He was tense.

Every muscle felt uncomfortably tight.

He ran through a series of relaxation exercises, working from his fingertips inwards. He concentrated on the flow of blood through his body, using it to draw the tension out like a panacea.

He left the house, but not by the door.

He took to the thieves' highway, travelling across the rooftops of the city, keeping low, and sticking to the lower buildings so that he wouldn't be exposed to the guards on the city walls. He couldn't risk a light, which meant he had to go more slowly than he might have liked, giving his eyes time to adjust.

The fourth bell after midnight tolled sonorously through the dark city, echoing down the abandoned streets. A light drizzle began as Felix traversed the rooftops along the banks of the dry gulch that had only a few days earlier been the Reik River. Without water to drive it the huge mill wheels were no longer turning. He hunkered down on the slate roof of the old stone mill house. The drizzle made the slates treacherous. It also wet the tar on his toes. He prayed fervently that they would be sticky enough when he needed them. Coupled with the web of clothes lines and forgotten laundry that criss-crossed the rooftops the slick tiles were a hazard he could have lived without. Occasional lights bobbed by below, carried by watchmen. The light broke the shadows. He waited patiently for the torchbearers and lantern carriers to move on. Now he had committed himself to the job his sense of overwhelming urgency had gone.

He moved on, ducking under a hemp rope that had been stretched between two chimneybreasts and hunkered down again beside a third, using it to keep him out of sight of the archers on the city wall while he scanned the nearby rooftops, picking out the best path between where he was and the Imperial counting house.

The boarded-up windows of many of the surrounding houses made his job so much easier. No prying eyes to worry about and more than a few wrought metal balconies that could be borrowed if the rooftop traverse was interrupted. He picked his path and started to move, keeping low by habit even though there wasn't a moon to silhouette him. Peripheral vision had a way of noticing movement that direct line of sight would often miss. There was no point in taking risks he didn't have to.

Felix moved almost entirely on instinct; he had been a thief long enough to know when to trust his gut feelings about something. He scuttled forward, right up to the edge of an overhanging eave. The next building was a three-storey house, but both the second and third floors had wide wrought iron balconies. Neither, thankfully, was cluttered with plant pots or other potentially noisy bric-a-brac and shutters had been secured over the large windows. The gap between the buildings was ten feet at most, but it was a jump that he really didn't want to make. Felix backed away from the edge and moved carefully along the roof until he had convinced himself there was no alternative. He moved back into place, taking a moment to judge the jump.

It was far from easy.

The second floor balcony interfered with what otherwise would have been a fairly straightforward jump and catch because any kind of impact with his lower legs could easily dislodge his grip on the railings above.

It was a long way down.

He took two steps back, and with a short run-up launched himself off the roof. For one sickening second Felix thought he had misjudged the distance then his wrists slammed into the metal filigree of the upper balcony as his legs continued to swing. He barely managed to catch a hold with one hand, fingers slipping down the iron spike as he hung there precariously, dangling high above the street. He kicked his legs, giving his body the momentum he needed to reach up and grab a firm hold on the trelliswork and hand over hand haul himself up onto the balcony. Sweat beaded on his forehead.

The balcony overlooked a baker's dozen of flat roofs, one of them crowding close to the rough-hewn walls of the barracks across the street from the Imperial counting house. The shadow of the counting house hulked just beyond it. One glance was enough to confirm that the rooftop security was minimal. He clambered up to stand on the balcony's handrail and reached up to grab the guttering, praying silently that it was secure enough to bear his weight for the few seconds he needed. The metal drainage pipe groaned and began to pull away from the wall as he scrambled up it, the tar on his toes sticking and giving Felix the purchase he needed to drag himself up onto the roof.

He lay flat on his stomach, listening to the sounds of the night.

He rolled over onto his back.

Altdorf was oblivious to his roaming. Felix rose in one fluid motion and stalked cat-like across the flat roof. His foot dislodged a tile, which fell forty feet to the cobbles below and shattered with a sound that could have been thunder. He froze, waiting for cries of alarm that didn't come. Thanking Ranald the Night Prowler for small mercies, Felix scaled the outer wall of the Imperial barracks, his boots slipping occasionally despite the tar on them as he pulled himself up. There were plenty of handholds in the pitted stone of the wall where the rain and wind had weathered them and the cement joining them.

And there it was, in all its dark splendour: the Imperial counting house. Among the criss-crossing washing lines a single thick hemp rope had caught his attention earlier in the day. It ran from the roof of the barracks to the roof of the counting house opposite. Smiling despite himself, Felix tested the rope, seeing what kind of strain it could take. It was secure. He knelt beside it, ready to lower himself and traverse the small gap between the two buildings.

The sensation that crept over him was unmistakable. He was being watched. Staying stock still, Felix scanned the rooftops opposite and the walls, then turned slowly, taking in the sweeping rooftop panorama of the city. He couldn't see his stalker but he knew better than to believe that meant they weren't there. He could feel their eyes on him. A good thief soon learned to trust his instincts. In this case his gut reaction was to turn around and go home, better to be alive and poor, than weighed down with treasures and very, very dead. There was always another job. Skills like his didn't just fade away. Thievery was a mindset. 'One last job,' he promised himself. 'It will be all over in an hour.' He swallowed, struggling to ignore every instinct that told him what he was about to do was a very bad idea, and lowered himself onto the rope.

It sagged slightly under his weight, but held firm as he swung himself forward hand over hand. He made it to the other side. He could still feel the eyes on his back.

He knew his way in. There was a ledge above the courtyard, and beneath the ledge a small balcony. By coming to it from above he kept himself out of line of sight of the guardhouse. Felix crept up to the edge, and then shuffled forward a few steps, readjusting his position so that he could lower himself and drop soundlessly onto the ceramic tiles. Working quickly now, he examined the lock, then selected the appropriate pick from his canvas wrap. It only took a second to pop the lock.

Grinning, Felix Mann opened the door and stepped through.

Something hit him in the chest, punching the wind out of him and knocking him off his feet. He tried to get up, but he was somehow being pressed to the floor. Dazed and disorientated, Felix tried to look around – but couldn't move his head. The air around him sparked blue as he struggled to break free of the trap. No net was holding him, no paralysing darts had struck him.

Magic! It was the only answer… But the practice of magic was outlawed. All sorcerers were hunted down by witch hunters, and destroyed. And witch hunters got their authority from… received their orders from…

His thoughts swam. He had been trapped. Him, the greatest thief the Empire had ever known. 'Stupid, stupid, stupid,' he cursed himself for a fool, a stupid bloody fool. The fact that he could talk through the spell did nothing to calm him. The subtlety of the magic only helped convince Felix that he was in deep, deep trouble. The kind of trouble you woke up dead from – or rather didn't wake up at all from. The lack of guards, the convenient rope from the roof of the barracks. Someone had grifted the grifter. He had been set up and fallen for it, hook, line and sinker. A groan slipped from his lips.

All he could do was wait and see what kind of mess he had gotten himself into.

The grating sound of a chain being drawn though brass handles carried up to Felix. It sounded like a death sentence in his ears. At least they weren't going to make him wait long.

Footsteps: two pairs, one heavier and more laboured than the other, echoed in the stairway. The footsteps stopped as one of the people approaching gave in to a fit of convulsive coughing. It didn't sound good at all. Three more steps and then the coughing began again; deep, tubercular hacks.

Flickering yellow light announced the pair long before they were at the top of the stairs. The light cast its jaundiced glow over the room's dark green wallpaper and rows of equally dark oil paintings. Each depicted a grim faced and forbidding chancellor long since buried. The guardians of Kaiserliches Kanzleiamt met Felix's predicament with blank stoicism. He was an invader in their house and judgement was coming slowly up the narrow stairs.

The methodical climb and the bobbing taunts of the light only served to increase his discomfort. Felix wanted it over.

'If you intend to kill me, get it over with would you?' he called out, but he knew they wouldn't, whoever they were. They wouldn't have gone to such lengths to snare him if death was all they had in mind; a quarrel in the back would have seen to that. They had had plenty of opportunities while he negotiated the treacherous rooftops. No, they had plans.

Which was worse, by far.

He couldn't even close his eyes.

The pair walked along the landing and into the green room. They were as mismatched a couple as their footsteps suggested. One was tall, emaciated, his hair drawn up in a topknot, the sides shaved high above his ears, the other was considerably shorter and moved with the arrogance of a natural born fighter but wore the robes of a priest.

'Felix, Felix, Felix,' the priest said, something approaching a smile on his ruddy face. It didn't last. The climb had taken its toll. He broke off into another fit of coughing. Felix saw the flecks of blood that spattered the priest's handkerchief as he took it away from his mouth. He secreted it in his robes, his smile returning. The priest's obvious delight at Felix's predicament had a cold chill quickening in his gut. He was face to face with the divine grifter, the Grand Theogonist himself. 'This is a pretty little pickle you've gotten yourself into, isn't it?'

Even if he had wanted to, Felix couldn't look away from the priest's scrutiny. He felt like a slab of meat being weighed out on the butcher's block.

He waited for the cleaver to fall.

'You could say that, but you could also say that it is getting more interesting by the minute,' Felix said finally, filling the uncomfortable silence. 'I mean, not so long ago I was all alone up here in the dark, thinking I'd probably rot here for months while the vampires had their fill below, and now look at me, blessed with an audience with the Grand Theogonist of Sigmar himself. Not what I would have expected, given the circumstances.'

'Well, my friend, desperate days call for desperate acts, isn't that what they say?'

'The grift,' Felix said, as though that explained everything.

'I'm sorry?'

'The grift, that's what this is all about isn't it?'

'I'm not sure I understand,' the priest said but the manner with which he said it gave lie to his words. He knew full well what Felix was talking about.

'The grift, the con, the big fat lie you just sold to half the people in this damned city.'

'Interesting, don't you think?' the priest said quite matter-of-factly to his partner. 'How our good thief here is in such an uncomfortable situation and yet he manages to turn the whole thing around so we appear to be the malcontents in this little scenario. It is quite a skill.' His smile fell away. What Felix saw was the face of a very, very tired man. Almost four days locked in the darkness beneath the cathedral had done nothing to help him and he obviously hadn't slept more than a handful of hours, if that.

'You're dying, aren't you?' he said, taking a wild guess: the tubercular coughing fits, the sallow skin, lack of sleep evidenced in the eyes, maybe it wasn't so wild after all.

'Aren't we all?' the priest offered, the flicker of a smile returning to his face.

'Some faster than others.'

'Indeed.'

'Never grift a grifter, that's what my old mum used to say, but that's what you are doing, isn't it?'

'Indeed,' the priest admitted. 'But quite irrelevant to the current situation we find ourselves in, wouldn't you agree?' Felix would have nodded, if he could have. 'I believe, and my friend here can confirm this, that the punishment for being caught *in flagrante delicto* as you have been, is quite steep.'

'You have seen the gallows outside,' the second man said, leaving Felix to put two and two together.

'And, alas, a defence of "I was tricked, yer honour" won't cut it. You're here, and your intentions are pretty plain. Once a thief, always a thief. You can dress up in fancy clothes and attend the society parties but that doesn't make you a gentleman, Felix. You're a thief.'

'And a damned good one,' Felix said.

'Well, present circumstances excluded, eh?'

'Can't really argue with that, can I? So, priest, what do you need a thief for? That is what this is all about, isn't it? You're hiring me for part of your grift.'

The Grand Theogonist bowed slightly. 'Very good, very good indeed. I can see why you come so highly recommended, Herr Mann. The price I am offering is an official pardon for all of your previous transgressions, including this one, and enough wealth in gemstones to reinvent yourself somewhere you are less well known, and live well for years to come. A small fortune, you might say. In addition, you are never to return to Altdorf, understood?'

'Sounds too good to be true so far, priest. Let's say I am waiting for the inevitable knife between the shoulder blades. No offence meant, but you religious types, well you aren't exactly trustworthy, far as I'm concerned.'

'A colourful way of putting it, but on the contrary the charge is a very simple one. I need you to steal a ring for me.'

'Steal a ring?' Felix repeated doubtfully. 'Whose?'

'Ah cutting to the quick of the matter, good, good. This is the situation: four days ago I retreated into the vaults of the cathedral, ostensibly to pray for wisdom. I was waiting for a very earthly sign though. This morning my visitor arrived with precious information. His message might very well save our beloved city from the beast at our doors.'

'And that secret was a ring?'

'So it would seem. I want that ring. I would have asked you out of public spiritedness, but this arrangement seemed far more practical. I do hope you will forgive me for taking advantage of your natural, ah, shall we say curiosity rather than greed? Greed is such an ugly word don't you think?'

'How did you know I would come in through this window?'

'Oh, I didn't. But all the other ways in have been blocked up, or are obviously guarded. This was the most obvious way in. Desperate times require desperate measures, and my colleagues convinced me that a man in their custody – Nevin? – could be "persusaded" to help us catch you. All I needed to do was sit and wait for word of your capture. Sometimes, I have found, it helps to think like the scum around you. I did not take long to deduce that in the citywide panic we find ourselves in, a profiteer like you would look to score an otherwise impossible job. I forced myself to think big. After that, the secret was to make a few of the plum pickings appear tastier – and easier – than the rest and let your – ah – curiosity do the rest.'

'So we could have been having this conversation almost anywhere in Altdorf?'

The priest nodded. 'Under identical circumstances.'

'I am impressed,' Felix said.

'Thank you. So to the crux of the matter: I want you to steal me a ring, a very special ring, tonight. If you agree, you will be freed from your bonds and given safe passage out of the city. If not, well, we won't go there just yet. So, do we have an agreement?'

'There's something you aren't saying, priest. It all sounds too easy. I can't work out why you need me, any one of your holy goons could steal a ring for you.'

'Ah, not quite. You see it is this ring that grants the vampire von Carstein his immortality. Without it, he can die like the rest of his filthy horde. You will find it, along with von Carstein, in his coffin in the white pavilions that have been erected on the mud flats before the Meadows Gate.'

'You have got to be out of your bloody mind!'

'Oh no, no. Think of it this way, Felix: the ultimate theft. No one but the very greatest could even dare, never mind achieve it. The next few hours offer you your very own slice of immortality. Imagine: Felix Mann, the greatest thief of all time, stole a ring of immortality from the hand of the Vampire Count while he slept in his coffin – in the middle of one of the largest armies the world has ever known. Come on, Felix, you have to admit that the notion intrigues you.'

'Scares the bloody life out of me, you mean. You'd have to be a fool to step out into the middle of that lot.'

'Or a dead man,' the Grand Theogonist said, bluntly. Suddenly, with that one sentence, Felix understood the full horror of the priest's threat. The gallows was more than just a death sentence for his crime, it was the promise of resurrection into the ranks of the Vampire Count's mindless undead. Damned if he did, very much damned if he didn't. What they were doing to him was monstrous.

'My god, there's no difference between you, is there? You're as bad as each other. How could you? How?'

'In the face of great evil, the end justifies, always, the means,' the priest said, sympathetically. 'I am sorry, Felix, but that is the reality of your situation. Now, you won't be alone out there. You will have help though most likely you will not be aware of it. My visitor is even now making arrangements to ease your passage through the enemy forces. According to him von Carstein ought to be sleeping for hours to come. I suggest we do not waste any more time.'

He had no choice.

CHAPTER TWENTY-THREE
The Left Hand of Darkness

ALTDORF
Winter, 2051

FELIX MANN WAS in hell.

He lay in the thick undergrowth beyond the city wall, watching von Carstein's men secure the perimeter of their huge encampment. Their torches burned, throwing hellish shadows over the scene. The dead lay where they had fallen when the Vampire Count had retreated to his coffin; the mud flats were covered with thousands and thousands of rotting bodies and bones.

The Grand Theogonist had given Felix a small double quarrel hand-held crossbow and directions to an inn on the outskirts of Altdorf, owned by the temple. It was surprising how far Sigmar's financial influence spread but it made sense that they would want some kind of back door out of the city to hide the comings and goings of their flock when necessary. The cellars connected to a subterranean labyrinth that offered escape from the city away from prying eyes. The tunnel came out two hundred yards beyond the wall, opening out into a cleft in the riverbank, a few feet above the fast flowing Reik. The cleft was sheltered from sight. It was perfect for what he had in mind.

He had been there for twenty minutes studying the movements of the enemy's soldiers. Already he had seen things he didn't want to believe.

They weren't all dead, nor were they all monsters.

There were normal people swelling the ranks of the undead.

Normal people. The idea that men would willingly choose to ally with the Vampire Count troubled him deeply. It was one thing to fight against monsters and lose, becoming one of them, but quite another to willingly align yourself with them. Felix had no idea how many living – breathing – humans he faced. The few he had seen strutted around the mud flats arrogantly. It would have been nice to see their smug grins slip when von Carstein realised he had been robbed of his precious ring. If the Grand Theogonist were right about the ring's nature, those traitors would be the first to face the vampire's wrath.

Felix saw a body swinging from a silver birch. It had been stripped and a sack had been put over its head. Something moved inside the sack. He stared for a moment, sickened by the slick, almost sinewy movement of the thing in there with the man. A ferret? A rat? Felix thought sickly. They had put vermin in the sack. It would have eaten half of the man's face before he died. It was a ghastly punishment.

How could they not understand that alive or dead they were worth as much to their twisted master?

Come dawn the zombie would tear the sack from its ruined head and rejoin the fight.

Felix shuddered.

Four of von Carstein's men stood talking less then fifteen feet away from his hiding place in the undergrowth.

'I tell ya, I heard summink, Berrin.'

'Nah, it's in yer head, lad. We're all alone with the dead out here.'

'That's what I'm saying, man. I heard summink and I'm thinking we should tell someone, because it might be important.'

'An' what good will that do, lad? They'll thank you kindly 'n then they'll wet themselves laughing 'bout you jumpin' at ghosts. Ain't none of us happy we're shacked up wif the dear departed so I say keep yer trap shut 'n wait for some other bugger to tell 'em about it's my advice.'

Good advice, Felix thought with a smile. *Now be a good boy and listen to it*. He lay very still but his fingers itched to nock an arrow and make sure the boy wouldn't live long enough to tell a soul.

'What if one of them's out there?'

'Then most likely he's running scared and no danger to anyone, right?'

'I ain't sure, Berrin. I mean–'

'You think too much lad, that's yer problem. Life ain't all mystery and intrigue. We's soldiers. Soldierin' is what we do and that means we do what we're told, no questions, even if it means we hafta do our business in a field a long way from home and don't get to feel them warm legs of our women wrapped around us when we go to sleep. It's our life, lad. You don't want the vampires thinking yer frightened of yer own shadow, now do ya? They'll just make yer life hell for it.'

Felix smiled at the veteran's logic. *What you don't see doesn't hurt you*, he added silently, willing the boy to let it drop.

The boy mumbled something that he couldn't make out and then started to wander off. The others followed. Felix watched them leave and didn't move until they were out of sight. He rose slowly into a tight crouch, scanning the line of white pavilions to make certain no one was watching. Satisfied, he crept along the rim of the riverbank.

He knew what he had to do. It was suicide, he knew, but the priest knew how to play his ego. Not for the first time that night he cursed his stupidity. The Grand Theogonist was taking a massive gamble, but if it worked… On the humiliating walk down through the counting house the priest talked about an army being like an animal.

And what do you do to a wild animal? You cut its head off, Felix thought, the voice in his head sounding very much like the priest's.

He didn't have much of a plan beyond sneaking in to the Vampire Count's tent, taking the ring and running for his life. Felix had already reconciled himself to the fact that he was unlikely to reach the third step of the plan.

In a way, that didn't matter.

The first few fat drops of rain fell. In five minutes it was pouring from the heavens. The moon was a thin silver sliver in the cloudy sky.

He counted forty-three fires scattered across the mud flats, and guessed there were a dozen men per fire out there warming themselves on the flames. These were the living contingent. About five hundred men, give or take. He didn't want to think about the rest of the Vampire Count's malignant army.

He waited, giving them time to get tired.

Tired men made mistakes.

He closed his eyes and pictured himself walking among them. Cutting their throats while they slept. The image wrapped a chill around his heart not because it was murder but because it was useless. Dead or alive they served the count.

Dead or alive.

The camp had been quiet for more than an hour, soldiers lying in their bedrolls around the dwindling fires.

Felix laid his crossbow in the tall grass and rested the quiver with his extra bolts in it across the wooden shaft. He wouldn't need it where he was going. He took first one dagger and then the other from his boot sheaths and tested their edge with his thumb. Satisfied, he kissed both blades and slipped them back into their sheaths and rose into a crouch, creeping forward a dozen paces through the litter of corpses, his eyes on the nearest fire.

Carrion birds picked at the dead.

He moved slowly. His heart hammered as he lowered himself to the ground again and scanned the circle of fires. It was so loud in his ears it was a wonder von Carstein's soldiers didn't hear it. He didn't move a muscle. The soldiers there were oblivious to his presence. Some slept, others talked, their conversations muted. He couldn't make out what they were saying but as long as no one was yelling and pointing in his direction they could say whatever the hell they wanted for all he cared.

He knew what he had to do even though it revolted him. He looked around for some particularly wretched corpse, ripped his clothes and smeared himself in its blood and rotting flesh until he looked like one of the count's disgusting flesh-eating ghouls.

The darkness was his strongest ally. He clung to it as he crossed the no-man's land between the dry river and the officers' pavilion. To his left, someone moved, rolling over in his bedroll. Felix stood still.

'What you doin'?' the soldier grumbled sleepily.

'Takin' a leak, man,' Felix muttered, hoping he sounded aggrieved enough to mask the sudden swell of fear he felt rising.

'Well, hurry up about, would ya, some of us are tryin' to get some shut-eye. Next time drain the snake before ya hit the hay.'

He waited. Sweat ran down into the palms of his clenched fists. He felt so exposed and vulnerable his skin itched. He looked up into the rain and savoured the feel of it on his face. The kiss of the rain was seductive. He could have stayed there savouring the sensation of it running down his face because he knew it could so easily be the last pleasant sensation he ever felt.

Felix started to move, quietly. The soldiers slept on.

Von Carstein's pavilion was in the centre of the camp, ringed by smaller tents, but none of them were close enough fall into the pavilion's shadow.

A slow grin spread across Felix's face when he saw that there was no one guarding the entrance and the oil light in front of the opening had been left to burn low enough that even the peripheral shadows remained untouched. The rain masked the sound of his footsteps. Instinct told him to be wary. It was too easy. This time he listened to it. The spot of skin between his shoulder blades prickled. It was almost as though von Carstein's men were being deliberately sloppy, letting the lights burn low so that the unguarded flaps of the count's pavilion were nothing more than the bait on a trap set to lure him out into the open and into their steel jaws.

He stopped dead in his tracks.

The figure of a tall, thin man stepped out from between two of the pavilions. The man was hooded but Felix recognised him from the way he moved. It was the stranger from the alleyway; the one who had told the priest about the ring's supposed powers.

The priest had promised help. Felix understood the seemingly lax defences around the count's tent now. The stranger had had a hand in it, he was sure.

The stranger nodded, but said nothing before he strode away into the heart of the darkness beyond the flickering lanterns.

The stranger moved with grace, barely making a sound, barely even disturbing the air with his passage. It was, Felix knew, unnatural.

A priest and a vampire, strange bedfellows indeed, Felix thought, gliding between the canvas walls of two pavilions. He could hear the muted sounds of conversation coming from inside. Rain drummed on the canvas. He walked slowly toward the count's pavilion, waiting for the challenge that never came. He looked over his shoulder, towards the dark shadows of the spires of Altdorf, and slipped through the opening into the tent.

It was darker inside without the lantern to illuminate anything beyond the vaguest of outlines. Felix drew the tent flap closed behind him again. The soft regular sound of his breathing filled the darkness.

He couldn't allow himself to think about what he was doing or he wouldn't be able to do it.

Reaching out, Felix felt his way through the darkness toward the coffins at the rear of the tent. There were two: one had to be the count's, the other his wife's.

The air had a strange tang to it. Some kind of perfumed wood had been burned in the makeshift hearth and the residue still clung to the air.

Felix knelt beside the first coffin as though in prayer. It was considerably larger than the other, decorated with black iron clasps that were open. Steeling himself against the sudden swell of fear, Felix eased back the coffin lid.

The rain was loud on the roof of the tent.

He looked down at the dead man in the coffin. In the flickering light he appeared surprisingly young. Lush dark hair spilled loosely around his shoulders. He was handsome, his smooth, almost aquiline features giving no hint of the depravity that had replaced his soul.

The Vampire Count's hands were folded across his chest. He wore an extravagant signet ring on his right hand, with a garish gem set amid what looked like wings, the tips studded with precious stones. It was ostentatious. On his left hand the count wore a dull band of what looked like black iron.

Felix didn't dare move.

He stared at the ornate ring with its dark gemstone setting for a full five minutes, barely sparing a second glance for the plain iron ring, before he reached into the coffin and began to prize the signet ring off the count's cold dead flesh.

Von Carstein didn't stir.

Felix weighed the ring in his hand. It was undoubtedly worth an Emperor's ransom but... something about it nagged at the back of his mind. It didn't make sense. Surely the priest wasn't thinking of collecting treasures – and the best grift is the one you don't see. Felix smiled to himself and pried the plain black iron ring from the count's other hand. He laid signet ring on the vampire's chest.

Felix caught himself in the process of slipping the ring onto his index finger. 'Stupid,' he muttered, realising he hadn't brought a pouch or purse to carry the stolen trinket. If it was magic who knew what kind of damage wearing it could do? He had sudden flashes of being paralyzed and being held helpless in von Carstein's pavilion until the count rose.

He closed his fist about the ring and backed cautiously out of the pavilion.

He stared at the coffin, expecting the vampire to come raging out of it at any second, fear hammering against his breastbone as he crept toward the tent flaps, conjuring a mass of putrefied zombies to swarm over him as he slipped out of the tent into the everlasting night, but, mercifully, the dead didn't rise.

He ran for his life.

CHAPTER TWENTY-FOUR
Out of the Darkness, Rising

ALTDORF
Winter, 2051

IT WAS A night for ghosts, ghouls and wraiths, for zombies, ghasts and wights.

It was a night for the dead.

The theft of his ring had unleashed von Carstein's wrath. The Vampire Count stood on mud flats before Altdorf, gripped by a feverish, wild rage. His fury had summoned a blizzard, the elements buckling beneath his black madness.

The rain turned to snow, the snow fell thick and fast without settling on the sodden ground. Jon Skellan and Jerek von Carstein stood beside the count as he raged against the heavens and threatened to tear down the walls of Altdorf with his bare hands. Neither had ever seen the count so utterly devoid of reason or control. It was truly frightening. Von Carstein stood in the centre of the mud flats, his hands raised and head thrown back, shrieking as the wind and snow buffeted him. It was as though his furious incantation drew the storm to him.

Lightning appeared to dance across the tips of the Vampire Count's fingers before it clawed its way back up into the heavens, piercing the dark heart of the night with its ribbons of jagged blue.

Thunder cracked.

The ground beneath their feet and all around them rippled with unnatural life. Small tremors and their aftershocks ran in concentric circles out from von Carstein's feet as the summoning took shape. Drawing strength from nature and all that grew around him, Vlad von Carstein channelled his raw anger into the pattern being formed by his fingers, feeding it to the fallen buried beneath the snow and dirt.

'RISE!' he shrieked. 'RISE!'

All around them the dead were rising.

The trees along the riverbank nearest Skellan had already begun to wither, the needles of the evergreens tinged brown as the life was leached out of them to feed the count's black magic.

The dead lurched and staggered to their feet, even as the ground beneath them buckled and trembled with revulsion. Ghouls cried out in anguish. Wights shrieked as they wound themselves around the rising corpses and tore off into the night sky.

Von Carstein's fury was terrifying.

A moment later the first dead fingers breached the wet surface of the mud flats, clawing at the air for the life that had already been taken from them once.

'Here they come,' Skellan said unnecessarily. His awe at von Carstein's strength resonated in his voice. That the Vampire Count could draw the long dead of Altdorf out from beneath the damned city and onto the plains was incredible. Even fuelled by von Carstein's wrath it was an agonizingly slow process. Bone by bone the dead crawled out of their graves, impelled by von Carstein's ranting spell. At first they came out of the earth one or two at a time, but then they clawed their way free of the dirt in their tens and twenties, all the poor souls who had fallen on the fields before the greatest city of the Empire. Friend or foe, it no longer mattered as they were born again into von Carstein's army.

And they weren't all whole.

Some of the dead rose in pieces, an arm clawing the surface, torso and head dragged up behind it, without legs to support itself where the rot of decay had eaten through it. More and more body parts rose, drawn by von Carstein's hateful summons.

The snow swirled around the mud flats, whipped around by the bluster of the wind. Gradually the snow turned to hail. Hard pellets pelted the dead as they rose.

The Vampire Count's face was taut, his lips moving as though with a purpose of their own, reciting over and over again a litany of pain and anguish as he drew the dead from the dirt.

When he was done close to five thousand dead had risen to swell the ranks of his pestilential force, looking once more with amazement upon the walls of their beloved city. Their bodies were in various states of decay, from the stripped and yellowed bones of the long dead to the rotted flesh of the newly deceased. Von Carstein screamed at the heavens, his voice ringing out the death of a thousand seasons as it duelled another thunderclap.

'Look upon the fall of mankind! See death before your walls. The dead rise. The dead reclaim what once was theirs. Look around you. Behold the Kingdom of the Dead! Behold. Behold! Tremble before its majesty. Fear its might. Fall to your knees. The dead rise and the living fall!'

When his gaze came down, Skellan saw Vlad's eyes were glazed with a wild staring madness.

'The dead are crawling out of their graves, even Morr can't hold them back,' Jerek seethed. 'Ten thousand today, another ten thousand tomorrow? Next week? A world full of dead men and cattle.'

'I know,' Skellan said, savouring the delicious thought. 'The Kingdom of the Dead. Who could possibly stand against it?'

Von Carstein pointed his finger at the wall and the bone siege engines rolled forward. The dead screamed and yelled and shrieked and wailed, and threw themselves at the huge stone wall. Others clung to the towers, riding them as they rolled remorselessly toward the high walls, sixty feet high, twenty feet wide, ballistae, catapults, and ladders. Suddenly von Carstein was the calm amongst the storm.

Frightened archers fired wild arrows from the battlements.

Skellan watched it all in mute admiration, though at times it was difficult to see through the driving hail.

Along the walls the defenders set up notched poles to help repel the siege ladders while others lined up hundreds of clay jars filled with oil as soul-searing screams rent the darkness.

Skellan's mind was icy calm as he took it all in. He let von Carstein waste his energies with fury. Wrath, vengeance, they were all human emotions. Surely the Vampire Count understood that? It was nothing more than pride and arrogance.

The siege engines lumbered toward the walls, straddling the mud flats like something out of myth, colossal giants of flesh fused with living bone. Fires burned at their tops, casting ghastly shadows down the lengths of the infernal machines. The dead clustered around them, heaving them relentlessly toward the high walls.

The city would fall, Skellan knew. It had no choice.

That was the apocalyptic reality of the Risen Dead. Nothing would ever be the same again. The skeletal arms of the onagers cranked back and released scores of flaming and rotting skulls, catapulting them high over the walls. The second volley was different. The buckets of the catapults were loaded with huge chunks of granite, basalt and other hard stones that the dead had scavenged from the land around Altdorf.

The archers on the walls looked on in frozen horror as the sky filled with deadly stone rain that hammered down all around them, shattering the stones, fracturing the walls of buildings and caving in slates and roof tiles as though they were tissue paper. The third volley was, again, fire. The flaming skulls whistled as they swooped through the air. This time, they burned where they hit, the fires catching inside buildings as well as outside. The fourth volley was stone.

The boulders crashed into the battlements and arced over the walls in a monstrous rain of rock and debris.

The noise was horrific.

But the silence that followed it was twice as terrifying as the carnage revealed itself from beneath the clouds of smoke and dust the bombardment had caused. Fifteen archers and another thirty pikemen died beneath the crushing weight of the gate tower as it collapsed beneath the onslaught of huge granite boulders. Moments later their broken and battered bodies were jerking around awkwardly trying to stand on shattered bones as they answered von Carstein's summons to undeath. With the enemy suddenly risen within their midst the defenders along the wall fought for their lives as their brothers in arms turned on them in death. Silver blades flashed in the firelight as they threw themselves at friends they had been talking to only moments before. Von Carstein's curse was sick. It shattered the morale of the defenders to see their friends fall only to rise again as puppets of the beast. There was no safe place. Death could come from any side, in any guise.

Skellan couldn't begin to wonder what they were thinking as they threw the broken corpses over the crenulated wall as though they were garbage.

Still the pile of broken bones writhed at the foot of the city wall, desperate to rejoin the fighting.

The walls withstood the first wave of horror.

For five hours the deadly rain of stone and fire continued, smashing the bodies of the defenders to bloody wrecks, powdering huge segments of the city walls, completely obliterating the spires of three temples and setting light to hundreds of houses. It was merciless. The hail ceased but it was still bitterly cold out there. Stretcher-bearers had two grisly jobs, to tend to the wounded and hack up and burn the dead. They couldn't allow sentimentality to get in the way. They built massive funeral pyres in the squares across the city, dragging the fallen into the flames before they could turn on them and attack the defenders on the wall from behind.

The city reeked of burnt flesh.

Skellan breathed deeply of the smell.

He stood silently, watching the smoke billowing up from the city. The city would fall, broken, like the bodies of its defenders crushed beneath the rain of boulders.

The siege towers rocked into place snug up against the high walls and the dead poured from them, zombies burning and falling away where the Altdorfers soaked them with oils and ignited them with flaming arrows, and skeletons shattered beneath the battery of warhammers and maces as the defenders fought desperately for their lives.

Their desperation gave them strength; they fought like savages.

And still, fresh horrors came, mocking their defence. The onagers and mangonels launched rotting body parts riddled with plague and pestilence over the walls, and the dead followed them with hideous battle-cries, throwing themselves at the city walls as arrows and oil and fire rained down on them. The dead hauled themselves up the giant siege engines and onto the battlements where they were met by Altdorfer's steel. Swords clashed with bone and steel, the archers were joined by axmen on the wall-walk. They fought side by side. Men screamed and cried out, fell and were sickeningly raised again by the dark magic von Carstein had woven over the battlefield, parts of their bodies smashed beyond all recognition, bloodied, cut, ruined.

Vengeful death descended on the city of Altdorf and all along the walls the exhausted men knew dawn offered no respite. The sun would not rise to save them.

This was the last stand.

Already the battlements were slippery with blood and the foot of the wall cluttered with bodies. As the defenders threw the fallen off the battlements they poured oil onto the corpses and lit them with flaming arrows, the oil and flame searing the flesh from the bones of the dead. And still the skeletons rose, charred, lumps of flesh clinging to the bones where it hadn't burned away.

It was a glimpse of hell on earth.

Bloody hour followed bloody hour as the dead surged up the ladders of flesh and bone and the siege engines lobbed horrors from the sky. It was endless: hacking, slashing, tearing, rending, clawing, biting, flaying, dying and burning. As more and more zombies spilled onto the wall-walk more and more of the dead went unburned and rose jerkily to join forces with them. Always though, they were beaten back, albeit barely. Sheer weight of numbers, coupled with the exhaustion of the Altdorfers, would drag the city down eventually. Skellan judged the defenders had perhaps another few hours worth of spirited resistance left in them as it stood, but von Carstein had held back his vampires. Unleashed now, the humans wouldn't stand a chance.

The hours were filled with agony and the screams of death.

The siege engines were ablaze, the living dead fused in the skeletal towers crying out in agony as the flames consumed them. The defenders poured hot oil on the towers, stoking the fire. It made no difference. The towers were only constructs, the day had yielded enough deaths to build twenty more towers if von Carstein so desired.

One by one the towers collapsed in on themselves and toppled over, giving the defenders precious minutes to catch their breath before the onslaught redoubled.

One man strode like a giant along the battlements though, clad in the white of Sigmar, his huge axe bloodied, defying the dead, encouraging the defenders to stand and fight once more even when exhaustion threatened to betray them, tapping on reserves of strength they didn't know they had: the Grand Theogonist, Wilhelm III. The man had a warrior's soul. He may have taken to prayers but he was a fighter. Two decades older than some of the men at his side, the priest shamed them with his stamina and determination.

'Vampires! To me!' von Carstein commanded. It was almost as though he had read Skellan's mind but of course he hadn't, the count was a supreme tactician and an excellent reader of men. He knew the defenders were weakening.

He pointed at the walls.

Skellan grinned wolfishly. Beside him Jerek nodded.

It was time.

Finally there would be blood enough to satisfy even his darkest thirst.

Skellan threw his head back and howled at the flawless black sky.

The others took up his cry as their features twisted and mutated into the bestial muzzles and elongated jaw-line of the beasts they carried within them.

The vampires answered Vlad von Carstein's call.

CHAPTER TWENTY-FIVE
The Fallen

ALTDORF
Winter, 2051

'THEY'RE COMING AGAIN!' someone yelled.

The men were beaten. Exhaustion lay heavy on them. The damned dark would never lift. The respite had been pitifully brief. The Grand Theogonist hefted his axe and walked along the allure, offering words of encouragement to the men in the face of the nameless death swarming up the ladders and over the battlements. He braced himself against a splintered merlon and watched the dead charge.

'Sweet Sigmar…' an archer beside him said, seeing the bestial faces of the vampires as they swept forward, von Carstein himself in their midst.

'Stand tall, soldier. The next few hours determine whether we live or die today.'

The archer nodded sickly. 'Aye, we'll fight the devils 'til we drop, an' then…' he let the thought trail away bitterly.

The priest's shoulder burned and his knees were aflame; every step cost him but he couldn't afford to let the men see his weakness. That was why he had worn the white of his god over his mail, so that every man along the wall-walk could see him and take heart from his presence even as the darkness overwhelmed them. He was an old man and he was dying. Both were irrefutable facts, yet when they looked at him they saw Sigmar himself striding down the battlements, smiting foes and lifting hearts.

He would not fail them.

Blood spattered his white tabard and the silver rings of his mail. None of it, blessedly, was his.

He looked at the archer. The man's eyes were red-rimmed with tiredness. He looked like a beaten dog. Along the line men sat with their backs to the wall, recovering what little strength they could. A few had closed their eyes and dozed, taking advantage of the lull in the fighting. With the siege engines buckled and destroyed they believed themselves safe for the moment. Others stood, staring out at the vampires as they swarmed toward them, looks of sheer horror frozen on their faces as they squared up ready for the fighting to begin again in earnest.

'Look at them, tell me what you see?' the priest said, resting a steadying hand on the archer's shoulder.

'The end of the world.'

'Not while I live and breathe lad, not while I live and breathe. Look again.'

The archer scanned the lines of the vampires, his gaze drawn back to von Carstein himself. 'He looks… like a daemon possessed.'

'Better. It is the blood lust. That and fear. We've done that to him, soldier. He looks up at us and he knows fear.'

'You think?'

'Oh, I know, believe me.'

The vampires reached the wall and began scrambling up it like flies swarming over a corpse. They scuttled up the stonework.

The priest laughed bitterly.

'What's so funny?' the archer asked. It was obvious the priest's lack of fear horrified him.

'My own stupidity,' the priest said. 'I thought we had bought ourselves a few hours. Instead we face death again, grown faster and more lethal even as we have tired and weakened. So be it. Up, soldier, let's make them earn our corpses, shall we?'

The priest sent a runner down the stairs to warn the reserves that the fighting was about to begin again, and had them divided into three groups, ready to plug any gap in the wall should it be breached. There would be no escape from the wall for him or the men around him. He had resigned himself to dying on the walls, the only comfort being that he would be dying free and that had to be enough for him. He coughed, a hacking tubercular rattle, and spat out a wad of blood and phlegm. The bout of coughing served as a wake-up call; he wasn't going to live forever, instead he had to make his death count. Make it meaningful.

'Oil!' he yelled, sending the message down the line. In seconds the last few clay jars were being thrown down at the monsters scaling the city walls, some bounced while others broke. The thick black oil splashed down the stonework and covered some of the vampires. 'Fire!' Arrows dripping flame skidded down the wall, igniting the oil with a dull *crump*. A dozen of the vampires fell away from the wall blazing like human torches as the oil caught light and seared away their flesh. Their screams were terrible as the flames engulfed their bodies. The others came on, like demented spiders, faster, stronger.

The priest drew himself to his full height and hefted his huge double-headed axe.

'Come on then, my beauties, sooner you get up the wall sooner we send you back to hell.'

The men around him stood, bracing themselves for the attack.

They knew what was coming and yet not one of them gave in to the instinct to run. He was more proud of them then than he had been for a thousand days through a thousand different circumstances. They were good men. They were going to die like heroes. Each and every one of them. He felt a swell of grief and pride at knowing them, being part of this with them. It was one thing to share your life with someone, it was quite another to willingly share your death.

'FOR SIGMAR!' he bellowed suddenly, holding his axe overhead.

'ALTDORF!' someone answered down the wall-walk. The cry went up:

'ALTDORF! ALTDORF! ALTDORF!'

They might not have been spiritual men but their words shook the foundations of the city wall. Spear butts and sword hilts clanged off the stonework adding to the chant.

'Sigmar help us,' the young archer said as the first of the beasts crested the battlements. A spear thrust in its face sent the creature spinning away from the wall, clutching the bloody weapon where it stuck between soft flesh and hard bone.

The next vampire over the wall was one he knew, a man he thought dead. In another life Jerek Kruger had been a friend. Now the priest stared at the lord of the White Wolves, still dressed in his ceremonial armour and furs, huge warhammer in hand, his face pallid and tinged blue, and knew that his friend was gone. The thing that stood in his place was a cold-blooded killer. The Wolf howled and threw himself into the thick of the fighting, his warhammer cracking the skull of the first man to get in its way. More vampires surged over the walls even as the defenders hacked and slashed at them, trying desperately to drive them back.

The preternatural speed of the vampires coupled with their awesome strength made them a deadly foe. On the narrow wall-walk where the press of bodies made it almost impossible to swing a sword, they were overwhelming. They fought like daemons possessed. For every one vampire slain eight, ten, twelve, defenders fell.

The priest swallowed back his rising horror.

This was why Sigmar had chosen him. He was a fighter first, a man of god second. He threw himself into the fray. Against the fury of the vampires he fought with curious detachment, instinct governing his actions; he caught a sword blow on the shaft of

his axe, turned it against his would be killer and drove
the flat of his axe head into the vampire's face, bursting the cartilage of the creature's nose and staggering
it back the step he needed to roll his wrists and
deliver a killing blow, slamming the honed edge of
the axe blade into the vampire's throat. It was a massive blow, the priest's full strength behind it. The
metal sheared through dead flesh and crunched into
the bone vertebrae. The creature's head rolled back,
half decapitated, hands fluttering up weakly to clutch
at its throat even as its body collapsed under it.

He kicked the monster from the wall and met the
next attack head on.

Around him good men died.

He couldn't allow himself to mourn them.

The wall had to hold. If they lost ground here von
Carstein would be inside the city. Images of slaughter
filled the priest's mind as he hammered the twin-
headed blade of his axe into the chest of another fiend,
opening the creature up from throat to sternum. The
vampire's guts spilled onto the wall-walk. The beast
clung to the handle of the priest's axe as it died, its face
shifting back to that of a handsome young man. The
priest fancied he saw, in that death mask, a look of
peace that defied the vampire's violent death. A third
vampire fell beneath his axe, its head splitting like an
overripe pumpkin as the axe bit into it.

Ducking beneath a slashing sword, he turned and
disembowelled a leering vampire with a staggering
backhanded sweep of his massive axe.

He stepped over the dead body and moved in to support part of the wall's defence that was crumbling
under constant assault from the dead.

A flaming skull shattered at his feet, splashing fire up in front of his face.

The priest backed up a step, waiting for the flames to abate.

The sounds and the stench of death were terrible. It was a bloodbath.

Defenders fell from the wall, broken and bloody, their bodies torn to shreds by tooth and claw, slit open by cold steel, shattered by the crushing blows of warhammers and smashed by falling stones as the catapults renewed their barrage.

Here, at the end of his life, on the walls of Altdorf, he was returning to what he had been before Sigmar saved him and raised him up: a killer. He had come full circle. Though not quite, in taking the name Wilhelm III he had left behind the brute he had been, a drunk, shunned by family and friends, given to rage and violence. He had been shaped by the will of Sigmar, forged by the fires of worship and atonement, to die here, giving his life in defence of the greatest city mankind had ever known. He was Sigmar's hammer made flesh.

'I will not fail you,' he pledged, stepping over the dying flames.

He saw von Carstein.

If ever he had wondered about the lord of the dead's humanity, this ended it. Von Carstein was no man; he was everything the priest had feared, a daemon possessed.

A killing machine.

The enraged Vampire Count was fighting his way along the battlements to face him.

The sounds of battle crystallised in his ears. He remembered them, each and every one, as though

they were the last he would hear: cries, screams,
curses, pleas, steel on steel, steel on flesh. Another
blast of fire roared around his head, black smoke cur-
dling his vision. The priest forced himself to go
through it. As the smoke cleared he saw he was standing in a swath of burned and blistered flesh as men
lay wounded and bleeding. They had been caught in
the fire. Smoke curled up off their bodies. Strips of
their flesh were charred black. The priest shielded his
nose with his arm. Still it smelled sickeningly of
roasted meat.

A scorched face, weeping blood and pus, cracked
and completely unrecognisable, reared up in front of
his, a ruined hand reaching out imploringly for his
help.

He stepped over the fallen. There was nothing he
could do for them.

Von Carstein cut down two defenders, his wailing
blade cleaving through the right arm of one, severing
it just below the elbow, and the head of another.

'I see you, priest!' he yelled above the tumult.

Out of the cacophony the priest heard a whistling
shrillness followed by shattering impacts and screaming. Below the wall-walk men were running, shields
over their heads. Some had already fallen. Others
were trying to reach them, drag them away, destroy
them, before they could rise and turn against them.
Small fires burned everywhere.

'Come to me then! Come and face your doom,
vampire!' the priest rasped, trying to stop his voice
shaking as he moved to meet the vampire.

Flying splinters of rock and dirt sprayed him; he felt
their sting as they cut his face.

The vampire barged another soldier aside.

They were fifteen feet apart on the wall-walk, the allure slick with blood and dust. The Grand Theogonist hefted his axe, feeling its reassuring heaviness in his hands.

Behind him, a chunk of masonry fell, cracking the wall-walk. More rocks and stones followed as the machicolations caved in beneath the barrage of debris. Part of the wall-walk broke away.

Ten feet apart.

The Vampire Count's mouth opened; he roared his anger and hurled himself at the priest. The priest let the monster's momentum carry him through as he brought his axe up to anticipation of the savage blow. The beast hit him full on, staggering him back four steps. He drove the butt of the axe handle up toward von Carstein's face, catching the vampire a glancing blow on the cheek. Von Carstein bellowed, driving the priest back with the sheer force of his anger as he hit the man, three times, with dizzying speed. The blows snapped the priest's head back three times in quick succession. The Vampire Count was rabid.

The Grand Theogonist shook his head. His own blood from his ruined nose sprayed his arms. He winced, tasting blood where it spilled into his mouth.

'Time to die, holy man,' von Carstein rasped vehemently.

The vampire launched a double attack, swinging the wailing sword high and wide with his right hand and slamming his left into the priest's face. It was a punishing blow but physical pain didn't follow. He was numb to it. There was no feeling. The priest grunted at the impact and cracked the shaft of his axe

off the vampire's elbow, bringing the flat head of the
axe round to hammer into the side of von Carstein's
head. The vampire vaulted backwards, easily avoiding
the wild blow – but it bought the priest precious
breathing space.

'You talk a lot for a dead man.'

'The same could be said about you.'

The priest pressed his offensive, windmilling his
axe forward. Von Carstein ducked under two blows
but two more rocked him, one cracking against his
jaw the other crunching into his left shoulder. The
vampire rubbed a hand across his mouth; it came
away slick with blood. He countered with a
lightning-fast jab that nearly took the priest's eye
out. Blood ran from the gash in his brow, into his
left eye. The eye socket itself swelled up purple and
bloody quickly. Half the world blurred as he lost
most of his vision from it.

'How does it feel to be mortal?' von Carstein
goaded. The count laughed deeply and whipped his
blade out in a slashing arc, keeping the priest on his
back foot.

'You tell me?' the priest said contemptuously. He
swatted away the vampire's lunge with the butt of
his axe. 'Without that damned ring of yours how are
you going to come back this time?'

Lunatic rage flared in the count's dead eyes. He
held up his right hand contemptuously, showing
the priest the ornate signet ring on his middle finger.

'Your man failed, priest.'

The priest raised his head high, catching the first
fresh flakes of white as the snow returned, whirling

in the air. Life, hope, drained from him. Mann had failed. They were doomed, all of them.

Von Carstein hit him.

He felt as if he had been slammed face first into a stone wall. A pang of fear went through him, rising up from his gut to his throat, a desperate urge to vomit. Terror dried his mouth, seized his body. Cold specks of snow kissed his face, melted and slid down his neck and beneath his armour.

The darkness closed around him.

He was an old man, his strength slowly fading with each blow given and received, whereas his enemy was immortal, strengthened by the blood and death all around him. He knew deep down in his bones his death was inevitable. They traded blows, hard blows. Fits of coughing shook him. The vampire was merciless, driving his advantage home. His blade whipped out again and again, nicking the priest, shallow cuts that stung more than they bled. Two cuts were bad though, slicing deep into his upper left arm and low on his left side. Both bled profusely, yet still he faced von Carstein, defying him with sheer bloody determination.

He winced at another stabbing pain as the wailing blade slammed into his left side, forcing the rings of his mail into the deep cut. The pain was incredible. His vision blacked out for a heartbeat, his head filled with the sheer agony of the blow. He staggered but refused to buckle. The priest lifted his head up.

'Come on, vampire. Is this it? Is this the might of Vlad von Carstein? Stealer of souls, king of the dead?' He shook his head. 'I am an old man. I haven't lifted a weapon in thirty years. You are *nothing*, vampire. Nothing. It ends here.'

The fighting raged on around the two combatants, death a constant companion on the battlements and the streets below. Screams of anger and pain met the clash of steel and the insidious rasp of fire.

He was dying. He was bleeding out his strength ounce by red ounce.

'You're a fool, priest, like all of your kind. You talk of good, of evil,' von Carstein said, advancing once more. His eyes blazed with naked savagery. 'There is no good, there is no evil. I have passed beyond death, priest. Understand that, there is nothing. I have been there. I have seen the lie of your promised land. My body died a long time ago, far, far away from here, yet here I am. Living. There are things – powers, priest, powers – so far removed from your philosophy they would dwarf your mind, things so old death no longer touches them. Death no longer weakens them. Look at yourself, priest, and then look at me. You can feel it in you, can't you? You can feel it creeping through your limbs, from the cuts in your side and your arm reaching down through the tiring flesh into your soul. Into you. Death. It's in your eyes.'

A huge boulder smashed into the wall-walk; the floor didn't split but it shivered beneath his feet and the existing cracks began to tear themselves apart under the strain.

The priest ignored the rumbling. He did not look down. He only had eyes for the vampire.

'Cling to your half-life, fiend. Live in an eternal dark, for all the good it will do you. You have failed. Here, this is where it ends. Look around you. Altdorf stands defiant. Through the smoke and the dust the people are already beginning the process of healing. They go on living, it is what people do.'

'They go on dying,' von Carstein rasped, slicing a cut deep into the priest's right arm. The steel chain linked rings splintered and broke, gouging deep into his flesh.

He bit back on the pain.

With an immense effort he hefted his huge axe. He could barely see though the veil of pain the vampire's cuts had pulled down over his eyes.

'You can burn us and bleed us, von Carstein, but you won't crush us. Cut me down, another will rise up in my stead. You have failed, vampire. An old man and some brave-hearted boys have beaten you.'

'Hardly, fool. You can barely stand, let alone fight on. You're done. It's over… but,' the Vampire Count added, almost as an afterthought, 'you would make a good vampire, priest. I have never taken a priest.'

The priest tilted his neck, exposing the hard pulse of his jugular. His hands clenched around the shaft of the axe. He straightened his head up and snorted. 'I thought not.'

Wilhelm III, Grand Theogonist, drew himself erect. It took all of his will and strength not to cry out against the biting pain of his wounds. His head swam. He didn't have long left and he knew it.

Von Carstein cut him again, a slash that sliced through his ear and buried itself deep in his shoulder.

He staggered a step forward, barely keeping his feet under him. The pain was unbearable. His vision misted momentarily, then cleared, and he saw with stunning clarity what he had to do.

Tears stung his cheeks.

Von Carstein rammed his sword into the priest's left shoulder; the pain of withdrawal as the vampire wrenched the wailing blade out of his flesh was blinding. A second thrust plunged into his chest, between his ribs, and into his lung. He had felt nothing like it in his life. He was dead, living on borrowed seconds, a final gift from Sigmar. He knew what he had to do. The axe weighed heavily in his hands. He dropped it.

Von Carstein laughed, a bitter mocking sound.

'It seems you were wrong, priest, when you promised me I would die here. This is my city now. Mine, priest! It is you who has failed, you sanctimonious fool. Look at you. Look at you! You are a wreck of a human being. You shame your god do you know that? You shame your god.'

The priest swallowed the pain even as it consumed him. He looked at his lifeblood leaking out of him. There was nothing left. Nothing. He could barely raise his head to face the monster.

Instead of wasting his life on words the priest screamed, embracing the rawness of it, using the blistering pain to drive him on, and in that scream he became like an animal, primal and deadly.

He threw himself at the Vampire Count, his body slamming into von Carstein, his staggering momentum carrying them both back into the bracing wall of the machicolations.

They hung there for a heartbeat, balanced precariously between the wall-walk and thin air, von Carstein using every ounce of his incredible strength to push back against the priest but even as it looked as though the priest's last desperate lunge would end in futility his foot stumbled into a deep fissure in the stone floor. With the full weight of the priest pressing down on him von Carstein couldn't recover his balance. He was helpless. The priest had his arms pinned. He couldn't even reach out to grab hold of something. The priest's grip was iron.

The priest couldn't make out more than a blurred outline of black where von Carstein was trapped in front of him.

With a massive grunt and the very last ounce of his strength, the priest pushed. The vampire strained, struggling to keep his footing but there was nothing he could do. In desperation the priest found the strength to take them both off the battlements.

They fell, locked together in a deadly embrace.

Neither screamed, even as their bodies were broken by the fall. The arc of their descent carried them out into the closest of the shallow ditches, behind the fast flowing moat of the Reik.

The ditches lined with sharpened stakes.

The stake pierced von Carstein's back, bursting out of his chest even as it sank into the priest's. The vampire's eyes flared open in shock even as the weight of the priest drove him deeper onto the spike.

A sound like thunder cracked through the world. He felt it bone-deep.

The vampire gagged, blood leaking out of his mouth as he tried to speak. The priest couldn't make out a word. It didn't matter. The blood told him all he needed to know. He could walk the path of souls now to Sigmar's side.

'I did not fail you...' And though no one heard him, it didn't matter.

There was no pain, only blessed relief.

He bowed his head and let his life go.

The first chink of sunlight broke through the black sky, the ray of light a column of gold on the black of the battlefield.

They died there, trapped together in the sun, vampire and holy man.

CHAPTER TWENTY-SIX
Streets of Ash and Hope

ALTDORF
Winter, 2051

CITIES, UNLIKE MEN, are immortal.

A scholar had said that. Felix couldn't remember
whom – Reitzeiger perhaps? He agreed with the sen-
timents completely. Where flesh and blood failed
stone stood firm, and when bricks and mortar failed,
well it could always be rebuilt surpassing its former
glory. That was how cities flourished. They healed
themselves and in doing so they rose like phoenixes
from the ashes, resplendent. Those early dark days
would slip from the memory as moments of beauty
and ingenuity replaced the ruins.

Over the last few days, with the rebirth of the sun,
Altdorf had begun the long painful process of survival. Those left behind had said their goodbyes to

loved ones fallen defending their right to freedom; normal men who neither wanted nor asked to fight were buried alongside soldiers who had given their lives willingly. That was the cost of survival. Innocent blood.

It weighed heavy on the populace.

An innocence had died among the people of the city. Safety, the most basic of liberties, had been stripped from them. They no longer took the sanctity of their homes for granted. This was a double-edged sword. Good, because it meant they suddenly appreciated what they had. Bad, because the lesson it taught was that anything good could be taken away without a moment's thought. It heightened the grief the city felt. Buildings could be rebuilt, fortified. People would survive, but that sense of comfort, of being protected once the door closed at night, that took a long time to recover. Some would never get over it.

The city was in ruins. It would be a long time before the spires of Altdorf commanded the majesty they once had; broken slates exposed the burnt timbers and gaping holes where homes had stood. The architects of necessity and desire would fix that of course, roofs and walls were only stone, but the wounds betrayed the true hurt Altdorf had suffered. It wasn't about bricks and mortar, it was about children growing up orphans, about wives kneeling at grave markers unable to think beyond what might have been, about mothers wondering if they had enough love, enough strength, enough hope to face the world each day. It was about people.

Felix Mann walked through the ruined streets, listening to the dawn chorus breaking out all over the city.

This was his home. These were his people.

Despite the fact that days ago he had been ready to abandon them to their lot he hurt with them. In the last few days he had become a part of this great city, and soon he would be leaving it never to return. That was his loss to bear. For the first time, emerging from the vampire's tent carrying the iron ring, he had found a sense of belonging, and now he was turning his back on it.

He looked up at the windows of his house. He couldn't go home. That was the crux of it. Things had changed. He couldn't go home. He found himself clutching von Carstein's ring all the harder, pressing it into his palm. Was it truly possible that a trinket had kept the vampire alive?

The talk on the streets, of course, was far more miraculous. The Grand Theogonist's holiness and the grace of Sigmar, they said, had finally undone the monster. They were far more willing to believe the ridiculous than they were to accept the mundane.

Felix loved that about people.

The bigger the lie the happier they were to embrace it. Already they spoke of Wilhelm III with the reverential tones normally reserved for a saint or a martyr. Felix was sure the old man would have approved; it was the icing on the cake as far as his grift was concerned. And, surprising himself, Felix didn't begrudge the holy man in the slightest. The people of Altdorf needed heroes now and magic or not, that was exactly what the priest was, an honest to gods hero.

He walked away from his apartment. He knew where he was going: the Sigmarite cathedral. This morning it felt as though every street led there. The press of people was claustrophobic compared with the emptiness the last time he had walked these self-same streets. Even the smallest avenues were teeming with life.

Felix looked around as he walked, bumping between people. Their relief was palpable. They were talking. Laughing. A few days ago the thought of laughter ever ringing out again in Kaiserplatz had been inconceivable. But there it was. People survived. Adapted. Found joy in the smallest of things.

Still, it would be a long time before anything even remotely resembling normality returned.

Indeed, so heavy were the losses to the men of Altdorf that even with Vlad himself dead, and more than half of his damned vampires vanquished, the rest were able to flee without serious pursuit. It was difficult to watch the enemy flee without giving chase but to do so in their condition was suicide. Reluctantly, the heroes of Altdorf had manned the walls, jeering as their enemy fled the light.

Felix walked slowly, not in a hurry to get to where he was going. He would say his own quiet goodbye after the pomp and circumstance of the state funeral. It was a matter of practicality. He had a price to collect from the lector before he headed north to Reiksport and took the boat. He wondered if it would be difficult to disappear and decided it probably wouldn't. He knew the lies he needed to say for people to accept him as someone else; he had been lying most of his life. He would miss the city though, and the house, but both were just stones that could be rebuilt elsewhere. It was time to start thinking about a different kind of life: a scholar's. Perhaps. He could picture himself locked away in dusty libraries growing old surrounded by even older books.

Then again, he was a thief, and there was a reason for the adage once a thief, always a thief.

No matter what he called himself he knew in his heart he would still be Felix Mann, thief, even though he wouldn't be able to take credit for the greatest job of his career. It didn't matter. He knew and he would take the secret to the grave with him.

It was his second funeral in as many days, though very different to yesterday's, a quiet affair within the walls of the cathedral grounds that he wasn't actually invited to, when the lector had interred von Carstein. Curiosity had Felix taking up residency among the rooftops where he had a good view of the cemetery grounds. The creature's grave had been dug beneath the holy ground they intended to use for Wilhelm, a last defence against the beast's rising.

The lector had decapitated von Carstein's corpse, taking the head and scooping the grey matter and soft tissue out to burn, and buried the rest of the head in an unmarked grave, a white rose in its mouth, his eyes replaced by cloves of garlic.

There were only four people at the vampire's burial, Mann, the lector, Ludwig the Pretender and lastly, Reynard Grimm, the new captain of the Altdorf guard. The body was buried face down, the arms bound behind its back with wire, kneecaps shattered, von Carstein's black heart cut out of his chest and burned along with his brain. He was not coming back. Not this time.

They levelled the inside of his grave and prepared it to receive Wilhelm's body. The Holy Father would serve one last duty for Sigmar, as eternal guardian watching over the Vampire Count even in death.

Felix had expected tears but the outpouring of grief as he entered Domplatz was unlike anything he had ever witnessed. Mourners lined the streets. They sobbed hysterically, a babble of voices choked between gulps and hiccoughs:

'He saved us.'

'Without him we'd be living in the dark.'

'You have to believe… You have to… He was sent by Sigmar to save us.'

'The way he looked at you, he saw into your soul.'

'He was special. There will never be another man like him.'

'He wasn't a man at all, I tell you, he was Sigmar himself.'

'He shone out as a beacon against the dark times!'

'He was the light of our lives!'

'He was our saviour.'

And to them it was all true, to degrees. It didn't surprise Felix to hear talk of the Grand Theogonist's sainthood. It was the perfect end cap to the greatest grift of all time. He had sold a miracle to the entire world and they bought it.

Some had wrapped themselves in flags of Altdorf and banners of Sigmar, others sat quietly on the cobbles weeping openly as though they had just lost their best friend. Felix pushed between them, working his way toward the side door into the cathedral. He wouldn't be going in through the gates.

A young novitiate answered his knocking, obviously expecting the thief, nodded and ushered him inside.

'The lector is in the vaults, dealing with the… ah… prisoner. Captain Grimm has yet to return from the field with his finds from the vampire's pavilion. Would you care for a drink while you wait? The interment will be a few hours, no doubt. You could of course avail yourself of the chapel.'

The novitiate scurried away down the cold corridor gesturing for Felix to follow. The cathedral was surprisingly simple, lacking in ostentation. It had none of the gilt-edges or plush velvets he expected from the priesthood. It was simple, bare, even austere. It was a place for worship without the trappings of the material world. Felix liked it. It reflected well on the personality of the Grand Theogonist. It was unassuming. Down to earth. Of course the public face of the cathedral was anything but, but back here, out of sight of the common man, the hand of Wilhelm III was most noticeable.

'He was a good man,' Felix said to the novitiate's back.

'He was. He listened, you know. He cared. He truly cared.'

'I'm sorry for your loss.' And he was.

'We do not mourn his passing, we celebrate the time we shared with him.'

He led Felix to a small chamber, barely large enough for it to be considered a room at all. There was a hard wooden chair, a small table and a jug of water. Felix couldn't help but smile to himself; the young man had led him to what looked like a penitent's cell.

'Wait here.' With that he left Felix alone.

With time on his hands to think, the thief was forced to do just that.

The last few days had been a strain. He had learned some things about himself he wasn't entirely comfortable knowing.

He heard footsteps a while later, and the flickering light of a candle lit the corridor outside the small room. A man appeared in the doorway, his long shadow reaching deep into the room. He was dressed in the formal robes of the clergy, and did not look pleased to have been dragged away from whatever it was he had been doing.

'Yes?'

The curtness put Felix off balance slightly. He had expected to come, be paid and leave. Business was business, after all.

'I've come for my price.'

'What are you blathering on about, man?'

'My pardon and the money I was promised. I've come to collect.'

'Is this some kind of joke?'

'Hardly. I was… ah… hired… by the Grand Theogonist to do a job for him. I held up my side of the bargain, and now I want you to hold up yours.'

'No such bargains were made, I assure you. Our most benevolent brother did not treat with thieves.'

'No, he walked with hand in hand with Sigmar. Yes, yes, very well, I am scum. I know that. Now give me my money, priest, a deal is a deal. Where's the lector?'

'He's detained currently, now I suggest it is time for you to leave. Whatever business you believe you had with our beloved holy father, I assure you does not continue with this office today. Good day.'

Felix bristled. He stood, the wooden chair grating back on its legs as he pushed it out of the way. 'I don't think so, priest. A deal is a deal and I intend to collect, with your blessing our without. You do know who I am, don't you?' His lips twisted into a grim parody of a smile.

'I know who you are and I know that you will be leaving here empty-handed.'

He grabbed the priest, throwing him up against the wall. His fists bunched in the priest's cassock, pressing up hard into the man's Adam's apple. The man gagged, his arms flapping ineffectually at Felix's, unable to break the thief's grip.

'I don't make a habit of hurting priests but in your case I'm willing to make an exception. Now, where's the lector?'

'In the vaults,' the priest gasped. 'With the captain.'

'Take me to them.'

'No.'

'I said take me to them. I am not in the habit of asking twice.'

'I can't,' the priest pleaded.

'Don't make me hurt you, man.'

'I can't.'

Felix hit him, once, hard, driving a fist into his gut. The priest doubled up in pain. Felix slammed him up against the wall again. 'I could lie and tell you that hurt me almost as much as it hurt you but it didn't. Actually it felt pretty good. Now, we'll try this one last time, priest, take me to them.'

The man's head came up defiantly. 'They are in the vaults with the prisoner, you can wait or you can leave.' Felix raised his fist again. 'They are not to be disturbed. Hit me again, my answer will be the same no matter how many times you do so.'

Disgusted, he pushed the priest out of his way and walked out of the room.

'Where are you going?' the priest shouted after him.

'Where do you think?'

He stalked down the chill corridor, listening but only hearing the echo of his own footsteps. The entrance to the vaults would, he reasoned, be off the main chapel, assuming that the vaults were part of the crypt or could be reached through the mausoleum. The other logical choice was the kitchens. There was no guarantee of course. With these old buildings the vaults could actually be some long forgotten dungeon with a secluded stairwell hidden away somewhere. He stopped at a corner as a whiff of nutmeg and cinnamon hit him. He followed his nose and found the kitchens, but more importantly, he found a staircase leading down to the depths of the cathedral's cold stone heart.

The air was noticeably colder as he descended, prickling his skin. Even the texture and quality of it changed. It was older air. Stale.

He paused at the bottom of the stairs, listening. He could hear muted voices from deeper in the darkness. He followed the sounds. Warm orange light suffused the corridor.

They were torturing the prisoner when he walked into the cell. The priest and the captain, Grimm, stood over a man who was bound by thick chains to a chair in the centre of the room. The prisoner's head was down so Felix couldn't see his face but it was obvious he had taken severe punishment. His clothes were stained darkly by blood, his hair matted with the stuff. The cell smelled of vomit and urine.

'What in Sigmar's name are you doing here!' the lector spat, seeing Felix in the doorway.

'I've come to collect the money promised to me, then I will be on my way.'

'Get out, fool!'

The prisoner's head came up. It was bruise-purple, swollen and bloody from the beating he had taken. Felix stared at the wretched man. The beating had rendered him barely recognisable as a human being. The sheer brutality of it shook Felix. His eyes darted about the small cell, saw instruments of torture, tongs and pincers, a brazier of hot coals. Grimm held a bar of red iron to the prisoner's throat, the skin sizzling blackly even before the kiss of the metal seared away the top layers of flesh. The prisoner's scream was harrowing. The man bucked and writhed against his chains.

Felix backed out of the room. This was wrong. War drove men to extremes, he knew, but they were extremes of necessity, not wanton acts of evil. The torturing of a prisoner moved very definitely into the realms of evil.

The prisoner's screams haunted the passageway.

The lector came out to join him, sweat blackening his forehead. The man was clearly exhausted.

'This is not for your eyes,' he said, closing his own as the prisoner cried out once more. When he opened them again Felix was surprised at the depth and intensity of grief he saw in them.

'I made a deal with the Grand Theogonist, I rendered him a service, ah, appropriating a piece of jewellery he desired. In return I was promised a pardon and coin enough to begin a new life away from here. I want what is my due.'

'Impossible,' the lector said bluntly.

'I really do urge you to reconsider. I have a feeling that someone would pay very handsomely for this trinket, and in the wrong hands it could almost certainly prove to be far more trouble than it's worth.'

'Are you threatening me, thief?'

'Not at all, threats are idle. I will have my due, priest. Your temple owes me. A deal is a deal.'

'So you say, but I see no evidence of any such deal. Do you have a notarised contract? Do you have a shred of evidentiary proof to support your word? No, I thought not. So as far as I am concerned, thief, you are also a liar. You are wasting my time.'

'You would be dead if it wasn't for me!'

The priest laughed at that. 'I think not, thief. We are all alive by the grace of Sigmar and his divine hammer, Wilhelm III. Now leave before you try my patience further.'

Felix turned on his heel, disgusted, and left them to torture the prisoner. He wanted to be as far away from this godforsaken place as possible. He would take his price and be damned. He didn't need their permission, a deal was a deal. Their coffers would open long enough for him to take his due. He took the stairs two and three at a time, almost running up them. He was seething. At the top, he looked left, then right, and plunged into the heart of the cathedral, following a narrow passage as it opened into the grand chapel. The huge vaulted dome was magnificent, humbling, with its murals and gilt décor. Marble statues of the beatific Man-God Sigmar stood watch over the holiest of holies, impassive to the comings and goings his chosen sons. A scattering of the devout knelt at prayer in the wooden pews. Felix walked through the middle of them, looking left and right for something of value to take.

He saw nothing. For all the obvious wealth on display it was art, sculpture, the decoration itself. In frustration he overturned a pew and lashed out at one of the multi-pronged iron candelabra lighting the room. It fell, the candles snuffed out as the rolled across the stone floor. Felix stalked out of the chapel, slamming the huge oaken door behind him.

The first dark blush of dusk was drawing in. He had lost all track of time while he waited inside the house of Sigmar.

Three novitiates were tending what looked like a funeral pyre in the cathedral garden. There was no body; they were feeding the fire with scraps of paper, drawn one sheet at a time from the old tomes spread out by their feet.

The flames sparked and hissed as the sheets were fed to them, blazing blue in the instant of immolation before being consumed by the red flames.

Felix barged through them in his hurry to be away, kicking aside one of the books. It fell open on a vicious scrawl of unintelligible black ink. His eyes were drawn immediately to the brittle pages that so obviously weren't paper. He was an intelligent man. He could read and write but even a cursory glance was enough to know this was no language he had ever seen before. Instinctively, he knew it to be a grimoire.

He would have his price.

Whatever secrets the book contained they were dangerous enough for the Sigmarites to be burning them. That made them the kind of secrets someone would pay a lot of money for.

Without thinking he grabbed the book from the floor and ran for the street.

CHAPTER TWENTY-SEVEN
Let Us Not Go Gently Into That Endless Winter Night

DRAKWALD FOREST
Winter, 2051

THEY WERE LOST within the dark heart of the old wood.

They were the last. It was hard to believe.

A few days ago they had been part of the most awesome fighting force the world had ever seen.

They had been invincible. They had been immortal. Warriors of the Blood!

What were they now? A few stragglers, beaten, driven from the field of battle, forced to run, to flee, to cling to the shreds of their unlife as their world unravelled. The von Carstein bloodline was all but extinguished, those few that remained pale shadows of the great vampires that had fallen. They were third, fourth, even fifth generation gets. They were not their

363

sires. They lacked the awesome strength of those who had fallen. They were shadows. They were weak.

A spent force.

The Kingdom of the Dead had crumbled on its foundations of dust. The horrors of von Carstein's army, the skeletons and the zombies that had ravaged the country, had sunk slowly back into the dirt as the necromantic magic of Nagash binding their bones came undone with the count's death, transforming the ground before the bleak stone ramparts of Altdorf into one vast garden of bones.

Jerek von Carstein blundered through the undergrowth, dead leaves mulching beneath his feet as he drove himself on, slapping aside the cut and sting of withered branches even as exhaustion suffused his limbs and muddied his mind. They followed him blindly even though he was lost both physically and metaphorically.

All was quiet save for the passage of the dead.

A single raven sat on a skeletal branch, watching them pityingly. The castle's ill-omened birds had followed them from Drakenhof itself, feasting on the offal and carrion the army left trailing in its wake. They scavenged the fields of blood beneath the walls of Altdorf, cawing and shrieking and picking at the rotting flesh of the fallen. While the others lingered to feed this lone bird haunted them. It was always there on the edge of his vision, black wings blurring as he tried to focus on them. He had seen the bird four times since they had entered Drak Wald.

He didn't know if they were following the bird or it was following them.

It didn't matter.

They were all dead.

It was only a matter of time before the humans abandoned the security of their walls and set about finishing what they had begun. They had days, a week or two at best while the enemy regrouped and healed, then the bloodline would be wiped out in one almighty purge.

In a way it was a relief – an end to it.

Jerek was finding it harder and harder to remember who he had been. At times, like now, it saddened him that his personality had slipped, been subsumed by the monstrous beast von Carstein had sired, though these moments were fleeting and few and far between. A pang. Nothing more. Hour by hour he lost himself. Facing von Carstein in the bell tower he had imagined it would all be over in a heartbeat, that his mortal soul would be wiped out, he had never considered the possibility that he might remember what it was like to be Jerek Kruger. The torment was pulling him apart. The need to feed went against everything he had been, and yet it represented everything he had become. Jerek loathed himself and the monster von Carstein had made him.

But that was who he was: Jerek von Carstein. Kruger was dead and gone but for a few rogue memories.

There had been a dark presence inside Jerek, ever-present like a second heartbeat, an echo that tied him to his sire. It had been a comfort of sorts, binding him to von Carstein's twisted mockery of a family. Now nothing lived on. The vampires had lost and in doing so became hollow creatures. The link had been severed brutally and suddenly they were bereft. They all felt it: the ache of loss. The emptiness engulfed them

all. They had lost their father and without him, suddenly, they were nothing. It seemed inconceivable. In
a few hours the Kingdom of the Dead had come
undone. Vlad had fallen, returned to dust by a rag-tag
army of humans.

'We need to feed,' Pieter said, sniffing the air for
even the faintest trace of humanity, his teeth bared.
He had regressed almost to the point of becoming
animalistic. Grief brought out his base nature. The
man was a weasel: a dangerous creature not to be
trusted despite its innocent appearance. 'We need
blood and I smell cattle.'

The others crowded around, their faces betraying
their desperate need.

'Then go hunt,' Jerek said. 'The woods are filled with
trappers' cottages and tiny settlements. All of you, go
hunt, feed. Do what you need to. Leave me alone.'

No one moved.

'You heard me,' he said, turning his back on their
hungry faces. Their expectancy disgusted him. He
hefted his warhammer, felt a thrill course through his
fingers as his flesh came into contact with the
weapon. It sang in his blood.

Still none of them moved to follow Pieter.

They looked to him for guidance, he realised,
because for all their finery and sophisticated ruthlessness, he was the only true warrior left amongst them.
He understood their enemy better than any of them
because he had led them. They were rats, weasels, fer-
rets, and stoats, animals used to sneaking, hiding,
fighting from the dark, striking fast and moving on.
In contrast, he was a White Wolf, fearless, powerful, a
majestic beast. They grasped and grasped at the twin

illusions of strength and power, desperate to cloak themselves in the stuff, to wear the trappings they offered. Avarice pumped the dead blood through their veins. Hunger for power and hunger for blood, were, he knew, the twin dimensions of the vampire's world. Jerek von Carstein might have been Vlad's get but before his birth into the Kingdom of the Dead he had been born and raised in a world of fear and violence. Raised a warrior from birth, he was a knight, but more than anything else he was a survivor. Their diffidence wouldn't last. He knew that.

Once they were safe the murderous succession would begin. They were liars, cheats, thieves and killers, each and every one of them. There was no honour in their dead hearts. They feared power. They respected ruthlessness. They coveted everything they lacked. Some, no doubt, were already planning his downfall simply because he was Vlad's get and in terms of the blood his claim was stronger than all of theirs.

'Go!'

They scattered, some transforming into their lupine aspects, others loosing the beast within.

He was alone. He sat on an old tree stump, rotten to the core. He heard them crashing through the trees, heard the screams when they came. They were animals.

'You should have forced her to return with us'

Jerek turned to see Emmanuelle, Pieter's wife, standing behind him. She had come up on him without him hearing a sound. Blood dribbled down her chin. Her porcelain skin looked so fragile in the gloom. In contrast her eyes were flint.

'She was beyond that. To leave would have robbed Isabella of the man she loved. In her madness she believed that staying there, where he fell, she could somehow keep his memory pure, alive, but to return to the castle without him, he would weaken, fade and eventually cease to be the man she loved.'

'So instead you left her there to die.'

'I took pity on her.'

'Pity is for dogs.'

'So what would you have had me do? Drag her kicking and screaming to Drakenhof?'

'If needs be, yes. She is one of us, we don't abandon our own to the cattle. We owe her. We owe Vlad.'

'We owe no one!' Jerek said vehemently. His ferocity surprised him. He mastered his anger quickly. 'We didn't ask to be sired, they chose us, we did not choose them. Now we start fighting for our lives because behind us the humans are coming and they intend to exterminate us like vermin.'

'Humans,' Emmanuelle said contemptuously.

'Yes, humans. Like it or not, the cattle stand on the verge of wiping us out.'

In the distance a woman screamed. Her cries died out quickly.

Emmanuelle's smile was cold. 'Did you hear that? That is how we deal with humans.'

'I know,' he said, afraid of himself, afraid of what he had become, afraid of what his future held. 'I know.'

CHAPTER TWENTY-EIGHT
The Stalking Ground

ALTDORF
Winter, 2051

FELIX MANN CRADLED the book to his chest as he ran.

He pumped his one free arm hard, mouth open as he ran. The spine of the book banged into his chin. His heart hammered in his chest.

He skidded around a corner into one of the seedier districts of the city. Two dogs fought over scraps still on the bone. They snarled as he dodged around them, nearly tripping over the foot still attached to the shinbone they were fighting over.

Two of the Sigmarite novitiates gave chase while the third raised the alarm. Cries of: 'Stop! Thief!' rang through the narrow back alleys but they didn't slow him. People heard and turned and by the time

they did he was past them and careening down the
street, around the corner and away.

He ran on, through the narrow warren of streets,
crashing through laundry hung so low it almost
dragged on the cobbles as the wind stirred it.

The sky shifted into dusk, clouds obscuring what
little was left of the sun. Night, for the first time in
what felt like forever, was his friend again. It
promised shadows – places to hide. It was his time.

People stared at him. They would remember the
way he had come. He stopped, breathless and gasping, back pressed against a wall, listening for the
sounds of pursuit.

He began to understand what he had done.

It wasn't just a book, he knew. He could feel it. The
thing was vile. Corrupt. He felt its taint wherever his
skin touched the skin of the binding. He didn't want
to hold onto it any longer than he had to. It had
seemed like a good idea, a means of securing pay-
ment and forcing the Sigmarites to keep the old
man's word, but like so many good ideas it was not as
simple as that. Felix tore a strip out of a laundered
sheet and wrapped the book in it. He tucked the book
under his arm. The cloth did little to shield him from
the book's taint but at least he didn't have to feel the
dead skin.

He hurried away from the wall, pushing aside
another sheet. He heard footsteps behind him. When
he turned there was no one there. He carried on
through the alleyway. He didn't know where he was
going to go. None of his usual fences would handle
something like this. Despite the fact that the ring
looked like a worthless trinket, it wasn't. Like the

book, it had power of that he had no doubt. He would need to find a specialised seller but who in the Old World would be prepared to traffic in dark magic. And that is what it was, Felix reasoned. It had to be, judging by the way the Sigmarites had been tearing the books apart page by page and feeding them to the fire. Even the fire hadn't been natural – it had burned blue with the taint of the accursed pages. He put two and two together: von Carstein had animated an army of the damned, bringing them back from beyond the grave to do his bidding. Was that was this was, some dark grimoire containing the secrets of reanimation?

Felix shuddered and cast a frightened look back over his shoulder.

As much as he wanted to think otherwise, raising the dead wasn't outside the realms of possibility. The Vampire Count's war had proved that. If the book he had stolen contained anything close to dark magic powerful enough to raise the dead that made it dangerous in so many ways, not least of which was to him.

He had to think. He wanted to move it on quickly, get his price and leave Altdorf. He could try Albrecht's down by the Reiksport, or Müllers in Amtsbezirk, though that would mean working his way back along the west bank of the Reik to the Emperor's Bridge and then over the Three Toll Bridge. There were a lot of dangerous places for a thief along that road, governmental ministries and influential nobles, and of course Schuldturm, the debtors prison. The prison would be guarded. A cry of alarm could see the chase become a lot more deadly that a pair of blathering priests shouting, 'Stop! Thief!'

No, Müller's was out of the question; too many opportunities for things to go wrong. That left Albrecht. Rumour had it he had a taste for the outré. Perhaps he would know someone interested in the book *and* the ring. A collector perhaps? A lover of antiquities or a scholar with a taste for the obscure. Together they had to be worth a small fortune. Hell, if the book was even half as dangerous as he believed it was, it was priceless.

He paused at an intersection between two streets. Looked left, where an old maid was on her knees scrubbing down the stoop of her tenement house, and right, where children chased each other in circles in the street. He nodded to the woman when she looked his way and scuttled across the street.

He could of course smuggle both items out of the city and sell them to the surviving vampires. They would know the true worth of the book and von Carstein's signet ring. He was angry enough to consider betraying the city and just walking away, leaving them to their greedy fate. The anger would wear off, he knew, and be replaced by bitterness. Without the righteous anger fuelling him Felix knew he wouldn't be capable of selling the lives of friends and neighbours for a few coins, no matter how much he detested the priests.

He would have to hope Albrecht knew someone interested in the kind of arcane curiosities he was peddling, and if not, knew a man who knew a man whose brother's neighbour's nephew knew a man who might be.

His thief sense tingled, the hairs along the nape of his neck bristling as his skin crawled.

Someone was watching him.

He had no idea how long they had been following him. He slowed his walk, giving a chance for them to catch up or reveal themselves by slipping into a shadowy doorway.

He felt their eyes on his back. He had been a thief long enough to know to trust his instincts. He had gone against them once already this week.

'Fool me once,' he muttered. 'Shame on you. Fool me twice, shame on me.'

He looked left and right furtively, scanning the streets.

There was no sign of anyone but that didn't mean there was no one there. It paid to be paranoid in his line of work. He waited, counting to eleven, concentrating as he listened. He tried to pick out any out of place sounds.

Nothing.

He knew that if he stalled much longer his hesitation would tip off the watcher. He needed to move. His instinct was to make for the Reikmarkt but there was no guarantee it would be anywhere near busy enough to lose the watcher in. The siege had decimated trade. The Süderich Marketplatz was closer, and now that a few trawlers had started arriving again, the chances of there being some fresh fish to sell increased, meaning the chances of there being people to disappear amongst increased. Fresh produce was at a premium still, with the trade caravans only just beginning to arrive in the city.

He moved away from the wall. It was difficult not to look around. He was conscious of his every move. Felix pictured himself as he walked, visualising the street in his head, the points of access, places where it was overlooked, places where he would have hidden if the roles were reversed. There were three obvious vantage points but two were useless because they offered little or no chance of pursuit. The third though was a gem, good cover to see without being seen and it covered any number of possible escape routes. Felix had a philosophy: he always considered the predator at least three degrees more prepared and therefore more dangerous than the prey. He was in trouble here and he knew it. Whoever was following him knew about the ring; that was the only logical explanation he could think of. They couldn't have known about the grimoire, the theft had been far too spontaneous and his stalker was far too skilled in the hunt to be one of the novitiates from the temple. So it was the ring they were after.

He knew then who it was.

The stranger with the ancient eyes he had followed out of the Sigmar cathedral before all hell broke loose. The one who had materialised out of thin air and told him to forget what he thought he'd seen. It made sense, of course. He had suspected that the stranger was one of the major players in the Grand Theogonist's grift. This proved it. It stood to reason that he knew about the ring, Morr's teeth, the man had probably told the priest of its existence. That was the Grand Theogonist's divine intervention. Extrapolating the thought, it made sense that if anyone in Altdorf knew the signet ring's true nature it was the stranger.

Felix couldn't fault his reasoning, which didn't make him any happier with the mess he was in.

He couldn't help himself; he cast a worried look back over his shoulder. His eyes instinctively sought out the best of the three vantage points available to the hunter. It only took a fraction of a second to see that the hiding place was empty. The man wasn't as skilled in the hunt as he feared. Felix smiled, a wave of relief washing over him.

He had a chance of getting out of this alive.

He turned to check the remaining vantage points – which of the two the stranger had chosen decided his escape route for him.

Both were empty.

Doubt flooded through him.

Had he misjudged the street?

Had the stranger somehow worked his way around in front of him without him realising?

And then it hit him: the cold hard realisation of just how much trouble he was in. The stranger could have been anywhere, stood right at his shoulder even, and without the slight shifting of the shadows to give him away Felix wouldn't be able to tell until it was too late and the assassin's blade was slipping into his chest or his back or his throat.

He bolted.

He didn't care if the stranger knew he'd been rumbled, he just wanted out of there, away, somewhere less exposed. Somewhere he could dictate the terms of the encounter, though of course Felix knew no such place existed. He ran because it was a matter of survival.

His heart hammered against his breastbone. Adrenaline coursed through his body. He ran – really ran.

He didn't look where he was going. It wasn't important. All that mattered was getting away. Within two minutes he was breathing hard. His head swam. He crashed into an old woman on the corner of Rosenstrasse, sending her sprawling. He tumbled and rolled and was up again and running as though nothing had happened even as her curses chased him down the street.

The sounds of pursuit haunted him, the slap of running feet on the cobbles, the ragged breathing, but every second Felix wasted looking back over his shoulder revealed nothing but empty streets. Occasionally he thought he saw a glimmer, a peculiar refraction of light, a snatch of shadow moving oddly but he daren't risk slowing to look properly. He ran because anything else meant almost certain death.

He ducked down a narrow alleyway and scrambled over a low wall into an overrun garden, weeds and junk sprouting out of every nook and cranny. He scrambled over the next dividing wall and the next into another back yard full of weeds and broken planks. The back door of the house was open.

He didn't think about it. He ran inside, through the kitchen and down the hall before anyone had even noticed he was inside. An emaciated stick of a man with greasy hair and sweat stains ringing his tunic stood between Felix and the door, a scowl set on his bony face. He crossed his arms.

'What do you think you're doing?'

'Move!' Felix didn't wait. He hit the man full on, slamming him into the door. The man buckled. Felix dropped the grimoire and drove a fist into the man's gut, doubling him up, then a vicious uppercut with his left. The man went down and Felix put the boot in, kicking him once, twice, three times in the stomach and a fourth time between the legs. The man writhed on the floor in agony. Felix stepped over him and opened the door. The fight had lost him precious seconds.

He turned back to pick up the book and saw the light coming through the kitchen door shimmer strangely, the doorframe bowing as though bending around something that plainly wasn't there.

He didn't wait. He grabbed the book and ran.

Behind him, the hunter laughed: cold mocking laughter.

He was being driven further and further away from the busy streets into the slums of the city.

Worse though, by far, he could feel himself tiring. His legs burned. His knees felt it worst; the impact of each frantic step triggered another fiery burst of pain. He cast a desperate look back over his shoulder and his legs betrayed him. He stumbled and fell, sprawling across the cobbles.

The laughter was close: almost on top of him.

Felix scrambled back to his feet and managed five more steps before he stumbled again, sheer exhaustion tying his legs up. He didn't fall this time and he didn't look back. He ran on expecting the stranger's blade to slam into his back at any moment. In desperation he ran into a gap between two houses; it was too narrow to be called an alleyway. It was barely a passage. Halfway down it he realised sickly that he had run himself into a dead end.

This is where I die, he thought desperately. *Here in a piss-stinking alleyway. For a stupid lousy ring.* The irony of it wasn't lost on him. All the distance he'd put between the slums of his childhood and all the privileges of the life he had stolen for himself, the fancy clothes, the gourmet dinners, the pretty women – and the ugly for that matter – and here he was, returned to the filth and stench to die.

He turned to face the hunter as the man shimmered into solidity right before his eyes. The effect was disconcerting. It was as though the stranger simply stepped out of the shadows where he hadn't been a moment before.

Felix backed up a step, shaking his head as though trying to dislodge the stranger from his eyes.

The man's expression was somewhat pitying as a black-edged blade whispered clear of its sheath. He held the sword naturally, with all the assurance of skilled swordsman; as though there was only one way in his mind this encounter could play out. His balance was good; he moved lightly on his toes, narrowing the gap between them.

'You want the ring?' Felix said holding the grimoire out in front of him like a shield. He hated the way his voice sounded: weak, frightened. But he couldn't master his fear.

'Yes,' the stranger said coldly, eyeing his clenched fist. 'And the book.'

'Take them. They're yours. I-I don't need them.'

'No I suppose you don't,' the stranger agreed matter-of-factly.

'Here–'

Before he could finish the sentence the stranger rocked forward on his toes and the black sword lashed out, snakelike, slicing clean through his wrist.

The pain was staggering. Hand and book fell to the ground as Felix screamed in agonised shock. The ring chimed on the cold stone as it rolled away. Blood gouted from the stump of his wrist, spraying everywhere.

Felix screamed, insensate, his shrieks a babble of wretched pleas and curses that rose in an agonised spiral. He staggered forward clutching at the stump, every trace of colour gone from his face as his lifeblood spewed from the wound.

There was a reason the stranger had shepherded him into the heart of the slums: violence was a way of life. People could scream blue murder without the locals raising an eyebrow.

'Hold out your other hand,' the stranger commanded.

Felix shook his head stupidly, the world span wildly out of focus. The pain was overwhelming. Sunbursts of pure white agony flared behind his eyes. The street was gone. There was only a world of pain. He lurched forward another step and slipped on cobbles slick with his own blood, stumbled and fell to his knees. He held his hand up to cover his face and saw only blood red darkness as the stranger's black blade severed it mercilessly.

Felix fell the rest of the way to the floor. He felt his blood, warm, on his face. The cobbles swam in and out of focus.

He saw the man's shoes as he knelt to pick up the ring.

'You don't look good, Felix,' the stranger said conversationally. 'The way I see it, if you live, your days as a thief are over, but I believe beggars can scratch a living on the streets of most cities in the Empire. So that is a small mercy. It would obviously be better if you died, because, well, your legend is assured. Your name shall live long into the future, when they realise what you have done they will laud you as the greatest thief of all time. The fact that you simply disappeared, well that only adds to the enigma. It makes it into a story. For my own part, I am indebted to you for securing my... ahh... inheritance. And the book, such a wonderful, wonderful surprise. Who could have known Vlad had such treasures? I cannot thank you enough. The night, however, is running away from us and I must, alas, leave you to the whim of Morr. Farewell, thief.'

The stranger walked away and he was alone, bleeding out onto the cobbles.

He couldn't move. He felt warm liquid trickle down the inside of his trousers and didn't know if it was blood or urine – and didn't care.

He just wanted the pain to end.

'Help... me.' It was barely more than a croak. It didn't matter; no one would come to his aid.

He lost all track of time, all sense of self. It just slipped away from him in the pain.

Felix tried to crawl towards the mouth of the narrow passage but he blacked out long before he reached the light waiting at the end.

CHAPTER TWENTY-NINE
All That Remains

ALTDORF
Winter, 2051

CAPTAIN GRIMM WAS torturing the prisoner when the novitiate hammered on the cell door.

The lector was glad for the interruption.

He had no stomach for Grimm's brutality or the obvious gusto with which the man went about his task; it made him sick to the core. His head swam. More than once he thought he was about to pass out. And still the prisoner wasn't talking. The man stared straight ahead, the madness of pain blazing in his eyes as Grimm applied red-hot tongs and other instruments of torture to his flesh.

The stench of burned meat clung to the small chamber. The sizzle of hot metal on skin would haunt the lector for years, he knew. He struggled to rationalise it with thoughts of the greater good; one monster's pain set against the suffering of his entire congregation. It was difficult.

He answered the door.

'Yes? What is it?'

The young priest in the doorway was pale, shaken.

'Your holiness… things… you need to come up stairs. The guards have taken a prisoner… a woman. She was raving and trying to dig up the Grand Theogonist's grave. They have her in the tower. The chirurgeon sedated her with laudanum. She is most disturbed, your grace. Her face… she is one of *them*. The creature tears out of her face as her grip on reality slips, your grace. She is incoherent. Before the drugs she was throwing herself at the walls. She tore her fingernails bloody trying to claw through the stone. She was ranting and raving about her beloved. Now she merely whimpers. There is no talking to her. Her sanity is gone.'

'I see,' the lector said thoughtfully. It was possible then that the damned creatures shared similar bonds to the living, love, friendship, the ties that bind brother to brother. Could it be that the woman was in some way tied to the dead count? 'Come, walk with me. I have no liking for the business of torture. It is time I saw the light of day. Now, you say she was found trying to disinter the Grand Theogonist? Perhaps you have read the situation wrong. Think about it. Is it not more probable that she was trying to get to von Carstein's remains?' The lector closed the heavy cell door on the prisoner's screams and walked the dank corridors back toward the sun.

He had no idea whether it was day or night. Time and hours and minutes had lost rhyme and reason in the vaults beneath the cathedral.

The novitiate said nothing until they reached the stairway back up to the surface.

'There is more, your grace.'

The lector stopped, one foot on the stair and turned.

'Tell me, lad.'

'The books given to us to destroy...'

'What about them?'

'The thief... stole one.'

'Then find him and recover it. Those damned books cannot be allowed to stain the world any longer than they already have. There was a reason I bade you destroy them, lad. They are dangerous books. I have no idea if they were original or copies, but I do know they contained the necromancer Nagash's dark wisdom, his incantations, and his defilements. Their presence in the Vampire Count's horde explains his army of living dead. This kind of power cannot be let loose in the world again. Find Mann and get that book back.'

'We have... ahhh... Mann was found in the slums of Drecksack in the shadow of the Muckrakers' Guildhall.'

'Then I see no problem. Mann is caught, the book is returned. We were lucky this time. See to it that the book is destroyed immediately, lad. We can't risk any more mistakes.'

'Ahhh... but... you see... the thief didn't have the book, your grace. He had been attacked. Both of his hands lay on the cobbles beside his body, severed. He was barely alive when they brought him back to the cathedral. Whoever attacked him has the book.'

'Then let us pray they do not know what it is.'

'We will know more if the thief ever regains consciousness, your grace, but I fear his fate is an ill omen. The attack was made to look like natural comeuppance for his thievery but according to the muckraker who brought him to us the only words Mann uttered before slipping into unconsciousness were: "Shadows... shadows... he walks in shadows." It could be a thief turning on his own, I suppose. The whole concept of honour amongst thieves is ridiculous, after all, but it doesn't ring true.'

He walks in shadows.

Those words froze the lector's blood in his veins. He knew.

There was no doubt in his mind.

Wilhelm had bargained with the devil and the devil had already claimed his due. It wasn't over. Far from it, it was just beginning in earnest. His mind's eye swam with visions of slaughter, fields of blood, corpses being picked over by carrion birds even as they stirred back to unnatural life. How many more would die?

'If you are fool enough to treat with daemons, you get what you deserve, I suppose.'

'Your grace?'

'Just talking to myself, lad. Just talking to myself.' He suppressed a shudder. 'So, one problem at a time. Take me to her.'

Together they climbed the stairs to the highest spire in the cathedral, the Tower of the Living Saints, to the barred door. Two guards stood watch. Both as wooden as the door, both distinctly ill at ease with the task they had been charged with. The lector nodded to the bar. 'Open it.'

'Your grace, the prisoner was drugged incoherent an hour back by the apothecary because she was a danger to herself and to those near her.'

'I will take my chances, soldier. Open the door.'

The man nodded and slipped the bar out of place. The door opened on a threadbare cell. Once, in a past life, the room might have been majestic with its vibrant red velvet drapes and its sumptuous divan but the moths had been at the fabric and decay lay heavy on the furnishings. The woman was huddled in the far corner of the room, a wild animal cornered. Her black hair fell in lank ringlets across her face. She craned her neck to look at him. Her eyes ached with the pure madness of grief.

'Do you know where my pretty one is?' Her voice was painfully childlike in the way it trembled. The hope in her eyes was heartbreaking. And then, as quickly as it came, the innocence was gone and the woman's face was split and stretched by a ferocious animalistic howl as the beast within tore free for a split second before being harnessed again. She twisted and writhed, slapping at her own face, clawing at her eyes fiercely enough to draw runnels that ran like bloody tears down her cheeks. Gasping and panting, the woman looked up at him beseechingly. It was difficult to reconcile the beast and the beauty owning the same form.

The lector made the sign of Sigmar in the air before stepping across the threshold.

'He is dead.'

The woman thrashed about wildly as though being beaten. He saw then that she was shackled and chained to the bedstead.

'No he is immortal! He cannot die! You are a liar!'

The chains jerked and gouged at the wood but they held.

He knelt before her. There was nothing but pity in his voice when he told her: 'I am many things, woman, but I promise you this, the Vampire Count is no more. He is gone.'

She pressed herself up against the wall, shaking her head, drawing her knees up to her chin, wrapping her arms around them and rocking. The chains dug into her bare legs. 'No, no, nonono. No. Not my pretty one. Not my love. He wouldn't leave me here like this. He loves me. He does. He wouldn't leave me.'

'He had no choice in the matter,' the lector said, resting a hand on her knee. She laid her hand on his. It was a moment of false tenderness. She snarled and gouged long claw-like fingernails through the back of his hand, tearing the skin before he could pull away. The wound stung. Blood dribbled between his fingers as he clenched his fist.

Someone entered the room behind him.

'Put the bitch out of her misery, priest,' the newcomer said, harshly.

The lector turned to see Ludwig, pretender to the Imperial throne, both craven and coward, with his personal bodyguard.

'You are not welcome in the temple of Sigmar, pretender,' the lector said, turning his back on the pair. 'Neither is your thug.'

'You forget yourself, priest. Remember, in your secular world I have considerable sway, including for instance, the power to confer the title of Grand Theogonist on whomsoever I see as a valid recipient. If you have any ambitions in that quarter I suggest you remember yourself quickly. Now, I say again, put von Carstein's whore out of her misery and let's be done with it.'

The lector ignored the Pretender and reached out for the woman's chains. With great compassion, in part triggered by the fact that she looked so vulnerable, in part through the survivor's guilt of still being alive when others better than him had gone, and, no doubt because of the atrocities he himself had been party to in the dungeon, he took her hands in his. Despite the revulsion her daemonic aspect inspired he held her hand for a long moment. 'Let me release you, you are not an animal and should not be treated as such.'

'Do you know where my love is?' she asked again, real tears mixing with the blood streaming down her cheeks as she held out her wrists. 'Will you help me find him? I need to bring him home. If I can bring him home everything will be all right.' Without the keys there was nothing the lector could do.

'Use this,' Ludwig said, holding out a sharpened wooden stake. 'Put the beast out of its misery. We have more important things to concern ourselves with. These things must be exterminated.'

The lector stared at the piece of wood uncomprehendingly.

'Do it man. She's not a woman. It's all lies. She is an animal. Worse, she is an animal that has gone rabid.'

'Murder is never the answer,' the lector said.

'Don't think of it as murder, priest. Think of it as offering her salvation.' The Pretender rationalised. 'You are giving her a way back to your precious Sigmar, or at least a path into Morr's underworld.' He pressed the stake into the lector's hands, his face implacable.

The transformation of Isabella von Carstein was both immediate and shocking. Her face contorted in a feral snarl. The snarl betrayed other subtle changes; her rich full lips peeled back on sharp incisors that grew into brutal fangs, her back arched and her brow and bone ridges elongated, thickening. Her nostrils flared and her eyes radiated sheer hatred. She lashed out at him, claws raking down his cheek, drawing blood.

The lector reeled back, falling on his backside and scuttling away from the beast that was the countess. She could, he realised, easily kill him. She wasn't an innocent to be saved, she was a monster to be slain. It was the nature of the beast. She couldn't be tamed. She couldn't be brought back to the light with the love of benevolent Sigmar. Moreover, she didn't *want* to be saved. The woman she had been was long gone; all that remained was an abomination of nature, a by-blow of death, a daemon.

He knew what he had to do but still his hand trembled.

'Do it man, drive it into her heart, kill her.'

He stared at the stake in his hands: a tool of death. He held it poised to strike. Despite her bestial strength the woman was helpless. It was nothing short of butchery. Cold-blooded slaughter. The thought stayed his hand. He was a priest – he cherished life, creation, and all things holy. He did not bring death. He was not some filthy servant of the murder god. He had given his life in service of Sigmar. His nature was to nurture, to treasure, and to save, not to wipe out.

'Are you a coward, man? She isn't human. She is everything your faith abhors! You can feel her taint beneath your skin. She is evil! Do it! Purge the world of her vile existence.'

'She is not the one demanding murder, Pretender.'

'How dare you!'

'I dare because I am not a killer,' he said softly. He couldn't do it. He let the stake slip through his fingers and pushed himself slowly to his feet. 'You though, I could make an exception for.'

Ludwig the Pretender was apoplectic. His face was purple with rage. A vein pulsed in his forehead dangerously. Spit frothed at his mouth as he swore and cursed at the priest. Beside him his bodyguard remained curiously impassive, as though he were used to his master's fits of pique.

'As I remember it you were the one who suggested ceding Altdorf to the vampires and begged the Grand Theogonist to open the gates to save your own precious hide. So, I believe of the two of us, life has cast you in the role of coward, Pretender.'

'You will pay for your insolence, priest!'

'No doubt,' the lector agreed. 'But not with my immortal soul.'

'*WHERE IS HE?*' the woman shrieked then, her anger more than a match for the Pretender's as she fought against her chains. She pulled, twisting and kicking, lashing out again and again until the bed leg cracked with a sound like breaking bone. *'WHERE IS MY HUSBAND?'* She had grabbed the stake from where the lector had discarded it and held it to her own breast. Tears streamed down her face. The blood made her look like something spawned from the blackest of nightmares. She knew the answer but she needed to hear it out loud.

'GONE! DEAD! ROTTING IN THE DIRT!' the pretender yelled. Ludwig backed off a step behind the safety of his bodyguard. For all his anger he was still a coward at heart. *'WHICH IS WHERE YOU SHOULD BE!'*

For a split second it was impossible to tell which of the two was inhuman. The anger in the Pretender was vile to see.

Her voice broke, barely a whisper: 'Where is he?'

'He is gone,' the lector said.

'Where is he?'

'Gone,' the lector repeated but there was no getting through to the woman. 'He is dead. Truly dead. He is dust.'

'No... I don't believe that... He is immortal.'

'All things must die.'

'No.'

'Yes,' he said sadly. 'That is the indifference of the world. It doesn't care. We are mere motes, specks in the eye of time. We are all born of dust and to dust we return. He is gone, woman.'

'HE WOULDN'T LEAVE ME!' and softer, with less confidence: 'He wouldn't leave me...'

'He had no choice,' the lector said for the second time since entering the room, his tone of voice more than anything conveying his mixed emotions. 'He was destroyed. There is no way he can return for you.'

'Then I have nothing,' Isabella von Carstein said.

The lector nodded. He made to reach out and brush away the hair from her face but she was too quick, ramming the sharp end of the stake into her own breast. There was a sickening sound, the tearing of wet flesh, and the splintering of bone being forced apart as she impaled herself on the wooden stake. Her eyes flared open as the pain registered in her brain and in them he pretended he saw relief.

She couldn't finish what she had begun. The wooden stake protruded from a shallow wound in her chest, not deep enough to finish her.

'Please…' she mouthed, the word barely audible. Her hands still clutched the shaft of the stake. The lector closed his hands over hers and pushed, forcing the point deeper and deeper until he felt her body yield beneath it and it plunged into her heart, stilling it once and for all. Her tainted blood leaked from the wound, over his hands and down his arms.

He backed away, staring at the woman's blood on his hands. He had killed. No matter that there was mercy in it. He had killed.

Isabella slumped to the floor, her skin already beginning to desiccate as the years of unnatural life gave way to accelerated decay. The skin crumbled, the flesh beneath rotting and collapsing in on itself as the air itself seemed to strip away the flesh from the bones. In the end there would be nothing but dust.

The lector turned away only to see the Pretender gloating.

'You have got your way.'

'As I always do. You are a strange man, priest. You grieve for a monster and yet thousands of our own lie dead and buried at her hand. I cannot pretend to understand your loyalties.'

'She was a girl once. I grieve not for the monster she is but the girl she was, the woman she might have been.'

Behind him the dissolution continued apace. Isabella von Carstein's face crumbled and powdered. The sound was sickening, like a plague of insects feasting on flesh, skittering and chittering. And then she was nothing more than dust.

The lector pushed past the Pretender and left the tower room. He made a decision halfway down the narrow winding stair. He looked in on the thief. 'The man is to be cared for, and when he is recovered he is to be offered a new life, here, in the cathedral. He does not deserve the life of a beggar. The man is a hero, one of the last, I fear. We shall treat him as we would any brother.'

The young priest tending to Felix Mann nodded understanding and returned to his tender ministrations.

That left the monster in the vaults.

Steeling himself, the lector descended deep into the darkness.

Captain Grimm was still about his work when the lector pushed open the heavy door. The prisoner was barely recognisable as human, which of course it wasn't, not any more. Blood had swollen one eye shut and the man's flesh was a mess of charred streaks and burns. A single deep bloody gouge ran from throat to groin, almost a hand's breadth, in places burned through to the bone. The room stank of seared meat and fat.

Grimm looked up from his labour.

'End it, I have no stomach for this, captain. Don't you see what we have become? How we have fallen? In a matter of days we have reduced ourselves to the level of animals. We have stripped ourselves of the dignity and compassion that served as our humanity more effectively than von Carstein's brood ever could have hoped. We have looked into the abyss, Grimm, and instead of conquering the beasts within we have embraced them and become monsters ourselves. That is our reward for surviving. We have become more monstrous than the things we were fighting.'

Grimm ran a sweaty hand over his brow, his eyes blazed in the reflected sickness of the brazier.

'He is stubborn, I'll give the beast that,' he said, as though he hadn't heard a word the lector had said. 'But I'll break him. Mark my words, your grace. I'll break the beast.'

'No, Grimm. No more torture. No more death. I'll have no part of it.'

'But the beast is breaking, I have him!'

'At what cost, man? At what cost?'

'It costs me nothing!'

'It costs you everything, you fool. Everything.'

'You have no idea what you are talking about, priest. This thing has no right to life. It doesn't breathe. Its heart doesn't beat. The blood in its veins is rank. It isn't alive. It doesn't deserve your compassion. It is evil. Pure evil, plain and simple, priest. Save your sorrow and regret for something that deserves it. The beast is an abomination. If we can learn from it before it dies then it has served its purpose. No matter how weak your stomach is the beast must die. There can be no reprieve. You cannot save the man he was. The man is dead, long gone. Now only the beast remains. And believe me, priest, the beast must die. Good men died for us and they deserve nothing less.'

The prisoner laughed then, a sick dead rattle. 'Deserve, deserve, deserve. You speak a lot of deserving, soldier. Now listen to me. The beast has a name,' he said, his voice cracked and broken almost beyond understanding. There was madness in his one open eye. 'It is Jon… Skellan. And believe me, I have no intention of dying, not for a very, very long time.'

*Coming soon from the Black Library: the second
volume in the Vampire Counts trilogy*

DOMINION

by Steven Savile

GRUNBERG
Late winter, 2052

IT WAS DESPERATE.

Kallad Stormwarden knew the tide of the battle
had turned. The young dwarf prince stood side by
side with his father, matching the gruff dwarf blow
for blow as Kellus's axe hewed through the swarm of
dead storming the walls of Grunberg Keep. The
dwarfs of Karak Sadra had chosen to make their last
stand against the Vampire Count together with the
manlings.

The walkway was slick with rain.

Kallad slammed the edge of his great axe,
Ruinthorn, into the grinning face of a woman with
worms where her eyes ought to have been. The blade
split her skull cleanly in two. Still the woman came
on, clawing desperately at his face. He staggered back

a step beneath the ferocity of her attack, wrenching the axe head free. Grunting, he delivered a killer blow. The dead woman staggered and fell from the wall.

He knuckled the rain from his eyes.

There was no blood and the dead didn't scream. Their silence was more frightening than any of the many horrors on the field of combat. They surged forward mercilessly as axes crunched into brittle bones, splintered shoulders and cracked skulls. They lurched and lumbered on as arrows thudded into chest cavities, piercing taut skin and powdering it like vellum. And still they came on relentlessly as heads rolled and limbs were severed.

'Grimna!' Kallad bellowed, kicking the woman's head from the wall. His rallying cry echoed down the line as the dead shuffled forward. Grimna: courage. It was all they had in the face of death. It was all they needed. Grimnir gave them strength while the stubbornness of the mountain gave them courage. With strength and courage and their white-haired king beside them, they could withstand anything.

There was an air of greatness about Kellus Ironhand. More than merely prowess or skill, the dwarf embodied the sheer iron will of his people. He was the mountain: tireless, unconquerable and giant.

And yet there was a chill worming its way deeper into Kallad Stormwarden's heart.

Only in death did moans escape their broken teeth, but these weren't real sounds. They weren't battle-field sounds. They were sussurant whispers. They weren't human. Nor did they come from the living. They belonged to the gathering storm and were terrifying in their eeriness.

It didn't matter how hard the defenders fought, how many enemies they killed, they were trapped in a losing battle. The ranks of the undead army were endless, their bloodlust unquenchable.

Bodies surfaced in the moat, their flesh bloated and their faces stripped away by the leeches that fed on them.

Kallad stared at the tide of corpses as one by one they began to twitch and jerk like loose-limbed puppets being brought violently to life. The first few clawed their way up the side of the dirt embankment. More followed behind them: an endless swell of death surfacing from beneath the black water.

The futility of fighting hit him hard. It was pointless. Death only swelled the ranks of the enemy. The sons of Karak Sadra would be dining in the Hall of the Ancestors by sunrise.

Kallad slapped the blade of Ruinthorn against his boot and brought it to bear on a one-armed corpse as it lumbered into range. The bottom half of its jaw hung slackly where the skin and muscle had rotted away. Kallad took the miserable wretch's head clean off with a vicious swing. The fighting was harsh. Despite their greater prowess, the dwarfs were tiring. Defeat was inevitable, but it would never lessen their resolve to keep fighting.

Behind, someone yelled a warning. A cauldron of blazing naphtha arced high over the wall and crashed into the ranks of the dead. The fire burned bright as dead flesh seared; tufts of hair shrivelled and bones charred. The pouring rain only intensified the burning as the naphtha reacted violently to the water.

The stench of burning corpses was sickening.

Kellus brought his axe round in a vicious arc, the rune of Grimnir slicing into a dead boy's gut. The blow cracked the boy's ribcage open. His entrails spilled out like slick loops of grey rope, unravelling in his hands even as he struggled to hold them in. The dead boy didn't bleed. His head came up, a look of bewilderment frozen on his features as Kellus put the thing out of its misery.

Kallad moved to stand beside his father. 'There's no better way to die,' he said in all seriousness.

'Aye, lad,' his father agreed.

Three shambling corpses came at them at once, almost dragging Kellus down in their hunger to feast on his brains. Kallad barged one off the walkway and split another stem to sternum with a savage blow from Ruinthorn. He grinned as his father dispatched the third creature. The grin died on his face. Down below, one of the dwarfs fell to the reaching hands of the dead. He was dragged down into the mud of the field where they set about stripping flesh from bone him with savage hunger. The dwarf's screams died a moment before he did.

His death spurred the defenders on, firing their blood with a surge of stubborn strength – until the desperation itself became suffocating and closed around their hearts like an iron fist, squeezing the hope out of them. On the field below, another dwarf fell to the dead. Kallad watched, frozen, as the creatures ripped and tore at his comrade's throat, the fiends choking on his blood in their urgency to slake their vile thirst.

Kallad hawked and spat, wrapped his hands around the thick shaft of Ruinthorn and planted the axe head between his feet. The last prince of Karak

Sadra felt fear then, with the understanding that his wouldn't be a clean death. Whatever honour he won on the walls of Grunberg Keep would be stripped from his bones by von Carstein's vermin. There would be nothing glorious in it.

The rain intensified, matting Kallad's hair flat to his scalp, running between the chinks in his armour and down his back. No one said it was going to be like this. None of the storytellers talked about the reality of dying in combat. They spun tales of honour and heroism, not mud and rain and the sheer bloody fear of it.

He turned to his father, looking to draw courage from the king, but Kellus was shivering against the rain and had the look of determination in his old eyes; determination and defeat. There was no comfort to be drawn from him. The mountain was crumbling. It was a humbling experience, to be stood at the foot of it and witness the rock crack and fall. It was nothing more than scree now where once the mountain had stood tall and proud. In that one look Kallad saw the death of a legend at its most mundane.

Kallad looked out across the fields where countless hundreds of the dead shuffled and milled aimlessly among the piles of bones, waiting to be manipulated into the fray, and beyond them, the black tents of Vlad von Carstein and his pet necromancers. They were the true power behind the dead, the puppet masters. The corpses were nothing more than dead meat. The necromancers were the monsters in every sense of the word. Every last trace of humanity had abandoned them. They had given themselves to the dark magic willingly.

Kallad watched as five more fiends clawed their way up the wall of the keep to the walkway. Would these be the ones who sent him to the Hall of Ancestors?

'They need you down there,' Kellus said, breaking the spell of the creeping dead. 'Get the women and children out of this place. The keep's fallen – with it the city. I'll have no one dying who can be saved. No arguments, lad. Take them through the mountain into the deep mines. I'm counting on you.'

Kallad didn't move. He couldn't abandon his father on the wall; it was as good as murdering him.

'Go!' King Kellus demanded, bringing his own axe around in a savage arc and backhanding the head into the face of the first zombie. The blow brought the creature to its knees. Kellus planted a boot on its chest and wrenched the axe free. The creature slumped sideways and fell from the walkway.

Still Kallad didn't move, even as Kellus risked his balance to slam a fist into his breastplate, staggering him back two steps.

'I am still your king, boy, not just your father. They need you more than I do. I'll not have their deaths on my honour!'

'You can't win… Not on your own.'

'And I've got no intention of doing so, lad. I'll be supping ale with yer grandfather come sunrise, trading stories of valour with yer grandfather's father and boasting about my boy saving hundreds of lives, even though he knew to do so would be damning this old dwarf. Now go, lad. Get them manlings out of here. There's more than one kind of sacrifice. Make me proud, lad, and remember there's honour in death. I'll see you on the other side.' With that the old dwarf turned his back on Kallad and hurled himself into the thick of the fight with vengeful fury, his first blow splitting a leering skull, the second severing a gangrenous arm as King Kellus, King of Karak Sadra, made his last, glorious stand on the walls of Grunberg Keep.

More dead emerged from the moat. It was a nightmarish scene: the creatures moving remorselessly up the embankment, brackish water clinging to their skin. Cauldrons of naphtha ignited on the dark water, blue tinged flames racing across the surface and wreathing the corpses. And still they were silent, even as they charred to ash and bone.

The black bodies of hundreds of rats eddied across the blazing water, the rodents racing the bite of flame to dry land.

Kallad turned reluctantly and stomped along the stone walkway. He barrelled down the ramp, slick with rain, and skidded to a halt as the screams of women and children tore through the night.

Heart racing, Kallad looked around frantically for the source of the screams. It took him a moment to see past the fighting, but when he did he found what he was looking for: a petrified woman staggering out of the temple of Sigmar. She clutched a young baby in her arms and cast panicked glances back over her shoulder. A moment later a skeleton emerged from the temple. Dust and cobwebs clung to the bones. It took Kallad a moment to grasp the truth of the situation: their own dead were being drawn back from the dirt and the cold crypts and turned on them. Across the city, the dead were stirring. In cemeteries and tombs, loved ones were returning from beyond the veil of death. The effect on those left behind would be devastating. To lose a loved one once was hard enough, but to be forced to burn or behead them to save your own life... Few could live through that kind of horror untouched. It made sense, now that he could see the pattern of the enemy's logic. The necromancers were content to waste their peons in a useless assault on the walls. It didn't matter. They had all the dead they needed inside the city already.

The impossibility of the situation sank in, but instead of giving in to it, Kallad cried: 'To me!' He brandished Ruinthorn above his head.

He would make his father's sacrifice worthwhile. Then, when the women and children of Grunberg were safe, he would avenge the death of the King of Karak Sadra.

The terrified woman saw Kallad and ran towards him, her skirts dragging as she struggled through the mud. The baby's shrieks were muffled as she pressed the poor child's face into her breasts. Kallad stepped between the woman and the skeletal hunter and slammed a fist into the skull. The sounds of metal on bone and the subsequent crunch of them breaking were sickening. The blow shattered the hinge on the right sight of the fiend's head, making its jaw hang slackly, its broken teeth like tombstones. Kallad thundered a second punch into the skeleton's head, his gomril gauntlet caving in the entire left side of the monstrosity's skull. It didn't slow the skeleton so much as a step.

The twin moons, Mannslieb and Morrslieb, hung low in the sky; the combatants were gripped in a curious time between times, neither the true darkness of night nor the first blush of daylight owned the sky. The fusion of the moon's anaemic light cast fitful shadows across the nightmarish scene.

'Are there more in there?' Kallad demanded.

The woman nodded, eyes wide with terror.

Kallad stepped into the temple of Sigmar expecting to find more refugees from the fighting. Instead he was greeted by the sight of shuffling skeletons, in various states of decay and decomposition, trying to negotiate the rows of benches between the door down to the crypt and the battle raging outside. He backed up quickly and slammed the door. There was no means of securing it. Why would there be, Kallad thought bitterly? It was never meant to be a prison.

'More *manlings* woman, not monsters!' He said, bracing himself against the door.

'In the great hall,' she said. The overwhelming relief of her rescue had already begun to mutate into violent tremors as the reality of her situation sank in. There was no salvation.

Kallad grunted. 'Good. What's your name, lass?'

'Gretchen.'

'All right, Gretchen. Fetch one of the naphtha burners and a torch.'

'But… but…' she stammered, understanding exactly what he intended. Her wild-eyed stare betrayed the truth: the thought of razing Sigmar's house to the ground was more horrifying than any of the creatures trapped inside.

'Go, woman!'

A heartbeat later the dead threw themselves at the door, fists of bone splintering and shattering beneath the sheer ferocity of the assault. The huge doors buckled and bowed. It took every ounce of Kallad's strength to hold the dead back.

'Go!' he rasped, slamming his shoulder up against the wood as fingers crept through the crack in the door the dead had managed to force open. The door slammed closed on the fingers, crushing the bone to a coarse powder.

Without another word the woman fled in the direction of the naphtha burners.

Kallad manoeuvred himself around until he was bracing the huge door with his back, and dug his heels in stubbornly. He could see his father on the wall. The white-haired king matched the enemy blow for savage blow. With his axe shining silver in the moonlight, Kellus might have been immortal, an incarnation of Grimnir himself. He fought with an economy of movement, his axe hewing through the corpses with lethal precision. Kellus's sacrifice was buying Kallad precious minutes to lead the women and children of Grunberg to safety. He would not fail. He owed the old dwarf that much.

The dead hammered on the temple door, demanding to be let free.

Gretchen returned with three men, dragging between them a huge iron cauldron of naphtha. There was a grim stoicism to their actions as the four of them set about dousing the timber frame of the temple in the flammable liquid while Kallad held back the dead. A fourth man set a blazing torch to the temple wall and stepped back as the naphtha ignited in a cold blue flame.

The fires tore around the temple's façade, searing into the timber frame. Amid the screams and the clash of steel on bone the conflagration caught and the holy temple went up in smoke and flames. It took less than a minute for the building to be consumed by fire. The heat from the blaze drove Kallad back from the door, allowing the dead to spill out of the temple.

The abominations were met with hatchet, axe and spear as the handful of defenders drove them back mercilessly into the flames. It was nothing short of slaughter. Kallad couldn't allow himself the luxury of even a moment's relief – the battle was far from won. Soot smeared across his brow. His breathing came in ragged gasps. The heat of the blaze seared into his lungs. In his heart he understood that the worst of it was only just beginning.

Kallad grabbed the woman and yelled over the crackle and hiss of the flames: 'We have to get everyone out of here! The city is falling!'

Gretchen nodded dumbly and stumbled away toward the great hall. The flames spread from the temple, licking up the length of the keep's stone walls and arcing across the rooftops to ignite the barracks and beyond that the stables. The rain was nowhere near heavy enough to douse the flames. In moments the straw roof of the stables was ablaze and the timber walls were caving in beneath the blistering heat. The panicked horses bolted, kicked down the stable doors and charged recklessly into the muddy street. The stench of blood coupled with the burning flesh of the dead, terrified the animals. Even the mightiest of them shied and kicked out at those seeking to calm him.

The dead came through the flames, pouring over the walls in vast numbers, lurching forward, ablaze as they stumbled to their knees and reached up, clawing the flames from their skin even as the fires consumed their flesh.

And still they came on.

The dead surrounded them on all sides.

The conflagration spread, eating through the timber framed buildings as though the walls were no more substantial than straw.

Kallad dragged Gretchen toward the central tower of the keep itself, forcing his way through the horses and the grooms trying to bring the frightened beasts under control. The flames chased along the rooftops. No matter how valiant the defenders' efforts, in a few hours Grunberg would cease to be. The fire they had lit would see to that. The dead wouldn't destroy Grunberg. The living had managed that all by themselves. All that remained was a desperate race to beat the fire.

No direct path to the great hall lay open, though one row of ramshackle buildings looked to be acting as a temporary firewall. Kallad ran towards the row of houses, racing the flames to the doors at the centre. The hovels of the poor quarter buckled and caved in beneath the heat and caught like tinder. Kallad was driven towards the three doors in the centre of the street. The intensity of the blaze forced him to skirt the heart of the fire. Only minutes before, the crackling pile of wood before him had been a bakery.

Kallad swallowed a huge lungful of searing air and, taking the middle door, plunged through the collapsing shell of an apothecary as demijohns of peculiarities cracked and exploded. Gretchen followed behind him, the child eerily silent in her arms.

The lintel over the back door had collapsed under the strain, filling the way out with rubble. Kallad stared hard at the obstacle, hefted Ruinthorn and slammed it into the centre of the debris. Behind them, a ceiling joist groaned. Kallad slammed the axe head into the guts of the debris again and worked it free. Above, the groaning joist cracked sharply, the heat pulling it apart. A heartbeat later, the ceiling collapsed, effectively trapping them inside the burning building.

Cursing, Kallad redoubled his efforts to hack a path through the debris blocking the back door. He had no time to think. In the minutes it took to chop through the barricade thick black smoke suffocated the cramped passage. He slammed Ruinthorn's keen edge repeatedly into the clutter of debris and, as chinks of moonlight and fire began to wriggle through, he kicked at the criss-cross of wooden beams. The smoke stung his eyes.

'Cover the bairn's mouth, woman, and stay low. Lie on your belly. The best air's down by the floor.' The thickening pal of smoke made it impossible to tell if she'd done as she was told.

He backed up two steps and hurled himself at the wooden barrier, breaking through. His momentum carried him sprawling out into the street.

Coughing and retching, Gretchen crawled out of the burning building as the gable collapsed and the roof came down. She cradled the child close to her breast, soothing it even as she struggled to swallow a lungful of fresh air. The flames crackled and popped all around them. Inside the apothecary's, a series of small but violent detonations exploded as the cabinets stuffed full of chemicals and curiosities swelled and shattered in the intense heat.

Kallad struggled to his feet. He had been right: the row of buildings acted as a kind of firebreak, holding the flames back from this quarter of the walled city. The respite they offered wouldn't last; all he could do was pray to Grimnir it would last long enough for him to get the women and children out of the great hall.

He ran across the courtyard to the huge iron-banded doors of the keep and hammered on them with the butt of his axe until they cracked open and inch and the frightened eyes of a young boy peeked through. 'Come on, lad. We're getting you out of here. Open up.'

A smile spread across the boy's face. It was obvious he thought the fighting was over. Then, behind Kallad and Gretchen, he saw the fire destroying the shambles of his city. He let go of the heavy door. It swung open on itself, leaving him standing in the doorway, a length of wood in his trembling hand: a toy sword. The lad couldn't have been more than nine or ten summers old, but he had the courage to put himself between the women of Grunberg and the dead. It was that kind of courage that made the dwarf proud to fight beside the manlings – courage could be found in the most unlikely of places.

Kallad clapped the boy on the shoulder. 'Let's fetch the women and wee ones, shall we, lad?'

They followed the boy down a lavish passage, the walls decorated with huge tapestries and impractical weaponry. The hallway opened onto an anti-chamber where frightened women and children huddled, pressing themselves into the shadows and dark recesses. Kallad wanted to promise them all that they were saved, that everything was going to be all right, but it wasn't. Their city was in ruins. Their husbands and brothers were dead or dying, conquered by the dead. Everything was far from all right.

Instead of lies he offered them the bitter truth: 'Grunberg's falling. There's nothing anyone can do to save it. The city's ablaze. The dead are swarming over the walls. Your loved ones are out there dying to give you the chance of life. You owe it to them to take it.'

'If they are dying why are you here? You should be out there with them.'

'Aye, I should. But I'm not. I'm here, trying to make their deaths mean something.'

'We can fight alongside our men,' another woman said, standing.

'Aye, and die alongside them.'

'Let the bastards come, they'll not find us easy to kill.'

One woman reached up, dragging a huge two-handed sword from the wall display. She could barely raise the tip. Another pulled down an ornate breast-plate while a third took gauntlets and a flail. In their hands these weapons of death looked faintly ridiculous, but the look in their eyes and the set of the jaws was far from comical.

'You can't hope to–'

'You've said that already, we *can't hope*. Our lives are destroyed. Our homes. Our families. Give us the choice at least. Let us decide if we are to run like rats from a sinking ship or stand up and be judged by Morr side by side with our men. Give us that, at least.'

Kallad shook his head. A little girl stood beside the woman demanding the right to die, crying. Behind her a boy barely old enough to walk buried his face in his mother's skirts. 'No,' he said bluntly. 'And no arguments. This isn't a game. Grunberg burns. If we stand here arguing like idiots we'll all be dead in minutes. Look at that girl – are you prepared to say when she should die? Are you? For all that your men are laying down their lives knowing that in doing so they are saving yours?' Kallad shook his head. 'No. No you're not. We're going leave here and travel into the mountains. There are caverns that lead into the deep mines and stretch as far away as Axebite Pass. The dead won't follow us there.' In truth he had no idea if that was the case or not but it didn't matter, he only needed the women to believe him long enough to get them moving. Safety or the illusion of safety, at that moment it amounted to the same thing. 'Now come on!'

His words galvanized them. They began to stand and gather their things together, tying cloth into bundles and stuffing the bundles with all that remained of their worldly goods. Kallad shook his head. 'There's no time for that! Come ON!'

The boy ran ahead, the toy sword slapping at his leg. 'That stays here,' Kallad said, dipping Ruinthorn's head toward an ornate jewellery box one woman clutched in her hands. 'The only things leaving this place are living and breathing. Forget your pretty trinkets, they ain't worth dying for. Understood?'

No one argued with him.

He counted heads as they filed out through the wide door: forty-nine women and almost double the number of children. Each one looked at the dwarf as though he was a saviour sent by Sigmar to deliver them to salvation. Gretchen stood beside him, the child cradled in her arms. She had eased the blanket down from over the child's face and Kallad saw at last the reason for the child's silence. Its skin bore the bluish cast of death. Still, the woman smoothed its cheek as though hoping to give some of her warmth to her dead baby.

Kallad couldn't allow this one small tragedy to affect him – hundreds of people had died today. Hundreds. What was one baby against this senseless massacre? But he knew full well why the sight of the dead child was different. The child was innocent. It hadn't chosen to fight the dead. It represented everything they were giving their lives to save. And, more than anything else, it showed what a failure their sacrifice was.

Then the baby started to move, its small hand wriggling free of the blankets. The child's eyes roved blankly still trapped in death even as its body answered the call of the Vampire Count.

Sickness welled in Kallad's gut.

The child had to die.

He couldn't do it.

He didn't have a choice. The thing in Gretchen's arms wasn't her baby. It was a shell.

'Give me the baby,' he said, holding out his hands.

Gretchen shook her head, backing up a step as though she understood what he intended, even though she couldn't possibly.

Kallad barely grasped the thoughts going through his head they were so utterly alien. 'Give me the baby,' he repeated.

She shook her head stubbornly.

'It isn't your child, not any more,' he said, as calmly as he could manage. He took a step closer and took the child from her.

'Go,' Kallad said, unable to look her in the eye. 'You don't need to see this.'

But she wouldn't leave him.

He couldn't do it, not here in the street, not with her watching.

He moved away from her, urging the refugees of Grunberg to follow. He held the child close, its face pressed into the chain links of his mail shirt. Glancing back down the street to the ruin of the stables Kallad saw the dead gathering, the last of the moonlight bathing their rotten flesh in silver. They had breached the wall and were pouring over in greater and greater numbers. The fire blazed on all sides of them, but they showed neither sense of fear nor understanding of what the flames might do to their dead flesh. The last of the men was lining up in a ragged phalanx to charge their enemy. Their spears and shields were pitiful against the ranks of the dead. Even the sun wouldn't rise in time to save them. Like their enemy, they were dead, only Morr had yet to claim their souls.

Kallad led the women and children away from the last hurrah. He had no wish for them to see their men fall. The fires made it difficult to navigate the streets. Alleyways dead-ended in sheets of roaring flame. Passageways collapsed beneath the detritus of houses, their shells burnt out.

'Look!' one of the women cried, pointing at part of the wall that had collapsed. The dead were clambering slowly over the debris, stumbling and falling and climbing over the fallen.

'To the mountains!' Kallad shouted over the cries of panic.

Avoiding the pockets of fire became ever more difficult as the fire spread, the isolated pockets becoming unbroken walls of flame.